FUTURE LIBRARY

Contemporary Indian Writing

∽

EDITED BY

Anjum Hasan & Sampurna Chattarji

Red Hen Press | *Pasadena, CA*

Future Library: Contemporary Indian Writing
Copyright © 2022 by Red Hen Press
All Rights Reserved

No part of this book may be used or reproduced in any manner whatsoever without the prior written permission of both the publisher and the copyright owner.

Book design by Mark E. Cull

Cover art *Flight* by Tanmoy Samanta, courtesy the artist and TARQ Art Gallery, Mumbai

Library of Congress Cataloging-in-Publication Data

Names: Hasan, Anjum, editor. | Chattarji, Sampurna, editor.
Title: Future library : contemporary Indian writing / edited by Anjum Hasan & Sampurna Chattarji.
Description: First edition. | Pasadena, CA : Red Hen Press, [2022]
Identifiers: LCCN 2021035535 (print) | LCCN 2021035536 (ebook) | ISBN 9781636280318 (trade paperback) | ISBN 9781636280325 (epub)
Subjects: LCSH: Indic literature (English)—21st century. | LCGFT: Short stories. | Poetry.
Classification: LCC PR9494.92 .F88 2022 (print) | LCC PR9494.92 (ebook) | DDC 820.8/0092—dc23/eng/20211203
LC record available at https://lccn.loc.gov/2021035535
LC ebook record available at https://lccn.loc.gov/2021035536

The National Endowment for the Arts, the Los Angeles County Arts Commission, the Ahmanson Foundation, the Dwight Stuart Youth Fund, the Max Factor Family Foundation, the Pasadena Tournament of Roses Foundation, the Pasadena Arts & Culture Commission and the City of Pasadena Cultural Affairs Division, the City of Los Angeles Department of Cultural Affairs, the Audrey & Sydney Irmas Charitable Foundation, the Meta & George Rosenberg Foundation, the Albert and Elaine Borchard Foundation, the Adams Family Foundation, Amazon Literary Partnership, the Sam Francis Foundation, and the Mara W. Breech Foundation partially support Red Hen Press.

First Edition
Published by Red Hen Press
www.redhen.org

FUTURE LIBRARY

Acknowledgments

The editors would like to acknowledge the contribution of Ravi Shankar, who initiated this project—originally conceived as a multigenre anthology—in 2017, with Sampurna Chattarji as coeditor. Anjum Hasan came on board in 2018. Thanks are due to Aaron Hauptman for his help with the earlier avatar of this book, and to Tobi Harper, Natasha McClellan, and Rebeccah Sanhueza at Red Hen Press, for their dedication and support.

The title of this anthology comes from Sohini Basak's "Future Library" poems, which were triggered by Katie Paterson's public art project (of the same name; "Framitidsbiblioteket," in the Norwegian), which involves tending to 1000 spruce trees that were planted in 2014, somewhere outside Oslo, to create and curate a library for the future.

CONTENTS

Introductions

xix ~ **ANJUM HASAN**
All Is Addition

xxviii ~ **SAMPURNA CHATTARJI**
Making Our Alliances Visible

Future Library: Contemporary Indian Writing

1 ~ **ARUN SAGAR**
Black Leather Shoes
Naming
The Fourth Day

4 ~ **ROHAN CHHETRI**
The Blueprint among the Ashes
Visitation

7 ~ **EUNICE DE SOUZA**
Learn from the Almond Leaf
Compound Life
Western Ghats

11 ~ **JASWINDER BOLINA**
Country, Western

13 ~ **ARVIND KRISHNA MEHROTRA**
Three Questions for Prabhu S. Guptara Concerning
    his Anthology of Indian Religious Poetry in English
Ballad of the Black Feringhee

16 ~ **RALPH NAZARETH**
The Song of the Plumber On the Fourth of July

18 ~ **SUJATA BHATT**
A Neutral Country
Notes from the Hospital

23 ~ **MONIKA KUMAR**
On Seeing a Watermelon
Window Seat

25 ~ **KIRUN KAPUR**
Girls Girls Girls

27 ~ **MANOHAR SHETTY**
Taverna
Carried Forward
Jackfruit

31 ~ **SHARANYA MANIVANNAN**
The Chicken Trusser

33 ~ **SUBHRO BANDOPADHYAY**
Dog Days
About Presences
Glass Pronouns

37 ~ **TABISH KHAIR**
Who in a Million Diamonds Sums Us Up?
    Or, Fru Andersen speaks to me across two centuries

40 ~ **ROBIN S. NGANGOM**
Marriages and Funerals
Saint Edmund's College
Understanding

44 ~ **GIEVE PATEL**
Postmortem
The Multitude Comes to a Man
Of Sea and Mountain

47 ~ **MONICA MODY**
stayed home with language

49 ~ **ANDAL**
The Song to Kamadeva, God of Love
Take Me to His Sacred Places

56 ~ **MEENA KANDASAMY**
Celestial Celebrities
Eating Dirt
Things to remember while looting the burial ground

60 ~ **LAL DED**
Verses from *I, Lalla*

61 ~ **SUMAN CHHABRA**
Home Body
this life is mock containment

63 ~ **MANGALESH DABRAL**
Description of the Mad

65 ~ **NABINA DAS**
Anima walks borderless

66 ~ **KEKI N. DARUWALLA**
Winston to Cyril
Some Poems for Akhmatova

70 ~ **TSERING WANGMO DHOMPA**
After Sunset
Before Sunrise

72 ~ **SUBHASHINI KALIGOTLA**
Interior with Particulars
Grammar Lesson

74 ~ **ANAMIKA**
Hands Up

75 ~ **MONA ZOTE**
Rez

79 ~ **MUSTANSIR DALVI**
Effigy Maker
Teo'ma

81 ~ **ANAND THAKORE**
Elephant Bathing

82 ~ **KALIDASA**
Cloud-messenger

87 ~ **ARJUN RAJENDRAN**
Mail from San Juan
Sea World
Refilling

90 ~ **VIKAS K. MENON**
Devayani
    Nair Marriage Ceremony, Kerala, India (photo, b&w, 1934)
    King James Bible (cloth binding, 1900)
    Wedding Reception (photo, b&w, 1934)
    Bed, South India (rosewood, 1900)
    Coda

96 ~ **MEDHA SINGH**
Chair
An Answer

99 ~ **LALNUNSANGA RALTE**
Afzal
Dear Baruk
Fak You.

102 ~ **VINITA RAMANI**
Wildling

103 ~ **SRIKANTH REDDY**
Scarecrow Eclogue
from *Voyager: Book One*

107 ~ **NIRENDRANATH CHAKRABORTY**
Being Means
Hello Dum Dum
Amalkanti
Flag

112 ~ **JAY DESHPANDE**
Pennsylvania, Pittsburgh
Page Ripped from Rockbottom's Own Invented Book of Prayer
That's the American Dream, Is to Have a Green Lawn

115 ~ **NIRALA**
Little Princess, or the One-Eyed Girl

116 ~ **LEEYA MEHTA**
Black Dog on the Anacostia River

118 ~ **KUTTI REVATHI**
We are women with three breasts!
A Spectral Horse

120 ~ **K. SRILATA**
Breasts/*Mulaigal*
Because I Never Learned the Names of Trees in Tamil
A Brief History of Writing

123 ~ **SHELLY BHOIL**
the way we write

125 ~ **JOY GOSWAMI**
50

130 ~ **MICHELLE CAHILL**
Red Scarf

131 ~ **TISHANI DOSHI**
O Great Beauties!
The Women of the Shin Yang Park Sauna, Gwangju

134 ~ **MONICA FERRELL**
In the Fetus Museum
A Funfair in Hell
Savage Bride

138 ~ **SHIKHA MALAVIYA**
Botany 101 (For India's Daughters)

139 :~ **MEENA ALEXANDER**
Little Burnt Holes
Fragments of an Inexistent Whole

142 :~ **K. SATCHIDANANDAN**
The Unknown Tongues
An Old Poet's Suicide Note

145 :~ **MUHAMMAD IQBAL**
Ghazal

147 :~ **AKHIL KATYAL**
Dehradun, 1990

148 :~ **VIVEK NARAYANAN**
Poems After Valmiki
    Rama
    Manthaara, the Hunchback
    They Saw No Longer the Battlefield

151 :~ **USHA AKELLA**
Nov 1/16
Nov 2/16

153 :~ **SHRIKANT VERMA**
Disillusionment of a Courtesan from the Time of the Buddha
Trauma
Return

159 :~ **RAJIV MOHABIR**
Vapsi: Return
A Mnemonic for Survival
Underwater Acoustics

162 :~ **MANI RAO**
from *Echolocation*

165 :~ **VIJAY NAMBISAN**
On First Looking into Whitman's Humor
Lint
Bhima in the Forest

168 :~   **SALEEM PEERADINA**
         Heart's Beast

171 :~   **SIDDHARTHA MENON**
         Eclipse
         Evening
         Retired Swami

174 :~   **INDERJEET MANI**
         Ali G does Kabir

175 :~   **SURJIT PATAR**
         The Magician of Words

177 :~   **JASON SANDHAR**
         oak creek: 5 aug 1919

179 :~   **AMIT MAJMUDAR**
         The Gita Variations: Gloss 10
         Godhra Sequence

184 :~   **VINOD KUMAR SHUKLA**
         "That man put on a new woolen coat and went away like a thought"

185 :~   **IMTIAZ DHARKER**
         The Knot
         Out of Line

187 :~   **RAFIQ KATHWARI**
         The Day I Was My Sister's Chaperone
         For My Nephew Omar on His Engagement to Nadia

189 :~   **ARYANIL MUKHERJEE**
         from *code memory*: *dead fish buoy above the living*

192 :~   **ANITHA THAMPI**
         Alappuzha *Vellam*

195 :~   **RANJIT HOSKOTE**
         Sand
         Shoe
         Market
         Hunchprose

199 :~ **HEMANT DIVATE**
Praha, I'll be back
What Happened to Language?

204 :~ **PRIYA SARUKKAI CHABRIA**
Great Mosque, Xian
Prayer as Three Camera Movements

207 :~ **KAZIM ALI**
Divination

212 :~ **ANON**
Prakrit Love Poetry from the Gathasaptasati of Satavahana Hala

213 :~ **ARUNDHATHI SUBRAMANIAM**
When God is a Traveler
How to Read Indian Myth
Leapfrog

219 :~ **ROBERT WOOD**
We Seed
Week of Rose
To Be Rice

222 :~ **KUNWAR NARAIN**
Reaching Home
They are not crowds, they are us

225 :~ **SHARMISTHA MOHANTY**
What Holds Together

227 :~ **IRWIN ALLAN SEALY**
crossing the line

234 :~ **SOHINI BASAK**
Future Library: Some Anxieties
Future Library: A Footnote
Future Library: Alternative Ending

238 :~ **ROSALYN D'MELLO**
Something New, Something Borrowed

241 :~ **SHAMALA GALLAGHER**
Mooncalf

248 :~ **SASHA PARMASAD**
The Village

250 :~ **PRAMILA VENKATESWARAN**
from *The Singer of Alleppey*

251 :~ **PALASH KRISHNA MEHROTRA**
Double Bed

262 :~ **JEET THAYIL**
from *The Book of Chocolate Saints*

274 :~ **RAVI MANGLA**
Feats of Strength

276 :~ **ARUNI KASHYAP**
from *The House With a Thousand Stories*

282 :~ **ANEES SALIM**
from *The Blind Lady's Descendants*

290 :~ **K. R. MEERA**
Ave Maria

295 :~ **SEJAL SHAH**
Climate, Man, Vegetation

296 :~ **GAIUTRA BAHADUR**
The Stained Veil

304 :~ **KUZHALI MANICKAVEL**
The Statue Game

311 :~ **SUBIMAL MISRA**
Wild Animals Prohibited

315 :~ **GEETA KOTHARI**
I Brake For Moose

325 ~ **SAIKAT MAJUMDAR**
       from *The Scent of God*

331 ~ **SAMPURNA CHATTARJI**
       Insectboy

337 ~ *Contributors' Notes*

355 ~ *Credits*

INTRODUCTIONS

ANJUM HASAN

"All Is Addition"

"Anyone who is concerned with Indian writing should, at some stage, state his limitations," wrote the poet and anthologist Adil Jussawalla in his introduction to *New Writing in India* (1974), striking a note that runs through many anthologies of Indian literature—a note of caution to do with that seemingly all-encompassing and apparently simple category, Indian. Who can claim to know or be able to fairly represent all of Indian literature, and who has a handle on the many languages in which this literature is written? Arguably, no one is privy to that "omniscient Himalayan" view. Jussawalla's project is familiar in another sense as well—it is conducted in English and interrogates what it means to write in English in contrast to other Indian languages, what happens when we translate this literature into English, and how to approach this wide field through that one language.

And so, as is often the case when talking about Indian literature, language itself becomes the object of the discussion—language not just as the instrument of writing, but as a history that shapes writing, a history with both modern as well as antique roots. Language has been the determining factor in subsequent anthologies too. The present collection follows on two other notable ones that were imagined not as mere compendia, in the way projects often are, but as forceful arguments about the literature being presented.

Amit Chaudhuri's *Picador Book of Modern Indian Literature* (2001) challenged the fashionable late 1990s view that the best Indian writing was taking place in English. While Jussawalla's emphasis was the contemporariness of the selection, Chaudhuri's was a historical project, a sensitive curation of writing from the nineteenth and twentieth centuries in several Indian languages, reminding us that vernacular literatures were the result of colonial-era cross-fertilization and that these languages started to produce modern literatures some two hundred years ago, at the same time as English did in India.

Jeet Thayil's *60 Indian Poets* (2008) is perhaps the most wide-ranging anthology of Indian poetry in English ever published, appearing in a slightly expanded avatar in the UK as *The Bloodaxe Book of Contemporary Indian Poets*. By bringing together in one collection Indian English poets from across the world, of different generations, working in different styles, Thayil made the argument that this poetry, wherever and however it is written, should be seen as a continuum—"one language separated by the sea" was his characterization of Indian English. He sought to both give renewed credibility to this language as well as tie the genre to it rather than to the physical boundaries of India.

The editors of all these three anthologies are writers themselves and their projects were inevitably personal—not only in the limited sense of being expressions of individual taste but also in how their stances came from a need to work out their place in the literature they claimed and contributed to. And if there were defenses these writer-anthologists felt compelled to mount—such as Jussawalla's sense of the Herculean impossibility of grasping the whole of India or Thayil's championing of English as a language of Indian poetry—then an awareness of these limitations also became the means of taking the measure of their own inheritance.

This anthology brings together contemporary writing in English and in translation from Indian languages—in poetry, fiction as well as something in between—the prose poem, flash fiction, or the poetic vignette. It seeks to present new Indian writing—by the local as well as the emigrant writer. Of course that term, with its associations of self-imposed or forced exile, is no longer quite accurate for a second or third generation émigré who is nevertheless, as several selections show, often still writing about an abiding sense of loss and dislocation. Even though English is used as a creative language by Indians all over the world, including in India, it "is not an Indian language, the way it is an American language, nor is it an Indian language the way Bengali or Urdu are," pointed out Chaudhuri in his introduction.

Nothing illustrates this ambivalence as vividly as translation. Literary translation from Indian languages has come into its own in this century and some of the many genres—from medieval poetry to contemporary fiction—being translated into English are represented in this collection. In fact, translation itself tends to be seen as a genre in India, bracketed off from what is written in English, which only ends up limiting engagement with it. And yet there *is* a sense in which translation creates paradigms of its own. We have the word "contemporary" in the subtitle of this anthology, even though it includes some writing from several centuries ago, because these translations are contemporary—thus signalling the independence, in some ways, of a translation, from its source. At the same time, literature in translation is, quite obviously, no one thing—given the many-sided traditions in the several languages from which translations take place.

While the bulk of this anthology features writing in English, we have also included poetry and fiction from Hindi, Tamil, Malayalam, Kannada, Bengali, Urdu, Kashmiri, Punjabi, Marathi—all modern languages with old roots, as well as work in translation from two much older languages—Sanskrit and Prakrit. This modest variety will hopefully reveal to the reader something of the original literature, but also how we use English today to convey, for want of a better word, our Indianness. My coeditor Sampurna Chattarji elaborates in her companion piece on the complex nature of this Indianness.

There are many idioms of English at work here and several strains of English audible. Nothing at first glance appears to unite, say, the late poet Eunice de Souza's astringently clear and unsentimentally sad Indian English voice ("Fling my ashes in the Western Ghats / They've always seemed like home. / May the leopards develop / A taste for poetry") with Inderjeet Mani's rap rendition of medieval poet-saint Kabir ("Bruvvers, me life's been pissed away / In silence, widout thinkin to pray") with Anitha Thampi's poem of origins both literal and figurative, the English in J. Devika's translation seeking to recreate the compounded adjectives of the original Malayalam:

> She, of Alappuzha,
> the girl with palm-thatch braids,
> daughter of the muddy water,
> rotting-coconut-husk-reeking water
> faintly-briny-tasting water
> bright-tea-burnished water.

And yet the attentive reader may be able to trace lines of connection between de Souza and other Indian English poets and writers of her generation—the sardonic sympathies evident in the poems of Gieve Patel and Keki Daruwalla—to name two of her contemporaries included here. And this consciously modern, distinct and yet unshowy English style, developed by the writers who were born around the time of the country's Independence in the midtwentieth century, seems to have become the natural choice for several younger poets and fiction writers, some of whom appear here such as Vijay Nambisan, Robin S. Ngangom, and Palash Krishna Mehrotra.

In a footnote to her poem, Thampi writes about how a "senior poet" asked her why she used the colloquial Malayalam word *"vellam"* for water in one of her poems, instead of the classical Sanskrit word *"jalam."* (What underlies this question is the fact that the written and the spoken diverge greatly in south Indian languages such as Malayalam and Tamil. Literary Malayalam, unlike the vernacular, has a high percentage of Sanskrit words.) Thampi's poem, which distinguishes between the local *vellam* of her childhood and the more impersonal *jalam*, is, in addition to being a translation, a comment on translating oneself, and a response to the question of which vocabulary best suits this self-explication. We cannot reach, through English, the cultural associations of either word—and skeptics will say context is untranslatable—but the instinct behind the poem is clear: to describe the highly personal nature of those associations.

This instinct can express itself in other, subtler, ways as well. In Anees Salim's "Blind Lady's Descendants," the metaphor is a shadow. The young narrator, wasting away in a small seaside town, wants to migrate to the West and latches on to an elderly British tourist couple who might be his route out.

> I walked to them, looking innocent and orphaned, squinting at my shadow, which appeared to be more eager than me to be with them. A thought struck me as I dragged

myself across the hot sand: if they took pity on me and opted for an adoption, my shadow would be the only thing I would be taking to my new life. I could already see it thrown on unfamiliar landscapes, hovering around me in my new environs, sitting pensively by me as I happily wrote Mother a letter of fake nostalgia.

Like Thampi, Salim's milieu is Kerala, though he writes in English rather than Malayalam. His fiction creates a sense of location—often accompanied by the yearning to escape—not through referencing culture or language but with the literary figure of the brooding local, deeply implicated in and yet at an angle to personal histories and family lives.

This translation of the self through literature is evident in several other pieces here. In his poem, "Who in a Million Diamonds Sums Us Up?" (the title taken from a Wallace Stevens poem), Denmark-based Tabish Khair arrives at himself through the voice of Fru Andersen, mother of the famed nineteenth-century writer of fairy tales, Hans Christian Andersen. The poem performs a complex dance, as the speaker—through a moving account of her loneliness and poverty, the trials of raising a misfit child, and the subsequent distance between mother and famous son—manages to form a bond with the stranger she is addressing, that is, the sharp-eyed poet.

> To arrive anywhere you have to come from afar,
> As he did, as shadows like you do, you ugly black man.
> In his fairy tales, they find peace,
> But I see you lay mines between his lines.

Marathi poet Hemant Divate in Mustansir Dalvi's translation, "Praha, I'll be Back," wanders in Kafka's city and finds himself slowly leaching into the writer's identity.

> Or, am I the man in the Kafka coat
> and while I say that I am moving along,
> am I actually standing in one place
> waiting for the punt under Charles Bridge,
> while possibly, a man in a Kafka coat
> is in the boat, slowly approaching me
> as I stand here eating chickpeas?

It is often assumed that because India is capacious and crowded, its literature will be similarly busy. (One recent example of this view is the blurb text of leading poet Arvind Krishna Mehrotra's *Collected Poems*, which appeared in 2016 from the Australian press Giramondo. "We think of contemporary Indian writing as sharing the same teeming quality as the country itself. But the simplicity and clarity of Arvind Krishna Mehrotra's poems point to another Indian literary tradition [. . .]") That other tradition is modernism which has had an incalculable influence on the country's twentieth-century literatures. It meant the encounter in writing with the individuated and lonely self, an encounter in which it was the strangeness of being human and the singularity of consciousness that enlivened more native preoccupations, so that, as in the poem above, the man in the Kafka coat was both out there as well as, somehow, oneself. The distinctive hallmarks of such modernism can be seen in Mehrotra's poetry as well as Hindi poets such as Vinod Kumar Shukla, Shrikant Verma, and Kunwar Narain, and Bengali poet Nirendranath Chakraborty, all included in this collection.

We are poets who also write fiction (Sampurna) and fiction writers who occasionally write poetry (Anjum). There is significantly more poetry in this collection than prose, though this is in no way a reflection on the quality of contemporary Indian prose vis-à-vis poetry. Some of the fiction featured here—short stories, which have been the favoured form of many Indian writers, as well as excerpts from novels—is by those who have only recently been more widely discovered through translation such as K. R. Meera and Subimal Misra; others like Irwin Allan Sealy write in English and have been published transcontinentally. Realism, in different registers and put to varied uses, is the preferred mode for most Indian writers of fiction, while the poetry ranges from a quietly observational lyric style to the epic mode as well as an adventurous looping back to the underlying elements—language, location, self, consciousness.

There is as much in this anthology distinguishing these almost one hundred writers from each other as there is shared ground. The word "Indian" in the subtitle, applied to this diversity of writers, becomes then a means of exploring multiplicity rather than enforcing commonality. To say this is to state the obvious, for the insular category of the nation and the aspiring borderlessness of literature do not sit well together no matter which the country in question. American readers, however, are likely to come to this collection with the expectation of learning from the literature something about its cultural sources. A well-read Indian encountering a similar anthology of American literature is unlikely to seek education in a national culture—simply because she knows enough American writing to be able to judge the thing on its own terms. Without such a context of reading, all literature acquires the character of an object lesson.

And so, the question of a discernable literary tradition. Despite our wide scope and the fact that our lens is the kaleidoscopic one of English, there are clearly predilections and preferences, echoes and reflections. One is an interest in the subject of tradition itself. Indian mythology, that is, the prehistoric epics of *Ramayana* and *Mahabharata*, and legends about the lives of gods in the Hindu pantheon, forms the subject of many of these pieces.

In her poem "How to Read Indian Myth," Arundhati Subramanian provides several routes into the field, including "Read it like you would read a love story / Your own." A startlingly persuasive suggestion to the question appears in Meena Kandasamy's poem "Eating Dirt" which draws on the well-known story of the mischievous child-god Krishna and how his mother miraculously glimpsed all three worlds of Hindu belief when he opened his mouth. Only here, a pregnant woman craves mud and when her child is born he has the same urge, so that in his mouth she sees, "the truth of the three worlds—/ sand everywhere, everything / turning to sand." This puncturing of myth is as much in evidence in this collection as reminders of its sublimity. In Srikanth Reddy's "Scarecrow Eclogue" the speaker tacks the page of a poem to a scarecrow in a sugarcane field, where it is quickly reduced to a minor element of the pastoral scene, a poem which turns out to be the narrator's version of the Bhagavad Gita, "what the god dressed up as a charioteer said / to the reluctant bowman / at the center of the battlefield." And Amit Majmudar glosses more explicitly on the Gita in his poem on this theme, his Krishna telling that reluctant bowman, Arjuna, "[. . .] I am Mother / Kali, Mother Mary, / Gaia and Maya / And Kwanyin in one." Meanwhile in Kuzhali Manickavel's understatedly hilarious short story "The Statue Game," Krishna is reduced to a broken piece of masonry that its feckless and accidental owner is unsure what to do with. Instead of "idol"—the expected usage—Manickavel tellingly calls the sculpture a statue, one that "was chipped all over, as if he had been pecked at by millions of tiny birds. Both his hands were missing and there was a large hole where his right knee should have been. His flute had been reduced to a rusted mess of wire that stuck to his cracked lips."

Not all of the tradition is connected to religion. "Unable to count / The days of separation / Beyond her fingers and toes / The unlettered girl broke down." These and other astonishingly accessible poems of romantic love have been translated by Arvind Krishna Mehrotra from an ancient verse written in one of the country's prakrits, that is, vernaculars. Compiled by a king in southwestern India in the second-century CE, but likely to feature poems going even further back, this is one of the earliest extant anthologies of Indian poetry. Romantic love is also the theme of Kalidasa's fifth-century CE lyric drama, *Meghadutam*—excerpted here in a playfully interpolative translation by Mani Rao. Though gods and their myths feature in the play, the story has a secular theme—a lovelorn yaksha (demigod) seeking to send a message to his distant lover through a cloud.

"Men die into ghosts, ghosts have no place to go," writes Sealy in "crossing the line," a prose except from his books of poems *Zelaldinus*, in which contemporary characters exchange notes and make journeys with the sixteenth-century Mughal king Jalaluddin Akbar, who was known in Europe by the latinate name of the book's title. Several ghosts of the past feature in this anthology, but Sealy's is a substantial ghost, rife with memories, regrets, questions and advice. As much as myth, history has repeatedly worked its way into modern Indian literature, and there are some striking examples in our anthology—which Sampurna reflects on in her essay—of history as a record of violence.

The most intimate form of historical remembering is perhaps the homage—the contemporary writer invoking the dead one, such as in Keki N. Daruwalla's poems to

Anna Akhmatova; as well as Tabish Khair's and Hemant Divate's conversations with Andersen and Kafka mentioned above. Such recalling of precedents can also be an arguing against rather than for, evident in Jaswinder Bolina's disavowal of some of the hallmarks of Western culture:

> [. . .] the paintings in the museum all say,
>
> *This is life on Earth! This is life on Earth!* so I'm jealous
> of their candor, but that isn't my pasty duchess,
> that isn't my butchered messiah, that isn't my bounty
> of meat beside the gilded chalice, I'm no Medici

What counts out of all that past is ultimately how it speaks to me—the "I" of the lyric poem and the narrator or protagonist of the story. More than any other source it is personal history and private memory that is charted in these works, and in fact if there is one obvious theme to this collection it is today's painful obsession with the self—the self as body, the desolate self, the eternal return to the child self, the self as connected through family ties to other selves, the socially ostracized self, the self always observing self. "A self is a rickety structure, a home you / build on your back from the twigs of whichever earth," writes Shamala Gallagher in her prose poem "Mooncalf"—one of many references in this collection to this makeshift reality.

And perhaps nothing brings home this provisional quality as starkly as the experience of being an immigrant: there are several immigrant songs and stories here. Bolina's poem above addresses America obliquely in the voices of all those who arrived there "with less than a shekel, / less than a rupee, less than a kroner or any glinting / Kennedy, three pence short of a peso." And America—the word, the country, the experience, the dream, the nightmare recurs: Ralph Nazareth's plumber who raps, "Don't ever call furra plumber, never again! / Break it and fix it, thas AmeriCAN / Break it and fix it, fix it and break it / O America!"; Jeet Thayil's story of an Indian-origin Brooklynite in post 9/11 America, which has become "Post America, After America, the dream of equality curdled into race paranoia. Rights if you're white otherwise you take your chances"; America represents freedom after the humiliations of being an Indian in the Caribbean in Gaiutra Bahadur's story; and finally there is Amit Majmudar's sovereign Krishna, quoted above, who declares, with magnificent disregard for immigrant self-division, "Of nations / I am America, / Mother of ephemera."

Yet the urge to transcend—the limits of the self, the boundaries of nations, the burden of history—is equally strong and the natural obverse of these tendencies described above. The lyric poem especially is as often aiming at this transcendence as being put in the service of describing the minutely particular. Several inventive poets here—Joy Goswami, Ranjit Hoskote, Mani Rao to name three—stretch metaphor and invert language so as to nail the abstract, net the elusive. So does Kazim Ali in 'Divination': "Here I am a threaded bead impaled by decades / By prayers I can't see or hear but slide along the thread / Neither the one praying nor the prayer itself / Just a clot of muscle and bone counting."

The title of this essay comes from Arun Sagar's poem "Black Leather Shoes" which expresses a similarly visionary approach to contemporary existence.

> [. . .] All is addition, concatenation,
> collation, all is connected by the *and*. I can but swing forth
> and back, from *and* to *like*. Like, all is metaphor. Unavoidable
> as Swiss cheese.

Both *and* and *like* are escape he says later in the poem and, even later "There is no *and* or *like*, mere all- / usion, illusion, shadowy rhetoric." This insight into the essential connectedness of everything is undercut by a post-modern recognition of the utter contingency of everything. Read ironically this is a wonderful poetic manifesto for our century—as well as a worthy description for this book. The irony is essential though, because "all is addition" may well have been—all is illusion. Or—I'm still quoting Sagar—all is repetition.

Where does that leave us? To return to the question of tradition. As Indian writers who live in India, our own sources to a great extent lie in the modern pioneers of the previous generation, some of whom are featured here. One is Malayalam writer K. Satchidanandan who writes about the poet's total disenchantment: his life as a collection of "vain deeds," seeking after revolutions that did not come, books that didn't yield the truth, beauty that is not worth celebrating because it cannot hold up against cruelty and destructiveness. He ends with "Farewell. Call me when the world changes. / I shall come back if the hungry worms / and the obstructing angels permit me."

This is what many in this generation of Indian writers clarified for us—this sense of a moral charge, however muted, to literature, and a purpose, however subtle, to the writer's life. And even when the outlook is bitter, satirical or self-destructive, the writer remains aware that she is operating in a particular social landscape that necessitates the taking of some kind of a stand. In our own era that writerly engagement with society is often loosened or has vanished altogether.

What do we have in its place? A bottomless diversity of contexts and a lively equivocation. As Sohini Basak's sequence of poems on the theme of a future library shows, everything is potentially a story and no story is better than any other. But the leading question is: will there be any future stories at all? Perhaps, for in one possible ending:

> stories will stop sitting on fences, stories will ferry

cures [. . .]

stories will

    disown gods,

        escape frameworks, mouths, the market,

            stories will never figure out how they end,

                how lovely then that we'll be able to say we had a hand in this.

And so that exuberant and yet somewhat vertiginous feeling—*all is addition.*

SAMPURNA CHATTARJI

Making Our Alliances Visible

Let's argue with each other using literature as a tool to read the world.
—Tsering Wangmo Dhompa

Every anthology emerges from a sense of adventure. The impetus for this one, as the initial proposal stated, was to present a lively body of work, full of surprise, which, while overturning expectations, would provide a robust and varied portrait of the ecosystem that constitutes Indian writing in English. If there was to be any bias, that bias would be towards comparatively lesser-known writers deserving of a wider readership, as well as works in translation from other Indian languages. The idea was to capture the spirit of thriving literary communities, and allow selections to sit organically within the interstices of existing and ongoing dialogue.

That dialogue was multi-dimensional—including, but not limited to, an engagement with points of origin, interrogations of troubled histories, dismantling of oppressive constructs, homage to literary ancestors, reinvention of mythologies, and translations of the self. These concerns are true of any literature that deserves to be reckoned with; what, then, would be identifiably "Indian" about any eventual selection? How, after all, could such an amorphous (and endlessly debatable) notion as "Indianness" be defined? And how might the making and reading of this particular anthology unfold against traditions that serve both as locus and point of departure?

In India, as Gautam Chakravarty and Subarno Chattarji, editors of *An Anthology of Indian Prose Writings in English* (2004), point out, "literary anthologies began to appear from the early twentieth century, as the modern languages acquired body and a corresponding awareness of identity and literary history. But the practice has a longer ancestry in the *Subhashita*: medieval compilations of edifying passages from the Sanskrit scriptures and classical Sanskrit literature, which by the late-nineteenth century were rendered into more accessible vernacular *subhashitas*." While the Sanskrit *subhashita* meant "well-spoken" and the Greek *anthologia* "flower-gathering," both tended towards speech (later derivatives of *anthologia* specify "to speak, to pick out words"). Ranging further afield, the Welsh word for anthology is *blodeugerdd*, literally "flowers of poetry/art," most likely an eighteenth-century neologism based on the Latin *florilegium*. This pleasing confluence of meanings—a picking out of well-spoken words, a gathering of eloquences, arranged with an attempt at beauty, informed by the tastes of the gatherer—led me to a neologism of my own, "*subhashita anthologia*," an idiosyncratic/syncretic key to this project that springs from, and is shaped around, the shared heritage that Indian writers claim across time, location and language.

> time, intricate around language until
> only stubs remained
> —Monica Mody

The poet, translator and polymath, A. K. Ramanujan (1929–1993), who taught in America for over forty years, opened the way for "Indian literature" to be seen as many literatures, interconnected through folklore and women's tales as much as by classical poetry and mythology. In "Is There an Indian Way of Thinking? An Informal Essay" he unpacked perceived "cultural tendencies" with the expansive, easy erudition that was his trademark. The essay deserves to be read in entirety. What is germane to my reflection, however, is the following:

> No Indian text comes without a context, a frame till the nineteenth century. [. . .]
>
> Texts may be historically dateless, anonymous: but their contexts, uses, efficacies, are explicit. [. . .] not only does the outer frame-story motivate the inner sub-story; the inner story illuminates the outer as well. [. . .] The tale within is context-sensitive—getting its meaning from the tale without, and giving it further meanings.
>
> Scholars have often discussed Indian texts [. . .] as if they were loose-leaf files, ragbag encyclopedias. Taking the Indian word for text, *grantha* (derived from the knot that holds the palm leaves together), literally, scholars often posit only an accidental and physical unity. We need to attend to the context-sensitive designs that embed a seeming variety of modes (tale, discourse, poem, etc.) and materials. This manner of constructing the text is in consonance with other designs in the culture. Not unity (in the Aristotelian sense) but coherence, seems to be the end.

Not unity, but coherence. That is what I feel our anthological impulse aims at. And while it seems self-evident that any anthology, including this one, is a "context-sensitive design" rather than a grab-bag *grantha*, I would like to think through a few pertinent questions. Which larger narratives motivate and give meaning to smaller sub-stories; what are some of the interior/exterior illuminations; and how can a collection of voices—speaking from anywhere between Perth to São Paulo—be viewed within the frame of Indian writing (my coeditor, Anjum Hasan, addresses what makes it contemporary).

The concept of India as a nation-state is one that began as an "accident of administrative centralization by the British" (Chakravarty & Chattarji), but it was Henry Derozio (1809–1831), an Anglo-Indian poet, teacher and journalist writing in English, who first enunciated it in his poem, "To India—My Native Land." What's intriguing, though not surprising, is that many first-generation Anglophone Indian writers considered England their "native land," the source of inspiration and advancement. Michael Madhusudan Dutt (1824–1873) went to the extent of converting to Christianity in order (he imagined) to write authentically in English. Bombay-born Dom Moraes (1938–2004)—one of the foundational figures of modern Anglophone poetry in India—was lionized as a young prodigy during his years in London and Oxford. In his autobiography, *My Son's Father*, there is a poignant description of his encounter with Oxford scholar Verrier Elwin, who came to India in 1927 as a missionary for the Anglican Church (which he renounced in order to live and work with the Gond tribes). Moraes writes:

> I was delighted to find that Verrier Elwin, on one of his occasional swivels back from the jungle, was briefly in Bombay. I went to see him [. . .] "I don't think I've ever asked you," he said in his gentle way, "do you like painting?" I said yes, Samuel Palmer, Cotman and Crome. He laughed his little husky laugh [. . .] "What a very English trio," he said.
>
> Suddenly what had haunted me on this trip became explicit. My mother and my father had nothing to do with India itself: they were simply themselves, as I was myself, and our relationship had to be worked out independent of where we were. But the colors and smells of India [. . .] pulled me one way, and the new life I led abroad [. . .] pulled me the other.
>
> I told Verrier this, hoping he might explain: he was after all himself an expatriate only he had come the other way. [. . .] He said, "You're in a peculiar historical position, you know. All your family speak English, and, really, you yourself are a very English person. Your reactions aren't Indian, are they? I can't explain that, but there it is. You seem quite naturally to live in a world of English poetry and English painting, and you are an English poet."

As it happens, Moraes did not let his "peculiar historical position" prevent a very real involvement with the India that had once felt so alien to him. In an in-depth and context-sensitive introduction to his critical edition of Dom Moraes's *Selected Poems* (2012), poet-editor Ranjit Hoskote points out that belonging was, for Moraes, "a splendid paradox [. . .] a matter of being at home in a period or a predicament, rather than a place." This paradox is something several of our contributors recognize, as they refuse impervious definitions of nation, preferring instead—as Sejal Shah puts it—to make "each word a country."

> You are looking, I know, to oust that convent-English insect,
> frantically alive, trapped there since class one.
> —K. Srilata

The shift towards "Englishes" other than British appears to have occurred much less contentiously, perhaps for extra-literary reasons: popular culture, Hollywood, the embracing of American models of consumerism, "Amreeka" as the promised land. In this anthology, the subsequent curdling of this idyll is apparent; in the pragmatism of the young narrator of Geeta Kothari's "I Brake for Moose," for example, or the insouciance of Jay Deshpande's poem, "That's the American Dream, Is to Have a Green Lawn." Deshpande's poem took me right back to "Evenings in Iowa City, Iowa" by Dilip Chitre (1938–2009)—one of the first generation of Anglophone Indian poet-translators, prominently featured in earlier anthologies—where, in one fell swoop, he repositioned *expatriate* and *native*, reversed the gaze and reframed the narrative with these lines: "Are we already bitter or are we still bewildered / Filling our brown bags with the bounty of America / Wandering through libraries / Boozing and growing long hair or beards / The true exterior of the expatriate / And conversing in exasperated voices. / Sometimes even writing poems / While the natives mow their lawns."

Aligned to the bounty of America rather than the (fading) allure of England, English came accompanied by a guilt-free, buoyant atmospheric. The angst of struggling against accusations of un-patriotism (read "anti-nationalism"), the erosion of mother tongues, the invariably fractious conversations on "loss" and disingenuous arguments on "authenticity" could be neatly side-stepped, if not avoided altogether in this new domain. Or perhaps it only seemed so to those of us who continued to live and work in English from India, where the familial and fraternal could just as easily become an echo chamber for lingering disquiets.

The confidence to leave those disquiets behind—to be neither bitter nor bewildered—owes as much to the shift in traditional publishing hierarchies as it does to our at-home-ness in English. As writers and editors, Anjum and I are both inheritors and beneficiaries of a tradition of "earlier strugglers in the desert" (Arvind Krishna Mehrotra in his introduction to *The Oxford India Anthology of Twelve Modern Indian Poets*, 1992). I believe this lent our choices an exhilarating sense of freedom. Chakravarty and Chattarji note that "one reason for calling IWE (Indian Writing in English) a 'twice-born' literature is because it began with an expatriate community trying to reckon with a new home in an old language, the very obverse of what Indian authors in English began doing from the latter half of the nineteenth century: using a new language to reckon with the old home." Moving on—and away—from reductive binaries and anguished reckonings, what travels in these pages alongside the shapeshifting idea of belonging (still a work-in-progress) is the equally fluid idea of becoming. To borrow from Ramanujan, perhaps what distinguishes writing from India is its ability to turn "all things, especially rivals and enemies, into itself"!

> More than exiled. Unsettled.
> —Kalidasa / Mani Rao

Could such an absorbent, migratory, and protean sense of self be a useful guide to reading our anthology?

To understand this, I turn to thinker and social historian, Ashis Nandy. In his essay, "The Journey to the Past as a Journey into the Self: The Remembered Village and the Poisoned City," he writes, "while for Victorian England a journey might have been primarily the frame through which others could be seen, for South Asians it has been mainly the frame through which the self can be confronted." Travel was not just a "broadening of the mind," it was the mind itself, "at play with the past and the future of the self." Pilgrimages were centuries old, each "a play with the boundaries of the self." The *Mahabharata* and the *Ramayana* were "organized around the idea of exile," and had sustained existential validity. In the light of the contemporary Indian writer's preoccupation with retellings, as demonstrated by more than one text in our anthology, what is significant is this: "Of the two epics, the *Ramayana* is more loved, but the *Mahabharata* is the one that underpins the Indian consciousness. It serves as a mythography of the Indian self and, at the same time, as a record of the disowned selves within the culture—the non-selves and anti-selves that contribute to the final definition of the self."

It is precisely these disowned, non- and anti-selves that animate our selection. And while there can be no final definition of the self, what matters is the journey, the framing structure that enables a confrontation to segue into a conversation. As thirteenth-century Marathi bhakti poet Sri Jnanadeva put it—in twentieth-century poet Dilip Chitre's translation, "Life of the Opened Self"—"In that city / Beyond all action / Experience arrives / Like a throng of migrants / Stunned."

> Let the conditional
> begin its wordmagic
> —Subhashini Kaligotla

In our anthology, as Anjum establishes, a "translation of the self through literature is evident." I'd like to pause a moment on what might make this translation culture-specific, and to what extent that culture might be Indian—in ways more limber and inclusive than once imagined. Consider the following contributors, whose biographical notes alone indicate interesting trajectories, but whose work proves revelatory of deeper crossings.

Lahore-born Imtiaz Dharker, who grew up as a "Muslim Calvinist" in Glasgow, and now lives between London and Mumbai, has an early poem in which a woman—fed up of being quizzed about her origins—flips the exclusionary "You must be from another country" into the affirmative "I must be from another country." In her newer poems, her voice is more tender than combative; her "I" and "you" closer to the "I is you" offered by Kazim Ali (another of our transnational contributors) as she opens the primal knot of memory with the ease of a mother untying a dishcloth that has kept the parathas warm.

Sujata Bhatt—born in Ahmedabad, India, domiciled in Bremen, Germany, with abiding links with the US—whose early practice of embedding Gujarati script in her English poems was a self-declared way of "destabilizing the authority of English within the poem," can be found here contemplating the "strange brightness" of a neutral country, the fabric of which is as fabular as the idea of neutrality.

Meena Alexander, who was born in Allahabad, and lived and worked in New York, where she died in 2018, writes from a visceral desire for severance and continuation in "Fragments of an Inexistent Whole": "Syllables sieved through floating gates, / Metal clack of printer / Mortal rendition, Fortran—/ The future coming closer and closer." For Alexander, the bridge to cross over from the mounting "census of the dead" to the "grammar of redemption" is the "deliverance of Sanskrit / What I learnt without knowing that I did."

Here then are translations of the self that are indubitably Indian without once closing the door on the stream of visitants from other cultures travelled to, dislocated from, or immersed in. For the "inexistent" self, certainty is concomitant with instability. Memory is more than ancestral longing—it is coding. An attempt to apprehend the "flow of time-sensitive language," in the words of Kolkata-raised, Cincinnati-based Aryanil Mukherjee, who states that all writing is "made from human data / grilled in hominid memory." Internal, instinctive, almost simultaneous translations of the self are made explicit through process: Mukherjee's prose-poem, *code memory*, was "written in two languages, partly in English and partly in Bengali, and transcreated bidirectionally."

The capacity to code-switch between the languages at one's disposal, to be one's own translator, is something other authors in this gathering are blessed with. Translation is, in India, as elsewhere, an increasingly vital and political act. The band of translators is an intrepid (and often unpaid) one, keen to bring the pleasures of their other tongues into the English they think and write in. Poet-translators like Arvind Krishna Mehrotra, Mani Rao, Mustansir Dalvi, Ranjit Hoskote, Priya Sarukkai Chabria and Vivek Narayanan are represented here in both avatars, as is their due. The point, however, is not merely to do with translation as a critical component of this publication nor as literary practice. The point is to celebrate it, irrespective of proverbial losses or gains. "Semiology," Mukherjee writes, "is all about an assemblage of remembered relations." That *assemblage* could comprise fragments of a language one didn't really want to learn. Those *remembered relations* could attempt to embody, through words, a wandering anima.

"Anima Walks Borderless," a prose poem by Nabina Das, ends with the lines: "I'm stateless. I'm a *jajabor*." At once individualized and collective, the "jajabor"—Assamese for "wanderer"—seems to me emblematic not just of this project, but of our persistent authorial excursions. As we raid the tradition repeatedly, we renew it, repeatedly. But what could we possibly mean by "the tradition"? I turn to Octavio Paz's translation from the Sanskrit of Buddhist philosopher and poet, Dharmakirti (C. 7 CE).

The Tradition

No one behind, no one ahead.
The paths the ancients cleared have closed.
And the other path, everyone's path,

>   easy and wide, goes nowhere.
>   I am alone and find my way.

So many of the solitary pathfinders in this anthology have sought and found their own way to open up the overgrown tracks once cleared by the ancients. Their tradition is complex and catholic; their writing an open challenge to the aggressor's insistence on a single story of identity and allegiance. Their itineraries are textual, spiritual, physical, mythical. As Rajiv Mohabir (another poet-translator) puts it in "Vapsi: Return": "In my myth / I was promised a voyage back / home to an India, borders shifted, / my village renamed." In Srikanth Reddy's "Voyager": "Fact is the script of the unknown. / Its shadowy disclosure documents the further world. / [. . .] / He knew the topography of injustice. / It had neither inside nor outside, like love."

Here are the personal mythographies that Nandy posited—both record of, and play with, the boundaries of the self. The mutual illuminations of interior/exterior that Ramanujan spoke of are vividly realized in Arun Sagar's poems where—outside a ritual hall filled with prophesies and prayers—"all things continue / like before." Riffing and swaying between bilingual dictionaries and black leather shoes, this poet has nothing to lose, because "all is rhythm / and blues." Sagar's tradition here is as new as Elvis and as old as utterance. What begins in hesitation—"as each particular takes away / a part of my self"—ends in urgency: "I must speak / [. . .] / O white heat of summer, I must return, and speak to you."

This is more than what Wallace Stevens called the pressure of the imagination countering the unimaginable pressure of reality—this is self answering self, voice countering voice, tongue finding tongue, endlessly baiting words and their reverberations. The impossible task of eliminating the self is what Rosalyn D'Mello writes eloquently of in "Something New, Something Borrowed," where the irrepressible articulacy of inscribing the carnal self is traced back to the possibility of a devotional self.

>   my journey's end,
>   the shape of my waiting,
>   the palm of my devotion
>   —Usha Akella

With religious fundamentalism on the rise around the world, grappling with the sacred gains a new valency, subsumed within the writer's personal pilgrimage. The difficulty of communicating directly with "god" (which the ancients seemed to do so easily) is overcome by contemporary poets through a variety of positions and strategies. Prayer is reimagined as camera movements, *Allah hu akbar* is inflected in Mandarin. Saint poets and women mystics sit alongside other, often overlooked, aspects of "Indian tradition"—that of church committees and King James Bibles, of "Sunday ceremonies of mantraps / and *armageddon now!*"

It is through the improvisatory form, the powerful frisson and undercurrent of sadness in Mona Zote's "Rez" (from which the lines above are quoted) that we get an inkling of the troubles that count for normalcy in North-East India. Trapped between the triumphalist angel and the condescending bloodthirsty adult (symptomatic of mainstream India's attitude towards its outliers), the interiority of the kid's voice illuminates the exteriority of a hopeless environment. Aruni Kashyap's extract from *The House of a Thousand Stories* gives us a glimpse of Assam's late-twentieth-century insurgency and its brutal military suppression. Tsering Wangmo Dhompa says, "I've promised myself I will not write / about exile, or about home, but everything shifts from their positions, except my hope." Both her poems are shadowed by that very exile—of Tibetans to India in 1959, fleeing Chinese persecution.

Clearly, ongoing translations of the self do not imply shutting out the disturbing crackle of reality. Negotiating the slippery zones between belief and bigotry, preservation and ghettoization, the writer owns—greedily, somberly, irreverently—whatever the writing demands. Sharp new voices like Akhil Katyal and Jason Sandhar bring in new registers and resonances. In "oak creek: 5 aug 1919" Sandhar transposes the murder of Sikhs in colonial India onto incidents of racism in Wisconsin. For most Indians, 1919 is easily identifiable as the year of the infamous Jallianwala Bagh Massacre ordered by the British General, Reginald Dyer; while the "true name" that folds away in the face of "dyer's / shrapnel truth" can only be the "sat naam," central to the chanting of the Guru Granth Sahib, the holy book of the Sikhs. In Katyal's "Dehradun 1990," a child's inability to pronounce the letter R becomes a comment on religious chauvinism, no less cutting for its humorous play on language (Hindi). Both these poets tune into—and tinker with—the frequencies of their polyglot, polyphonic backgrounds. References that are both culture- and language-specific shimmer through like phosphorescence. There is neither false pride nor false modesty in having multiple access points, merely a delightful cheekiness, like the one expressed by Lalnunsanga Ralte, a young poet from Shillong. In a poem titled "Fak You" he writes, "Now that you have learned a word in my language / Maybe I will learn one in yours / And then maybe the boxes we have put each other into / Will start to take the shapes of people."

I feel deeply fortunate that we have been able to make this anthology a hospitable place for the shapes of so many people, speaking in so many colors, from the red-wrath of Shelly Bhoil's

> stamp
> of a
> gender
> atop
> the race of fridays's Master

to Subhro Bandopadhyay's "ancient language that breaks / in the silence of a white flower" to (once again) Meena Alexander's incandescent "black flash" of "any *me* I might claim." It is with regret that we have had to let go of prose and poetry by Vijay Seshadri, Manil Suri, Vivek Shanbhag and Anis Shivani. These could not finally be included due to lack of permissions and budget constraints. To all the contributors for whom this book might have felt like an eternity of waiting, I owe a special debt of gratitude.

After living so closely with the project for so long, after extensive readings over more than three years and intervening turbulences, the writing of this essay has been a necessary act of meditation, a looking back on the terrain covered. Revisiting old favorites, I realized afresh the extent to which they contained multitudes, as Anjum and I gravitated to the same texts for different reasons. I was moved by the writerly ability to refocus attention to the original meanings of the words—village, country, world—and fill them with forgotten specificities. I was struck by the contemporary Indian writer's acute sense—acute like loneliness, acute like vision—of the inhabited place as a function of the habitable self.

From who we are to where we live, from rest to flight, Elizabeth Bishop's pensive query—"Should we have stayed at home, wherever that may be?"—stays relevant. In the global context of dispossession and erasure, it seems any literary enterprise concerned with homelands, imaginary or otherwise, could only be undertaken (and read) as a participation, a marking of our place in the world, and yes, our displacement.

It is with this heightened awareness that I seek closure in words taken from Shamala Gallagher's luminous "Mooncalf":

> I am from parents of two different races [. . .] I wear a skin like my father's skin: pale. I wear hair like both parents' once was and which is (for now): black. I wear—or for some time wore—a belief in my skin as deep and tawny like my mother's, a warm and complex gold which showed that I belonged somewhere if not here. [. . .] Mooncalf, if my skin bore a color that told you I once came from a subcontinent in the heat, perhaps you'd look at me and know our alliance instantly. I would like our alliance to be visible.

To those interested in seeing "contemporary Indian writing" for the many-hued thing it is—going against the grain, free to align, re-group, un-belong, free to go renegade—this *subhashita anthologia* will be, we hope, a temptation to seek the plenitude that exists outside the confines of these covers; an acknowledgment of tangled genealogies; a way of making our alliances visible.

FUTURE LIBRARY

ARUN SAGAR

Black Leather Shoes

All is wordplay, word as play. And as each particular takes away
a part of my self to fill in the gaps in myself, I can only speak
of the unnecessary—the images and ways—the flock that sprays
itself across the evening. And so all this is but the comforting
resolution of the mind, over meniscus and radii, the future that
is *waiting on eBay*! And I am left alone with winter's stock
of images, Christmas trees in January, black leather shoes.
And all is perfect in decrepitude. All is addition, concatenation,
collation, all is connected by the *and*. I can but swing forth
and back, from *and* to *like*. Like, all is metaphor. Unavoidable
as Swiss cheese. *Il a fallu qu'on introduise le corps*, the old
man said. The body is a tyrant, yes, and *and* and *like* are both
escape. Bilingual dictionaries, black leather shoes. All is rhythm
and blues. All is comprehension, interpretation, summation, in
between, coming from, moving to. I got nothing to lose, I got
my black leather shoes. There is no *and* or *like*, mere all-
usion, illusion, shadowy rhetoric. All is introduction, refrain,
intermission, repetition, refrain; I must speak to you. I must
speak to you, *from the scented lemon groves, from the
hot sun*. In summer blues and lavender, and shoes of black
leather. And all is September, October, drawing back towards
you. O white heat of summer, I must return, and speak to you.

Naming

Sind wir vielleicht hier, um zu sagen: Haus,
Brücke, Brunnen, Tor, Krug, Obstbaum, Fenster
—Rilke

                It's useless, but I'm trying
to name the trees across the river, testing
my beginner's eye, wanting to say
              cedar, cypress, pine,
but the words dissolve in clear greenness,
pure *tree, arbre, baum.* So much is nameless
              or too easily named:
Friday, Rouen, France, wings over the Seine,
cormorant, kingfisher, crow, names
              made up or made familiar,
syllables settling on my tongue. Creatures
are living in my earlobes, unpronounceable,
              crawling up my legs,
milling about my head, *fly, mosquito, midge,*
names conjured from air, *lightning, raindrop,*
              names built of stone,
cathedral and *spire,* shadow and silhouette;
la Tour du Beurre, a tower made of butter,
              cumulus clouds,
woman, stranger, wife, figure on a bridge,
statue of Corneille, house where Flaubert lived,
              sunset on the ridge,
Bois-Guillaume at evening, name on a photograph
or said aloud each morning, things that one can spend
              one's whole life naming.

The Fourth Day

So this is the smell of death: lilac
and frankincense, a charred
winter freshness
filling the ritual hall.
The prayer book
speaks forth in tongues, and there
remains the need to praise
or prophesy. But
outside all things continue
like before, the petty
robberies upon the steps, the forceps
twisting in the bone.
Last time we met,
you spoke of lust, and how it
should take precedence. And here I
stand with offerings
of petals, and sunlight
on white cloth, and armfuls of leaves
fresh from the trees.
The elegy must be of these.

Note:
The Hindu memorial ceremony *chautha* ("fourth") is held on the fourth day after a death.

ROHAN CHHETRI

The Blueprint among the Ashes

The old man loved his sleep,
my father remarked to the visitors
a week after Grandfather died.
I was twelve
& the cruel metaphor wasn't lost on me.
And indeed, that's how I remember
him in his final days, slumbering
through afternoons on end, alone
in the dank, half-constructed first floor
of the house we called "upstairs,"
with stray cats for company,
the other rooms crammed
with old wood & chests of rare coins,
brooding over this failing architecture.
This man once feared by the whole town
now reduced to a fetish
of hoarding lumber, an unreasonable fear
of hospitals, & a refusal
to face the waking hours.
So when he did die, for days
it felt like he would cough at the door
& enter & no one would dare say a word.
Upstairs, where I never went alone
for years until
my mother cleared a room
& opened a beauty salon.
One day I took my friend there
& plucked his eyebrows clean
gnawing at a thread wound round my fingers,
just the way I'd seen my mother do it.
Five years later, a fever killed him.
I came to the city.
My uncle married again & moved
to a room on the first floor with his wife,
& my mother closed down the salon.

Now when I'm back home & go upstairs,
sometimes there is a moment
when I walk across the balcony
& enter the hall. A moment
when the old hesitation comes back
in the cobwebbed dark when a bruised cat
slinks through a broken window,
& I smell Grandfather's musk
in the sunless air, fossilized in the dust
& old teak hollowed by termites.
I think of the dream my father had,
months after Grandfather's death:
the old man waking up here,
resigned & hysterical as the night he died,
making a soft noise of our names in the dark,
still hearing our voices downstairs,
tentative laughter testing the air,
us going about our days through
the quiet, forgetful grief,
& hearing too the gray clamor of the street.
I imagine him wanting to burst forth
into our bright static of flesh,
through my father's dream,
& now through this air I stand on
that his will is kneading so thin
& timeless, like a yawn that quietens
the whole world for a few edgeless seconds
to a seclusion of jaws.

Visitation

A bleak day, but for the pale sun bruising the air
to a color of wine. Across the street, a yellow
dollhouse on a tenement balcony & scrawled
across it in red, a little girl's initials I will not reveal.
But what it all stands for: the same flaring sadness
I felt leaving her house on mornings like this.
I remember the bright days after, how I leaned
my forehead against the fogged glass door of the train
each morning, undulating along the brief stretch
of the cantonment, where the forest thinned
into a few trees, burnt ground, & a rampart of concrete
and barbwire. I waited every morning to see them
grazing on the periphery: three brown antelopes
I couldn't name by taxonomy. Outside, soldiers
patrolled the morning with their mute rifles
across welted shoulders. And on some mornings,
I would see one of the three stray & break into
a careless lope, so gently, I imagined the underbrush
rising beneath the wake of its cloud feet must feel
something close to knowing you were loved.
The way I still felt then, towards the end,
as I lifted her brown hand from across
my collarbone, slipped into my poor clothes
in the half-light of the living room & tiptoed
out of the house into the deepening dawn, before
the morning's gleaming thumb could snuff out
any small fires we might have divined by night.

EUNICE DE SOUZA

Learn from the Almond Leaf

Learn from the almond leaf
which flames as it falls.
The ground is burning.
The earth is burning.
Flamboyance
is all.

Compound Life

1.
The first-floor procuress
takes the air.
Her bosom precedes her.
Ditto the pigeon
that follows her.

2.
She has a quacking voice.
He has duck-tailed hair.

3.
Mrs P's daughter never smiles
never talks
walks with her head down
looking for potholes and pitfalls.

4.
Mrs V beats her husband.
The churchman says:
Into every life
a little rain must fall.

5.
What can trees do in such a place
except light their own fires

6.
The night watchman
sleeps through the night.
Opening his tiffin he says
This is a good job.
The best I ever had.

7.
A compound full of silver cars.
The sky with not a single silver star.

8.
A bird hovers.
A word hovers.
A word is a bird
is a bird is a bird

9.
Hot, still, dawn air.
A rat, condemned to gnaw,
the only sound.

10.
The downstairs neighbors sing:
Yes
Yes Yes Lord
Yes

Western Ghats

Fling my ashes in the Western Ghats
They've always seemed like home.
May the leopards develop
A taste for poetry
The crows and kites learn
To modulate their voices.
May there be mist and waterfalls
Grass and flowers
In the wrong season.

JASWINDER BOLINA

Country, Western

Via carriage and steamer and saddle and rail,
via twin-prop and airship and ship of the desert,
via savannah, via steppe, via zip line and glider,
under moat and over rampart, over barb

and under wire, over three green seas, via burro, via grapple,
via ballistic trajectory, like broke satellites cratered
in alien dirt, like banged knuckles on the door
of an uneasy speakeasy, we were the party after

the party nobody wanted, sober and famished, we were
the parched fronds beggared and supplicant
to the clouds, the clouds cool and distant
as a bourgeoisie, and we without our sleet coats,

and we without our hail hats, with less than a shekel,
less than a rupee, less than a kroner or any glinting
Kennedy, three pence short of a peso, we arrived
over guard and under sentry, via catapult, via coyote,

via many genies blinking, we arrived bats in a manse no bat
should inhabit, so we grew fin and we grew talon,
we scrambled arachnid and jaguared in the canopy,
dissembled, reassembled, and it's true we piss now

in marbled closets and shower indoors as if we are clergy,
it's true no junta defiles us, no furious bomber
or hegemon's boot, but the faces on the currency
all watch me, the paintings in the museum all say,

This is life on Earth! This is life on Earth! so I'm jealous
of their candor, but that isn't my pasty duchess,
that isn't my butchered messiah, that isn't my bounty
of meat beside the gilded chalice, I'm no Medici,

and that isn't my life on earth I arrived in via wormhole,
via subspace, via mother ship descending, in a snap-button
sarong, in a denim sari, in my ten-gallon turban, I look
so authentic you'd almost believe it's the 44th of July,

and I'm the sheriff of this here cow town, I'm one jack better
than a straight flush, buzzards above the valley,
I can see the whites of your eyes, my name is Consuela.
you can call me *Mr. President*. You can reach for the sky

ARVIND KRISHNA MEHROTRA

Three Questions for Prabhu S. Guptara Concerning his Anthology of Indian Religious Poetry in English

1.
Dear Mr Guptara,
The day I got your letter
I'd had myself vaccinated against smallpox.
Do you think the vaccination will rise?

2.
Dear Mr Guptara,
I washed my shirt this morning
and it's still wet round the collar.
Do you think the earth
is pear-shaped?

3.
Dear Mr Guptara,
For heaven's sake.
But then that girl in red
bicycling down the road,
isn't she so utterly religious.

Ballad of the Black Feringhee

*I would rather sing folk songs against injustice
and sound like ash cans in the early morning
or bark like a wolf
from the open doorway of a red-hot freight
than sit like Chopin on my exquisite ass.*
—Carl Rakosi

India it is midnight the tenth of March and I open my palm
India the silver coin doesn't vanish, the matchbox doesn't fly
  into the trees, and I pick the wrong jack
India I've hung up my magician's gloves
India I've been betrayed by the tricks learnt in the
  long narrow rooms of Allahabad, Ljubljana, and Iowa City
India I've returned to the brightness of your streets,
  the regularity of your sounds, the evenness of your days
India I'm going to hypnotize your bricks
India listen to the grass, there's something going on in Ethiopia
India give me five pounds of rice and I won't ever leave
India give me a peanut and I'll shut my window
India my hands are tied and my footprints trapped
  like wild pigeons
India what are the first principles of ventriloquy
India I was born in the year of your independence
India I've been trying to procure a bottle of kerosene
India what will I do when the lights go out
India if you blindfold me I'll see you better
India will I always have to write in the dark
India the cats are nervous
India where's my horoscope
India you were an astrological mistake
India I'm afraid of your truckers, shopkeepers, postmen and herbs
India the man in the street is a shrewd animal
India you don't transport them in trains
India you don't tie them to trees and shoot them
India you kill them in "encounters"
India you kill them while they're trying to "escape"
India your police stations are little Siberias

India when they come for me I'll put on a clean shirt
India their bullets won't settle on me like flies
India I want to wrap you in an old newspaper and carry you from
 door to door
India there's no need to hide your large teeth
India what a big nose you have
India remember the pile of ash on Mandelstam's left shoulder
India don't destroy yourself in slow motion

RALPH NAZARETH

The Song of the Plumber On the Fourth of July

Re-born on the fo'th of July!
he among us
humongoUS!
—Mercury Jam in *Radium Roulette*

Wassup she ask me? What's the beef?
Ya see, I, ai, ai, aieee, I's turnin' o'er a new leaf.
Decision decision, make a sharp incision with precision
in the dead ol' brain and train out the new life
with fife and drum and bubble gum:
Not gonna sit on my buns. Gotta have maself some fun
befo is all done! Gonna ditch 'em
college words—they's just fo' de birds—
and switch to the bitch
of my rappin' 'n' clappin' imperial American
Buffalo Billy Johnny come lately marchin' hunk of self
singin' no mo' in low tones playin' dead bones,
pocahontasizin' sentimentalizin'
but hittin' the high note from C to whinin' C,
from Californication to Riker's Island nation

America, oh America, ah, how I love ya
for your deep dark whatever 'tis, big bad whatever 'tis,
the best the worst, bombs burstin'
the bushwackin' and tackin'
in the wind of a mind hellbent on bein'
clear as clear and simple for a change after all the years
of obfuscation. Ya, ya, but the question
is watchya gonna say, mon?! One thinga sur,
not gonna go hush under Bush.
Rockin' 'n' jivin' me gonna talk up a storm
'bout nuthin' but everythin',
wigglin' 'n' wagglin', fingas thrustin' 'n' dustin',
eyeballs mockin' 'n' rockin' in their sockets,
hip as hip, pokin' 'n' stokin',
murky me's now reborn on the fo'th of July ai ai ai

trappin' 'n' zappin'
all the liars in their lairs
rows and rows of Carly Roves
Rummy Felds Gonzalo Albertez.

When da plumber came to fix my faucet
he it was who told me
I'm a-crazy for not turnin' 'n' yankin'
and jackin' 'n' breakin'
and burnin' 'em bridges

This is the whole thang, he sez,
the whole kit and katzaboodle
'tis about good 'ol America, he sez.
Lemme tellya the secret of 'Merica, he sez.
You raise the ante in your panty, ratchet up the hatchet
dontya worry 'bout breakin' nothin'
thas the whole fuckin' secret, he sez, of America.

You better grow up, he sez, is time
to leave your land of sacred cow, genteel knowhow,
he sez, become American,
a bloody rare prime-rib American, thas what you're gonna be
when you swear by your balls and greasy overalls
that you CAN do, an AmeriCAN,
yessirree, an AmeriCAN
No CAN'T just CAN, get it buddy?
Don't ever call furra plumber, never again!
Break it and fix it, thas AmeriCAN
Break it and fix it, fix it and break
O America!

SUJATA BHATT

A Neutral Country

He just wanted to step out
for a walk—some fresh air
to clear his head—and on the way back
he told his wife, he'd get some milk and eggs.
But he found dead bodies in front of his door,
five dead bodies, all young, all so young,
he repeats. It will take him a long time
to recover from this.
Now he prefers to stay at home.

℘

One day a letter arrives,
an invitation, we accept—
we agree to visit a neutral country.

We cross rivers and valleys and mountains.
It is a quiet journey.
A strange brightness surrounds us.

℘

Over here the air smells of cheese.
The first light in the morning
comes through layers of fog.

White gauze—endless veils—

And somewhere along the paths
we cannot see, somewhere, they tell us
Psyche walks, Eurydice walks—

They want us to believe—

We know there are cows somewhere
                and church bells
waiting to be heard— But now
even the grapes are asleep.

*

They let us stay in one of their castles
and ask us to entertain their King.

Their King arrives with apples and honey,
           with chocolate and coffee.
Their King arrives with a violin
     and bottles of wine.

We never know what to say to him
and listen to his stories instead.

*

It's a castle protected by roses,
a castle protected by a lake.

Their lake smells of the dreams of birds—
there are dreams they call ghosts
and dreams they call fish.

Somehow they know what birds believe.

Their fish are alive and smell of nothing.
The lake's water smells of winter—
as if winter breathes within it.

The lake's water holds the memory
of a silver necklace once forgotten in the grass—

*

Afternoons we sit in their rose garden
and watch bees follow the sun.
Their roses are so fragrant

our hearts ache—our hearts ache
and we do not know why.

We watch lizards turn into leaves
and leaves turn into lizards.
We listen to the soft scraping, rustling sound
of their flight as they race down
the steps of the castle.
Even the oldest, most beautiful stones
cannot keep them.

But a nun follows the lizards
to a graveyard—and there she sings
to them until they dance.
She shows us how she does this
day after day—and we watch the way she turns
towards the roses.

༄

It is August, early August—
before sundown—
    and as we walk through
        their vineyards
we can feel shadows turn gold.

༄

We have forgotten to count the days,
forgotten why we came here.

They ask us to look at the stars,
at the moon— They ask us to believe—

Notes from the Hospital

There are three of them:
Love, Life and Death. Inseparable.
Now that I live in a hospital
I see them every day
when they follow the doctors
on their rounds. Inscrutable,
absorbed in their own world
just like the doctors.

Sometimes Death has the stare of a lioness.
Sometimes Life smells of the sea.
Sometimes Love sings a song no one can hear—
almost no one.

But these days Love stays behind
and lingers in my room.

You will find more stories of love
in a hospital than anywhere else.
And yet, somehow their computers have failed
to keep a file on love.
Somehow all their intricate instruments
have failed to record any sign of love.
But the peonies on the window sill
know everything—so much more
than you could ever understand.

The peonies stand tall
in their creamy richness,
all glossy silks and countless ruffled petals—
a milky softness, whispered hints,
and the shy awakening of petals touched by the sun.
Beyond splendor, beyond glory—
they are goddesses who have turned
into flowers. I can see their faces

and I know they are not aloof.
The peonies stand tall
but they are troubled
by the helicopters landing outside,
troubled by the smell of disinfectant.

The peonies can hear the legs
weeping for their beloved, lost lymph nodes.
The peonies have heard a lovelorn liver
plead with an unresponsive pancreas.
The peonies know that the kidneys
mourn the lost liters of blood
while the lungs, secretly in love with the kidneys,
can offer no comfort.
The peonies are worried about the heart
because it is confused. "Why?" it says,
"Why?" all day long.
The heart feels betrayed
and the brain, who loves the heart,
feels guilty and tired.
And yet, deep down the heart knows
that everyone is innocent
except perhaps the Universe,
except perhaps Fate.
Meanwhile the brain promises
to create dreams, dreams that might heal.
The brain promises so much.
And the peonies?
The peonies ignore their own sorrow
and become even more fragrant.

MONIKA KUMAR

Translated from Hindi by Sampurna Chattarji in collaboration with the author

On Seeing a Watermelon

Seeing a watermelon
was my introduction to vastness.

I can only approximate
how much I love you:

by the handful,
as much as the sea,
or not at all.

Approximations fail me
when I look at a watermelon.
How red it will be
how fleshy
how its meditative eyes would be arrayed inside.

You were stubborn in your insistence:
the earth is round as an orange.
You refused to accept
it could also be like a watermelon.

Anyway!
I lied to you
when I said I can tell you, approximately,
how much I love you.

All estimations are a failure of my language.
I need a few signs of exclamation
mad transports
that will gently translate my failures.

Window Seat

To be happy in life one needs very little.
That "little" can sometimes be no more than this:
when we are all set to travel by bus or train or plane
we should be lucky enough
to get a window seat.
And, having bought a ticket,
avoided arguments with co-passengers,
stowed away our luggage safely,
after all of this,
we should be lucky enough to slip easily into ourselves.

Between home and the wild how hard to find such places
where we can take naps light as flowers,
have hundreds of trees cradle our sleep
or the whiteness of clouds carry us towards nothingness.
To wake from this small sleep is a miracle,
this sleep repairs our dwindling being,
restores us to our position,
brings us back to the question
of who we are,
which we ask ourselves once again,
even if our only answer
is to burst into tears.

KIRUN KAPUR

Girls Girls Girls

Along the strip in Waikiki, past sailor bars
and clubs, the length of beach where lipstick
sunsets smudged and magazines would shoot
and caption, *Paradise*. Past posh hotels
where M. and I would wait for some nice man
to buy us drinks from the bar. We'd watch
the women walk like they were stars onstage,
dress like they couldn't wait to be undressed,
leaning over into idling cars. Out on the west side
of the island, J. tells me any man she dates
is more likely to hit her than pay for her dinner.
Teenagers holding babies spit at us when we stare:
What you looking at? You got nothing.
I have nothing, sobs L., today, on the phone.
I know it isn't my fault, but when I think of how I let him do it
over and over, even helped him cover it up, I hate myself.
I'm thinking of the man who owned the noodle shop,
the man who'd always sit with me and chat
about Hanoi, warm water in canals,
moms on bikes with babies tied down
front and back, how to tell a ripe papaya.
I saw him on the news a few years back,
for smuggling women in refrigerated trucks.
He owned the bar called *Girls Girls Girls*
a few doors down from where he served me pho,
the one whose sign was made of neon legs
that kicked and kicked until they were a stain of light.
We liked to swim along the south shore
when the tide was right. You had to time your dive
or crack your head against the reef. More than once
a girl washed up. Sometimes they named her
on the news. M. and I drank Kamikazes
on the lanai of the new Sheraton,
the chief of security coming out to check
we were the right sort of girls, regaling us

with stories of the wallets stolen off of businessmen
by ladies *visiting* their rooms, a theft
they'd later blame on the hotel maid.
I hate—L.'s voice, mine. *When I think
of how I*—how many times have I said it?
How many times have I said nothing at all
or tried to explain why we aren't at home—
the right sort of girl and the wrong,
why we're out under the orange street-lights.

MANOHAR SHETTY

Taverna

After twenty years of yoga
And mastery of its
Acrobatic asanas—forehead
On the floor, feet round
The neck, total breath control—
He tripped over the doormat
And died of cardiac arrest—
All of 44. Clean living,
As he put it once,
Is the path to nirvana.
At the Goodluck Taverna
Eddie, 74, pours three
Quarters of cashew feni
Topped by a shot
Of doutor's brandy
Down the hatch below
A picture of Mother Mary
Between sunset till
The bar shuts at twelve.
He goes home on his
Moped without
Troubling the potholes
Or the pigs and sleeps
The sleep of the just.
This his ritual the past
Forty years though every
Christmas doc warns him
It's his last.
I asked him once
Over a peg, boiled eggs
And a saucer of peanuts
The secret of his long life
And sound health.
He blinked behind his soda-
Water-bottle lenses and said,

Drink. Siesta.
And God bless.
What for you is poison
Is for me tonic
And medicine.

Carried Forward

Beyond Furniture & Fixtures,
Fixed Assets incl of Plant
& Machinery, Goodwill incl
Of Green Donation & Tree
Trimming Vehicle, Gross
Profits, R&D on WMD
Incl of Hospitality,
Sundries (in millions)
As Incentives to sundry
Inspectors (of Boilers)
& Miscellaneous Agents
Incl of Undercover
& an unnumbered account
In the Caymans, here is an
Asterisked footnote
In the fine print—words
Carried Forward for their
Own sake, but clear as a trickle
Of water dripping
In rhythm deep in a skeletal
Megalopolis
Buried one metric
Mile below the burning
White landscape.

Jackfruit

Something carnivorous in carving it open.
The two halves, sighing in a fragrance
overwhelming as incense,
rest on their domed heads.
The stem's acrid milk reddens
my skin, cleaves the knife-edge.
My hands grope in the wholesome
innards, the golden slippery ligaments,
the litter of flesh-colored seeds,
the plucked flesh heaped in a bowl,
the pimpled carapace
like something disemboweled.
Who would have imagined a blister
to bloat in the ripening heat
to this pendulous
softness and hardness.
Strange maternal fruit,
what unearthly roots
bring such seeds to bloom?

SHARANYA MANIVANNAN

The Chicken Trusser

Seven in the morning in the Chintadripet
quarter, and on the next street are women
with their baskets on the pavement before
them, threading jasmines on string to be
measured out to the lengths of their
forearms. Here, wire cages of white
birds are stacked one atop the other in
front of a blood-bright Vodafone wall.
I watch the chicken trusser emerge from
under the loud shutter of his storefront,
raising feathers with each step, like a
molting angel. He carries
nothing. He opens

a cage and in a swift movement has
a hen by the neck, then by the feet,
dangling it upside down so it stills in
that peculiar manner of poultry. "It's
hypnotism," someone told me once.
"They're comatose." It hangs slack
from his fist, as if caught mid-dive.
One by one, dexterous, he subdues
them this way, until in his hand is a
bouquet of fowl, suspended in sleight
before slaughter. In the cages, an
agitation of wings, packed tight.

With his other hand he loops a knot of
twine around their feet, lays the birds
against the asphalt, secures it, and
boutonnières them to the handlebar
of his motorcycle. Then he opens
another cage. When he is done,
a consecution of white chickens,
bound claws skyward, will move

through the city, bumping against the
bike like a heavy-tasseled shawl.

I walk away. I buy flowers for my hair,
and watch the women weaving jasmine,
their fingers twining and knotting rows of
small white buds, twining and knotting, and
when I lift a forearm of strung blossoms to
my braid, I can think only of those beaked
heads, garlanded together, the trail of
petals that will scatter through the city
this morning, soft as silence.

SUBHRO BANDOPADHYAY

Translated from Bengali by Ranjit Hoskote in collaboration with the author

Dog Days

What do we whisper to ourselves?
The ruling party drops a cadaver indifferently.
Will my friends in the city believe it?

I did not want a tropical breeze along the arctic gale
But when the bones curve through the finger
My hands want to hold something

There is only decay in the stony construction . . .

What do these mongrel-days find, scratching
The dusty roads of the heart?

About Presences
for Bhaswati

1.
It is not broken
Yet
We are walking through a lawn covered with glass

Why do we have to hide the dew
On the bodies of question-less evenings?

You moved away without saying anything
Serenity occupied your space

Your name is nowhere
Only your presence

2.
I stabbed a broken piece of mirror in my proper noun
No search left
Neither answer nor direction

Is a piece of stone enough for the Self?

You are the sole recipient

Of the presence that isn't there . . .

Glass Pronouns
for Bhaswati

> *Living in pronouns*
> —Pedro Salinas

1.
You are a broken song, nailed to the body of April.

This rocky fall of morning is shivered glass
Exposing
Liberating you to a fragrance
of boiling rice

A tune is born on the line of dawn
When the metallic trunk of a leafless tree grows violently—

Can the shadow of my cheek still offer flesh? To whom?
Why do the fletched blades fly towards refugee camps?
Time curdles on the yellow of classical music . . .

Tell me
are the old songs now
letters to be read alone?

2.
You could have been a blue leaf sometime

Your designed tread-path
towards the pilgrim's pale robe
vanishes into a glass cloud
colored
it is the ancient language that breaks
in the silence of a white flower
the evening that remains floating
is it the sound of your anklet?

Is this waiting
the rounded vibration
of cowbells in a valley?
You are a broken song, nailed to the body of April.

TABISH KHAIR

Who in a Million Diamonds Sums Us Up?
Or, Fru Andersen speaks to me across two centuries

> *The man who has had the time to think enough,*
> *The central man, the human globe, responsive*
> *As a mirror with a voice, the man of glass,*
> *Who in a million diamonds sums us up.*
> —Wallace Stevens, "Asides on the Oboe"

1.
The view from the bank is mostly bleak,
Though sometimes a barge passes by, lighted and loud.
With gin for warmth I have stood here washing
Those clothes I hoped he would get to wear.
Once when he returned with his face slapped,
I took him out of school.
Not you, I told the teacher, not you,
Life has blows enough in its bloody bag for him.
He was an outsider like you, and as ugly, black man.
Like you, he came from nowhere. Like you, he would sing.
He would do more: he would dance, float on a cloud,
With those long limbs of his, his heavy sunken face.

2.
Is he coming now, is he coming again, in his moment of glory?
What music is this that floats like milk on water?
I remember the first time he sailed by, in rich garments;
Like the clothes I had washed were the clothes he wore.
I stood here, just here, with gin for company,
And watched the music drift by on that lighted barge.
I believe he raised his hands in a surreptitious moment;
I know he called to me in the darkness of his art.
But the barge was too far away, the music too loud;
I stood silent like you, stranger, dark writer,
And watched him toasted on the barge of dreams.
He knew I never held it against him, the distance between us.
I had heard him croak; I had watched him stumble.
What did they know, those toasting him, how far away he was?

3.
At a certain time of the year, when the season grows cold,
Hands roughened by washing, mind deadened with drink,
I come and stand here to watch him pass in his glory.
Year after year, centuries maybe. Who knows?
Mostly I stand lonely, as on that day; sometimes I wave.
And sometimes I find a shadow by my side; today it is you.
Someone who watches him from a distance, silently like me.
I know the shadow every time, though it is always different.
Distance knits those shadows to him, and to me.
Silence too, for you are those who hear him in the silence;
He lives in you who do not toast him on the lighted barge.

4.
In some I see his stumble, in some I hear his croaking;
My steadfast tin soldier, my ugly duckling.

5.
Child, lover, friend, stranger
Are names for presence and absence,
Are terms to measure distance.
They speak of love, or fame, or success,
But what do they know who sail on lighted barges?
Do they know how long it takes
For the chilled body to get used
To another's warmth and shape?
Three months or two years, I would say.
In any case you ease the body along
On soft crutches to begin with, until
You learn to walk again,
Pour coffee instead of tea,
Talk just a bit differently,
Slant opinions unconsciously
To fit a different shoulder
Into your (re-grown) arms,
Consider perfectly normal
A new curvature of spine,
To stop yourself just in time
From leaning on ghost limbs.
It does not take long to anticipate a fall.
What do they know who sail on lighted barges?

6.
To arrive anywhere you have to come from afar,
As he did, as shadows like you do, you ugly black man.
In his fairy tales, they find peace,
But I see you lay mines between his lines.
I see you step on mines he laid between his lines.
You know where they are, the distance has taught you.
Each explosion shatters his mirror of himself
And multiplies it into a million diamonds.
It returns him to himself, the glass man,
The man with no reference and all.
You watch him from the bank where the view is bleak.
He listens for your explosions and not their lighted words.
Go ahead, writer from nowhere, silent shadow:

Blast my immortal son to bits.

ROBIN S. NGANGOM

Marriages and Funerals

I've stopped going to marriages and funerals. Any demonstration of grief or joy unnerves me. Solemnity withers me and dark sartorial elegance moves no one. It's not that I've forgotten kindness, or to wish people happiness if they can find it. I could help the bereaved furtively after the mourners have eaten and left. I have become truly unsociable.

I can't fathom why anyone would like to be comforted except by people they love selfishly. You only need hugs and kisses from people who give you, when pressed, your morsel of flesh. I cannot be comforted, except by the woman I love illicitly.

I often wonder about the efficacy of marriages and funerals. Could it be because others are as worried, as I was during my own wedding feast, that my friends would not show up for some mystifying reason? As regards funerals, I know that if the house of the dead cannot keep a demonic hold on me, my absence will not make any difference. But I don't want to be censured for not attending marriages or funerals. I wish people would not invite me to weddings or bring news of an old acquaintance's death. If I could, I wouldn't attend even my own funeral.

I remember the day I returned home, and without even seeing my father I went to my aunt's house when I heard my cousin had died during my long absence. I tried to match my aunt's grief by trying to show some tears in my eyes but ended up sniffing like a dog. After that, my cousin's sister, my other lovely cousin, in whose body I first sang a liquid tune, gave me pineapple to eat and we smiled at each other. I used to dip my hands into her blooming breasts, a pair of frightened pigeons. But later, my dead cousin appeared in my dreams to play and protect me again as he did during our childhood. He took a long time to go away and I had to spit three times to make sure he wouldn't haunt me.

I remember this film about slum-dwellers in Bombay and how after the tears and the burning they would bring out their bottles of orange liquor and get drunk and have a real ball. That's one funeral I would like to attend.

Saint Edmund's College
after Jotamario Arbeláez

To Basu, gardener, who marijuana kept alive
To an Irish Brother, shipwrecked in a hill station
Facta, non verba

Grafted at fifteen
On Lum Mawrie hill
One winter I burnt
Pine needles, cones, branches
On its sepia slope,
Avoiding fetes,
Fiercely intelligent classmates,
But lusting after the nymphs
Who came to smoke in the forest,
Or watching movies
In the school hall
While the principal smirked
At demurely horrified Loreto Convent girls
During a naked scene.

I avoided the principal's
German Shepherds
Lurked in the corridors
Severed nude Greek goddesses
Inside the library of gravitas
Took my turn at graffiti
On the toilet wall
The future is in your hands
Shake well after use,
If you shake it more than once
You're playing with it,
They said.

At economics class,
Adam Smith, the father himself,
Hawked and spat
And asked me if I didn't sleep the night before

While the brother who taught chemistry
Advised a classmate to take a formula on faith
When he failed to grasp it.
The geography teacher
During his frothy lecture on African rivers asked
Why my friend laughed like a crocodile.

On many fluid days
I inhabited parallel worlds
Of tailors and boarding houses
Of barbers and books
Of hostel and bar,
Speculated on sex and movies
With little money in my pocket,
And only one pair of shoes
But many roads.

Understanding

I can understand, on this virtual day,
even without smelling,
let alone touching it. So
I'll not say a word
about the sea giving up a toddler.
I can even understand
this groundswell of feeling
as if humanity were testing its waters,
after adapting a short brackish tragedy
despite pleas from the gentlest mourner not to use
the image of drowning
but only remember a child's smile,
in an age whose only metaphysical worry is
"what can be saved?"
trees, animals, or children, for instance,
late after the mocking "ecstatic destruction."

GIEVE PATEL

Postmortem

It is startling to see how swiftly
A man may be sliced
From chin to prick,
How easily the bones
He has felt whole
Under his chest
For sixty, seventy years
May be snapped,
With what calm
Liver, lung and heart
Be examined, the bowels
Noted for defect, the brain
For hemorrhage,
And all these insides
That have for a lifetime
Raged and strained to understand
Be dumped back into the body,
Now stitched to a perfection,
Before announcing death
Due to an obscure reason.

The Multitude Comes to a Man

The multitude comes to a man
When he acquires the power
To heal: slowly the multitude
Comes dragging
Its heel. What
Can the multitude want
As I join it to visit
The man who can heal?
The multitude sees its own power
Accumulate before
The healing man, and exchanges
Willingly power
For power.

Of Sea and Mountain

When at a friend's exhibition of paintings
The works are wonderful
And the crowd substantial
And you feel a sinking boredom
Which you would not have felt
Had the paintings been yours

Or at a friend's exhibition of paintings
The works are not wonderful
But the crowd as substantial
And you feel pity and anger
For and at your friend
For and at the crowd
And at yourself

And on both occasions you rush from the gallery
On to the road
To fill your lungs with air
That is not bitter with your imperfections

Then, O Sea, I think of you—
Your unbroken chain
Of deep salt waters.

MONICA MODY

stayed home with language

i.

stayed home
stayed safe

stayed between languages like an old sheet
ghost-specter drawn with dust

scared not a child
not one

turned a corner & longing leapt at my hem
dog-like

hem bleeding
him with his bleeding triggered my flood
I built a boat

language refugee on a curled paper boat

ii.

so I'd lost what I'd set out to find
longed for
& set out to find

when language pulled me to itself like an old sheet
wrinkled with overuse

I wore tatters for my crown
my beard reached the ground

with birds & cairns & shouts
syllables & nests

& mice chased time for a bit of game
walnuts passed between us—it was a game
of passing time

time, intricate around language until
only stubs remained—
       cracked shells

he had long wiggled out of shells
& bled, shifting to bone

his eye still looked at me & we loved
& I inched on formless limb towards his eye
or was it love

ANDAL

The Song to Kamadeva, God of Love
Translated from Classical Tamil by Ravi Shankar

In January hoarfrost, I sweep the ground
to draw sacred mandalas with fine sand,

intricate adornment of stars and matrixes
of dots in rice powder that will disperse

in the afternoon void. The art of engaging
beauty for its own form and transient sake.

Enraptured, flushed pink, I turn to you
& your brother to ask, *how do we still live?*

Untie me with the hand that holds the discus
ringed in fire so I might adorn more streets

with sand dripped through my fingertips.
I bathed alone during the vast song of dawn,

& tended the fire with tender, smooth twigs.
My vow to him courses through my body

like a ripened blossom strung on your bow
to release with keening motion the name

of the only one capable of ocean-breaths
dotted with song cleaved from between beaks.

Draw the bow at me, loosening braids of reason
until I am an untied string without a knot,

united as wave and postulate. Concluded.
Three times a day I will worship at your feet

with fragrant blossoms of moonflowers,
my heart ablaze, from fiery tips of arrows

woven from efflorescence to spell his name,
Govinda, a musk essence of transcendence.

Aim the arrow at him & let it fly, to pierce
him until I might enter that succulent light.

O ancient Kamadeva, I paint cave walls
with your names, trace with glistening

forefinger your banner bearing glinting shark,
attendants waving fly-whisks, your sleek

black bow shining with filigreed carvings.
Do you even take notice of my obsession?

From childhood, I pledged all that in time
would ripen and swell to the one and only

lord of Dvaraka; I beg you unite me with him.
My surging breasts long to leap to the touch

of his hand which holds aloft the flaming discus
& the conch. I shudder to think of my body

being offered to mortal men when it was made
to wait only for him, like *darshan*, the sacred

offering anointed by learned Brahmins versed
in the Vedas, but instead of being consummated

with the divine, sniffed & pawed at, desecrated
by forest jackals who'd eat decomposing bones

easily as blessings. Even through springtime,
I will keep my word Kamadeva & praise you

for rousing the insatiable, sleep-heavy limbs
of young people into exquisite mutual enticement.

All day, I will sit within myself, waiting for the dark
lord hued & arrayed overhead as rain clouds,

then as dusky blossoms from a blackberry bush.
Please coax his glance this way! Persuade his lotus-

eyes to consider my lithe bud, to shower down grace.
O Manmatha! Take him my simple gifts: sugar-

cane, freshly harvested grains steamed, sweet rice,
flattened paddy; ask him to eat them from my hand.

Coax the world-measurer to caress my waist,
to encircle the twin globes of my breasts

& your glory will resound for generations to come.
See my body is filthy. My hair unravels. My lips pale.

I eat but once a day, grudgingly, already engorged
on longing. O radiant and mighty Kamadeva,

please take note of my vow. I have nothing left
to say except for this singular wish: grant me

the pleasure of fielding the flux of the force
that claimed my womanhood. Let me share

its roar. I will worship you three times a day
& bring you fresh flowers, unless you refuse

my wish to serve my lord. Then I will flood black
ocean with my tears, will rend the air with grief

& cry out with unfulfilled love *amma*! *amma*!
until you hear no other sound no other time.

I labor unaccompanied under the heaviest yoke,
a beaten ox left in barren fields to starve.

So Kotai of the kingdom of Putuvai, from the city
of towering mansions cresting like mountain peaks,

sang this garland of flowering Tamil to plead her case
with Kamadeva, God of love, with his sugarcane

bow & five-flower arrows, to help him unite her
with her love, the lord who hurled an elephant

by the tusk & ripped a bird from beak to beak
like a blade of grass. The dark one lustrous as a gem.

All those who wail these blues will remain forever
at the becoming of Being, from which we all arise.

Take Me to His Sacred Places

Translated from Classical Tamil by Priya Sarukkai Chabria

Dear mothers, can't you see I quiver when you say "Madhava"?
I'm cut bowstring vibrating for his touch. Your counsel's
incomprehensible like the deaf talking to the dumb.

> His mother he left to be reared by another. *Will he recognize
> me? Will his love hold fast? Confusion wrings me.* In
> Mathura he killed mighty wrestlers; *I crave his
> stranglehold*

I implore: take me to his holy city.

Uncover me. Why should I wear modesty when the world knows
of my barefaced love? If you wish to be dazzled anew by me
there's only one cure: I must see the lord of illusion.

> He appeared as a dwarf but covered worlds; *he's seeded and grows
> bursting boundaries. Why clothe me in convention? Let rapture
> recapture me.*

I flame towards trembling stars. Take me quick to the magician of Ayarpati.

Don't try to protect my honor, my mothers. Word spreads I've
deserted father mother family for him.

> The lord of mystery has revealed his form; *his beauty entraps.* He's
> playful,
> delighting in lure and scandal. *I'll play his game,
> become invisible.*

Drape me in stealth, carry me through night's *inky throat* and abandon
me at Nandagopal's door. *I'll sneak into his family like a kicked pebble.*

Mothers, experienced ones, don't you see my condition?

> *Though blindfolded* by saffron paste the eyes of my breasts *open
> to* seek him who clasps the discus's *ringed* fire. They shrink
> from mortal sight but search for his mouth's *dark hold*. I'm *inferno*
> longing for Govinda.

Don't find me another; leave me on Yamuna's moon drenched
bank. *I'll quench.* Here I shan't survive an instance.

None of you understand my divine disease, O tender mothers,
don't suffer for me.

> Only his wild caresses *black as the star-tossed ocean* can cure
> me. *I'm flaying fish and flood.*

Take me to the riverbank, to the *kadamba* oak there. From its
leafy hood he leapt to trample Kaliya's reared heads. In that
battleground alone shall my passion be quelled. *I'll calm
in him as tree becoming seed, potential expanding.*

> Vast dark clouds, flowers burning amethyst as his eyes and sapphire
> as his body, lotuses tender *as his skin* urge: "Go to him!
> Go!" to Hrishikesha who though chief among gurus waited sweating,
> belly pinched in hunger. He waited long for his share
> of sacrificial food at Bhaktilochana.

Take me now to that sacred grove. *I'm hungry, I'm rapture's offering,
I'm his food, he's mine to devour.*

I can't eat. Pallor seeps from lips, my skin's muddy. My mind
liquefies. I'm a shameless woman *streaming after him.* My soul's
color drains *into his sapphire splendor.*

> Go quick fetch and fasten around my neck his thick garland of
> dewy dark basil, *its drape weight will revive me*

Lay me at the banyan where Balarama crushed Pralamba to death. Amidst
bone shrapnel I'll fruit wet and heavy.

Don't rain abuse, you sinners. Don't say: "He's a cowherd, that's
all." "He's a vagrant." "He was tied to a mortar." Don't speak
of what's beyond you and I shan't scorn you.

> He's triumphant Protector. During the deluge he effortlessly
> scooped the mountain
> to serve as an umbrella for cows *and souls.*
> *My love torrents fiercer, I'm drowning.*

If you seek my survival take me fast to Govardhana, *it's my*
refuge too.

"Govinda! Govinda!" my pet parrot calls from its small cage. As
punishment I don't feed it. It torments me further: "He measured
the worlds!" it shrieks, expanding my longing for him who
pervades.

> Friends, don't earn the city's dishonor. *Your punishment only*
> *pulses my love faster. Release me from this cage.*
> *My bruised wings beat his ecstasy.*

I pray: send me swiftly to Dvaraka, his city of *expanding* light.

Determined to reach the dwellings of her lord
—From the everlastingly celebrated Mathura
To welcoming Dvaraka where he reigns—
Kotai of glossy curled tresses
Of Vishnucuttan, lord of Srivilliputhur of shining mansions
Demands her people take her to all the places of her beloved.
Those who chant her sweet garland of verses will
Forever live in his highest heaven, Vaikuntha.

Note:
Andal, the ninth-century CE teenage Tamil mystic, declared herself to be the bride of Vishnu, the Preserver in the Hindu pantheon. *Take Me to the Land of My Love* is part of her second and last composition, *Naachiyar Thirumoli (The Sacred Songs of the Lady)*. Andal draws from the living landscape of myth as her passion mounts—she must be taken to meet her Beloved, here avatared as Krishna, the radiant, dark-hued lover. Her tone swings between plea and command. Each verse has two parts, though connected. In the first, she pleads with her mothers to stop their suffering—and hers—by taking her to Krishna's many dwellings; in the second, she recounts the mythological events that occurred at these spots.

MEENA KANDASAMY

Celestial Celebrities

because they had established a reputation
for being wild and unrestrained and indiscriminate
when it came to men
because they never cared
who left sediments inside them
because they looked forward to going down
when an opportunity presented itself
because they went dry
when it got muggy and unpleasant
because they froze to frigidity in their beds
when they were in the unlucky lands
of those who had fallen out of favor
because they were rapid in youth
because they mellowed and became maternal
when they met their match
because they followed the jagged, moody course
they chose for themselves
because they loved erosion and erasure
because they threw tantrums and triggered wars
because they lacked secrets and loved catfights
because they held the magic key
to the corridors of power
because they were fond of running off
and running away
the rivers here bear the names
of fallen women exiled to earth
when the heavens found them
too bloody hot to handle.

Eating Dirt

her famished tongue feasted on dreams
and she catered to its cravings—
green mangos clay cloying chalk
citrus soap crusty coal raw rice
crushed ice cubes crayons ash
powdered glass pickled garlic
salt sieved rain-scented soil

a son was born, he was fed
and he learnt to feed
soon he was caught eating mud
a son taking after his mother
a son inheriting her tongue

she tied her speechless moon to a millstone
and after some frantic spanking
she saw in his cloudy mouth
the truth of the three worlds—
sand everywhere, everything
turning to sand.

Things to remember while looting the burial ground

- Don't go alone[1] or as yourself.[2]
- Don't be afraid of the police[3] or the rationalists.[4]
- Don't permit animal slaughter[5] as a substitute ritual.
- Don't be fussy as regards the antiquity or antecedents of the bones.[6]
- Don't hesitate to go wild with the skeletons.[7]
- Don't worry about the extra calories.[8]
- Don't forget to smile for the camera[9] at every stage.

1 Such a precaution is not meant to subscribe to the commonly held worldview that hauntings/possessions are possible because a person who is unaccompanied is more susceptible to otherworldly forces. On the contrary, since this ritual is designed to foster male bonding and preserve cultural traditions, it is recommended to go in groups of three or more.

2 It is advisable that every participant disguises himself/herself as Lord Shiva. Such an appropriate masquerade can be achieved by smearing oneself with leftover ash from the cremation of dead bodies and stripping down one's clothes to the bare essentials.

3 According to human rights activists, the police track record of brutality towards the living (including those with fundamental rights, and those specifically protected by the Constitution) is unrivaled. Therefore, the uniformed men lack the moral high ground and the legal right to actually prevent anybody from practicing their religion.

4 The claim of the rationalists that this is a superstitious practice followed by the people in a blind manner can be refuted by explaining the reason behind the observance of the contested ritual. It has been widely documented through the oral tradition that when his father-in-law's skull caught hold of Lord Shiva's hand and refused to let go, Shiva rushed to the burial ground, where the skull, tempted by the presence of scattered bones, released its grip on his fingers and instead began to restlessly chew bones. Sociologists who have probed into the metaphysical connotations of this ritual have pointed out that such an activity is aimed at purging and expunging feelings of hate and anger by providing a harmless outlet.

5 Besides the fact that it is exciting to go for the real, raw stuff, it is worth remembering that PETA and Maneka Gandhi hold the firm opinion that animal rights are non-negotiable.

6 Since the selection has to be made between parts of a skeleton, the deciding criteria ought to be size and succulence.
7 It is a scientifically proven truth that once the human heart stops pumping blood to the brain, the transmission of signals denoting pain to the related neurons is suspended.
8 The milk of human kindness oozing from the nibbled bones is rich in calcium and assorted minerals, while being low on calories. Moreover, the increased intake of calories will be adequately compensated by the energy expended on frenzied dancing in the graveyard.
9 An analysis of television footage across six regional and three national channels from last year's Mayana Kollai festival reveals that a drunken participant in this ritual got ten times as much play on prime-time news than the President of India who was visiting Cambodia then.

LAL DED

Translated from Kashmiri by Ranjit Hoskote

Verses from *I, Lalla*

13.
     Love-mad, I, Lalla, started out,
spent days and nights on the trail.
Circling back, I found the teacher in my own house.
What brilliant luck, I said, and hugged him.

14.
     I wore myself out, looking for myself.
No one could have worked harder to break the code.
I lost myself in myself and found a wine cellar. Nectar, I tell you.
There were jars and jars of the good stuff, and no one to drink it.

64.
     Whatever my hands did was worship,
whatever my tongue shaped was prayer.
That was Shiva's secret teaching:
I wore it and it became my skin.

111.
     What the books taught me, I've practiced.
What they didn't teach me, I've taught myself.
I've gone into the forest and wrestled with the lion.
I didn't get this far by teaching one thing and doing another.

140.
     This body that you're fussing over,
this body that you're dolling up,
this body that you're wearing to the party,
this body will end as ash.

142.
     Don't think I did all this to get famous.
I never cared for the good things of life.
I always ate sensibly. I knew hunger well,
and sorrow, and God.

SUMAN CHHABRA

Home Body

I list
thistle, wonder,
night fall, braver

I'm getting to
abandon
the fear of it
the debate, within, of what constitutes

how many cells
still miss them
trauma deep in my right hip
the need to stretch out
but the demons' camp set up
tents lifted
what they spin over purple fires
at night they circle the sacroiliac
chant. step. dance. step.
the vibrations of their plan
I try to decipher
anticipate how they will permeate
the next day
I unwrap the kindling log for the fireplace
the one a robin flew through
and mom chased until it chased us
press my face into the mesh flame guard
I will walk out of this house
and still see it every dream

this life is mock containment

reader. reader in your sunlit bungalow
holding the paper in one hand
glass of lemon water in the other
you start your day sunlit inside
eager with your laughter
and love for love's sake,
expanding everywhere, even the Hindu Rope Plant
that sits on its own stool in the kitchen
even the sounds of basketball and commercials
from the next room
even the ache in your own shoulders
even the breath
even the list repeated in your head
fear of fear of fear of

reader. reader i left you a few hours ago
waiting upstairs
rather, i left myself upstairs
along with any logic that i search to gather
by knocking on cells, hoping them open
and asking: can you help me?

mitochondria murmurs zip in response
and i press:
now would be great

to observe the chemical wave
i, in a white coat
pour hollow beaker into hollow beaker
bend down so eye
can recognize universe in glass

MANGALESH DABRAL
Translated from Hindi by Arvind Krishna Mehrotra

Description of the Mad

Since there are few rules for growing mad
The thousands who are
Are each mad in their own way
With their different temperaments
Each one's behavior is the opposite of the other's
Their worlds like parallel lines
The instructions that could have kept them from going mad
They've long forgotten
The books on how to make the body beautiful
In which healthy minds can live
And be reflected in the face as in a mirror
The methods to achieve this
Improving by the day

Those who have lost their minds
Suddenly appear
With dry morsels tucked inside rags
Sometimes terrifying to look at sometimes meek and submissive
They don't know where they're from
Whether they were even born
Or if their birth was celebrated
And what the meaning is of the eternal running
From this pillar to that post

A lunatic sits in a corner and nonstop
Abuses the prime minister
Another stands on the sidewalk
And plans his next move
In the long war he's waged against the system
A mad woman recognizes
Her unfaithful lover in the crowd
And pelts him in anger with invisible stones
An old nutter mistaking the town square for a cave
Makes his home in it
And narrates the bloody history of mankind

Those with healthy minds often go past
These madly gesticulating people
They look fleetingly into their eyes
But taken aback they walk on
As though shaking off a bit of their own lives
Some anger some love some protest
Some fire of their own
That now wanders separated from them
On busy squares and street corners
Clothes torn hair unkempt dry morsels preserved

No one knows
Where lunatics go at night
Which doors open for them
And let them in
Maybe they knock at a gate
And alluding to an old friendship ask for shelter
We're the victims of a widespread conspiracy they say
Or they ask for a cup of tea
Before leaving again to attend to the day's business

NABINA DAS

Anima walks borderless

The forests are deep-cleft and dreaming. From Barak's beautiful sky-trees to upwards north of the darklike ranges of a mountain kingdom I walk. *Charaiveti, charaiveti*, the distant locomotive wheels mumble running through the tunnels. And then I walk back to my Dihing where the journey had first started. The elephants are going to rest in their groves, no more hunted down by poachers. The speedboats are wrapping up their fishing nets in benevolence so the rivers are free. All hate is flying out on coordinates spanning our guide maps, and all love is fleeting in fast. How's this possible, you ask. We've seen vast graveyards of people dead. They were whisked away from homes, from children's sides, lovers' arms and disappeared for as long as one dew season went to the other. No one asked for maps for them. I remember the young girl whose country never came to her till she was of gray hairs and mourning for her lost love. What is it? you ask. The sound of military boots at night in a new tongue. The red river redder with poison-bombed fish and weeping limbs. *Charaiveti, charaiveti*. The government map officers are here to scout a new route to send the hornbill flying to another border. I walk to send them back.

I, Anima, am a wandering body. From river to river, from one coal field to another, dam to dam, I look for my own. I want my measuring tape, my own marker. I speak of woman body, turtle body, bird body. I speak a verse body across those cartographies. Our bard poet sang it in his silver voice across the red river: Mark Twain with his body of stories, Gorky with his benevolence seeping down the murmuration of our spine. The bard's body in our quest, our long trudge back home. For I've let geography slip up through my river-sense. I'm stateless. I'm a *jajabor*.

KEKI N. DARUWALLA

Winston to Cyril

We haven't met, in fact I don't think
I or anyone ever heard of you
till Clement handed you a knife to oversee
the autopsy of this benighted country.

Don't touch the ground here or people; you could
invite a hit on your liver or lungs;
if lucky you could get by with a skin disease.
don't worry about knives, post mortems;
procedures never bothered the Indian;
no doctor here touches a corpse himself.
The sweeper calls out—skull-wound three inches
deep; brain? not there, Sir, never was.
It is just like their anti-graft outfits—
they may piddle in the streets, if not down the stairwell,
but no one will soil his hands with the corrupt.

Am told by fellow Tories that you don't know
a thing about easting and northing. Maps, dear man,
are geography raised to metaphysics,
something almost occult.
Don't worry, flunkies will shout out square mileage
and population densities—you just draw the lines.

Muslim League chaps in their karakul caps
and harem pants are our friends; they never failed
us, none of them were ever jailed;
shoulder to shoulder with us they stood—
they'll guard the north against Stalin and his brood.
Though this August will see twin abortions, two black dawns
in the Great Game, at least we'll have our pawns.

Some Poems for Akhmatova

In the disgraced poet's room
terror and pity watch by turns;
Night gets switched on—endless black—
    at its taper-end no dawn will burn

1.
You knew your eyes
were transparently radiant

You knew how to love
and to look into others' eyes

You were so slender
I thought you were as light as your curls

You were young
so was the century

But even as you talked of lilies,
their petals tremulous with dew

You walked the abyss with others
the abyss was always with you

2.
Where did this vein
of dark prophecy come from?

Ten years before the War,
thirteen before the Revolution

you heard the wind's howl
ricocheting over the void

and you saw or foresaw
a grave abandoned by its inhabitant,

the cross on the headstone gleaming
ghost-white in the phosphorescent air

3.
I have a poem like yours
the ewe talking of the shepherd
and his throwing stick
and her lamb being roasted
for the prodigal son.
Then I came upon your
"Imitation From the Armenian."
But your black ewe is addressing
the Padishah that was Stalin.

That upped the scales. My ewe
was only talking to the shepherd, the Lord.
Stalin was a different samovar of tea
altogether, a bigger bowl of goulash.
What can the black ewe ask
now that the lamb is cooked, I wondered.
Yet I started sinking when you said to the walrus moustache
"Was he tasty, my little son?
Did he please you, please your children?"
I sank—there are hearts which keep sinking
even after they hit the sea floor.

4.
In the disgraced poet's room
Terror and poetry watch by turns
And night is switched on interminable;
At its taper-end no dawn will burn.

5.
To the Woman in the Prison Queue

Woman with the blue lips
standing in the cold,
woman without a name
perhaps without bread
awaiting your turn
to see a loved one, lover

or husband, frozen behind bars
as you turn blue under a frosty sky,
you are immortal in a way
except that your name has been
swept away by the years.

Your face, though, stares out of her poem,
your momentous question;
and when Akhmatova agrees,
the wintry smile trudging across
what had once been your face.

TSERING WANGMO DHOMPA

After Sunset

There was a deer in his backyard, Rob covered it with maple leaves,
biding his time to think of the next step. What happens afterwards?
I told him my aunt was petite, but she'd become so thin the family
had to cut up yak meat when she was offered to the sky. He said
the coyotes skulked around, they were probably the reason. We didn't
talk about death, funny, how poetry works. How the vultures circle over
the burial ground or burial sky, and the living understand someone else
is being dead, or moving into the *bardo*, which is also a metaphor for the
statelessness I was born into. My aunt had a perfect *kapala*, the medications
she had to take all her life did not show there. It is hidden in her husband's room,
I hear. My aunt's heart, who knows. This morning my uncle tried to speak
through the oxygen mask, his words humming, translated, *How is your health?*
Are you doing well? I do not know how to grieve in my language, to say
to a loved one who is sure of nothing but death, to say, what? This is
what exile does, the dying and the ones who cannot return. My mother
always said, *Poor thing*, when she spoke of her younger sister. She'd suffered
the most of all the siblings, even the ones who spent a decade in camps and prisons
for being born. I thought my mother was assessing her own life in exile
as something more livable. Rob has a bed in his office, it is his meditation chair,
or, as he shrugs, it's something that had seemed like a good idea. He thinks he'll
get rid of it, but it takes planning to empty one's place. Strange, how death is
the poem, or maybe it's what I'm translating from the edges of the page. Every
other poet says it so much better. Thank God! It's hard to know if I enter any
conversation at the right time or from the right position. I feel like a firecracker
that is not the right one for the occasion. My uncle reminds me about life as
he lays dying. We wave at each other into the phone. We will never meet. The
deer, Rob says, was attacked by a coyote. But not finished up. I feel he's asking
a question about something else, another kind of burial that I have never seen
but have interpreted from a distance, reading the black cloud of wings in the
air. Praying for the long life of those I know, praying the dead will go into their
next. My aunt had a lot of antibiotics in her system, we wonder what that means
to the environment we continue to live in. He thinks the bed is out of place, it's
something he has to explain as though there has to be a story or a reason for
things to be there.

Before Sunrise

The morning sun sets on fire what in the course
of the day turns out to be an indented metal cap of a bottle, a safety pin
with rusted edges, a square of paper foil. The plot changes with the setting.
In a class meant for poetry, for poets we look for a third option, not antonyms,
not synonyms, something that skips the preface *before 1959* and *after 1959*
the way the elders do as they wait to return home. I've promised myself I will not write
about exile, or about home, but everything shifts from their positions, except my hope.
I collect facts that might come to use some day: bamboo grows 35 inches in one day;
air bubbles in cranberries cause them to float in water. I learn that the smell
of fresh cut grass is a distress call. What do I do now, knowing this, and what do I do
when the setting is there and history keeps me on this side as alibi.
Let's argue with each other using literature as a tool to read the world. A woman takes
down the walls of the hut built by a man in the woods and invites him to lie
with her under the stars. Thus, begins his resentment; plot is the highway
managing cars from colliding into each other. She should have built a garden
outside his hut, or walked past the hut to the valley beyond and built her own house.
A wall of bamboo. She should have let him be. He should have resisted, he should have
spoken up. I am stitching a blanket for you, for the days when you are hot. It will cover
up your childhood, scorch the tissue of sadness that is not able to stretch. The smell of
grass, the before and after of love.

SUBHASHINI KALIGOTLA

Interior with Particulars

I visit you often in that room. I revisit your expression.

The odor a sign of your newly acquired foreignness.

I touch you. I notice the long stubble. Evidence

of some of the body's parts still running:

some part of you

still ticking   with leftover life.

I realize the old arguments about the body

are meaningless when the body belongs

to the beloved.

Did they treat yours kindly?

Respect your modesty? Lower you gently

onto the bed?

Grammar Lesson

Transition to past participle complete. Disparu.
Disappeared. Dead. Why not call it lifeless
present. One instant he is

warm and healthy in the pitch, ready to kick
a football with his friends, then, asystole,
speeding pointlessly to the unknown

doctor who will call time of death. Let the conditional
begin its wordmagic, speak for the no-longer-able,
premised as it is on their somehow existing

in two states at once. Expressing their views
through our mouthpieces. Double agents playing
for both teams. And so the chorus: he wouldn't want to live

like that. He wouldn't want to live. Who wouldn't want to live.

ANAMIKA
Translated from Hindi by the author

Hands Up

Do you remember, dear, those
Doctors in the films of the sixties?
How they got down from their buggies
The patient's family all trotting behind!
All important, with heavy footsteps
They came to examine
The heroine's mother.
Stethoscope here, there,
Lips pursed
How they raised their hands to the sky
And then, in a solemn voice declared,
"No medicines now, just prayers!"
God only knows what's gone wrong.
All hands today reach just for the sky!
Are we praying still?
Or
Has someone with a pistol
Roared hard behind the scene,
"Hands up!"

MONA ZOTE

Rez

     A boy & his gun: that's an image will do
to sum up our times
        to define the red lakes
and razor blade hills of our mind. Out here *this place never changes, never will*
     we will keep choosing gray salt, bad roads,
      some thin yellow flowers to grieve, *alcohol over friendship* . . .
cash for peace, God's grin of despair. If you think *I'm starting to regret
sticking around* and kicking at the tombstones
            (if not pulling out the ak-47)
remember   the water lilies will bind you back.

Trenchcoat todesengel bringing *meaning to life thru death*, thru
an intimate if facile study of pain
               and that other *mental stuff* like drawing
      pictures of war
      people getting shot
      houses pulled down
      heads shorn
      traditional law custom kultur
        junkies runners bootleggers scum scum scum
We too have spent our brutal spring *exacerbated*
          by a long tradition of self-enforced isolation,
     continued into a cold-blooded summer (I feel
                                nothing
                      I fear
                                nothing)
           we said *it wasn't intentional*
and the grasshopper susurrus of our blood tells us
                      how
      you feel almost an ability to be worse than what you are
(Perhaps this explains why today in the middle of my room
                  a black hole soundlessly spins).

Look, kid, thank you for the demonstration
       & don't forget to take your angel home
         even if you don't *feel like going back to school*
& if they ask you about life on the reservation
       if they say they want to hear about stilt houses
       and the dry clack of rain on bamboo
       and the preservation of tribal ways
         give them a slaughter.

2.
Let's hear from you, Angel. *Incredibly,*
              He spake: "Four a.m. I rose from
the silicon box, wings quivering triumphant
if bleary-eyed, knuckles cramped,
having gunned down Virtual Viktor the smiling Rooskie, my erstwhile
friend, piss-full of vodka as he went—like the young in one another's arms
drowning among the waves. You remember
          Star Trek via Doordarshan?

Do you remember?—Those Sunday ceremonies of mantraps
and *armageddon now*!, logic and adventure,
new worlds braver than the last, those tinpan ships from an
interstellar Nineveh: amok times, yes. Also aboriginal
                        My shoes are Japanese

Christ, I can't forget Yaqob, surefire bet in the pro wrestling ring—
man's champ or scapegoat, who can tell? He got the better
of me in the end but I . . .
          I nailed his dreams to the cold ground.
In the distance, the guitars of Byzantium wept.

No, don't go there!
There be whales, cap'n, and pearls and eyes.
Thus let us venture to the noodle bar—"
                        The immortal game

"—Mister Nighttime, what say? Admit modernity in, sepia anime! Who
mourns for Adonis or Umrao Jaan? D'you remember what the children sang—
    *Your warriors are gone with Billy Bowlegs
        and Billy Budd swings from the mast*

O moments that have passed like tears in rain

Toke this: things have to be the way they are
because gods can't remember, we angels do. In this
we are as mortal as you
                              though fiery we fell.
Swaraj: acid anthem in our veins.
                                      But heart is truly Hindoostani

So many have fallen . . . these cinnamon groves. I swear . . .

I swear by the Wumpus, by Alphaman,
—the world's become
one big reservation. I should know,

I'm the Angel. I'm
in charge. You feel
that tightening of the temples as at some
momentous corner-turn of history? This tale, I fear, has just
begun to unfurl. Don't be afraid. Have a tsing pao—else, coffee?
                                    Stay with me, boss. Stay."

Screw it, let's *dance*!
or do origami.

3.
A mindless year of mindless action.

If the moon looks gray tonight, if you think she weeps,
                          it is because
                        you live on a reservation

If as you walked the houses rose on all sides threatening,
                        it is because
                        you live on a reservation

If the wind brings no news of love, if the villas are silent
                           and empty, it is because
                        you live on a reservation

The things you have to say, no one can say them for you
The places you have to go, no one can go there for you
The hills you have to burn, no one can burn them for you.

MUSTANSIR DALVI

Effigy Maker

Build me a torso to set alight,
haute-coutured to burn all night,
if you are half the tailor you are cut out to be.

Choose fabric that is retentive and slick.
Make your stuffing bleed; let a thousand cuts
allow for a thousand wicks.

Pay attention to extremities.
Keep the digits dry and pudgy,
stuff well with cotton balls and rags.

Matchstick heads with broader shoulders,
so that when they burn, they smolder,
and don't skimp on the number of flags.

You are overworked; I know, I know,
but for this I can pay more.
It's the season of burning, and I'm earning
credit with every conflagration.

Teo'ma

I am my master's vehicle.
I have been his camel, his pack-horse, his mule.
I have been his dhow, his canoe and his coracle,
I want to be a bird now and fly with his faith,
free of the cords of duty.
I want to lay down my scepter
and pick up my wings.

ANAND THAKORE

Elephant Bathing

He will never go there again,
Hip-flask in pocket, camera at hand,
Far from the crowded confines
Of the human animal he could not trust,
To the lush cricket-choired thickets
He so jealously loved;
Dense, creeper-canopied spaces
Where he would listen eagerly
For the sudden slither of a python's tail,
Or the persistent mating calls of leopard and crane,
Studying the stealthy ways of predator and prey,
Till panther, bison, hyena and stag
Seemed part of a single guileless continuum
He had only begun to see his part in.
Now home and city hunt him down,
Building about him their busy labyrinth
Of doctors, nurses, brothers and sons;
Though tiger and spotted deer remain,
Frozen above his bed in black and white.
An egret pecks noiselessly at a crocodile's jaws,
As pale flamingos, stripped irretrievably of their pinks,
Leap into a flight forever deferred.
Where you are going, they seem to say,
You will have no need for us or all you remember.
And yet the thought of getting there is not unlike
A great lone tusker taking the plunge,
His vast gray bulk sinking below the riverline
Against a clear black sky,
Till there is no more of him to see
Than a single tusk,
White as a quarter-moon in mid-July,
Before the coming of a cloud.

KALIDASA

Translated from Sanskrit by Mani Rao

from *Meghadutam*
Cloud-messenger

1.
Some yaksha who made a mistake was cursed by his boss:
Suffer!
One entire year

An ordinary yaksha
Not a hero

When even a season's separation's unbearable
Imagine six

What mistake
Kalidasa does not specify
Some lapse of duty
Same word for "duty" and "right"

Has the "hero" lost the reader's heart
In the very first line?

Heavy the pangs of separation from his beloved

His prowess gone like a sun that set
Year-long night

He lived in hermitages on a mountain
named after Rama

Groves cool, waters pure
Sita once bathed here

Remember Rama remembered Sita
Remember messenger Hanuman
Flying like a cloud

Why hermitages, in the plural?
More than exiled. Unsettled.

2.
Separated from her for months wasting on that mountain
The yaksha looked lovesick

His gold bracelets had given his forearm the slip
Good lovers pine thin

Looked at a cloud
embracing a ridge on day one of the rainy season
like an elephant butting a rampart

Elephants sharpen tusks
on termite-hills or trees

The simile's a stretch
Kalidasa knows
Wait two stanzas . . .

And Kalidasa calls the yaksha's girlfriend
"abala" : "without-strength"

Just a generic word for a woman
in a stanza where a particular yaksha
seems bereft of "bala"

3.
In front of the cloud the stirrer of ketaki flowers

The servant of the king of kings
The yaksha, servant of the yaksha-king
barely stood

Brooding
A long time
Tears pent

At the sight of a cloud even the mind of the contented
goes for a spin

Imagine a man whose beloved who longs to embrace him
lives faraway

4.
Foreboding in the skies . . .

For the life of his love he wanted the giver of life the cloud
to carry news of his well-being

With a gift made of fresh Kutaja blossoms
and pleasing words—"welcome!"

5.
What! A cloud? A tumble of vapor, heat, water, wind

To deliver a message from sense-able living beings

Not figuring that the eager yaksha
asked it—him—cloud

The lovelorns' dna is so—poor things—
They cannot discriminate
animate-inanimate

Kalidasa calls him "guhyaka"
It means yaksha, but also, "mysterious"

Wearing his heart on his sleeve
Our yaksha is anything but

6.
I know you—

You're born in the world-famous family of

Pushkara and Avartaka clouds
You're Indra's main aide
You take any shape you please
As for me
Far from family by a twist of fate
I've come to this state of imploring you

It's said
Plead to a superior even if in vain
Not to inferiors even if successful

7.
Raincloud, you're salve for those burning in love

You've got to take my message
Me—ripped by the wrath of wealth-god Kubera

Take my message to Alaka, city of the yaksha-king

Palaces washed by moonlight from the moon
on the head of Shiva situated templed
in the outer gardens

8.
Tossing curls
sighing

Wives whose husbands are away will gaze at you
riding the wind-route

When you're here all ready
Who can ignore a pining wife?
No one

Unless—like me—slave to another

9.
Go without delay and you'll surely see
your brother's faithful wife alive

absorbed counting days

Women's hearts : like a flower prone
to wilt in separation—

Hope's the tie that holds it up

Our yaksha says "not-dead" for "alive"
Hurry, cloud! She's in dire straits

10.
As a cool breeze nudges you slowly along
A proud lark sings sweetly to your left

Your entourage in the sky a flock of cranes
in spectacular garland-formation
to mate undercover

11.
Hearing that fortuitous sound the rumble
that makes earth a field of mushroom-umbrellas

Noble swans with delicatessen lotus-stem-shreds
Eager for Manasarovar in the Himalayas

will fly along, your companions
all the way to Mt. Kailash

12.
Hug your dear friend, the high peak
Slopes marked with Rama's footprints humans adore

Say bye

It's a friendship shaped by recurring meetings
and long separations' warm vapor exhalations

The mountain's resonant
with devotion and separation

ARJUN RAJENDRAN

Mail from San Juan

The concierge who found my copy of Lolita
in our room in San Juan was kind enough to mail

it to me. Maybe he was an admirer himself,
and felt it's cruel for stories about old men

and orphaned girls to be parted from their readers.
But it's more interesting to forget my book

was mailed, that the concierge inadvertently
discovered Nabokov while trying to replace my fallen

bookmark. That she reminded him of *tostones*
in bad weather. Of *alcapurria* from a shack across

the beach, freshly stuffed with pork and fried
by ladies who only spoke Spanish. He'd return there,

pretend the youngest is his adoptee. Become less
the islander trapped by his job, weary

of seeing blue cobblestones unleash holidayers.
Admit it, such perversions are lovelier than

any mail: where a poor concierge smuggles
a book into the honeymoon suite, opens it in a bath

to feel its lavender bring her to life—his dainty slave,
his underaged plate of *mofongo*, orphaned no more.

Sea World

Depravity is paying to see a 60-kg human
command a 9-ton orca. In 1989, I saw a torso being sawed

in half by P. C. Sorcar; the horror
I bought into then was ersatz.

That's what magicians do: mock entropy.
Now, as the whale earns its feed with a sensational aerial feat,

my camera imprisons even that semblance of freedom,
just like the one being honored by the lady in her scuba suit

as she distinguishes, in the audience,
men in uniform who've served this nation in Iraq,

and everyone claps. But it's not just
the children who don't really know what they are clapping for.

Refilling

      How now to describe that anguish when my father got off
the train at platforms to refill a water bottle;

because nobody then had yet learnt to sell water.
When everyone started buying it, I was older, unlike the time

my feet didn't reach the compartment floor. I sat
by the window thinking the whistle will sound any second now,

he'll never make it, till he'd materialize beside coolies
or a ticket collector and grin at me after

stubbing his cigarette. Now that I travel alone everywhere,
the loss of that uncertainty is just another adult fact.

But I always carry a bottle inside me. I keep
refilling it with memories from taps I often forget to close.

VIKAS K. MENON

Devayani

In memoriam: my maternal Grandmother, Ammukutty Amma, from whom I was vouchsafed the story and keepsakes of my Great Aunt, Devayani Velliamma.

Nair Marriage Ceremony, Kerala, India (*photo, b&w, 1934*)

A flare of whitelight shears across their faces
and startled, she loses herself,
blinking away the magnesium flash
as the crowd
murmurs around them.
The nasal, reedy call of the nagaswaram
blares from behind
and her arms lie at her side,
limp as the jasmine
in her hair.

King James Bible (*cloth binding, 1900*)

An artifact the size of my palm with an exposed spine and gilt-edged
pages. It is moldstained, its red fabric shorn
and stained with amoebic tears.

Inscribed within:

ON THE OCCASION OF HER
PASSING THE ENTRANCE
EXAMINATION AT THE
UNIVERSITY OF Madras

THIS COPY OF THE NEW
TESTAMENT AND PSALMS IS
PRESENTED BY THE BRITISH
AND FOREIGN BIBLE SOCIETY
TO Devayani K.

FOR Her CAREFUL READING
AND REVERENT STUDY.

Wedding Reception (*photo, b&w, 1934*)

In the background are skeletal trees. A plate of cakes sits untouched. Bored men in ties slouch at a long table. Devayani's betrothed wears a garland.

Her husband is smiling but all she can think of are her sister's faces, so far from her for the first time, for the first time traveling with a man not her blood kin.

She, like her mother before her, will learn to tuck the housekeys into her petticoats, maintain watch over the hearth, silent in the dark, his strange bulk in the bed next to her.

Bed, South India (rosewood, 1900)

My mother was born on this bed of heavy rosewood.
I sit, feel neither breath nor heartbeat.

My mother was born in this home of heavy wooden beams
and black stone floors, the first child born after the death

of Devayani Velliama. Immediately after her birth,
my mother's aunt began sewing furiously for the newborn.

I imagine reams of cloth falling from a sister still mourning,
strands of cotton unraveling at the edge of her scissors' cut.

Coda

Years after Devayani's death, my mother is hand
in hand with a friend, no more than seven years

of breathing for each. They giggle their way
through a narrow, winding alley, its walls of red

clay topped by thorny branches,
their shortcut to school.

Their skip and squeal is clouded
by men's shouts and across a bend

they see the curving horns toss
as the water buffalos strain towards

them, hides blueblack in the sun
and they turn in unison and run,

dust bursting from their feet
but can't outfly the thunder behind

them and some instinct sends
them up the walls, skating

on its concavity up and over
and they drop to the other side,

thorntorn, scraped
and bloody, hair slipping

from their braids, mouths
agape, gasping

for air, dust mingling
with the blood

bitten from
their tongues

the taste
of salt

filling
their mouths.

MEDHA SINGH

Chair

There is a dead chair, sitting across,
solitary and anticipating,
like one grandmother I never knew
or another perhaps,
that I should have known.

There is a chair, sitting across,
brooding,

with absolutely no one
to interrupt her.

An Answer

There is a new boy
in the classroom
introduced
as "Hasan,"
children hiss
about him in
bold suspicion,
he is shy, but
appears aloof.

One day,
his bones
turn twenty.

The winds are somber,
they carry his thoughts
back home;
grains of dust
spiral in the
desert wind
the evening dims—
the sky a ripe peach
now a violet grape.

Upon this thought
he returns
to
quiet.
In the moment
his silence arrives
there is no time
hence, no memory.

Neither the wind
nor the children
care to hiss anymore.

He always mistook them
for desert snakes.

LALNUNSANGA RALTE

Afzal

When Afzal refused to talk about violence
There was a hushed murmur of confusion,
A rechecking of notes.
Who is to play the other now?
An idea was expected to appear
Instead, here was a man, human.
Who is to play savior now?
There is no meek, no blind, no leper
Just a man, with white beard and hair
Steady as the spotlight shining on him.
His eyes pierced an audience
Waiting to salt the wine and cheese
With horror stories, full of pain and loss
And darkness and stench
Dry and dusty and burning
Each word he wrote, branded,
Burned into his skin.
After all, he is Muslim,
An Indian-Bangladeshi-Pakistani,
Exiled from two countries,
A child of two wars, and,
He writes poetry.

Afzal refused to talk about violence.
Instead, he recited a beautiful poem
Of love, of a man in love.
Goethe and Rilke were not there
Only a world waiting for him
To talk about violence.

Dear Baruk

Dear Baruk,
I have often tried to imagine the sunsets that you described.

How you say they fall with a satisfied sigh
Dipping into the white sands of Gokarna Beach
And merge the shadows into the palm trees.

Or the ones that you see now down there
Amidst protest signs and occupying Aotea Square.
Do you still pause to look?
How strange and yet familiar they seem
Like death.

I imagine we have sunsets here too.
But in our rush to get home and ready
For churches and committees
We have missed them.
We only have white walls and bright lights
Taunting an indifferent sun.

Adamant that the world is bad and ending
And our little lives worthless and suffering
We offer up prayers convinced of their worth in volume.

I sometimes wonder, Baruk,
If God is not in here
But out there, busy making sunsets.

Fak You

Fak you.
And before you take your head back
Understand
I am from a people with names
Such as *Faka* and *Faki*
And coincidentally you probably have guessed their gender correctly.
See, in my language,
Fak, spelled F-A-K, is a good word.
It is a word that blesses,
It means to praise or to exalt.
So fak Eliot and fak Shakespeare
And fak you!!!!

Now that you have learned a word in my language
Maybe I will learn one in yours
And then maybe the boxes we have put each other into
Will start to take the shapes of people
Standing across each other amidst the rubble
Arranging the stones trying to make something beautiful.
Maybe my word will replace yours
And yours mine
Maybe then the falconer will hear the falcon
And things won't fall apart so often
But until then,
From inside this box,
Dreaming,
Fak everybody.

VINITA RAMANI

Wildling

They say they fuck in jungles, but in truth, they fuck in small fragmented patches of state-owned reserves with secondary growth dipterocarp trees. They say they fuck by a vast lake, but the lake is a reservoir with very little fish and too many red-eared sliders, an invasive species that isn't much to look at. Still, they fuck and a clouded monitor lizards waddles by, comes to a dead stop and then slides quietly into the water, as if it's too shy to have witnessed such brazenness. They fuck by the drain pipe while children run on the boardwalk above them and lions roar in their enclosures. The lions don't roar. The lions are lethargic because it is midday and they're on display when they really want to be asleep. The roar is the guttural yearning in their throats that comes unstuck and mingles with the high-pitched ringing of cicadas vibrating their tymbals. They fuck at the open concept zoo in which no animal will ever leap over the carefully arranged boulders, or wade through the shallow moat to actually exercise a moment of pure instinct. She climbs him as if he's a tree and wraps her legs around his trunk. He thrusts. He sinks so deep that afterwards he's rooted to the ground, ankle deep in mud and she has sprouted leaves that unfurl on strands of her hair. They clean each other up, swallow each other whole and then use sticks to remove the mud from their shoes. People have been killed in zoos, she thinks afterwards, and people have come to zoos to kill themselves, jumping into enclosures and provoking an attack. She smells the sex on herself until she passes the zebras and wildebeest, at which point she smells apathy.

SRIKANTH REDDY

Scarecrow Eclogue

Then I took the poem in my hand & walked out
past the well & three leveled acres
to where the sugarcane built itself slowly to the songs of immature goats
& there at the field's shimmering center
I inserted the page
into the delicately-woven grass of the scarecrow's upraised hand
where it began to shine & give a little in the gentle
unremitting breeze sent over from the east.
I stepped back several paces
to look at what I'd done.
Only a little way off & the morning light bleached out my ink
on the page so it simplified
into a white rectangle against a skyblue field
flapping once, twice
as if grazed by one close shot after another.
The oxen snorted nearby
& there was a sense of publication
but not much else was different, so I backed off all the way
to the sugarcane's edge until the poem was only a gleam
among the fieldworkers' sickles surfacing
like the silver backs of dolphins
up above the green crop-rows into view, then down from view.
How it shone in my withdrawal,
worksongs rising
over it all. So then I said the poem aloud, my version
of what the god dressed up as a charioteer said
to the reluctant bowman
at the center of the battlefield.
How he spoke of duty, the substance
of this world,
with the trembling armies ranged.

from *Voyager: Book One*

The world is the world.
To deny it is to break with reason.
Nevertheless it would be reasonable to question the affair.
The speaker studies the world to determine the extent of his own troubles.
He studies the night overhead.
He says therefore.
He says venerable art.
To believe in the world, a person has to quiet thinking.
The dead do not cease in the grave.
The world is water falling on a stone.
He would have no objection to the study of nations.
Nations occur.
For a time, Finland.
Likewise, Namibia.
The Namibian people journey through the story of Namibia.
The Congo depends on Angola.
Nations are responsible for the failure of nations.
The Soviet Union is an interesting case.
He also will one day collapse. A world is a world is a world.

༄

Is is.
There is no distinction between ideology and image.
One.
He records his name on a gold medallion.
Two.
The philosopher must say is.
The world is legion.
The self is a suffering form.
Is is.
Waves rise and fall, but the sea remains.

༄

If there is a story, it is this.
He had a professorship at the university and had been out of contact with his
　　personality as a result.
His parting words made mention of the dark work of fact.
Fact is the script of the unknown.
Its shadowy disclosure documents the further world.
Was he some obscure thwarted figure in byzantine constraints?
The question arose.
He knew the topography of injustice.
It had neither inside nor outside, like love.
Like a long ago fire in the world.

⁂

War is.
War is the failure of form.
Thus sink each day's dead softly in the hearth.
The world the world he said.
Gravely he said.
Some suffer within flagrant circles.
Some take refuge in the avenues of the cross.
He was seeking an interpretation of arms and the man that would not further
Legitimize the regime.
Autumn was in pieces all across America.
Death surely lives in a mobile home.

⁂

Is.
Because.
The two are alike.
There the resemblance ends.
Form is because.
Is is is.
He laid down his work in peace.
Is is an unending series.
What is the case is more than the world.
The globe in the work arose.

Is not because.

Is desire present throughout the line?
Yes she said.
He said the final object is the cross.
Is the world one muted figure cut down with hands tied?
Carry out the bodies.
The body in the line means little.
Weigh voice.
Namibia Namibia Namibia Namibia.
Within seeds, increase.

Within uncertainty, understanding.

NIRENDRANATH CHAKRABORTY
Translated from Bengali by Chandak Chattarji

Being Means

Being means some books, a writing table.
Being means the blue of the sky,
The sun on the pond, the green of the trees,
Two birds on the cornice of a roof,
Some hidden current in the water,
The gradual going out of sight
Of a lonely boat in evening silence.
Breaking the humid air, the breeze that rushes in bringing news of rain
Comes and strikes at the heart.
Being means the faces of people, sweat, weariness and melancholy,
All that comprises the world.
Being means having a hold on happiness, unhappiness,
Aversion and attachment.
Being means a picture painted in light and dark,
A picture that's full of significance yet completely meaningless.
Being means, somehow, living within it.

Hello Dum Dum

In my hand is the telephone;
At my feet
Play *surjomoni* fish.
Rowing a boat
On the tarred road,
I want to go from the three-fourths of water on this earth
To one-fourth land.
I am waiting for that boat;
And every five minutes
Turning the dial I shout:
Hello Dum Dum . . . Hello Dum Dum . . . Hello . . .

Above my head burns a neon light
And swirling around my ankles
Rising to my knees
Black, dirty, spilling-over water from
The sewers of Mohenjodaro.
On my walls psychedelic pictures have blossomed.
Looking at those pictures I keep thinking,
My jasmine is blooming now
Under five feet of water.

But I don't get time to think too much.
Suddenly
I remember,
A rescue boat will come from Dum Dum Police Station.
For that promised deliverance, once again I start shouting:
Hello Dum Dum . . . Hello Dum Dum . . . Hello

Wading through the water I come to the bedroom.
My daughter is burning with fever.
After taking her temperature, once again
I wade back to the telephone.
In the meanwhile, finding the door open,
A heap of water hyacinths and a pye-dog

Swim
Into my drawing room.

I am not surprised.
I arrange the water hyacinths in a flower vase,
And with great care, make the pye-dog
 Sit on my sofa.
Then, holding the mouthpiece of the telephone
At his mouth, I say,
"If you want to live, you bastard,
 Then come, say in chorus with me,
  Hello Dum Dum . . . Hello Dum Dum . . . Hello . . ."

Amalkanti

Amalkanti is my friend,
We were together in school.
He came late every day, couldn't answer questions in class.
When asked about word-roots
He looked at the window with such surprise,
We felt sorry for him.
Some of us wanted to be teachers, some doctors, some lawyers.
Amalkanti did not want to be any of these.
He wanted to be the sunshine.
That shy sunshine on a rain-stopped crow-cawing afternoon,
That stays like a little smile
On the leaves of the rose- and star-apple trees.
Some of us have become teachers, some doctors, some lawyers.
Amalkanti couldn't become the sunshine.
He now works in a dark printing press.
Sometimes he comes to see me,
Has tea, talks of this and that, then says, "Well, I'll be off."
I see him to the door.
Among us, the one who teaches
Could have easily become a doctor;
The one who wanted to be a doctor,
It wouldn't have done any harm if he'd become a lawyer.
Yet, everybody's wish was fulfilled except Amalkanti's.
Amalkanti couldn't become the sunshine.
That Amalkanti—who, thinking of the sunshine
Thinking and thinking
Had wanted one day to become the sunshine.

Flag

One has to take a little rest, from time to time.
Turning around from time to time
One has to look at
The people left behind, the houses,
Farms and granaries.
From time to time one has to wonder,
Was it necessary?
For me to go up to the abode of the gods at the peak of that hill,
Putting one foot after another on these stone steps?
I have gripped tightly in my fist
That flag
Which I will hoist
Atop the temple
Having climbed all the way up
Putting one foot after another on the stones.
But now, turning around I see
Houses
At the foothills,
I see farms and granaries,
I see hordes of people.
This is the danger of turning around.
It seems
Some mistake has been made somewhere.
I could have left this flag
Right there, amidst the hordes of all those people.

JAY DESHPANDE

Pennsylvania, Pittsburgh

As a boy the names seemed equal, and I couldn't tell
which to put inside the other. Matryoshkas
with their waists the same, or siblings sleeping holding hands
so the darkness won't know which to take.

Equally plosive and foreign, each of these words could be
a city or a state. And when I visited, how could I know
the stacking order? A place can be anything; it doesn't cry out
its meaning. So the world unfurled, and left me misreading.

I didn't want to be the innocent. But problems found a way
into each other. Through the backseat window I saw a single flag,
its bright broad banner wave, and wondered if this one
was the truth, original, and all the rest were copies.

There is an urge in me to know what comes first,
what follows. More than what's inside, now I like it
when the origins cloud: the flags blanched out
in blurry number, like eyes go wide before a faint.

Page Ripped from Rockbottom's Own Invented Book of Prayer

God if you ever dare get near me
I will demand answers
to so many questions I want to know
what the river sounds like just before dawn
and when there are people talking
on and on for years sometimes
getting nowhere what are you
sewing between them what stitch
in the land keeps me from entering
the wood across the field
and why do they say you're here
in the midst of the city why
don't you look at me through the light
of that small girl's hands what
is keeping the carnival going all this
time you'd think no one appeared
to wet his lips for a game
you were watching weren't you
God is there another
whose bed you sleep in
when the music is turned
down low what noble
compulsion keeps certain
words off my lips
like a nail collar are you
angry at me God are you angry at me
if you're not I don't know how to live

That's the American Dream, Is to Have a Green Lawn

        Almond green or oxford green
        road-teeth-baring chartreuse or the neon
        sewn into the spines of animals we would
        rather rub up against then let
        them breed at home we roam
        noctilucent sensor green or brilliant
        appearance of the mage green hue
        of soft father trembling in the corner
        or dead in my sights green or
        teensy weensy picnic problem
        set between the fork & knife
        green of we found it there &
        green of we'll take it from here
        to the sod put down in trails
        in tears we keep our thumbs or
        green like your first lover brought to
        silence by the great field the invasive
        species acts in moral commons here I'll
        mow & inhabit we feel so good as it's
        getting easy being green by
        chemical love & love you put
        the good bed down turf or faux you
        cover up let's sleep now ssssh green sweet
        sleep let's sleep let's cover it in money

NIRALA

Translated from Hindi by Arvind Krishna Mehrotra

Little Princess, or the One-Eyed Girl

Her mother calls her Little Princess,
Affectionately, as the name suggests.
The truth, however,
Is a pock-pitted, flat-nosed, bald,
And one-eyed face.

Little Princess has come of age.
She cuts and threshes, pounds and grinds,
Trims the wickers till her hands are raw,
Sweeps the floor, throws the rubbish out,
Fills the pots with water.

Still, her mother's heart is troubled.
It feels like a box a thief has emptied.
Where will she get
A husband for her daughter?
She despairs if someone
Says in the neighborhood,

"All said and done,
Little Princess is a woman.
Who wants a one-eyed wife?"
When Little Princess hears this

Her body shivers.
She sees her mother's grief
And a tear fills her good eye.
But the blind left one
Stays dry, alert.

LEEYA MEHTA

Black Dog on the Anacostia River

Suddenly alone, she runs down the hill
Through Japanese gardens

In search of signs
That will tell her she is home in this new life

In this American city ten thousand miles
Away from her own choking Arabian Sea

The Anacostia River appears,
A brown knot of sludge

A dragon aching, its old feathers
Listless in the afternoon sun

No forty-foot glittering wingspan rising up to
Ripe cornfields, towering sunflowers

This is how she finds it this September day
A flooded marshland resting

Then out of nowhere, a flash of black,
Shining, molten, fast moving

Rottweiler, circling, its jaws set square,
Its eyes on her, all menace

She thinks, the heart of an animal is unseen
It could harm her, go for the jugular right now

But the dog flashes out of sight along chain fence—
Maybe it knows she is with child

Even though she does not—
As if it wants distance too

As if it is the heart of man that is unknown
As if she is the omen of how we abandon the things we should love.

KUTTI REVATHI

We are women with three breasts!
Translated from Tamil by Ethiraj Akilan

My ammamma's mum
Had made her vagina a huge urn.
And her granddaughter had made it a granary of paddy.
With potent seeds she grew a great forest.
Her daughter and daughter's daughters
Had learnt the art of creating a sea.
They remained buxom like rocks in an endless tidal space.
When you place your ear on the mouths of the urns
You might hear the hundred-year-sea's song.
They made a stream of the secrets of burning hearts
And let it flow in the sky.
In the blissful space of the firmament where stars swam
The stream ran non-stop.
My mum's mum made a sunflower blossom in the stream.
The flower's petals sent the sun to the earth.
I squeezed the sun and got him into my body.
I converted him into a huge cave of proliferating revelry.
How many moons arose I do not know.
With the water-feet of the water-ecstatic waterfall
I trained to walk like a hanging creeper.
I sounded the alarm of a no-alien entry.
The cave expanded and grew big,
And became a space of illuminated whiteness.
There turtles pulled time and moved along.
When time ripened to bury my vagina in the earth,
Another turtle would get up to climb the mountain.
And that day, my vagina would turn into a sylvan space
Where even my ammamma's mums could assemble
And whisper their gossip.

A Spectral Horse
Translated from Tamil by Vivek Narayanan

The body for my friend is a kind of exhibit
A riddle without end for my sister
For my mother it's enduringly sacred   God's dirt
For my father an asset to be protected and conserved
In the village pond entangled among the fish nibbling my body
that was when it opened by itself   my body
they stole my innards and on lotus leaves rolled and
rolled and played with them calling them, "diamond dew-bubbles"
I've heard grandma say that the body   for her   was an ornament
For the tiger the body itself   is wilderness
For my child it's a never-setting sun
To the lover a lake where the lotuses bloom
For me   my form is a spectral horse I straddle
my self isn't locked in any of my organs
on the horse of everyday feeling I see freedom
For me my form is a spectral horse I straddle
to bring the flown-away organs flying back
For me my form is a spectral horse I straddle
Not female not male not in woman
nor in man is this spectral horse I tend

K. SRILATA

Breasts/*Mulaigal*
for Kutti Revathi

He smuggles it out the theatre
and into pathology,
the small man,
heedless of that which is in his hands,
still warm with blood,
and pleading, for a last minute reprieve.
I think: what if he is a cannibal, what if.
I picture him licking his lips after lunch,
his hands on his swollen belly.
Mulaigal, I think,
the Tamil coming to me unbidden.

Orange slosh of Adriamycin,
teeth on standby carrying traces
of daily gritting and forbidden sugar-love,
that slow switch to crumpledness,
and nurses with breasts
who come and go,
and she talking of Kannagi, of Otta Mulachi,
and me thinking of that which is in his hands,
still warm with blood,
pleading, pleading,
and the night's dark ceiling
sprouting a million missing breasts.

Because I Never Learned the Names of Trees in Tamil
After Rod Jellema's "Because I Never Learned the Names of Flowers"

You pour it into my ear,
the warm oil of tree names in Tamil,
and not one of them in soft, cool italics.
You are looking, I know, to oust that convent-English insect,
frantically alive, trapped there since class one.

Manjanathi, you say, and murungai,
aalamaram, roots you can swing on, girl,
airy wings of thatha poochi
that will tangle
with your hair.

In my support, I cite, the carefree impunity
of lovers who carve their names
on trees they don't know the names of.
Palaamaram, you say, not giving up.
Poovarasamaram, vepamaram, magizhamaram.

The insect stops beating its wings,
learns to luxuriate in this unfamiliar oil,
acquires a certain sparkle.

It is something else entirely
that flies out my ear.

A Brief History of Writing

In this forgotten city park,
a man inscribes his lover's name
on the bark of a tree,
heedless that
in the twelfth century,
two hundred and fifty calves
lost their skins
to the Winchester Bible,
that it took thirty men sixteen years,
back in the thirteenth century,
to carve the Tripitaka Koreana
into eighty-one thousand wooden printing blocks,
that only seven centuries later,
the Japanese imperialist army
engraved their tongue
on the living bodies
of Korean independence activists.

Writing has made its violent way
into hide, skin, wood and paper,
squatting down in two-dimensionality,
no longer kinetic,
slicing through our minds
with its alphabetic, linear whiteness.

For the present,
we have forgotten,
the gentle, dancing shapes of things.

Notes:

Kannagi of Madurai, the central character of the Tamil epic *Silapathikaram*, is celebrated for her chastity. When her husband, Kovalan, is falsely accused of stealing the Pandyan queen's anklet and put to death, Kannagi protests the injustice, tearing out her breast, flinging it at the city and burning Madurai down.

Otta Mulachi, an orphaned tribal girl believed to have lived in Wayanad, Kerala, was so named because she was one-breasted. Left to fend for herself in a forest, she was raped by three men. Legend has it that Otta Mulachi killed them and drank their blood; and thereafter took to attacking young men from the village and drinking their blood. She was feared as an evil spirit or Yakshi even though she wasn't.

SHELLY BHOIL

the way we write

t   i
h   s
e
       w
w   h
a   y   we define
y   the crow for black   for example
              and black as blank
w
e

W
R
I
T
E
            for them to *write* WHITE words
                                      h
                                       a
                                  n
                              g
                           i
                      n
                g
        smaerd deredrosid ni

  - d - I - s - s - e - c - t - e - d
                                            with a penis
                                              by Freud
stamp
of   a
gender
atop
the race of fridays's Master

                        on a footnote
                          are two frogs
                             buried
    in debris
    off their hands
                       left with little sky
 to see from their land

JOY GOSWAMI

Translated from Bengali by Sampurna Chattarji

50

Is the sky no good once it's written?

Incessant new shout

Such unbroken tears brawl

My childhood books
Moon stars glowworms

That's why I'm dew why I'm dew

In the morning in the mouth of grass, in lotus leaves, dazzling anniversary diamonds
When new books are gold

Why don't you take a good look at me?
The horizon's hardly your agenda!

Surely there's some horrible lightning-tinted meaning
Surely the past is a handful of jubilant fire-tinted trees
Surely a handful of vast fields fly with the trees

After all, I did take the moon to my lips of my own free will
The minute I did, I saw it wax speedily to the
    Full

    Fortune drips
    Into the mouth-cave

After all, I do know that death saves itself by covering its ears
I know there's a debt even in your flawless lotus
I know how harshly the night dries up
I know the day is a tight restraint
And the last battlefield is blue

Surely, you too must've heard blue from a stranger's mouth
Must've heard Picasso's blue experience and the ocean's

I, too, am nothing but blue
I sleep so often with such replete frankness
In poetry's absorption

I heard the weaver-bird called the sparrow
And uttered four incomparable sky-wide threats:
One—texts, books, alphabets
Spread them all out and hold them open
Letters drizzle down mothers fathers great-grandfathers constellations all . . .
Two—shoes that will personally make you tour abundant dust
Will gain you admission into strings of rippling roads
The kind who wear small smiles
And are always home
Or up on the rooftop

Immediately after the shoes, the shoulder-bag. That's number three.
In which are present numerous excellent medicines,
I'll give them to you, I'll take them myself.
Fourth—the umbrella—how automatic!
Opens at a touch, in a blink not an umbrella but the ozonesphere
That saves this precious pate of mine
                              From ultraviolet rays

Got it, but why sky, even?

The sky, close to me. Near you, these, the masters of the birds.
              Tell me, are they after your own heart?
Their peacocks are a matter of peace.
What are you saying? Are there no other birds in the world of peace?
What about doves? There *are* doves!

The doves have become old.
Do you know what we call "old"?
The aged black wood of the window will call you grandson
The new-age chandelier will call you great-grandson
Breathing heavily from both nostrils filled with cobwebs
The swing hanging from the wall will declare:
Come on in, sonny boy, sit down!

Like an old house, the dove, too, is a spent bird.
Didn't I often tell you, between you and me let there be a
Spontaneous peacock
                At least once!
That's no longer possible.
Didn't I say, *that's* the noble remedy in the direction of sunrise!
The paintbrush copied me a blue waterfowl.
No, blue isn't blue in all cases—ability is colorless.
Remember? Of course you know him
The ravager of wind and wing, desireless flame!
The resolute pencil accepted the poison eagerly, on its own.
Thirsting hot iron dies as it reaches your lips
Forgets the ocean of creation
That college-going aunt who in her adolescent past
Tenderly simmered lofty love-and-blessings blood-red—
She wasted her words on me. In seas rivers pitchers
      Pots glasses sweet salt
That word I'm drinking, shouldn't I think about it?
What I'm thinking is curiosity—show me show me
        What you're copying into your ex'cise book
They don't show me a thing, the two of them like twins
        Simply pull the sheet over their heads . . .
Providence sees my whirling
Providence was mighty amazed at my whirling
Believed I would arrive at the water well in time
Those days are gone, yes sirree!
Everyone says:
Don't go away without hearing the end!
Says: Come on, let's go to pasture to understand grass
Says: Oh look-look, see those tumultuous young girls
        Paintbrush young girls cuddling kitty-cats
        Turning turtle in rippling waves
Everyone says: I won't do it again
Refute all fault, priest
Everyone says: I got nothing from life
I'm a desert I'm a dromedary

So much noise, my love, so much noise

Hiding below the piled-up noise
His life in his hands, he sits down, Mister Rainbow Himself—lightning!

Such a thunderbolt—today he curled up into such a tiny
                              centipede.
Therefore, from today
I become the overseer of stealing and eating another's food!

Every day at dawn poison at the root of austerity
The one who climbs into the sky
East of the mountain from which the sun rises
     Her face half-burnt by acid
Day comes home from field upon field
     Picking up the nests of returning birds
Such clambering high, leaning on the branches of evening
Such stringing of the moon chain-link by chain-link
     Hour upon hour the swinging of the bell
After sounding it for enthusiasm, filled with restless winds
     That relationship flies off, becomes a paper bag
Even the evening knows no acquittal, keeps showing up at your doorstep
Fear like the light of day

In a distant trench what burns is mere play
What floats in the upper sky—mere trees
What falls into the vast vessel of a dark plateau
                              Mere stars
They fall, they melt

In this poem all meanings merge with the unknown moon

Does the sky go bad once it's written?
Language for the sake of any language
Is my thief, and I her thievery
All I ask is that you make me a gold coin, break me normally
Come on, be like birth, one blow of the blacksmith's hammer!
Fear and courage are clearly one's own
O End, O Chief of Absolute Shadow
Your tomfoolery is the last drag of dope on a dead river
Whatever else happens
I won't roam the streets as a madman
Plenty of sights will still be strewn around in the fields
The days will be so perceptible. Gathering so many amazements
Tossing up ash
From so much burning

Breaking and remaking my destiny with my own two hands of my own free will
Lounging around on the warm red sea of sand
I will live on for so many more days
Copying so many hundred suns

Just as long as it takes for the dream to come

MICHELLE CAHILL

Red Scarf

She is wearing her favorite apron, hand-embroidered, beaded with dahlias. Sunlight floods half the garden, catching the yellow and pink aprons she has left out to dry. There are auras and scotomas, ripples of emerald over bruising-green. It is a day for make-up—a bluish tinge to the eyelids, bridled champagne lips. Her crème suitcase is packed with vintage cotton, pleated satin, hessian, hand-dyed silk, feathers, fur, glass beads, rouge and Raymond Chandler. She leaves this behind on the path. The brown suitcase is almost empty, and hence of no consequence in her arm. The sun outlines her limbs, falls across hedges, pooling in the hollow of her clavicle, warming a vein that connects a circle of blood in her brain to her heart. Beyond the shrubbery are white picket fences, a park gazebo, the trim downtown avenue where instead of having great sex people are watching sitcoms. The photographer finishes his shoot. Cindy and Rose hop into a white Cadillac headed for the soda parlor as pink cherry blossoms swirl. A man enters the garden. He takes the brown suitcase from her hands. Click, click, it's unlatched. Inside is a red satin scarf. She unfastens her apron, steps out of her dress. She pins both garments tenderly over the roses as thorns catch a rip in the cloth. Taking a few steps back she is naked in low white heels. Her eyes avoid the sky where the light pearls. She cannot even look at the sun without burning. The man begins to push the red scarf inside her, compressing and pleating the yardage, inch by inch, until there is no external trace of the fabric. Her eyes shun him, prudently her gaze lifts from the floating hem of his shirt to his shiny torso, his angled jaw. He shakes his head as if he is weeping. She turns away from him. She leaves him rather serenely, the make-up smudged, the light shimmying. By the time she reaches the gate, the red scarf is saturated like a sponge sodden with household spills.

TISHANI DOSHI

O Great Beauties!

O fatty dishes of love!
—Wisława Szymborska

O Great Beauties, I have encountered
you in museums across the world,
observed you and your ilk burst against frames—
bonneted, corseted, hiding from rain.

I've coveted your wardrobes of lace
and silk. Dreamt of renaissance gowns
and acres of pickadils. O the majesty of ruff,
of petticoat tails, mantuas, farthingales!

Not to mention the excellent headgear!
Fontages and feathers, chignons and wigs.
And the sleeves, such a dizzying variety of sleeves!
Slashed, dropped, poofy, fastened back.

In my study of beauty I've also made note
of the suitable props of babies and embroidery,
viola da gambas, pianofortes, hankies,
to distract or accentuate bosoms, according

to the chronology of fashion. Of the paleness
of brow, and eyes riven with requisite
sadness as Pooch snores gaily at your foot.
But Ladies, fripperies aside, I must hasten.

I must ask dear daughters of important houses,
heroines of epics, Helens, whores, how did you know
to obscure your true selves? Wherefrom the maturity
to swallow your grins and hide your teeth?

Even you—Ms Cornelia Burch, barely two
months old, oppressed in swaddling bands
clutching your sharktoothed golden *rinkelbel*.
How did you perfect the art of staring so well?

Were there sisters banned from immortality
for being too tan or toothy? For guffawing
into their hands while the maestro said, *Please,
Madame, a little concentration on the stand*!

O Golden-haired Girls scoured of makeup,
could you know that your direct descendants
would dismiss your resplendence; call you
Plain Jane, or worse: Munter, Minger.

That the gargantuan fortress of your lives
could be captured so clearly in a single portrait?
I mean no disregard, Beauties, to the centuries
of devotion to serious women.

Just explain the mystery to me.
Did the darkness burn all around?
Or did you see, as I see—a quiet wood
outside the town, with a banquet

in a field of belladonna? Did spirits slide
among trees with amulets and potions,
loosening the knots of emotion in your diaphragm,
tongue, throat, lip, larynx, palate, jaw?

Did you strip the mutinies of silk
from the ridges of your ungodly body,
revel in tufts of skin and hair while the hunt
blazed around the edges of the lair?

And when the night-hag finally arrived,
did you invite her to bed, offer her a carafe
of your finest red, open the pearls
of your mouth to the world, and laugh?

The Women of the Shin Yang Park Sauna, Gwangju

Hello, I'm naked, the bubble above my head
says, translated into Korean for their benefit.
But they are busy with their breasts and cunts,
their dimpled, rounded, flat-dented buttocks,
busy washing disappointment from their houses
of sternum, busy with the dirt of summer lodged
around hillocks of elbow and whirlpools of navel.
In one room a woman is pummeling another,
rubbing oil into her flanks and well-worn back.
In another, the young ones sit in a circle on stools.
Their breasts are Jell-O to gravity, they undulate
and lift, undulate and lift. There is gossiping,
of course, world over there is a posture
that involves gleam, that involves lean all the way
in for a proper bitching. *Hello, I'm naked
and I've washed.* The older women's bodies
are segregated by hysterectomy scars.
They murmur in hot tubs with headwraps,
legs spread like avenues of thick black trees.
They are warriors—plundered or having plundered.
The threat of annihilation sits in cool dishes
of water beside them. *Do you feel destroyed,
girl?* One of them looks at me the way death
might look at life, with pity and all the sweetness
reserved for a person who cannot be shown
the way out. She lifts a dish of water
and pours it over her head, barely flinches
from the iciness. *So this is how storms blow
through us.* She beckons with one finger.
Come, she seems to be saying. You are me,
I am you, neither one of us immaculate.

MONICA FERRELL

In the Fetus Museum

1.

White, incorruptible, a slip of moon
filming the reed-bordered waters of a pond,
he sits, or rather slumps, against the glass.
He's in no hurry. The world is here,

now and then it drags up an agonized eye
to plead with him—Mahavir, tiny Nero.
Gently, almost wincing, he smiles
as though waiting for me to finish my sentence.

Unborn. A door through which possibility
never walked. Flute no one ever played.
Once his cells were assembling their lace,
his mother was blinking into the sunlight.

Perhaps his invitation was lost in the mail,
though perhaps it's just as well. After all,
he's not missing much—except everything.
The inventions of lust, the pageantry of *what*.

2.

You tiny Nero among peacock silks: you mother-
of-pearl-handled pistol, you mill of stillness
swaddled by dazzling chemistry petals,
shut up in a Mason jar—what are you
listening to, Brown-eye? Is that a smile?
Maybe right now you're dreaming of some distance,
heavens shaped from white, marmoreal fields
where your dead mother's frozen, witch-finger touch
finds your body, finally. It's not too different
outside: here, love is a currency everyone wants.
Where I am, you can't get enough of touch
and the sun is a bloom who drowns each night,
air is like that wine you sleep in. We walk around

on two legs, going places. I have a kite
in my chest I take out at times to fly.

A Funfair in Hell

While the proprietor looms at the center of the bar
in white linen suit, as though on safari,
I trace the grooves worn in this old wood,
I taste my beer and it is cold as some god.

The lights in hell must be something like these,
immortal as remorse, as words once they are spoken,
and the people in hell must be like these men
holding engines of heads spinning emptily in their hands.

The proprietor wears a flickering smile
pretty as the word *syphilis*.
He shines one beer tap, then another.
The silence in my mouth is a piece of felt.

I am ready for my annunciation, Angels.
I am ready for the enormity.
Bring out the unguents, the strigil and gauze.
Weigh my heart against a feather.

Savage Bride

You need me like ice needs the mountain
On which it breeds. Like print needs the page.
You move in me like the tongue in a mouth,
Like wind in the leaves of summer trees,
Gust-fists, hollow except of movement and desire
Which is movement. You taste me the way the claws
Of a pigeon taste that window-ledge on which it sits,
The way water tastes rust in the pipes it shuttles through
Beneath a city, unfolding and luminous with industry.
Before you were born, the table of elements
Was lacking, and I as a noble gas floated
Free of attachment. Before you were born,
The sun and the moon were paper-thin plates
Some machinist at his desk merely clicked into place.

SHIKHA MALAVIYA

Botany 101 (For India's Daughters)
A found poem from phrases in the BBC documentary, India's Daughter

Course Description:
Introduction to good looking, softness performance, pleasant flower; flowers in relation to gutter and temple. Lecture/laboratory course. (3 hours worship/lecture, 3 hours gutter/lab).

Prerequisite: Birth as an Indian girl

Upon completion of this course, India's daughters will understand:
- Why a *female is just like a flower*
- Why a flower *always needs protection*
- How *if you put that flower in a gutter, it is spoilt*
- How *if you put that flower in a temple, it will be worshipped*
- Why *a man is just like a thorn*
- Why *a flower is given less milk than a thorn*
- Why *Indian society should never allow its flowers to bloom after 6:30 or 7:30 or 8:30 in the evening with any unknown* thorn
- How under *the imagination of the film culture,* a flower *might feel they can bloom for anyone*
- A flower means *immediately putting the sex in his eyes*
- How *in our culture, there is no place for a* flower
- Why *only 20% flowers are good*
- How flowers and thorns *are not equal*
- Why *housework and housekeeping* is for flowers, *not roaming in discos and bars at night, doing wrong things, wearing the wrong* petals
- How a thorn *will put his hand, insert, hit, create damage*
- Why *when being raped, a* flower *shouldn't fight back*
- How *if a flower disgraces herself,* a thorn *would put petrol on her and set her alight*

REGISTRATIONS NOW BEING ACCEPTED ON A ROLLING BASIS

MEENA ALEXANDER

Little Burnt Holes

Stiff legged, my head and throat so cold, I quit the jury selection room.

I dream of a shop with red velvet curtains where hats, the color of bark lie on the counter.

The hat I want is cut of mink, fit for a brutal season. It has prickles of fur, dirt-colored like the faces of prisoners afloat in the courtroom,

Like the wool Basho wrapped around his throat when he called on The Lady of Trees.

All night she sits under a wild flowering tree, ready to judge both the quick and the dead.

She has a son who breathes fire. Basho whispers to me: In your country they fill the prisons with dark folk, that's all they care about.

Outside the courtroom, on Center Street, a cold wind rips the scarf off my head, blinds me.

At night I see the Lady of Trees. She pulls out a handkerchief, makes her fire-breathing son stop and blow his nose.

Sparks waltz. Her muslin is spotted with little burnt holes.

Fragments of an Inexistent Whole
Inspired by Alison Knowles's The House of Dust

Syllables sieved through floating gates,
Metal clack of printer

Mortal rendition, Fortran—
The future coming closer and closer

House of broken dishes / by the sea / using electricity

Black flash, strange as any *me* I might claim

The already gone, its music barely audible
00-111—000 cut and sizzling, swiveling repetitions

The mind falling from itself, into no *where*.
The desire for place not to be denied

What touch affords us, sempiternal hold.

༄

Imagine a woman with a veil over her head,
Black cotton or muslin

Of the sort that my grandmother wore, the edge of her sari
As she sat under the sun, by the well side.

Already the veil covers the garden
Mango trees split into the shape of harps.

༄

The artist decides on materials, timber, tar, tumbleweed,
Then light source—natural, electric, strobe, that sort of thing

She decides on location—
A bracelet, a brandishing of space

Scores for a masked ball, the self and its others
Clinging close, hips grinding, a distinct congress

Precise rendering of rhyme or its uncoupling
Underwater copulation = syllabic sense.

The artist decides on persons—girls with jump ropes
Boys whistling in the sunlight by hydrants gushing

Hot metals, the planet soaked in ether,
A scholar blinded by footnotes, scores of them,

Men and women, faceless now, joyful and inconsolable
Veritable census of the dead.

℘

House of Dust / on open ground / lit by natural light
Is that where I belong?

Lord have mercy!
Grandmother cried, when I was born

This child will wander all her life.
Grandfather tossed in a match

The bush filled with smoke, gooseberry bush—
With freckled leaves

—*Tat tvam asi*—
The deliverance of Sanskrit

What I learnt without knowing that I did,
Grammar of redemption

Sucked from fiery space
As grandmother's hands turn to dirt

The sky—cerulean blue

Sheer aftermath.

K. SATCHIDANANDAN
Translated from Malayalam by the poet

The Unknown Tongues
Ávila, August 10. Listening to the many tongues spoken by the pilgrims at St Teresa's Church

I don't know
Avadhi or Azerbaijani
Kashmiri or Kurdish
Konkani or Kokborok
Gondi or Kirundi
Bangla or Burmese
Marwari or Malagasy
Mundari or Mandarin
Sindhi or Sudanese,
a thousand tongues besides.

But I know the tongues
of cuckoo and gecko
leaves and elves
deer and fish
rain and earth
body and wind
sea and sky
flower and star
sun and snow
of mind, of mind,
and thousands besides,

for I know
Malayalam.

An Old Poet's Suicide Note

Walking in the dark
I grew blind
Wading across silence
I turned deaf

Teachers who speak ceaselessly about light,
How far above is it?
Prophets who taught me about revolution,
How remote is it?

My legs have grown weary
My heartbeats are slow
You still tell lies
Don't lie to children, said the poet
Who just died of the world.

I searched in all the books
For a word of truth
I dug every drought
For a drop of tears

I can no more speak of earth's beauty
Sitting on a sinking land.
Cannot speak of trees sitting inside a storm
Cannot speak of beginnings sitting inside a deluge

I had a country when I was born
Now I am a refugee
I was born in a single chain
Several chains fetter me now

I raised my hands to scream against injustice
I said "don't" to the vile hunter.
My life is a collection of vain deeds.

This is the first poem I write
Without corrections and revisions
This is the first song of the night
I sing without faltering.

The spring of my dreams has gone dry
I draw the curtains on this shadow play
Quickly, easily, like switching off a TV set.

Farewell. Call me when the world changes.
I shall come back if the hungry worms
And the obstructing angels permit me.

MUHAMMAD IQBAL

Translated from Urdu by Mustansir Dalvi

Ghazal

Quais has forsaken the city,
you desert the wilderness too.
If a glimpse of her is all you lust after,
why, cast off Laila as well.

O Reverend! Desires can be fulfilled
only by forsaking the world;
so while you abandon the earth
cast off all thought of heaven too.

Better to kill yourself, than walk
down that trodden path.
Make your own road now,
don't wait for the servant of God.

Like your pen, your tongue
declaims the words of others;
let go of your conceit
over these alien things too.

What use, this theological swagger
if you are numb to the darts of love?
You bear no wound, why then
do you keep crying out in pain?

Weep on the blossoms like dew,
then walk on, out of the meadow.
Abandon your idle dreams
of making a home of the garden.

It is quite the thing
to seek isolation when in love;
forsake then, the temple,
the mosque and the cathedral.

No give or take this, this is
the reverence of God.
Forget all hope of a reward,
You ignorant one!

It is only fitting that the heart
be guarded by the intellect,
but sometimes the reins of the heart
should be let loose too.

What is a life worth
if dependent on others?
Such servility will never lead
to honor and prestige.

There is courage, O Speaker,
in your repeated requests,
but the condition for answers
is that you stop these urgings.

Should you, Reverend Preacher,
bring proof of the worth of wine,
I, Iqbal, insist in turn I shall
stop drinking altogether.

AKHIL KATYAL

Dehradun, 1990

As a kid I used to confuse my *d*'s
with my *g*'s, and that bit of dyslexia

didn't really become a problem till
I once spelt "God" wrong. That day,

the teacher wrote a strongly worded
letter to my parents, and asked me

to behave myself. Also, as a kid,
I could not pronounce the letter *r*,

so till I was sent to some summer
vacation speech-correction classes

at age five, I used to say, "Aam ji ki
jai, Aam ji ki jai"—Then a teacher

taught me how to hold my tongue against
the ceiling of my mouth and then throw it

out quivering, "Rrrr," "Rrrr," she wrenched
it out of me, over many sessions—"Ram"

I did not know God was so
much effort, till I felt him tremble

on the tip of my tongue, God was only
a little joke about mangos.

Note:
"Aam ji ki Jai" is "Long live the mango" as opposed to "Ram ji ki Jai" which is "Long live Lord Ram."

VIVEK NARAYANAN

Poems After Valmiki

Free translations/reinventions, mostly based on specific passages in Valmiki

Rama

Rama   that hero's hair dark as a crow's wing
Your son is not your son
Rama   that boy still with the sidelocks curling
Your son is not your son
Rama   that he-man of the heavy lotus eyes
Your son is not your son
Rama   speechless and radiant with swords
Your son is not your son
Rama   tiger among men
Your son is not your son
Rama   that blank face turned to the face of Saturn
Your son is not your son
Rama   who will never grow sick or tired
Your son is not your son
Rama   three-headed cobra from behind
Your son is not your son
Rama   that forest torn up from the heart
Your son is not your son
Rama   that sip of clearer water
Your son is not your son
Rama   that empty gaping dark
Your son is not your son
Rama   that corpse within the corpse
Your son is not your son
Rama   your nipple in the rain
Your son is not your son
Rama   that sleep beyond all sleep
Your son is not your son

Manthaara, the Hunchback
Spoken by Kaikeyi in Valmiki's Ramayana: Ayodhyakanda, Sarga 9

Manthaara, bent
like a lotus in the breeze,
your humped back is a fount
of wisdom, I'll bring
my lips to it and kiss it.
Manthaara, your
  shining face,
your breasts that rival
your shoulders, your
slim unassuming waist
and your spiraled navel,
your generous hips
  and wide behind,
the tinkle of your girdle,
the sturdy legs on
your slender feet.

Your hump is a chariot wheel.
I'll know your steadfastness by it.
I'll hold you by it,
I'll anoint you with gold,
I'll cover you with gold.
And one day when you walk
proudly, and still yourself
in the street, people will know at last
you are, you are more lovely
than the white orb
that limns
  the sky at night.

They Saw No Longer the Battlefield
After Valmiki's Ramayana: Yuddhakanda, sarga 55

And then like the blindness of fury in WAR
a solid rising column of iron-colored dirt &
skin & blood & hair & pollen & chondrite

buffeted in the ten directions the combatants
of both (monkeysrakshasasboth) sides, all
beings wrapped and tossed in it—

and they saw no longer the battlefield

only nebulas of dust, red rust
or white, whiter than white people or
the white of silk. Then nothing.
Not limb nor cloth nor banner
Not horse not blade
nor chariot nor bow could
be told apart in
that wretched dreck.

The sound
of the roaring ones &
the attacking ones
split your ears and yet
no true forms to
be apprehended by the eyes.

Stoked only more delirious with anger:

monkeys slaughtered fellow monkeys then
rakshasas blindly struck down their comrade rakshasas

and all was as it will be in the last
time-ravished frame.

USHA AKELLA

Nov 1/16

You've left, really, that's all it is.
    What happened to "*I will.*"
   Really, you've left something within,
      a letter with invisible ink,
         do you read it?
    I stay my tears, I don't stir out of myself
(I stay like a dog obedient to a command,
my greatest act of courage is a poem
I pour words from the heart-spout,
I imagine everything as your teaching,
               I weave epics from a handful of your words).
Instead, the sky mourns, the grass is wet,
    I don't care for the moon,
        When people talk, I listen to language from another planet,
I fade from company like a shroud,
all relations are words, fluff, bluff,
              every breath leaving this body
              is one breath shorter in the distance
                from me to you, this is the only count of existence.
    I am not afraid.
I will blow away this life like a dandelion willingly
        Say the word

  Master.

Nov 2/16

There's a chair here—plastic of some kind,
    nothing fancy.

Only, that it held a form, two weeks ago
    as a spoon holds honey

        And now it could be a
          swan
              a white lotus,
my journey's end,
  the shape of my waiting,
    the palm of my devotion,
      an emblem of silence,
        a teaching, like the flower of Buddha,
          holy feet.

    I sit in it at times,
        your unequal   but unashamed

        And I am held   by what holds you.

SHRIKANT VERMA
Translated from Hindi by Rahul Soni

Disillusionment of a Courtesan from the Time of the Buddha

With each caress
the breasts quiver

From the navel a fragrance rises

Astride
these thighs
only the mighty
can ride their
horse into the river

In search of unending pleasure come
the general,
the prince.

Women swoon.

Malati,
it won't be the same tomorrow
The breasts
will be filled
with pus,
the thighs
will lie broken
like monuments

You'll only be able
to hear footsteps—
whose?
The general's?
Or the prince's?

The river of pleasure
will have run dry

They'll joke
those who rode their
horse—
you too will laugh.

Fetching a corpse from the river
people leave it
at the ghats
and say—
Here lies Time

No one sees Malati.

With each caress
the breasts
quivered.

Only the mighty
straddled
these thighs.
In search of
unending pleasure
came the prince.

Women swooned.

The irony
Malati,
you've always been
Malati.

Trauma

A full moon night.
A full moon.
A mirror.

In the mirror
looking just like
the moon
the moon's
reflection.

After resting
for a while
the moon
slowly
moved
out of
the doorway.

I said,
How
silent it is!
Just then
I saw her
in the mirror—

before I
could ask,
Who are you,
she had already
disappeared.

Years later
remembering
that day
that incident

it strikes me—
she was
Padmini!

"That's why,"
I say,
"That's why
we both
are
broken,
the mirror
and
I."

Return

I saw him leave
by this very road:

he was not alone,
there was an army,
elephants,
horses,
chariots,
music—
the works.

And him
in the midst of it all
on horseback
serene
passing by,
as if he
was in charge,
and the rest
merely following.

Twenty years later
I see him return
by this very road:

he is not alone,
there is an army,
elephants,
horses,
chariots,
music—
the works.

And him
in the midst of it all

on horseback
serene
passing by,
as if someone else
is in charge,
and he
merely following.

RAJIV MOHABIR

Vapsi: Return

> *My coolitude is not rock either*
> *It is coral,*
> *Fruit of an earth laden with speech of birds*
> —Khal Torabully

My spirit's marine, constant
in sea legs—featureless when you
regard only my skin. I make

skeletal sense, beached. In my myth
      I was promised a voyage back
home to an India, borders shifted,

my village renamed. I carry
home in ship-song sternum-deep,
fringed in reef. Put your ear to my chest,

dear heart, you will be overcome
      with voyage cut in half. Stay.
Transform. You will grow a fluke and moan

kindly to the Others underwater
in webs of melody, not atavist
but evoking in you *vapsi*

to the center, where you now spout.

A Mnemonic for Survival

Is it surprising that whale songs rhyme?
That amidst the tonnage of vibrations,
new notes wail for measures?

Some cries fill you; their shifts
joined in migration as hull to
hull they cross the swells

and rhyme with those of my Aji's Aji
who once aboard the Hesperus
repeated refrains, a relief

at the surface; the body's strain
for air, to search for how to continue
in Demerara where sunlight fails.

Even today off Hale'iwa
one verse leads into the next,
rolls for knots and nautical staffs

across an expanse of an ocean's scale—
each singer displaced, improvising.

Underwater Acoustics
for Sudesh Mishra

Imagine the bluest electricity
of the coral sea. Dive headfirst from the bow,

your arms stretched out
before you in hallelujahs.

A mother and calf slap the surface
and you are caught
in the crossfire of calls;

all of your organs quiver.

Once you immerse yourself in unending strains
the tones will haunt you:

ghosts spouting sohars you've called
since childhood. They breach

and crescendo inside the vessels
of your brine. How you long

to touch and to be so touched
by the dark giants under your skin.

In the ink of night
long voices vibrate in your throat.

Open your mouth and spit.

MANI RAO

from *Echolocation*

1.
The demon and the dog whirl in space, the knives are out, flashing, and shame.
    She makes you eat spit and he who gives you shelter is already a refugee. She is a carrier for screams fortified with use and he has lost his fuck.
    Everyone is innocent, contagious.

9.
The sky is fitted linen, stretched over sealine without a crease, pegged to the spikes and jags of mountains, kingsize, navy, preparing to be sunshot. Sooner than lovers can hide, no sooner than the taste of stars striking your lips, one by one stunned and falling to light.
    It's all been said and yet, need, blowing between our lips, streams inside a tree. We flowed out of time and back so soon eating eggs our own. Through each other we pass like water.
    At the sun to see how it never changes, at the moon to see how it does, algae slipping beneath our feet, roots traveling and dewdrops dying in visible speed. There is no such thing as a circular river.
    Unlike bread, the body becomes softer with age. We tag our children with our names, store the plaits of our daughters. Stash berries under rocks and look for them later.
    Held in the fangs of a wristwatch, a well-worn path of a nail in our veins, heart-hammered time trail.
    No matter who two are kissing, eternity arrives, jelly bean eyes black crystal balls. The longer we look, the more we recognize and anything we could say is too obvious. The songs we like are the songs we know, and every song on the radio is about us.

13.
We hear the swarm and then see churning over the lawn. Buzzing so fast it's a wall, molecules whizzing on the inside, making it impenetrable.
    Then the bees grow taller, whirlpool and vanish into a pottery class.
    Now we know. To walk on water, slower than water. To see trees, move slower than trees. To pass through mountains faster than mountains.

15.
Views not parodied by descriptions, allowed to live and die, a cusp, from appearance to dis.

Close your eyes, imagine the view, open your eyes, replace the view with edge to edge identical copy of the original.

Framed by the window, held by both eyes; if you close your blinds, the birds and stars cannot see you.

A bird's eye: Thinning rivers, half eaten mountains, bending lakes, mild agitations of sea fur.

Clouds rush their journeys, just in case.

18.
Eyes are emissaries, soft knocks, nibs. Eyes are tongues, mad riverbeds insomniac for salt. Eyes are fangs, bared chisel tattooing face on retina. Bite this word, lick that wound.

Eyes are the itineraries of shooting stars on the tail of new disasters. Faster than witnesses, slow as alibis, don't look! Phoenix of mirages, allusions, holy ash, rising mohair soot. Darkness caving into black diamonds. Lashes fan the air between.

Stones drown to measure water of expression, water nothing dissolves in, pure staring child. Soft convex pillows, seed of sleep.

A false door revolves, a roulette swings back to starting position, the masochists bring out x-ographs.

Unfurling, clitoris. Descriptions, insatiable.

Eyes, are braille.

19.
We burn eyes.

Slippery flambéed moon on water.

How similar, fire and rain, the lapping and the fizz.

Outlined in soot, a black curvature.

27.
Steamed rice spills from a neighbor's window and before you know, it has arrived like mail, bulging with photographs.

A flood :

: home

I am your history, your memory and your child amnesia—I cannot remember you. Erupted in fear from your dream, I knew then it was, and that I, was your dream. A river uncoiling from mountains, weightcrashing into the sea.

28.
Picture the children who will never be born. The things they might do with video cameras. The petitions they might send to Kofi Annan. The children with a plan.

Children who take magnets out of their pockets and rally the universe into a new polarity. Children who can save us, lead us out of here.

Who don't do that. Who become a live journal suspended in word web. Who become parents. Loss after loss, born.

VIJAY NAMBISAN

On First Looking into Whitman's Humor

A child said to me: What is grass? and I replied,
It is a weed, not good for much; but if you
Pick some carefully, and dry it several days
In the sun; and you lovingly pack it
Into a ceremonial pipe—
   No, he interrupted,
Not that grass! The green grass—do you perhaps
Think it to be the uncut hair of graves?
So I threw a book at him and went on smoking.

Lint

Those who sweep beneath beds know the smell of lint.
It is something like musk, murmuring of age
And wickedness: something less than ashes, more than dust,
Lighter than the air which wafts above the bed,
Yet heavy as that which weighs upon your head at night
When you want sleep and it will not come.
    Lint is light
Captured in windows, kept captive against the dark:
It is all of yesterday that we wished to forget,
Creeping silently back when we thought it was gone.

Lint is power, wicked only in its weakness. Lock
It in cupboards and it triumphs; sweep it aside
And it owns no master.
The smell of lint is thus
The smell of waking to the very ill, who need
No compassion, but it smothers them. Yet those
Who sweep beneath beds are also sometimes wise,
And they know enough to leave the lint alone.

Bhima in the Forest

Of the flesh of the bull
And the flesh of the fowl
And the flesh of the blue deer
I have eaten.

Of the blood
Of the hare, and the blood
Of the ram, and the blood
Of the peacock I have drunk.

Tell me, where is the snake
To spoil me, where is the tiger
To tear me, for I am brother
In my body, to all beasts.

SALEEM PEERADINA

Heart's Beast

> *A man's heart will learn feebly first to walk on all*
> *fours and then strain upwards to stand up.*
> —P. C. Kuttikrishnan (Uroob)

1.
The heart must be curbed lest it become angelic.
It has to toil
in the sun
bruise its eye,
burn its back sifting dirt from dung.
It must plant
a fence, learn to stay
hungry, suck its fingernails.
It must strip
to the bone, keep its ear open for thieves.
It must surrender all
pride, exalt
only passion. The heart must vindicate
the honor of its fate.
if it prove worthy, the dew
of mortality will then bless its forehead.

2.
Scatter their ashes, drive
them into the sea—
deer, dove, butterfly,
wings, flowers, fins—salt them,
spread them in slime,
bury them in prehistoric silence
ending in coal.
The heart's a rodent,
a hog with a hard nose, all
mouth and hands, hair
on end, nostrils flaring.
A toad, a crab, a creature
without antennae.
A goat, a baboon

bitten by a field of red pepper;
a bleeding bear, an elephant
in a pit, a bellowing wolfpack.
The heart's cave of sleepless bats.
A dragonfly
with a crocodile's tail-lash;
a hawk cocking a barrel eye,
a cock hawking his appetite.

The heart's a mud-cracked buffalo mobbed by crows.

3.
Once it is violated, it loses
all tact.
It will show itself plainly, spit
in the eye of custom,
lead its object by the hand.
It will yield
unconditionally, expose its tendermost
parts. It will suffer abuse, stoop
to keep its claim open.
It will tease, flatter,
fight to forestall a breach.
It can wound and be afflicted. It is
insatiable. It can only exult
or scream.

4.
Hounded
by his own lust, the heart
goes into hiding: if he looks
askance, it is for tints
of flesh that snare him.
The prickly scent of grass
will yellow his vision for a day,
then needle his urge for pacing.
He will not stalk back. Even
thick foliage has no hollow
safe enough or far. Hoof-beats
wake him in the undergrowth.
A sniff transports a whole herd's

silent grazing into his view.
He roots on his haunches—
paws, neck, the flint of his eyes,
whiskers, eartips, all in a state of
phosphorescence.

SIDDHARTHA MENON

Eclipse

Ancient explicators had it wrong:
they said it was being swallowed
by, of all things, a dragon.
Lunatics might say that now.

To cast a shadow upon a moon
that shadows us: this is our
prerogative. The shadow we fling

is brown, consumptive: the moon's
been singed unevenly
by a profligate baker. Why
do we rise for such a thing at 2:00 a.m.?

Earth's appetites are gargantuan:
the timely moon is delectable
and the dragon turns to the sun.

Evening

Seen just now the moon
a misshapen speckled egg
is poised above the valley—

like in egg-fights at school
when a hardboiled shell was struck
on another held with cautious

intent and the winner was the one
whose eggshell didn't crack—
over the darkening valley

in an autumn chill the moon
is poised to crack shells
as lights lean out of windows

and harvest smoke streams
towards the low-lying river
which splinters the moon on rocks

and twirls fragments wherever
childlike and in suspense
a hardened witness stops.

Retired Swami

You were a tall presence
in the quiet grounds of thirty years ago
where birds and the trees were dust-free
and people shook off the unquiet street.
Before you they would bow low
or touch their foreheads to the clean flagstones.
I would watch in embarrassment
and wonder if I should do the same.
But you were always reassuring.
The height, the shaven head, the hooked nose,
the voice that carried from a long way in:
such calm certitude.

In the crowded chamber of my dream,
retired swami, your voice
is wavering; before us all
the chanting falters and you are to blame, apparently.
You struggle out of a molded plastic chair
and you are shorter than I (and none too clean)
somewhat stout, in a shirt tucked in
(where is your saffron robe
and how are you wisped with hair?)
and you kneel apologetically, clasp
the feet of one who bowed to you in the past.
Against one wall a TV flashes.

Swamiji, I know it is not your doing.
The street is cancerous, and I
am growing wise to certitude.
If you are TV-ridden it's your affair.

INDERJEET MANI

Ali G does Kabir

Bruvvers, me life's been pissed away
In silence, widout thinkin to pray
Me shawty days wasted in play
Me macho struttin so totally passé.
Hear me, bonin blew all me mula away
But me brain still hankerin fer payday.
So listen up to what me man Kabir say
Dem wicked seers be in nirvana today.

SURJIT PATAR

Translated from Punjabi by Amarjit Chandan

The Magician of Words

I was sitting in Obrero Park in the town of Medellin
in Colombia.
I was there to attend a poetry festival.

A child came to me riding his bike.
Looking at my turban and beard he asked me:
Señor, es usted mago?
(Are you a magician?)

I was about to say: No I am not.
But I did not feel like saying so.

I said: Yes.
I can pluck stars from the heavens
to make necklaces for girls.
I can turn trees into musical instruments
and the leaves into tunes.
I can make the air the fingertips of the guitar player.
I can transform wounds into flowers.

The child was enthralled and asked me: Really?
If so, can you turn my bike into a horse?

Thinking for a moment, I said:
I do not make magic for children,
I do it for adults.

Then can you turn my mama and papa's house into a palace?

I am not a magician of things.
I play magic with words.

Ahora sé, usted es un poeta.
(Now I know, you are a poet.)

Saying this and waving at me and smiling,
he cycled away, out of the park
and entered my poem.

JASON SANDHAR

oak creek: 5 aug 1919

temple punctured
wisconsin sunday.
dyer blasts words
through page:
curb stomp towelhead
firebomb shitskins.
bleed bodies
because brown.

words burst
red and (waheguru?)
kartar melts
into gulab kaur's nihang
wrath. scatter
crocodile, no pandits
or mullahs do we need!

dear lord
your wondrous
blue fury
speaks our
akali marxist's
untrue name.
as martyrs we
shimmer.

and the poet
splits open dyer's
white page. unborn
before time his
swastika grin
spills ten.
some are givers
and some
beggars. o nanak

the poor
beings are wretched
and miserable! they
wait, mouths
open ready
for your
friend's word.
we eat dyer's
shrapnel truth
for this is all your
wondrous play.

gulab kaur's true
name yet to come
reveals larval
revelation. history
trembles inside
gobind's mouth.
his marble words
blocked glottal, her
name true. word
of words, the
true name
folds away.

AMIT MAJMUDAR

The Gita Variations: Gloss 10

I knelt with scissors
Trimming sprigs
As gingerly as eyelashes
In Gethsemane.

I am the Bo tree,
The lote tree, the poetry
Of the furthest limit.
I am the soar in the sura.

Fetal position, I gestate
Live-buried in the Ark,
Swaddled in three cloths,
Amnion, chorion, muscle.

Of races I am the master
Mutt. Of nations
I am America,
Mother of ephemera.

The prophets took
Dictation from me,
Private secretaries
In my secret service.

In Lebanon
I rained on the hill
That sprouted the cedar
That became the true cross.

In Chidambaram,
In the Alhambra
I played hide and seek
Among the pillars.

Arjuna, I am Mother
Kali, Mother Mary,
Gaia and Maya
And Kwanyin in one.

The Kaaba shelled
My pupil for its black stone.
Bodhisattvas
Are my subtle body.

Of letters, I am I.
Of numbers, I am one
Over zero,
Irrational.

Do you see my coat
Of many colors, Arjuna?
Do you see how catholic
My dialectic is?

Gods and Goddesses
Are species of beetles
Crawling the galactic
Galapagos of me.

I have made it easy
For you to learn my nature.
Just bring the eyes I gave you.
Be my naturalist.

Godhra Sequence
—Gujarat, 2003

The moon this night is a scythe
taken off its hook
and bobbing
above a crowd of men.

The moon will follow
anyone who walks her
anywhere, even me
into the hospital
where your pupils are new moons.

> *Qaidi, only the moon has a dark side.*
> *The sun is fire all the way around.*

If every call to prayer
is also a call for the dead,

no wonder by this moanlight
mosque and morgue
look like they might rhyme.

Hands to either side of his mouth,
a frenzied muezzin
is blowing on the sparks.

The fires catch.
The fires catch

us

doelike where we stand and listen,
turning to our futures.

Qaidi, your eyes, too, are luminous.
But not from within.

☙

In the middle of a modern city,
they show up with farm tools.

Not just machetes, either.
Spades and shovels.
Murder full service,
burial included.

Qaidi, she is thinking
how absurd this schoolboy looks
with garden shears

until the jab and
torque and
three quick jerks—

the legs
the handles
forced apart

ribs cracking
as the blades
work wide

the beet-red furrow that

invaginates her heart

☙

First of all, it was all true. Everything you saw.

You must trust your memory
no matter what the loudspeakers
mounted on those vans
are saying.

If you brush your skin
and paint comes off
keep rubbing
until you expose the purple
subcontinent
of the bruise.

> *What you saw was the truth, Qaidi.*
> *Anything else is the news.*

VINOD KUMAR SHUKLA

Translated from Hindi by Arvind Krishna Mehrotra

"That man put on a new woolen coat and went away like a thought"

That man put on a new woolen coat and went away like a thought.
In rubber flip-flops I struggled behind.
The time was six in the morning, the time of hand-me-downs, and it was freezing cold.
Six in the morning was like six in the morning.
There was a man standing under a tree.
In the mist it looked like he was standing inside his own blurred shape.
The blurred tree looked exactly like a tree.
To its right was a blurred horse of inferior stock,
Looking like a horse of inferior stock.
The horse was hungry, the mist like a grassy field to him.
There were other houses, trees, roads, but no other horse.
There was only one horse. I wasn't that horse,
But my breath, when I panted, was indistinguishable from the mist.
If the man standing at that one spot under the tree was the master,
Then to him I was a horse at a gallop, horseshoes nailed to my boot soles.

IMTIAZ DHARKER

The Knot

At Loch Lomond they are king and queen to me,
laying out their bounty on the brae
after the queasy ride from Glasgow, we
children making sick-stops on the way

until we tumble out at the mouth of water.
where light eats shade and makes us ravenous.
She unties the dishcloth with a flourish later
to set the parathas free, and as she does,

undoes this deep red knot of hurt in the heart.
Today, when scars have been allowed to deepen
around a silence, wrenching our lives apart,
she has come back to us at the loch to open

the tangle of her dying, our mistake,
the high, the low, the road we did not take.

Out of Line

Happy arrives with the moon on its shoulder. Glamorous.
You can tell it has crossed the line by the way it moves,
eyes glittering like wet roads in headlights, dangerous
and out of control, attention all over the place. It loves

the language and talks to strangers, asks your name,
looks in your face and offers its hand, no sign of a knife
or a gun, no respect for the rules, not a trace of shame.
Before you can stop it, Happy slaps your back and kisses
                                                your wife

on the cheek. This is no place for Happy. It leads to touching.
it could spread an infection, cause a contagion of glances
with that dirty laugh, wine on the breath, it encourages smiling
and unrestricted movement of hands and feet. Dances.

Happy is just asking to be buried up to its neck in sand,
a face like that, asking to be stoned

to death. Is Happy known to you? Tell Happy this
for its own good, to hide its ankles, cover its wrists.

RAFIQ KATHWARI

The Day I Was My Sister's Chaperone

Tall tan stranger in safari suit flew
from Kenya to Kashmir to woo her

at the Shalimar. She raised her shalwar
to her ankles at the fountain's edge

he rolled his cuffs to his knees. Their
toes touched. She waved—a shimmer

on her finger caught my curious eye.
"Amorous Lover" floated amidst lotus buds,

shikara-wallah slicing Dal Lake
with a heart-shaped oar.

For My Nephew Omar on His Engagement to Nadia

This small box conceals a porcelain elephant,
rigged up howdah, Kashmir-style sapphire
on forehead—an inner eye.
Conch shell ears fanning out,
supple trunk cradles a bird's nest
without breaking the eggs.
'A matriarch of her herd,'
the woman who sold it said.
'175 years old, maybe older; Japan seal on sole'
Parting with this I have long held dear —
a metaphor for trials of love
I myself have yet to endure.

29 October 2005
Beaver Dam, Wisconsin

ARYANIL MUKHERJEE

from *code memory: dead fish buoy above the living*

semiology is all about an assemblage of remembered relations. I keep the house wrapped in its scent as dementia writes on the corroded walls. blur fills all vessels except the Renoir still life—
   oil color flowers in the urinal hanging directly above the call of nature. above automatic aroma

   I didn't want action to supervise it all
   the verb is a pro
   that was my proverbial claim
   that all writing is eventually human
   made from human data
   grilled in hominid memory
   even when the fractal lyric of a birdsong
   is saved
   we alter its meaning

℘

   the momentary lapse between life and poetry
   is so hard to accept
   although lightning and thunder have attuned to it

   I avoid the circle
   but the cylindrical poem reconfigures it   open at both ends
   allows the flow   of waste water
   I don't need to underscore its grime
   just the pure passage of men, women
   and the metaphor

   feeling under its feathers
   the real bird body conforms now to the imagination of touch
   did it elude the birdcatcher?
   each spice lends itself to the gravy
   the cigar put out in wine
   lies astray beside the goblet

☙

the familiar buzz brings back. what initially assumes the mold of a formidable fuzzy. later we realize it is our terrific ability to conjure up the long-gone honey of our lives. the touch of the silvery selves of those dead fish marked everywhere on us. from sideburns to hidden hair. a devouring silverness reminding us that the roots of all life emerge from waterbase. gravity doubles in its medium and pulls me towards the black bees alive in the recesses of dead fish.

☙

that dead fish buoy like books—how much of that can claim our sanity? I don't know. and the little girl who came to us to unfurl her latest discovery, talked about what she found in their viscera—a miniature violin made with silver wire. book or violin? cognition or wine? smell or taste?

as we continued to argue about these binaries I thought about pearls. remembering brings out the train of thought to reveal to us its profoundly magical universal joints. process threads that fill the sewer system under the design of unseen cities. the same threads weave thy pearls.

an essential part of reasoning makes belief memory. it is connected in obscure ways with the flow of time-sensitive language. much of the shelf life of honey depends on the honeybee's age. the peculiar ways in which it is embedded in time. it's not the road that's runny but the sidewalks—an ageless bi-product. like wax. which we melt to coat the dead fish and alongside all of the silver hue that's now museumified in a mortal gallery.

☙

the violet boughs that gravitate towards you ma
ma earth
who taught them?
the art of being grave
weighty?
how much learned skill weighs down in the mist
towards the shape of our palms

can you guarantee ma   the recipes you wrote are all
exclusively yours?

never prefaced
nor role-played in
by another soul   another pair of hands
or another text?

far away down
the sea tidies up this afternoon   waxes it
like the apple in the grocer's bin
you climb down the hill in your skirt   yellow collar
a butterfly alights from nowhere and you said—
the ones that survive the winter
bring on the amber of new year
upon their designed wings

window opens
to the new amber shine—
the racks of antique books
of antique amber
yesteryear butterflies, cankerous
and of unspeakable flights
and a forgotten song—
catch me   catch me if you can
you float like a butterfly and sting like a bee

ANITHA THAMPI
Translated from Malayalam by J. Devika

Alappuzha *Vellam*

She, of Alappuzha.
She, of that soil's charcoal-tints.

When she writes in poetry,
she writes, *jalam*!

Attoor, the Poet, asked:
It's *vellam*, isn't it?
She, of Alappuzha,
the girl with palm-thatch braids,
daughter of the muddy water,
rotting-coconut-husk-reeking water
faintly-briny-tasting water
bright-tea-burnished water.

For her, *jalam*
means the clear liquid
that reigns
in Wayanad, Nila-land,
hill-land, southern-land.
That which falls off the sky
and is un-fallen on the earth,
that which has no smell,
the gift of the deep,
colorless water which beholds
far distances, towering heights,
water that does not wilt and lie still
in the plains.

It holds the gods,
charming temples,
daily worship, divine feasts
year after year, festive flags,
trunk-waving tuskers,
the brimming crowd.

Alappuzha's fine soil
gets the monthlies.
Thus is born, *vellam*.
It stains,
it washes, it bathes,
it stretches out in pain,
it gets up, walks,
it stays sleepless,
touching not its mate-water.
Untamed and sharp-tongued,
couldn't care less
for clarity.
Fitful are its depths.

Their-Selves are their Deities.
Sacrifice lies sprawled on
its stones, all over inner worlds and out.
Oars, wheels, coir-spinning ratts.
The songs of the shattered throat.
Headless flagpoles.
The nod of the yellowed
palm-frond ears.

The monsoon that dances
all agog, like the beach at fish-thronging *Chaakara*,
pitiless summer, spitting fire
as the white sand scorches, sears.
Vellam keeps step, it brims, it sinks
bowls and pans,
storing pots full,
fish-scaly skin that clings
stubbornly to them—the *vellam*'s pain.

Canals, boat-jetty,
Stone Bridge and Iron Bridge,
pond, backwater, rolling water-weed carpets,
hyacinth-bloom-smiles
the glow of coconut-fibre-gold
the tang of dissolved iron
the sodden scent of sweat

all in the waters of Alappuzha.
It wobbles, it dims,
dissolves in the distance,
melts into images
the birds alone see.

Decades have passed
and she's homed in southern waters.
Yet while writing,
delving the depths of memory,
she, of Alappuzha's hues
she, of Alappuzha's hair
still knows not: *jalam*, or *vellam*?
She turns, she knows
but she turns not, she knows not.

The throat stays parched.

Notes:

Chaakara: a unique coastal phenomenon in which fish congregate in large numbers due to the formation of mud banks during the summer monsoon.

Poet's note: Many years ago, Attoor Ravi Varma, a senior poet who was editing an anthology of new Malayalam poetry, asked me why I had used the word *jalam*, instead of *vellam* in a poem. (While *jalam* is a Sanskrit word one uses in Malayalam, *vellam* is the "local" Malayalam word for it.) I didn't answer him then, but the question followed me persistently over the years, carrying me back to Alappuzha town and the villages where I spent most of my childhood. That was the watery terrain where the seeds of my language sprouted. For those of us living in water-borne Alappuzha, *jalam* and *vellam* were not one, they represented life-forces and experiences of power that were worlds apart. Attoor's question dragged me to the originary sources and primal impulses of my language.

RANJIT HOSKOTE

Sand

In the kingdom of sand
    the three-eyed man is king
he measures the dunes
  by what's left of meteor trails
        and camel tracks
trusts only what he can smell
    cloth is a cage
    so he wears what's real
nudges the trapped horizons awake
    calls out to his horsemen
   in sparse flashes of lightning
   when the rain comes it will be war
and he can see this script unravel three ways
      every single time
    an eye for each tense
one tight eye to shut out the wind
one eye that was taken for an eye
   one eye wide as the ocean
       as forgiving
with which he once saw
   a bird swoop down
on a listing ship
   perch and take wing
circle and point
    across a tsunami of sand
      can it bring him home?

Shoe

    What is wrong with that tree parked at eight?
        Go clock it with the last shoe
left on the rack
        luminous glow-in-the-dark blue
one of a pair
        the hours laced tight
            a sentence for dragged feet
they'll never forget
        walking on countdown ice

Market

Never forget the salt-makers
    they can trap the sea

Never forget the makers of flint knives
    they can split the earth

Never forget the spice sellers
    they can tempt the tongue to sing in many colors

Never forget the kite-makers
    they can tease the wind into giant streamers

Never forget the carpenters
    they can build horses that breach walled cities

Never forget those who stretch hide into leather
    they can craft drums that bring down palaces

Hunchprose

He calls me Hunchprose but what's a word
between murderous rivals?
Across from me he strops his fine blade
smooth talker barefaced liar pissfart
teller of tall tales who wraps you up
in his flying carpet serves you snake oil
carries off the princess every time.
And I what can I offer you except
fraying knots coiled riddles scrolled bones
keys to doors that were carted away by raiders
betrayed by splayed light and early snow.
Lost doors I could have opened with my breath.
Call me Hunchpraise. I bend over my inkdrift words.
And when I spring back up I sting.

HEMANT DIVATE
Translated from Marathi by Mustansir Dalvi

Praha, I'll be back

1.
If, on our very first meeting, I could touch every nook
and cranny, I'd forge an eternal bond through easy
familiarity. That's how I now feel about this city.

2.
I have never been able to read a woman
as fluently as a poem; even my wife,
whom I consider entirely mine remains
a stranger in the end.
How easy it would be if a woman
could be interpreted like wine,
sipped at a tasting.
Like an unfinished poem languishing
in my mind, I am made uneasy
by my own femininity, inside and outside me.
It's a similar incomplete, unclear
and upsetting relationship I maintain with every city
but the moment I landed here, I remembered
already having spent an entire lifetime,
so I return—a substitute for Gregor Samsa.

3.
I pace this town, wolf it down like a glutton,
as if my father owns this town and everything in it,
as if I have been granted a boon:
the more I walk this city, the more it will be mine.
Shops are stacked up tightly here
between coffeehouses, bars and pubs.
I sneak out of these constricted slivers
and slip into a familiar home.

I cannot find the bed of my childbirth
nor the table, the chair, nor the books,
nor the shaving razor, nor its mirror

but I can see right through this glass,
back a hundred years, where I am abandoned
in this blasted cold by an unrepentant, shivering
Kafka, who could not even make good
the one life he was granted, while I,
steeped in my own ennui endlessly experience
birth, death and rebirth in many foreign tongues.

    Kafka, you left with so many of my desires
unfulfilled, so here I rise, again and again,
putting brakes on my bestiality
like you killed your own desires
and became human. How late was it
before you realized the greatness
of transforming into an insect?
Look up now, to the old clock tower and count—
how many writers need to suffer and die
to bring one insect to life.

    4.
    I cannot see the numbers. Right now,
women and men become numerals on Charles Bridge.
With no choice, I push my way through and descend
to a nondescript punt waiting for me,
a boat fated to drown fate, time after time.
A man waits for me there
dressed in a long coat like Kafka.
He waits for me, eating chickpeas;
the fucker hasn't rid himself of his old habits.

    Am I not going there
just to tell him that the remains of his snack
should be thrown into the garbage bin?
    Have I forgotten why I need to meet someone?
Who am I supposed to meet, and for what reason?

    Or, am I the man in the Kafka coat
and while I say that I am moving along,
am I actually standing in one place
waiting for the punt under Charles Bridge,
while possibly, a man in a Kafka coat

is in the boat, slowly approaching me
as I stand here eating chickpeas?
And, as I wait for the man to approach,
the breeze blows dry shells from my hand
and you say, don't you even know
how to eat chickpeas? This means that
you clearly think I am some kind of arsehole,
so let me tell you a story:
not one that you should not repeat
nor one that no one knows, but
metamorphosis means the transformation
of a city into an installation in an exhibition hall,
a human artwork to be regarded by insects,
an insect artwork to be regarded by humans,
where the dim light metamorphosed over the installation
is the one that bathes the poet's composition
in a soft, linguistic, biographical sheen
while the city, as it is now
is the detritus of screaming, blood-soaked geography
or of raw imperialism that, like a half-done omelette
is left to sizzle in the frying pan of history.

—and one more thing:
Kafka prefers to drink English tea over coffee.
There below the Grand Clock
he waits to see which will turn into piss first,
my coffee or his tea?
We have a wager, Kafka and I—
while the one who pisses first wins, the other
will have to run, micturating all over Prague.
It was ten past ten when I met him
and all around his coat rose the angel-dust
of Prague's magic realism.

5.
From where I stand
I can see the impending demise of Kafka's language.
What can you see from where you stand?
Can you see the tale of Gregor Samsa
or only the ongoing, unending story of Franz Kafka?

6.
      Wandering through Josefov Quarter,
I get this feeling of people screaming loudly in my ear;
those who but moments ago walked arm in arm
now lunge for each other's throats;
soft voices are now shrieks,
russet-tiled homes now collapse into debris.
I run, and the whole city gives chase
as if I am the alpha and the omega of their destruction.
      Inside Café Franz Kafka, I see people drink Coca-Cola
instead of coffee. I turn to leave and cups, saucers,
chairs, tables, coffee machines rattle and bump
and grumble loudly: fucking Coke . . .
      Slowly, without fuss, I transform into a two-inch cockroach.
Divining with my antenna, I reach Praha railway station;
even there, these bloody Coke bottles block my path.
      As I turn back, Kafka accosts me, whispers in my ear
that—scuttling down these cobbled streets with me—
for the first time, he realised Prague was sexy.
      Fuck! I never once paid heed to the city's sexiness.
Praha, I'll be back!

What Happened to Language?

    What happened to the language
of the boy sucking on a sugarcane stick?
What happened to his language, this vagabond,
rolling an old tyre all over his village?

    What happened to the everyday tongue
of this little boy, playing thabu and marbles?
What happened to the language of the child
who loved surparambya, gilli-danda, lagori,
tops, mummy-daddy, doctor-doctor?

    What happened to this free bird
who lustily blew his whistle during the jatra?
This brawling boy, who played appa-rappi
and cricket with a ball of rags? What happened?

    The same boy, who spoke with his friends later,
self-conscious of his obviously ghati tongue.
What happened to his language?
Kaay zhaala?

PRIYA SARUKKAI CHABRIA

Great Mosque, Xian

    Lacquered in late afternoon light
the ancient mosque constellates
    as a sacred chameleon sourced
from mingled memory: Toorki/
    Chini. The old desert dream
of water surfaces as turquoise
    tiles; the surge of the Dragon
sheens its winged roof of glaze.
    Here peace emanates
through the proportions
    of courtyards, clipped shrubs,
stippled carp in stone basins, fallen
    light and carved calligraphy
in lapis lazuli: *Allah hu akbar*
    The muezzin's call is inflected
in Mandarin. Here the hunting heart
    quells its hungers: the unfamiliar
is welcomed home through beauty.

Prayer as Three Camera Movements

Falconetti's Joan of Arc Face

Cracked sun the teardrop that hangs on a lash and falls bursts
skids down her pitted skin, down her brokenness as she, stone
flower, sunflower, turns towards the inquisitor's glare and her
sainthood is slowly hammered into chainmail breasts.
Her silent words are wrong whatever she says.
Extreme close-up: no let up to transformation. See the
trembling of cell, phrase & faith.

Kinuyo Tanaka's Nape in The Life of Oharu

She drops her head to staunch her eyes' rain as her
son who reigns walks past not knowing that sack of kneeling
woman is his mother who sinned & pulled herself out
of icy seas like a wounded seal, sealed to secrecy. See the
bent stalk of her nape, how soft, how ripe for the axe.
Crane shot ascends: suffering shrinks to dewdrop size.
Silence of the enfolding gaze.

Gauri's Back in Sant Tukaram

"Accompany me to heaven," her husband says. "Who'll feed
the kids & scrub the buffalo if I come with you? Go!" She
rolls out chapattis, rough as dung-cakes, as holy bread. The saint
mounts god's eagle & people chant. She flings the
sweat from her face on the earth. Her back sturdy as a tree,
and bowed.
Slow backward track: the unseen movement that remains as
time forgets the color of clay.

Notes:
Marie Falconetti was a relatively unknown French stage actress when the legendary Danish director, Carl Theodor Dreyer, cast her in the title role in *The Passion of Joan of Arc* (1928). The film condenses the trial of Joan and her death at the stake to a single day. Falconetti played the role with a profound spiritual power that was to change her for life—she never acted again. The film, celebrated for her portraiture of the saint, is shot in excessive, almost excruciating, close-ups that intensify the realism of the film. *The Passion of Joan of Arc* still figures in many Top Ten lists, as does Falconetti's performance.

Among the outstanding actresses of classical Japanese cinema, Kinuyu Tanaka acted in several of Kenji Mizoguchi's films. In *The Life of Oharu* (1952), adapted from Saikaku's seventeenth-century novel, Mizoguchi fashioned a great tragedy about a woman at different stages of life in feudal Japan—imperial servant, concubine, prostitute and, eventually, itinerant nun. In a distinctive Mizoguchian final shot, the camera cranes up to show the entire panorama. Tanaka was Mizoguchi's amanuensis; here she plays the eponymous character with rare conviction and sensitivity.

The most celebrated bhakti (devotional) film made in Indian cinema, V. G. Damle-S. Fattelal's *Sant Tukaram* (1936) won many accolades and was voted as one of the best three films at the Venice Film Festival that year. Gauri was a sweeper employed by the Prabhat Film Co. in Pune when director and movie mogul, V. Shantaram, spotted her. She went on to play numerous character roles in the 1930s, considered the Golden Era of the Indian studio system. Her best-remembered performance is as Jijai, the hardworking peasant wife of the seventeenth-century mystic poet, Tuka. As the earthy Jijai burdened by housework, caring for their sole buffalo and hungry children, she is the perfect foil to the saint's otherworldliness and spiritual aura, ably conveyed by Vishnupant Pagnis as Tuka.

KAZIM ALI

Divination

Square and circle my birth chart impresses

Drawn to separate a single clear note emerging

From a wash of ambient sound of stars and planets

Individual notes discrete revolve around the sun

Here I am a threaded bead impaled by decades

By prayers I can't see or hear but slide along the thread

Neither the one praying nor the prayer itself

Just a clot of muscle and bone counting

I spin how clouds condense amber from the tree

Driftwood on the Baltic smooth under the palm

All roughness eroded on a map of the mountain's ridges

In color liken themselves to some other place

Algeria rhymes with Paraguay or Taiwan and Morocco with Chile or Bhutan

Confusion and utterance

South wind southern

Shuttered shut torn as per usual

Devil and his split tongue gives a word as another word

In the Generalife of the Alhambra we saw an Arab couple with their lonely planet guide

And the cypress tree leaning over

It may have witnessed the assignation but it looks dead to me

How much we want to hold on to history

I want to hold in my arms

My many lives

The one when I flew with blue wings

Or when I was on my back covered in sculptor's dust

Or when I spied the Arab couple with a guide book in Hebrew

Or the time in the gray city I wanted to strangle myself

With flowers and mist stoking infernos in my rib cage

Reading the *Master Letters* in the coffee shop of the bus station

Solid cold sky wet on my skin

My chest a prisoned cathedral

Never told in the park the winter brought

I am forgotten how to draw myself

In ice on the glass that no one told shattered

Chapters of tinsel dark lust and angry loneliness

I disappeared then amidst thrum and hunger

If you want to know the edge of ocean or sky

Water and air unloosens itself

Pitched into the season of orange

No weapon but green

I lost myself in the sedimented time of petrified woods

You are a door leading nowhere in the slopes of ardor and crime

Heretics used to burn

Your heresy is you believe the body has a mind and a spirit too

That it is a ladder to god

That bones and muscle are

Bricks of Babel

Of course you could try to actually look at yourself

Lie and say so casually oh it just came to me in the rain

I put a jacket of mist and flowers in my suitcase

All the contracts of lethargy and forgetfulness

I've refused to sign and on the other side of the glass

A friend I don't recognize, the brave one

Who unpacked all my shirts of silence

And now who am I without them

When I open my mouth

There's nothing left inside

I am only myself to throw now, grown into bell and ghost garden bird

Third every night to soar

Petals in my mouth

I want a big pocketful of coins now

Cents crazy you will be and festooned

Yes I is you

The papers are all writing stories about you

It's the now that will be your lover

Stripped in summer suck

Stringed to the sky wingless

You will be a knot of cleverness

This crime is my second offense

Accordion to conventional wisdom

The wind that carries the siren-song landwards

A land word land bridge my second or third try

Ken you quickly tell me

Ken you quickly kell me

When I thought up logos I foundered

Old ghost caused almost

There built I in the roots of the earth

A stone laboratory my labor labial

Pronounce a nonce announce

I can't spell your sin

Spill to the rest

To the west the third most important shrine

To color always counting god by shade

This flower book dehisces not close to you

Feeling in wonder through

The powder of gold air flouring

Fleet that sluices through

You sailed yourself to the end of vision

You spent are spent passed hand in hand

Lust spawn sent in throes of flower

Now petal yourself astronomical

Sky flower throw your voice of light

Petal yourself labialalluvial

Soaked clear through luminous spent

Kneeling before intensity why should the vessel be always unscathed

Why should the I always be spared

Don't you want to know you have been passed through

ANON

Prakrit Love Poetry from the Gathasaptasati of Satavahana Hala
Translated by Arvind Krishna Mehrotra

307.
Unable to count
  The days of separation
Beyond her fingers and toes
  The unlettered girl broke down

417.
We're trugs all right
  And you're a paragon
But at least we don't
  Fantasize chiropodists

599.
All he wants
  Is to see her armpit,
So asks the garland-maker
  The price of a string.

701.
To bandits
  Lovers
Travelers
  The cock cries:

Loot
  Copulate
Speed well
  The night flies.

707.
Preoccupied with thoughts
  Of his desolate wife,
The absent traveler
  Now approaches his village
Now leaves it behind.

ARUNDHATHI SUBRAMANIAM

When God is a Traveler
wondering about Kartikeya, Muruga, Subramania, my namesake

Trust the god
back from his travels,

his voice wholegrain
   (and chamomile),
his wisdom neem,
   his peacock, sweaty-plumed,
   drowsing in the shadows.

Trust him
who sits wordless on park benches
listening to the cries of children
fading into the dusk,
   his gaze emptied of vagrancy,
   his heart of ownership.

Trust him
who has seen enough—
revolutions, promises, the desperate light
of shopping malls, hospital rooms,
manifestos, theologies, the iron taste
of blood, the great craters in the middle
        of love.

Trust him
who no longer begrudges
his brother his prize,
his parents their partisanship.

Trust him
whose race is run,
whose journey remains,

who stands fluid-stemmed
knowing he is the tree

that bears fruit, festive
   with sun.

Trust him
who recognizes you—
auspicious, abundant, battle-scarred,
        alive—
and knows from where you come.

Trust the god
ready to circle the world all over again
this time for no reason at all

other than to see it
through your eyes.

How to Read Indian Myth
for AS who wonders

How to read Indian myth?
The way I read Greek, I suppose

not worrying too much about
foreign names
and plots,

knowing there is never
a single point
to any story

taking the red hibiscus route
into the skin

alert to trapdoors, willing
  to blunder a little in the dark

   slightly drunk
         on Deccan sun

but with a spring in the step
that knows

we are fundamentally
corky

built to float,
built to understand

and the chemical into which we are tumbling
will sustain
has sustained before

knows a way beyond
a way through

                    knows
                    the two

aren't separate.

Read it like you would read a love story
Your own

Leapfrog

Anyone who has sufficient language nurses ambitions of writing a scripture
—Sadhguru

Not scripture, no,
but grant me the gasp
of bridged synapse,
the lightning alignment
of marrow, mind and blood
that allows words
to spring

from the cusp of breathsong,
from a place radiant
with birdflight and rivergreen.

Not the certainty
of stone, but grant me
the quiet logic
   of rain,
      of love,
of the simple calendars of my childhood
of saints aureoled by overripe lemons.

Grant me the fierce tenderness
of watching
word slither into word,
into the miraculous algae
of language,
untamed by doubt
or gravity,

words careening,
diving,
    swarming, un-
forming, wilder

than snowstorms in Antarctica, wetter
than days in Cherrapunjee,

alighting on paper, only
for a moment,
tenuous, breathing,
amphibious,
before
     leaping
to some place the voice
is still learning

to reach.

Not scripture,
but a tadpole among the stars,
unafraid to plunge
deeper
if it must—

only if it must—

into transit.

ROBERT WOOD

We Seed

we seed, link, sift, cruise
our mesh

we at the end of the street peck
still the inheritance
sweet after talk the pointy end where the wake up calls
and the flesh to flesh press of the nucleus becomes our god

Week of Rose

Last week, everything, all the elements—clouds, fire, mascara

in fact i felt my life was more than tearing
but things change, oranges green to peach

absolution in hints

and suddenly, nothing sensed
it was like crushpace in the logs, chip shoulders
chilli paste
lacking rupture, chrysanthemums
the bare thought cohering with
mourning, a memory of anchored darkness

this week, any thing of rose.

To Be Rice

To be rice, to be tropics, to be mountainous
to be tuk tuk, to be smoggy, to be moon cake
to be terraced, to be glutinous, to be fanning

to be mediating the world as it defines itself
as indefinable and begins to show what it is
to know where one can be at home yet still

KUNWAR NARAIN
Translated from Hindi by Apurva Narain

Reaching Home

We all wish to take
a direct train home

We all wish to escape
the bother of changing trains

We all wish a journey superlative
and a destination definitive

We presuppose that journeys are hazardous
and home is freedom from them

Truth, however, could be otherwise
that journeys might be occasions
and home a prospect

Changing trains
be like changing thoughts
and wherever whenever with whomever we be
that be
reaching home

They are not crowds, they are us

In a disaster near Patna
seeing his name in the list of the dead,
Hardayal was stunned—"But
I am still alive!"

Then who was that other who got killed?
Is it possible that there is another
just like me?

The explosion failed
They who should not have won
lost on their own.

Smoke rises from the fort

It is as though a gigantic disorder
is protecting us.

He who remained safe thought—
there is a chance
I should return now,
the full import of being human
can be collected
around a commune,
its representative on earth
can be elected by a majority.

Smoke rises from the kitchen

Surprise, even without armies
the house was safe: the wife
was happy like honesty
even in a tiny space,
the child who cycled to school

had returned safely from
the jaws of a ferocious traffic.

Hardayal said to his wife—
Perhaps I was seeing a dream.
Listen, now we are not safe,
an agitated crowd has seen us
hugging each other in joy,
we have been surrounded on all sides.
Tomorrow news will be printed that we
have been killed in some clash
or stampede

No, this will not happen—
the wife said with simplicity—
You have got scared.
They are our neighbors.
Their eyes are moist with our happiness,
give them the face of your trust—
they are not crowds, they are us.

SHARMISTHA MOHANTY

What Holds Together

The mochi is inside his wooden box, made to the height and width of him sitting cross-legged. His knees rest on a narrow ledge outside the box, amidst broken shoes, hammers, cans of glue, nails and an anvil. In the few inches of space behind him, within the box, he hangs the shoes that he has finished working on. Above this he keeps the smallest altar with faded pictures of the Devi riding a tiger, and Jesus, and a saint with a turban, and the Buddha smiling his translucent smile, and Ambedkar. The mochi is in the sky. The box, painted a blue lighter than this sky, rides the wind. A gigantic eagle hovers above and casts the shadow of its wings on the surface of the ocean. He perches on the mochi's box without weighing it down. He moves his wings, stroking the waves without touching them. The sun is about to set, its last light behind gathered clouds. My doctor says, now look down at the earth from very far above. Yes. Your life is a line of light inside a transparent, thin cylinder stretched out on the ground, over a vast distance. Do you see it? Yes. I see the line on the earth, next to the ocean. But there is no light in it, except very far away, towards the future. The universe is very old, says the doctor. I see only what I move towards, I tell him, not what I have been or what I now am. I pay attention to the past and the present only because they lead to what will come. The mochi lights a candle at his altar. It brings the dimmest glow to the chest of the eagle above, and to a shard of the water below. He stitches a sole on a shoe, lifting the large, thick needle high into the evening. Pin pricks of blood appear in the sky, like the last residues of sunset. The mochi, for a moment, looks out over the ocean. Only what is continuous, what is unbroken, gives rest. The eagle folds his wings. He comes from a high wilderness, from a place without dust, where the earth has not been broken open. He can see very far, to where the rabbit, his prey, moves under bushes two miles away, and right through to the other side of the human heart. The mochi and I face each other, as we have done for eleven years. My black, high heeled shoes lie on their side on his ledge. One of the heels is broken. I haven't finished yet he says, glancing at them. You had asked me to soften the edges of the two straps so they don't cut the skin on your feet. That takes time. I can wait, I say. So dark, he says, isn't it, a moonless night. Do you remember he says, there were two full moons last month. The doctor's voice rises and falls now, like a hawker walking down a long street. The universe has its own answers, he says. If you go into this ocean below, diving under water, with a ship coming in to anchor, you will go next to the quiet authority of the ship, through the frailest plants with leaves as thin as hair being swayed by the water exactly like a plant swayed by the wind above, over stones that may have come to rest on the seabed that very day or a century ago, through schools of small black fish, or a single orange one alone, the seabed itself gradually being extended by volcanic eruptions, as you probably know, that harden into a crust. The oldest rocks on the bottom of the ocean are approximately two hundred million years old. The doctor knows that only what is continuous, what is unbroken brings rest. But for how long? He takes a handkerchief and brings it down on my tears. He is tender but careful, he does not touch my skin even once. The saint at the mochi's altar would have used his bare hands. The eagle sits still on the box. His large pupils have taken in the gleam of the earth with minimal diffraction. He has passed it through his body. He has not finished considering it. He moves to the edge of the box, leans forward, and raises his enormous wings. The mochi looks up and sees him for the first time. A tear drops from his eye. This eagle is from outside time, like the human stain that nothing can cleanse, neither birth nor death nor life, nor rebirth. The eagle has seen the doctor and the mochi, both trying to make unbroken what is broken, endless work. He has seen the line of my life far below on which the mochi's candle now casts a distant glow, and far beyond that, to those interstices of the earth where ascesis and instinct are as one. He rises into the air slowly but there is urgency in the beating of his wings. Time is infinite but never enough. The eagle's attributes are his tools, the panoramic image on his retina, the manifold sounds in his ear. With these he gathers pieces of consciousness from which he will build his eyrie, high above the earth but unmistakably on it. The pills the doctor finally has to prescribe are to be taken thrice a day, called Stablon, they are small, smooth, brilliant white, and swollen in the middle, holding the chemical tianeptine, first synthesized by French researchers Antoine Deslandes and Michael Spedding, in the early eighties. It is known to be effective much of the time, but it is not known yet exactly why. The research into human misery, they say, has barely begun. But the homeostatic mechanisms of unhappiness bequeathed by evolution can be dismantled and replaced as research grows. What is stable is what holds together, able to bear every centrifugal force, unlike myself. The eagle flies towards land, gripping the sky with his talons, over dark holes gaping from earth, baring iron teeth. He leaves behind a diurnal awareness. The box shakes as the eagle flies away and a hammer falls from the mochi's ledge, like a dislodged mountain rock. Everything is precarious, everything hangs on nothing. The night takes the hammer's falling force, its surface swells with a bruise. "Come by tomorrow evening then," the mochi says. He doesn't say this is all I can ever do, make sure that your shoes don't bruise your feet, and I don't say my feet are always bruised, and they are unsteady, and I often stumble and fall, and he doesn't say I don't have time to look up, like everyone who hammers, sews, ploughs, digs, weaves, grinds, and gathers, and I don't say I am too much looking up, looking skywards, and we live every day despite the facts that make us, despite the hands that serve feet, and my own hands that do not ever shake, but are excessively at rest.

IRWIN ALLAN SEALY

crossing the line

If nine out of ten living creatures live in the sea and not one in ten land creatures lives in this salt waste, life is—what—a hundred times more precious here than anywhere else on the face of the earth? wonders Percy as he scans the seesawing Rann of Kutch. The King in unsteady outline on another camel up ahead calls back.

Give Me an elephant any day, Perce.

The noncommittal horizon rocking black and silver in the night.

Give me even Indian Airlines, Sir.

You have to hand it to Golightly though. He got Me here.

That shape to the south is not a phantom tree but Golightly on his gray camel. He waves and turns away. He has an appointment with dysentery in Gujarat.

The King frowns at the map Percy handed him when their camels conferred. The alleged road does not exist. Or once did and has been swallowed up. Or He's holding the map upside down. Or the day's glare got to Him.

He can't dismiss that vision of white windmills by the sea, turning silently.

The camels keep bearing north towards the sands. Where the ground turns marshy they fret and want to tread an invisible line between two kinds of wilderness. Northwards, the shifting sand dunes of the Thar where the wind erases every footprint before the next is made. Southwards, where long tides lap in great glass mirrors, stretches the Rann. Vast nothing on the country's flank. Grass and bush, the bustard, the wild ass, and little else living. No way across. Or ten thousand ways leading nowhere.

Last thread of moon in the sky at 5:00 a.m. Dawn is breaking.

Travel on the Rann is strictly by night so the pair call a halt and bed down for the day under cover of the only trees for miles. Three feathery gray *prosopis juliflora*. Percy's drying off, crisp and salted like a chip from a tumble taken with his only change of clothes on. When the muse transporting him suddenly bent to drink from a pool of rainwater in a cup of rock.

They're on a desert island. Firm flood-plain knoll, saltwater marooned. The encroaching sea has not yet drowned this tuffet. These stunted trees growing out of yellow rock are real, cast
a luminous shade like frosted glass.

Beckoning all day long half an inch above the horizon, the false trees.

Head down, Percy drinks, no hands, where the camel drank. The puddle stills, gives back a face he blows into because a mirror in the wilderness is obscene. Looks over at the King in plain clothes, a man among men.

Zelaldinus did the talking with the Rabari camelteer, persuaded the man with a small pierced coin. Trust. Bought four blackbrush camels that belong across the border. So the beasts follow their noses back home, leaving the russet breed that keep east of the Rann. A tracker can tell Pak from Indian camels by the size of the footprint. He'd report these as wild ones of theirs that wandered down.

Two days and a night since Perce and the King quit the Badali Pir's pilgrim party and set out on their own. The border is due north here, not west. The sea a murmurous crest of surf beyond the southwest edge.

The Rann shelves out to sea for miles and twice each day the sea washes back over it leaving a new crust of white that in winter glitters like a snowfield.

They lie on their backs and hear from far away a sigh that turns them on their sides to watch until a wide clear pane of water comes into view gliding in to lap at their feet on the verge of speech till the long slow suck begins again and it returns in mute obedience to the place from which it came.

Nightfall. A row of pylons stride north to south lit by the salt's gloaming.

They pass under the zinging cables, first manmade things since the tomb. Meet and cross a road running alongside the row of concrete gumboots.

Demented dervish songs howl from the slung wires in the head wind. Salt gnaws at the berm pushed up by bulldozers to take a sealed road.

Next day there's a shelf of rock beside a thorn bush with some wild plum that Zelaldinus smacks out of Perce's hand just short of his mouth. The Light of the World hobbles four beasts, then tethers each with a clove hitch and tests the ropes for flaws. Thank god for a handy King, Perce thinks as he twists the can openerlugs around a tin of Goa sardines. The camels nibble *juliflora*.

Hm hm, the Emperor chumbles, focused on cold fish, unmindful of vegetarian banquets past. Before the camels turned up he'd begun to contemplate a sea crossing. Pushing off from the westernmost cape in a lifeboat. Salvaged from one of the cruise ship hulks that litter the coast. Imagine thinking they could buck the swell at the Indus creek mouths! *And* outwit two sets of coast guards without a seasoned fisherman at the till!

I hoped to show you Percy, He says shaking his head, *fresh prawns in your shoe.*

They sleep in the scant shade, a hot wind fluttering their eyelashes. Perce too is imagining those treacherous delta currents where the Indus swarms out to the Arabian Sea. He never learnt to swim. Is Plan B any safer?

> **The lights of Karachi effervescing on that black water, near enough to touch.**

> **At teatime their eyes open together as a pink cloud sails overhead, honking.**

The King all excited because flamingos mean they're nearing his birthplace. *We were on the run that time too, Perce—just that way, a stone's throw from here—when I must have kicked. Mother chewed a little betel, the midwives fussing, hey? Father was informed and the palace guard spurred on to Umarkot to prepare a suite in the Raja's fort. And there I first saw light. Light this same off-yellow color, half sand half clay, I swear.*

A ghari later, Perce's knuckles whiten on the handle of his mug as he sees, no honk no flutter, a galleon go sailing past their bivouac. Zelaldinus simply nods.

Mine. We sailed it downriver from Lahore to the sea. I always wanted a chunk of the Arab trade. Which other of our kings braved the deep? Our cook made seaweed bread from bladderwrack. I touched an electric eel. The river ran much further east in those days, right by here. Once we ran aground on an eyot just like this and it took a week to dig us out. The carpets drying on the thorn trees like scarlet leaves. When I was a boy in Afghanistan I learnt to love piny greens and blues but now I think this whited ochre is the ground to which all color returns.

You know, says Percy, when the ship's gone, last night in that passing shower when it was pissing down for just two minutes I thought how nice to be a ghost and have the rain go straight through you.

No no! says the King, alarmed. *You just stay a body, Perce, or how do you expect to please young Naz across the border? Not that I mean to nose with Naz,* he grins, *but did you get on well?*

Perce's mouth goes dry at the thought of all the pleasing waiting to be done.

He crawls over to a rock pool for a drink and notices the beard the moment before it disturbs the water. She hasn't seen him any way but clean-shaven. Will there be time for a shave? Do they have roadside barbers like we do?

They must—it's the same bloody country! It's then he turns sharply—droplets flying— and sees the ghost is no longer an old man. Whiskers gone black, sideburns, eyebrows, eyelashes gone back from salt to pepper. This is the King who first built himself a home on the red hill. The crown's back too.

Zelaldinus returning from a leak taken squatting behind a tussock on the other side of the mound has a new stride not sprung by bent marram grass. *Okay Perce,* He says, rubbing sand between the fingers of His left hand. *We're leaving rock pools behind. This yellow flowerer's good for a drink if you're desperate. Slit the bulb like this. And mind it's not the* white *flowerer that grows beside it, or you'll be later than my late food taster.*

Now that night is falling they can risk a cratered fire and heat the leathery dalpuri pilgrim fare Zelaldinus brought and brew up real tea. But each man seems inclined to press on. The Dog Star has appeared high up in the sky and Venus down low, a quaking oyster on the horizon. They travel north all night in silence making for the Pole Star. A thousand kos back in Sikri, say, or Agra you'd have the Bear on your right. No moon tonight. The horizon this night simply a level end to stars. But starlight turns salt to snow.

An arctic waste, with camels. A greenish mantle flickers in the northern sky.

Pity you've not run guns, Percy, Zelaldinus says.

I'd have trouble running a temperature, Sir. Though at school I ran long distance.

You'll need that when we cross. We loose the camels on the other side. That's when you start running. Don't stop till you reach the track. You'll have all night. Take any train going south. That's left. I go right, but don't wait for Me. Don't even turn round, hey?

Then the east goes pale and it's time to find shelter. A hump that's not soremaking and camel-black but that same Ranny high yellow with a tree that's not mirage. Nothing offers itself so they push on. But now risk being seen. Then another line of pylons, strung east-west this time, which means the border's just beyond. Now they must stop, even if they spend the last day in the open. The fence a line of rust at the horizon.

Zelaldinus makes a square of four camels on the nearest thing to tussock, hobbling each one to the next. They bed down in the camel coign, hardly noticing the wind that howls in their ears. When a gust rips off the King's turban.

It goes rolling like tumbleweed beyond retrieval. Let it go, Zelaldinus decrees.

Giving it hardly a glance as He slides into a bird dream. The lone bushchat that kept them company yesterday is gone.

But a harrier passes overhead silent and pale and watchful, satellite rapt. Both men follow its passage where they lie, their heads shifting by degrees.

What the satellite can't see (yet), thinks Perce, enumerating as he drops off: Dreams. Real time misgivings. The writing on the wall. Any satellite higher than itself. Your face in my head—and then he's asleep. His head rolling off the pillow onto tiny warped tiles of crusted silt that shatter back into dust soundlessly.

Teatime again they wake to a thousand honking cranes going the other way. No water now except where the cranes were going. Each takes a small swig from the Bisleri bottle, then Perce screws the cap back on tight.

Their shadows lengthen, first bronze then violet on ash, as the sun declines. The sky goes a brief pale blue in the west and an unearthly clarity descends on the great salt pan.

Keep low, boy, Zelaldinus says. If you look carefully beyond the power line that fuzz on the horizon isn't tree mirage. It's not mirage at all. It's fence. Barbed wire.
Electrified. Look closely and you'll see the poles. Now run your eye along to where that pylon is. All right, just beside it, see that tower? That's manned. They have them every five kilometres all along the fence. Now see those taller poles? Those are floodlights, with sensors. But there's a gate in here I'm told (Birbal, who else?) where both sides do flag meetings. The only spot where the razor wire stops to let you through to no man's land. In there you don't tarry, okay? Not to read the legend on the concrete pillar, not for anything. Anyway all it says is India *on this side and* Pakistan *on that side. After that Umarkot's*

one way and Karachi the other. You have the wirecutters? Water bottle you keep. We ghosts need less.

And Perce answers, Sir. His mind's already racing ahead at the word Karachi.

That night he saw the city lights across the black water, he imagined her at one of those gleams, working out in her rooftop room. Pakistan's ace hurdler. Last time they Skyped she said in the sign language they've evolved she has her slow brother's passport waiting for him. The one he never used. Who says the dead are past helping us? You simply step into his shoes. And then we'll see. Madness? Yes. Madness. And then he's in that pleasing room he's yet to see.

But tell me, Perce. What was the worst thing you ever did? the King breaks in on his reverie. And Perce thinks back and says, I signed a petition to impeach a man who never hurt me. I let myself be stampeded. And at the public hearing I sneered at a man who got up and spoke fearlessly in his defence.

Zelaldinus nods. *Let go of him Perce, or he'll haunt you harder than any ghost. Abul Wasim haunts Me that way. The man whose exquisite wife I stole. And that's going back a way.*

Night falls. The Light of the World pisses the camels. They can't piss sitting so he walks them one by one, stepping back at each cascade. At midnight he counts out his Pak currency notes and gives Perce half. *From Todar Mal, our treasurer.* Not crisp, not limp, just middling. Then an attar vial from his pack. *For Naz.* He starts to sing a line in Raag Bhairavi but stops when Perce cringes. Tansen He's not. *Go serenade her, son.* Then he bows deeply: to north to south to east to west.

Now follow me. They pass under the hum of the slung cables and Perce feels a voltage in him so strong it could frizz the whole cat's cradle overhead.

Akbar holds up one hand. *Watchtower,* he whispers. Then points. *Sentry*!

Wait here, he says, *by this pylon*. And wanders off into the dark but doubles back. *Trust in god*, He whispers, *but fasten your own camel. Old Turki saying.* He ties them up one by one, then sets out again. Comes up ghostwise to the man on duty who sees him—and drops, gun and all. Akbar gags and binds the sentry. Reappears at the pylon where Perce is waiting. Unties the camels and takes the halter on the leader. Now all move off together to the fence.

Wirecutters. Perce passes them.

The King cuts once, twice, three times, up and up the gate. High enough to let the camels through. *I disabled the sensors*, He whispers.

Just then the sleeping guard wakes and comes down the iron ladder. Finds his comrade trussed up on the ground. Looks at the gate. Sees them. Shouts a challenge. No answer. Starts to fire.

Run Percy! Zelaldinus shouts and Percy runs. Only one camel has got through behind him. It takes the bullets meant for him. Lies kicking in the sand as he runs. The other three bolt back onto the Rann leaving the King to absorb the hail of lead.

He takes the whole chamber muttering a mad catch with the refrain, *Go Perce!*

Men die into ghosts, ghosts have no place to go. They die back into bodies. Next morning they'll find him, more hole than body, one of the nameless dead that keep appearing on the fence. Useless bodies by a useless fence on no man's land.

Which Perce who ran at school now crosses. *Bear left*, he remembers, *or you run into a watchtower on the other side*. He runs and walks and stumbles and gets up and runs some more. All night. And at last there's the railway track. He jumps a goods train to the next station and cleans up in the bathroom.

There's even a razor someone left behind. Wonders as he scrapes, did the bullets just go through like rain?

At dawn he funks the ticket window, hops ticketless on the next Karachi train.

SOHINI BASAK

Future Library: Some Anxieties

stories will be buried like children found dead face down on a beach, words printed
today will be read a hundred years from now, but who will have access? lines written

now will take refuge under soil and over them, a forest will keep growing, but in between
what if our language capsizes, syllables wobble out of a too-full boat? a hundred years

from now, everything will be different, but tonight stories will be taken to undisclosed
locations, stories will be rendered speechless, or declared a threat to internal security,

stories will be coerced, stopped at the border, or be photoshopped to look like someone
else, stories will be in possession of firearms, stories will be blinded by pellets, stories will

overhear a hypodermic's confession to needles, stories will forget their beginnings, and in
forgetting, will eat other stories, but then a hundred years from now things may be different.

while a thousand trees are growing, they said: we are not interested in your information, we are not interested in your gene pools, in your lives lived without passwords, without a common

currency of manufactured teeth marks. stories will be told to put the arctic to bed and tuck in polar bears under a warm blanket, stories will wonder what other forests can home them. stories

will google: dandakaranya. białowieża. juruá-purus. stories will look for patterns in stories about forests which are often stories of exile and often end in fire. stories will stop believing

that stories are endangered when they go to the mall and see a polar bear lift his
    head to the camera, stories will say extra cheese on pizza but say, a hundred
    years from now, will our

children still be reading? will knowledge still be bitten in fruits or like vitamins,
    sealed in pills? stories will google: earth, google translate: earth. stories, say:
    foliage, say: moon, scribble love

on palms or sit by our caves but stories will refuse, for tonight stories will go to
    war, stories will
take the storyteller hostage a hundred years from now, how lovely that then we
    will all be gone

Future Library: A Footnote

no children for me, when I said *our*, I really meant the collective world's; no children for me because I am not the fittest and I dislike Sundays for the same reasons I decline syrup or because flowers like hydrangea, dahlia, marigold make me uneasy.

                    mummy, have we ever thought as a species?

xerox, xylem, xylophone, phonetic, phony—it's an alphabet of losing sensation: first earlobe then shin. I hide behind the cryptic but tell me, is fitness mathematical? meanwhile, superbugs, meanwhile, planets with atmosphere, meanwhile, dinosaur eggs, meanwhile, bodies burnt, culpability framed, meanwhile, a new mall, meanwhile the sneer slant of spring saying hello, meanwhile more pills, or we measure our lives with expiry dates, meanwhile, the slow cancellation of our futures, meanwhile, nerve gas, meanwhile on the phone, in the next cubicle:

                    are you sure it will translate to sales?

I don't mean a thing in matter—pleasure texture textual pressure—but let's cultivate nurturing in a petri dish. lover beloved = mother child? hexagonal rooms, protein sequence browser history: foetus attempts to manipulate maternal physiology and metabolism for foetal benefits. mummy, was I as selfish? let omissions be only accidents, coded information convincing us that a nest is an extended phenotype, that a healthy body is whole. the probability of being replicated with errors is at times attractive but I am predictable.

                    mummy, what is the evolutionary incentive for lying?

a hundred years from now maybe we'll no longer need to dream a dream of the nuchal chord or maybe our self-pollinating heads will solve these problems—what's more optimal? I only believe in the body which feels pain. say, a hundred years from now, under those trees in the forest we are growing, will there still be children *reading*?

                    text me when you reach home.

Future Library: Alternative Ending

the opposite of dystopia
    is ~~not utopia,~~
~~possible, compassion,~~ unprejudiced
        participation

    stories will be passed on
        despite nations conspiring to be selectively inherited,

stories will remember every other story,
stories will be scavenged from threadbare dialects,
stories will be translated, stories will
    rise up from mass unmarked graves to confront
        the hypocrisy
            of storytellers,

stories that breathe underwater will gather on top of each other like spider crabs
    to discard their old shells and grow softly
    into themselves, into themselves bigger,
breathing through masks and armed with watering cans, stories in your neighborhood
will make a comeback
    like the saiga antelope,
    fill the sky
    with screeches like an echo parakeet,
        stories will stop sitting on fences, stories will ferry
cures, after counting 915 coins from the stomach of a turtle,
    stories will give up on miracles
        and take matters into their own hands,

stories will
disown gods,
    escape frameworks, mouths, the market,
        stories will never figure out how they end,
            how lovely then that we'll be able to say we had a hand in this.

ROSALYN D'MELLO

Something New, Something Borrowed

I used to think of the human tongue as a singular muscular organ. I have only recently become conscious of its complex topography; its surface texture rife with perforations; lingual papillae, invisible pore-like receptors that register taste; and eight interior and exterior muscles that not only hold it in place but allow for its maneuvering.

Can the tongue be an instrument of ecstasy?

In a diary entry in 1938, Simone Weil, the French mystic, claimed never once to have prayed before then, at least not in the literal sense of the word. "I had never said any words to God, either out loud or mentally." But the summer before, while learning Greek with some friend or acquaintance she refers to as T-, she went through the Our Father word for word in Greek. She and T- promised each other to learn the Lord's Prayer by heart. T- may not have, or we have no evidence that he did. But Weil did. She writes about how "the infinite sweetness of this Greek text so took hold of me that for several days I could not stop myself from saying it over all the time." A week later, when she was laboring for the vine harvest, she decided to recite the Our Father in Greek every day before work, repeating it often in the vineyard, eventually making it a regular practice during her day. Should her attention wander, should her tongue slip and mispronounce a word, she would begin again. Her condition, though, was to only go through the motions of the text if she felt the impulse. The consequence of meditatively mouthing the words and in doing so producing sound, inducing rhythm and movement was a state of near ecstasy. Weil found her body was elevated and transposed from its external environment. She writes:

> At times the very first words tear my thoughts from my body and transport it to a place outside space, where there is neither perspective nor point of view. The infinity of the ordinary expanses of perception is replaced by an infinity to the second or sometimes the third degree. At the same time, filling every part of this infinity of infinity, there is silence, a silence which is not an absence of sound but which is the object of a positive sensation, more positive than that of sound. Noises, if there are any, only reach me after crossing this silence. Sometimes, also, during this recitation or at other moments, Christ is present with me in person, but his presence is infinitely more real, more moving, more clear than on that first occasion when he took possession of me.

In a completely different text, Clarice Lispector's *Agua Viva*, a euphoric text about the temporal moment, the Brazilian writer demands profound joy and secret ecstasy, a space in which the world trembles inside her hands. She says, "I want the vibrating substratum of the repeated word sung in Gregorian chant." Through the word, the written word, she plunges into the almost-pain of an intense happiness.

II.

When Anne Carson was a very young girl, she received a book called *The Lives of the Saints*. As she flicked through each page, her instinctive response was to tear it out, crumple or fragment the paper and eat it all up. "I still remember how luscious those pages were," she says in an interview. "I don't know if it was some kind of specially printed book or I just hadn't seen many books with a lot of color in them but each saint had a crown or garland on the head and some kind of complicated cloak thing, all different colors, and they looked like jujubes. I just wanted to stuff them in my mouth."

Later, she is asked about her own observation about attention being a form of prayer, and how, from paying attention to who one is, one can then step beyond the border of oneself and move from there to the creation of a work of art. Carson, who cannot trace exactly when she had uttered that specific thought, tries to link it to her recent appreciation of the artist John Cage, and his own attempts to move to a place of complete stillness and attention within himself. She quotes him saying, "I want to get every Me out of the way in order to start doing whatever the work will be." Carson thinks of it as an ongoing struggle: to get every Me out of the way. Her interviewer asks, Would she like to eliminate the Me? "Yes. I would," she answers.

III.

I am trying desperately to eliminate my Me. It is not daunting as much as it is impossible. Because my inscription of my self is not an act of excess as much as it is an articulation of an irrepressibility. My tongue, even when at rest, at ease, flickers soundlessly, enunciating language that registers upon my fingers. My tongue endlessly baits words and their echoes. When I write, I transcribe my self.

"The Resurrection is a self-emptying process," Father Whatshisname said during his Easter Sunday sermon. I pulled out my notebook and my pen and recorded just this sentence. Could my irrepressibility ultimately lead to redemption?

IV.

What I remember most distinctly about his apartment was the single un-potted non-plant that was poised in the center of his windowsill. As I stared into its dry, un-watered depths, I thought of Susan Miller's forewarning for Cancerians, about the curveball the universe was meant to throw at me during the full moon. Maybe it was confined to my phone screen cracking when I dropped it just after I had messaged him. Maybe he is the curveball, a fated yet unanticipated event that was meant to come to pass upon and within my body; the fleshy evidence of a dream I'd had a day or two before I chose to encounter him.

With his tongue he drew upon my breasts. I paid attention to every sensation, recording it for later resurrection.

Could I, would I ever, was it at all possible for me some day to empty my self so profoundly that I could become that singular un-potted non-plant that sat on his windowsill, filled only with the conditions for regeneration but otherwise compelled to wait until I was made lush and fruitful?

SHAMALA GALLAGHER

Mooncalf

STEPHANO to CALIBAN.
Mooncalf, speak once in thy life, if thou beest a good mooncalf.
—III.2.21, The Tempest

Mooncalf, you woke in your body, where you were alone. Blood pounded hot in the cave that contained you. In there you felt a buried fringe glitter, so you touched the hot low dark till you shook. You ruined hours palming the shaking cave, your thought in its holes. At last you lifted the heavy arms and saw them smeared with hair.

You could not believe the oil-dark of the hair that grew from your body. It turned you into contortions of brambles. Looking at the ocean, seeking a mirror, you came upon your eyes. They blazed with rot like desperate fruit. They shone from the shadowed hulk of your form with the brilliance of a monster's eyes.

I am learning to look into the eyes of a monster: to watch them glitter from their tortured form and not turn away. Mooncalf, I am writing a book for you: for all those who hunker in ruin. A man came to your island and named you a monster, and so I am writing a book of holes.

Mooncalf, your name belongs to a story that begins with a storm. How the torment of silver and black begins to harbor itself behind the blue mirror. Flicker and surface in the soaking heat. Air soaks in itself and then the first shattering flash. In a tempest, your course muddles
    suddenly in flailing winds. A self is a rickety structure, a home you build on your back from the twigs of whichever earth.

The Tempest is a book about the invention of the self: about the solitary and glittering stuff it is made of and the solitary and uncertain theaters in which it unreels. Sometimes the self contains a stutter of whiteness, a blip of emptiness in the page of the story, and it is unclear what will continue. I had such a year: you palpate the floor of yourself and find there only a hole.

Mooncalf. You should write your book if you can, because your grip on your youth is loosening and you don't understand what comes next. For years you've been scared of age, as if fear could be real preparation. You reminded yourself: I am getting older— even when it seemed preposterous to think it. You counted the years in your head and tried on ages five years older. You thought: that is not so bad.

But then comes a year. You will look at your hands. You will look at your face. Your anger will not be reasonable. Youth is some glass of spilt gin, but yours was not spilt unfairly.

On one birthday you were defiant; you wore a small dress; you put to your lips glasses and glasses of hungers. Nights ended then still in makeshift dancing and unharbored kisses at someone. You found your beauty still evident. Anguish also was young and would unfold with glory but not with certainty. You broke the glasses and were senseless and later they asked you to leave.

And now it is later (years later) still. And beauty itself is a poisoned apple you forget to pretend not to want.

Mooncalf, you come forth bearing an imperfect form. You are encased in this form and what you have made of it and what you will make of it as it will tighten and wither, loosen and furrow, mold-dance and dustfruit, as it will slip and change.

Soon it will be inarguable that you are older. Then it will be inarguable that you are old. Then you are clawing the soil to get free or wishing your ash would turn to body again in the air.

Mooncalf, it is time for the calculus of being, time for searching the areas inside you to ask what's the use. Who are you, Mooncalf? It is time to ask.

I am from parents of two different races, so that when I grew old enough to name myself I didn't know which name to say. I wear a skin like my father's skin: pale. I wear hair like both parents' once was and which is (for now): black. I wear—or for some time wore—a belief

in my skin as deep and tawny like my mother's, a warm and complex gold which showed that I belonged somewhere if not here. But it is not true—the color—not visually. And since it is not true, I wear the color I first felt: a pale, untrue-feeling freak-color, a paleness that looks like whiteness but is not.

But Mooncalf, how can you make a book, when you are an abandoned house? You have rapped a long time at its window. A sentence is a pale monstrous girl and it is chattering its nightteeth. You open every notebook so that you will not look at the first you opened. And for work or meaning you'll walk where the city peters out, at the city's perimeter in an old small shop where they give you a raspberry beer in a bag. One you can open in your hands and then walk alone in the street. I don't want to walk alone in the street, you say. But in your hands lives, your hair's yanking.

Mooncalf, I am writing this book because I don't know how to make sense of the networks of longing that mean a person. The strands of aired anger sneak into the open home. I chatter my teeth before talking. I am here with this speaking mess and this unreeling of daytime.

Prospero was once a duke; then he grew fascinated with the shining tunnels inside his books, and he let what he ruled be stolen. Thus alone with his magic he lived on an island of failure, "master of a full poor cell" (I.2.20). Caliban, you were chained to this island of failure too.

You are not worthless, someone said to me in a bar. But onward, and night it sears itself closed.

Mooncalf: it is spoken in *The Tempest* by an ordinary, drunk fool. The storm has undone his certainty; he is drunk and is pacing the lost territory wildly. This is where *The Tempest* occurs, and this is the site of my questioning: when something wrests you free of your securely clasped relation to life, and now you are drunk and wandering the island.

Mooncalf is what the fool names Caliban, the enslaved native of an enchanted and uncertain island—the native of a bewilderment. Two fools encounter this mooncalf, one by one. Each fool encounters the mooncalf on its own. Alone you meet your double, your monstrous twin.

And so Caliban, our first mooncalf, is a man. I address you now as the first mooncalf, Caliban. Mooncalf, a wild-haired man on an island. Mooncalf. Caliban. Mooncalf. I am talking to you directly, Mooncalf, looking at you. When I am saying Mooncalf right now I mean you. And also, Mooncalf, I mean I.

Each time I read *The Tempest* it is for you. I don't even read it; I flip through and look for your name. I look for all your lines. I want to be stunned into joy by what they disclose. I want to see the real story glittering underneath and I want it to be yours. I want to unearth the lines you don't speak.

Mooncalf. You are a dark-skinned man I could meet on the street, walking alone late at night. I have met you like this in cities. I have met you in the neighborhoods we walk in, Mooncalf, the ones where pavements smear with dirt and funk, and women walking to cars clutch their keys. You and I have no cars, Mooncalf, so this is where we are: walking toward each other so that our paths cross.

I know what you look like, Mooncalf, because I have met you. When Trinculo met you, he didn't know if you were an animal, and he didn't know if you were alive. He said he didn't know what you were, because you smelled: a "very ancient and fishlike smell" (II.2.25–26).

Mooncalf, I know what a man can smell like. In the cities I have smelled men on the street. I have given them money or I have looked them in the eye and said no. I have hurried past or I have laughed at their banter. I have displayed solidarity or I have screamed. Last night a man with a beer in his pocket asked for a cigarette and a lighter. He put the cigarette in his mouth and he stood with the lighter and gestured. The lighter was orange and I watched it move in his hand where we stood on the curb in the full-on dark. We stood near an emergency hospital, which is on my walk to the bar where I meet my friends. I don't know how to feel about this walk to the bar, Mooncalf, on which, out for my own revelry, I walk past others meeting death. But revelry is close to death, you would tell me, Mooncalf. He moved his lighter in the nighttime, which was orange, as the flame would be orange if he sparked it. He moved it because it was in the hand with which he gestured. Mooncalf, this man was angry—he had been in prison—he had not committed the crime—he was angry and drunk—I was scared. I was scared, Mooncalf, of a man because he was standing in the dark with his anger and he was out of prison and he was holding my lighter that he would not light.

Mooncalf means monster, or fool, or stupid one; mooncalf means an aborted fetus, human or cow. The first OED definition of "mooncalf" is "a mole," meaning "an abnormal mass within the uterus, specifically one formed by the death and degeneration of the fetus early in gestation." Some people thought this was caused by the influence of the moon. Thus in 1594, Pierre de La Primaudaye describes "The moone calfes in the womb, which fall out often." In 1658's *Natural Magick*, Giambattista della Porta provides an example: "A certain woman . . . brought forth in stead of a child, four Creatures like to frogs." Later the word took on the meaning of "an ill-conceived idea"—a wasted thought, a notquite-being that should have been killed at its source.

But "mooncalf" is an ironic word. I like to stare into the star-drunk ironic space between the cruelty of its reference and the silky beauty of its sound.

Mooncalf, perhaps I could get people to forgive me when I told them I was scared of you on the street. I was a woman, I could tell them. I was a woman and he was a drunk man. And in this way we—those who were not, at that moment, mooncalves—could huddle together and could speak of our cruelty as fear.

When Trinculo meets you, Mooncalf, he is scared of you and your smell. But then the sky is wracked again with heaving dark and wind and he is even more scared of the storm that has brought him to this shuddering island. He smells his own confusion. "Misery acquaints a man with strange bedfellows," he declares, and he creeps under Caliban's garment (II.2.25–26).

Mooncalf, what is happening here? Trinculo huddles close to Caliban's flesh. Caliban stands still, perhaps, perhaps so still that Trinculo doesn't see him as a person, someone you need to ask if you're going to come close. What could have made Trinculo do this, climb in close to a stranger who smells? Can Trinculo smell Caliban still? Was he drawn toward Caliban by desire? Is Caliban paralyzed now by the strange mess of a person, not-him, in his clothes? Is there love in this scene or only violence?

Later in literature, Ishmael climbs into bed with Queequeg. And Mooncalf: I am writing this book in order to climb into bed with you.

Mooncalf, I don't mean to keep us straight: I don't mean to hold us apart from each other and say: you are this, I am that. The world is thick with such talk, Mooncalf, but it is not true. I want us to be full of each other. I want us to say: we are full of each other already.

Mooncalf, if my skin bore a color that told you I once came from a subcontinent in the heat, perhaps you'd look at me and know our alliance instantly. I would like our alliance to be visible. But, Mooncalf, my skin is pale. I have tried to believe in it as amber or dusking and I have burned it brown in the sun. Before it turns brown it needs to redden and smart—to take on a strange, delicious ache. I lived once where the sun was glorious and devastating, and for those years my skin glowed near my desire, and later I paid in wrinkles. Mooncalf, perhaps it is right to wear marks on the skin.

Mooncalf, I am not satisfied with anything I am. Purple flings itself against the night. Purple stains and stains itself against the night, which breaks in half, which bristles. Mooncalf, I write this from failure—I write starting inside my own failure to write, because it is a place to start. I stand with my back to the cliff of failure. I grip a handful of posies of error. I am walking forward in the error-night. I trip on error's names, which are boulders that crop up in the house. They smash their brains on the floor. I walk through. They rack their brains on staining.

Is this prose, Mooncalf? When I'm too scared to write it and I write it anyway, this prose slips out of prose's edges. And so it is a late stain, so it is a blunting of night and a mass of screaming and no state from which to eat the years, from which to keep them from staring madly at what they think of as home.

Mooncalf, what is prose, that thing that divides a book from a waste? This is the prose a mooncalf must write: prose asking what is itself.

In *The Tempest*, prose is what the ordinary fools speak when they encounter the monster, when they climb inside it and find therein one of themselves. (Though that particular mooncalf speaks in poetry—speaks in blank verse like a king.)

Mooncalf, that gorgeous word, is another sad barb of violence—spoken by a powerless person to someone still more powerless. But, Mooncalf, it is where we start. In our own tempest, then, Mooncalf, we will make ourselves, in the image of our own longing.

Last night two white men I know were smoking outside a bar in the Southern college hipster town where I now live. Each city of the South, I think I see now, is still two cities superimposed: a city of "slaves" and a city of "people." A city of mooncalves and a city of the guilty: conjoined twins of cities. I live in the guilty one, determined to disown it. But it is hard to disown your own ground.

These two white men were smoking and a black man came up to smoke with them outside in the night. He asked if they wanted to hear jokes. "Are you racist?" he asked.

"No!" they said.

"That's my first joke."

All three of them laughed wildly. Later the man said, "These college students. They'll buy you drink after drink but no one will buy you a burger."

Mooncalf, I cannot be neutral, because I live in a world of Prosperos. In this world exist Calibans too, but the world likes Prospero better. Prospero, Prospero, Prospero. If I stand there and choose neither, the world will simply go on: Prospero, Prospero, Prospero.

This time, then, I choose Mooncalf as the name of Prospero. I choose Mooncalf as the name of Ariel. I choose Mooncalf as the name of Miranda. I choose Mooncalf as the name of Stephano. I choose Mooncalf as the name of whatever their name is, those usurpers of the careless Prospero's throne, so that he and Miranda were forced to find this island and grow lonely and powerful and beautiful. I choose Mooncalf as their name. I choose Mooncalf as the name of Stephano and Mooncalf as the name of Trinculo, those forebears of *The Tempest*'s prose. I choose Mooncalf as the name of the island and I choose Mooncalf as the name of the storm and I choose Mooncalf, of course, as the name of Caliban, the kind name of Caliban that loves Caliban and casts him as beautiful. I choose Mooncalf as the name of Sycorax, his mother from Algiers, and the name of his absent father. I choose Mooncalf as the name of the stage, that "bare island" from which Prospero (Mooncalf) speaks out at the end. I choose Mooncalf as the name of the reader and the name of the writer and the name of the sucking dog under her desk and I choose Mooncalf as the name of my desperation that makes me write this, my fear of growing old without having created. I choose Mooncalf as the name of all my fears that I am a monster and I choose Mooncalf as the truth of the monster I am.

I choose Mooncalf as the name of the closeness that will grow between us, as the closeness that grows between monsters in the wasteland; Mooncalf as the name of the wasteland that is the name of the utopia too.

For a while I became convinced that because of my monstrosity I was glorious. Then an empty glitter ripped into my late twenties and I became for a while that thing close to monster: a ruin. I lived broke on a hard plain of snow. I lived far from anyone, save a few strangers who stared. I had gone to chase a vision, which wasted itself as sleet sank into the wheat.

Now I live somewhere else; somewhere new that holds hope for a life. Here I have begun contracting my madness and filling, again, the page. But it is clear to me now: this can happen. I have a different understanding of the terrain of being. It is a thicket, it is a wilderness, it is a city of mirrors, and to survive you need gratitude for whatever meager earth is this hour's stand.

Once I believed that I would redeem myself by writing; I believed I was stumbling toward greatness. But Mooncalf, I no longer believe in greatness. There is no greatness. When we call someone special, we are trying to escape the brute fact of the consciousness of everyone. We would like to say to ourselves that certain people matter: that an artist matters more than a drunk. But we are saying this because it is too hard for us to accept that everyone matters, because if everyone matters, everyone living briefly and starving, everyone wasted in jail, then our world right now is a spectacular failure, the greatest ruin there is.

Mooncalf, my body is full of every place I have walked, in streets and classrooms, and my skin is hardened and rutted and my mind cannot free itself of its knowledge of the costs of wildness. Still my mind believes in wildness: our terrain. In every town on the face of the real world live mooncalves, in every city and every stretch of forsaken agricultural land. In my daring I say: in every person. And so I choose to name myself Mooncalf, too, though I am not Caliban, though my skin is achingly pale and he is a man from an island I have never seen. But: he is from a lonely interior island where I am from also.

What is Mooncalf? I am calling you Mooncalf, someone who will snatch a glance at her own grotesque in a mirror. Her face is the wrong color and she can't understand why her belly bulges. Not with a child: with herself. Her own ragged being. I am saying she for Mooncalf but she is not what I mean. She is the year you saw nothing of yourself but your single hurt color. She is the cringe inside the room of children: they all exchange glances about her. She has no high school diploma. She has too many degrees and doesn't know the song that is playing. She is pale in a room where they're dark, or she's ink-dark in a room where they're gold. She lives on the street or she longs for the street. Angry at houses, she could cast herself into the street.

I am not saying those are all the same things, Mooncalf: I'm not claiming the same life for each. But I'm calling them the same name, Mooncalf, anyway.

The Tempest is barely a book. It is a play, a book for enacting itself upon the air. I love a book for its outer boredom. A book is a tangle of disobedient air shut up in a shell and hidden in dullness. It is not like a film, whose blaze parades itself and demands our looking. A book is strange for our age. It is a project of shyness. It is someone speaking to herself in a cave, alone in a chamber of a cave with a single candle and the phone in her pocket gone dark. But she is not after all speaking to herself. She is speaking to the cave's enchantment, to her deranged belief in the cave as an altering and pressing at wonders.

SASHA PARMASAD

The Village
Trinidad, 1990s

Call me a village—a late night at a junction in Caroni, an Amerindian name, but they long dead, breathless, now we are here; Indian music now: Sonny Man, a touch of Sundar Popo, call me "Trinidad-Tobago, the land of flambeau, steel-pan and calypso, every creed and race find an equal place, and sunshine wherever you go"; call me Doolsie: hand on waist, bottle in hand, barefooted on a cool, concrete floor, grinding the air slowly with broad, sweeping hips, lips smiling wide call me, Woodpecker cheering, straddling a corner bench, rain-soaked, rotting, his bearded cheek resting flat against Sonawa's sweating back; Sonawa hunched over a game of all-fours, *tulup-chaar*, call me *You mother-cunt!* followed by a scraping of chair legs, shuffling of slippered feet; call me that coasting of FM stations, the 90s through 103, and Doolsie thrusting into static, calypso, Madonna, more static, some Shaggy and Lata Mangeshkar, Frank Sinatra call me, and finally some sweet Chutney; her fingers curl in the air like centipedes; call me a gold tooth winking fire in her mouth as she calls to Woodpecker, *Come, Boy! Heat me!* cards splayed across the rickety table, laughter rising from rum bottles; *The maikaychode . . . he had the trump!*—green glass bellies shattering in concrete yard, startling Boysie busy writing his name in pee across the unpainted cement wall; call me night beating itself numb with music and rum, turning sorely over into a dawn trembling with the timbre of barking dogs patrolling sleepy streets; call me that cacophony of crowing: captive cocks pitching messages across long distances; five a.m. swelling with smells of garlic darkening in sizzling oil, roasting cumin seeds, burning cigarettes, dewy grass, asphalt, incense, milky *chameli*, green clogged drains, green mangos, and black tendrils of sugarcane ash call me; Doolsie sprawled across a pink bedsheet branded with flaring red hibiscus; call me her mother, *nanee*, putting her nine-year-old daughter, Lita, to lie flat, dragging the child's jersey up to the armpits, placing a lit candle on her gassy belly, *Beyt, you go be late for school!*; the candle covered with a tumbler, Lita's flesh sucked up into it, flame dying out call me; Nanee—*Where your brother dey?*—glancing out the slit door for fourteen-year-old Ronnie swinging Doolsie's cutlass in the field, breaking sugarcane stalks like bones for weighing; their ramshackle house call me, hot with smells, pot-spoon scraping the blackened bottom of an iron pot redolent of onions; Doolsie twisting in bed like twine call me, her brawny arm hauling a pillow over her throbbing head, a brown elephant saliva smudge just under her left eye; call me that eye slowly opening, closing, opening to the sound of Lita singing as she waits in line for water from the standpipe—*A riddle, a riddle, a ree, I see a old man pee, he pee so fast, he make me laugh, a riddle, a riddle, a ree!*—water patting down dust, Lita's feet, the aluminum bucket knocking her scabbed knee call me, hair gleaming blue with coconut oil, ratty ribbons woven through thinning ends of plaits; call me Grandpa, *nanaa*, heating tractor to seek Ronnie laying cane in rows for loading; Nanaa picking neem twig, chewing on it, cleaning his teeth, standing in the gap in front of the house, aiming spit at the slime-filled drain, *blagging* to neighbors standing in similar gaps, spitting in similar drains; call me seven-year-old Sunny rushing up—*I go beat you at brushing teeth, Nanaa!*—toothbrush anchored in mouth, on the sly eating Colgate, flavorful, white frothing lips, dazzling leaves where he spits; his *Sita-Ram* greeting tossed to neighbors amid talk of politicians' ploys, last night's bacchanal; Sundar Popo's tune flavoring, floating out of the kitchen window that Nanee has partially screened with a scrap of cloth; call me Sushila next door pausing, iron in hand, to listen to Sundar, staring through tears at her kiskadee-bright school overall, its slicing pleats; *The child have too much mouth*—her pappy, Woodpecker, call me, his bloodshot eyes, ponderous pacing in closed bedroom, slurred talking to Ma—*But she is still a nice child*; Sushila setting down iron, rubbing against rough wall to ease the ache in her back where Woodpecker hit her with a wooden clothes hanger; call me thickening traffic on the pockmarked road edging their house, blaring horns, and Lita next door pausing before wardrobe mirror, pinching budding breasts, wiping talcum powder from nipples; cane-laden tractors grinding past sand-piled trucks, and sand-piled trucks grumbling past bright streams of chattering, uniformed schoolchildren holding hands, call me; Nanee glancing out the window at them while *balaying*, flattening roti-dough with a rolling pin, singing hoarsely along with Sundar, *My nanaa and nanee went to tie a goat . . . my nanaa make a mistake and cut out nanee throat!*—her laughter, call me, Nanee calling out to Lita, *Bring the fine-tooth comb for me to make your part*! *You go be late, Beyt!*—washing hands of lumpy flour, lifting them to aching head, wrapping head in *orhini* pungent with bay rum; Nanee calling out to Doolsie, *Girl, get up and help me see your children off to school!*; calling out to Sunny, *Beyt, you sweep the yard yet?*; Sunny scampering through the yard like a wild 'gouti call me, washing hands and mouth with rainwater from barrel beneath roof-guttering, grabbing cokeeyay broom, bending low, sweeping away footprints of people and dogs, chickens and cats, ducks and rats, making unintended patterns across the earth, walking backwards, sweeping his own footprints away—here I am

PRAMILA VENKATESWARAN

from *The Singer of Alleppey*

Diary Entry, 1930

Yesterday something strange happened. Ambi was running in the yard holding an imaginary rifle, screaming "Doo-doo-thuppakki, police-kaaran pondaati." It is funny, but how does he know what a rifle looks like, what it does, how it sounds, how to hold it? He's never seen one. Unless he has been looking at the newspapers his father reads and has seen pictures of British soldiers with guns. I know war is on in Europe and the East Indies—radio broadcasts, news reels before movies at the local Lotus theater we have been to a couple of times with Ambi are filled with the smells and sounds of war—but Ambi's world is just school and cricket and pranks. Our police only carry sticks, not guns, and they are hardly seen in our neighborhood except when they come during Diwali for gifts. A sad lot, most of them, really, and their pay is so bad, they look hungry, barely able to defend themselves, let alone us. That stupid rhyme, I know, it's nonsense, lots of kids sing it, but it makes me shiver. I tried pulling that imaginary rifle from him and he chased me with it screaming that rhyme: I am the innocent wife shot by my policeman husband.

Diary Entry, 1948

I have stopped doing puja, reciting endless slokas, performing rituals. No one notices. I merge into the dark corners of the house, since I am never expected anymore in the main rooms cooking or cleaning. Not expected to perform puja is a new freedom. Now I can use the time, when I am not watering the plants or doing odd jobs, to dream up songs even if I don't sing them, imagine the path of a raga. This is like prayer, an invisible spire of smoke rising from my belly. These Sanskrit slokas are like bees buzzing in my mouth. I want to spit them out and relish the beatitude of a dry mouth, soft tongue and quiet ears. I don't torment myself with them anymore. Instead, I disappear to the back yard where the outhouses are and rest under a jacaranda when others are rattling off their orations. Listen to this Tamil song by Bharatiyar, like butter on my tongue. When I sing it, even my body feels supple. Yesterday I sang it to the daughters-in-law and my daughters lounging on their straw mats after lunch. Their smiles lit the room. The men in the other room fell silent.

Note:
Subramania Bharati, freedom fighter, famous for his songs and poems.

PALASH KRISHNA MEHROTRA

Double Bed

Vipin Dogra loved school. He loved school when he was a little boy. He loved school as a grown man. This is why he got himself a job in the school he had studied in, as soon as he finished his BA Honors in Geography.

He also liked the small valley town where the school was situated. He liked the rainy weather and the familiar cycle of seasons, the permanent wetness that moisturized everything that lay in its path.

Vipin went to college in Delhi, a five-hour train ride away. He had an okay time there. He worked hard at his books, played football and fell in love with a rich girl, Rakshita, who adopted him as a hanger-on, purely for the sake of the novelty he afforded her. She had never met anyone like him. He followed her everywhere, unless she had to go on a date, when she would banish him abruptly. He held her bag when she went to the toilet in KFC. He bought recharges for her phone. He photocopied study material for her. He drove her Etios for her.

After finishing college, Rakshita left for America. Vipin, who had by now resigned himself to the fact of her leaving, returned to his hometown, and to his school. He loved the routine and order of school life: assignments, assembly, exams, cricket and football matches, the beginning of term, the end of term, summer and winter vacations—these simple certainties calmed his frayed nerves, for, let's face it, Vipin was the nervy sort. Little things could throw him—a woman who was too beautiful, a new Dean of Studies, even a festival like Holi or Diwali.

He also liked the sense of equality that academic institutions bred in their inmates. In the hostel mess, everybody said grace, ate the same food, and had the same yellow custard for dessert. It wasn't that one person got to eat Alphonso Marvel ice cream while the other got a stained overripe banana. No. Everyone ate custard. That was good. Very good. The way it should be. Start the day as equals, end the day as equals.

In school, Vipin felt closer to some of the students than members of the faculty. Most of the staff was married and Vipin wasn't. This kept him out of dinners where only couples or families were invited. The new dean, a man called Nair, had taken an instant dislike to Vipin, his unruly mop of hair and his single status. It didn't help matters when one morning he detected alcohol on Vipin's breath. Vipin had been up drinking till late, and talking to Rakshita on the phone. She was back in Delhi for a break. He'd taken care to brush his teeth twice but the smell of alcohol lingered.

He got along better with the students. He knew the senior kids drank and smoked on Sundays when they were allowed out into town. Vipin wasn't much into policing. While his colleagues went around catching errant students and bringing them to heel,

Vipin quietly extended an invitation to them to come to his place and do what they did outside. So on Sundays, a bunch would land up with beers and cigarettes and spend the afternoon watching American sitcoms on television.

When he'd just joined, Vipin had it difficult with the students. A restless bunch of thirteen-year-olds gave him hell in the classroom, so much so that days he had to teach them the first class in the morning, he found himself waking up in the middle of the night, bathed in sweat. Chalks and paper airplanes flew around the classroom as Vipin stood helpless at the teacher's desk. The dean complained to the headmaster and asked for Vipin to be fired. Fortunately, the headmaster had a soft spot for Vipin. He told the dean, "Give him time, he'll find his feet."

∞

Every two months or so, Vipin would make a trip to Delhi to see his other college friend, Shailaja, an electronica musician. He'd usually go over on the odd long weekend when she'd be playing a couple of club gigs. He liked clubs. He liked the thumping music, the smoke on the stage, the cool, dark interiors, the chilled beer. This is where he picked up his taste for booze. In the beginning he wouldn't drink alone in his bachelor's quarters. It was something someone had told him once: never drink alone. He followed the advice for a few years. Then he decided to let it go. He realized he liked his whiskey too much. The cold and the rain and the lonely winter nights got to him. He became a regular drinker, especially on weekends. On week days, he was usually allotted early morning classes by the dean; it kept the drinking in check.

One winter when he was away in Delhi he met a Punjabi rapper at Shailaja's place. The rapper introduced himself as Pointy. He was from Queen's, New York, and was hanging around Delhi, looking to collaborate with local musicians. He'd landed in the city after playing a series of gigs across Asia: Shanghai, Hong Kong, Manila, Kuala Lumpur, Kathmandu, Bangkok, Hanoi, Tokyo, Osaka, Pune, Bombay, Bangalore.

The two sank some pints together and went for Shailajas's gig at The Living Room in Hauz Khas Village. They got along reasonably well. Vipin had never been to America and he asked Pointy many questions. Were cowboys still around? Do gangsters run Chicago? Were New York women as sex-obsessed as they showed them to be in *Sex and the City*? When Vipin told Pointy that he was a Geography master, Pointy said, "Man, let's get a map of the world and see how many cities from my tour you can locate on it." Vipin was close enough with his guesses most of the time. Osaka was the only city he was clueless about. They became friends. Pointy promised to remain in touch.

∞

A few months later, Vipin opened his Gmail to find a message from Pointy. He was back in the country for a bit and was going to be in an ashram in Haridwar the following week. He also had an aunt in Dehradun, where Vipin lived, who he wanted to look up. If Vipin was free, he'd come by and hang out for a bit. He'd rather, though, not stay with his aunt—could he, instead, stay with Vipin?

The summer vacations had just begun. This year Vipin decided to give the annual school trek a miss. He'd been doing it for seven years, and no matter how much he loved routine and unchanging regularity, he was beginning to tire of the mountains. The thought did strike him that he wouldn't mind being in a coastal place for a few days—the sea might be nice for a change, but he didn't know where to go.

Normally, he would have hesitated to host a guest. He was too used to his space being in a certain way and even the shortest of visits disturbed his equilibrium. He liked his coasters to be in the right place, his kitchen and bathroom to be a certain way. He liked to sit alone in the small veranda in the mornings and read the newspaper. His routine got upset when people came visiting. He had to adapt and accommodate when others were around and he hated doing that.

Lately, Vipin had been drinking more than he usually did. There was no school, so there was no reason not to. The thought struck him that it wouldn't be a bad idea to have some company in the evenings. The tedium of drinking alone to prime time news was slowly getting to him. Besides, he liked Pointy, the little that he knew of him. So he wrote back, inviting Pointy to come and stay at his place.

✿

Pointy arrived in a whirlwind. A week in the ashram without liquor, and he was raring to go. Vipin met him outside Crossroads Mall, where Pointy was engaged in an argument with the guard who wouldn't let him take his quarter of Blenders Pride inside. They had lunch in the mall, then drove straight home. Vipin showed Pointy the guestroom which was sparsely furnished, apart from a double bed and a chair. The floor was bare and a white CFL bulb spiraled awkwardly out from a yellowing plastic holder.

Vipin had called some of his former students over in the evening. They had been handpicked for a reason: they were all fans of Pointy. They knew the words to his songs, knew his discography, and had followed his solo career after he broke up with his band.

Vipin and Pointy began drinking in the afternoon. Pointy had been to Punjab recently, to visit his relatives. He had a stack of Punjabi pop MP3s which he'd picked up from the various bus stations he'd been at. Pointy said he couldn't wait to hear the new music. His own laptop he'd thrown into the river in Haridwar in a drunken frenzy. He had nothing to play the music on. Now he had Vipin's laptop.

Vipin's students started to arrive in the evening. Usually, they came alone. But today was special. They'd all taken effort to bring dates with them. They walked in to the sounds of hardcore Punjabi folk-pop. Two of them shook hands with Pointy and told him they were big fans of his. They said the right things: "Man, your solo stuff is way better than what you did with the band." Pointy had been drinking on the bus, through the afternoon with Vipin, and by now he was beginning to slip a little. Besides, he didn't like people much, and Vipin's apartment was full of strange people. A girl said, "Can someone please put this off and play some U2?" Pointy growled, "Not that shit."

Vipin had a small two-room place that he liked to keep clean, like hospital-clean. When people were over he worked like a waiter in a bar, picking up empty bottles and lining them up neatly in the veranda, emptying the ashtrays and sweeping up crumpled pieces of cigarette foil dropped carelessly on the floor.

Vipin liked to clean in real time—he cleaned briskly as the garbage was generated. A bottle would be in the veranda the moment anyone finished it. Ashtrays were emptied when they were half-full.

Today was a little different. There were way too many people. Since Pointy was not in the mood to talk to anyone, the others broke up into small groups. Vipin kept shuttling between the two rooms, drink in one hand, broom in the other.

Pointy was feeling restless. He said he wanted to sleep. Vipin said, "You can't." In order to wake himself, Pointy decided to turn Vipin's revolving office chair into a bumper car at an amusement park. He raced in it from one corner of the room to another, propelling it by holding the armrests and pushing back with his feet. He went chugging past a glass bookcase, accidentally scraping the handle of the shelf. The chair, being made to perform a task it wasn't designed for, gave up after a while and collapsed in a one-sided limp.

Pointy had broken his toy—the bumper-chair car. Now he said he felt hungry. Vipin said, "There are some eggs and an uncut loaf of bread in the kitchen." Pointy flew to the kitchen with the determination of a migrating bird. The next two hours were dedicated to eggs. Pointy had his own style of breaking an egg. He knocked the egg, once, twice, on the side of the stainless steel gas burner, until the shell cracked. Once he'd managed to open up a crack in the egg, he'd carry the dripping egg to the frying pan. There was an interval of a few seconds—between when the egg was cracked and when its contents were offloaded into the frying pan. That micro-interval was all the egg needed to cause damage. Trickles of egg white and yolk leaked through and fell on the Bajaj Popular gas burner, on the kitchen slab and floor. Someone would walk into the kitchen to take a beer from the fridge. He'd step on the egg yolk, then walk back out with squelching shoes, spreading the sticky smelly egg-wet wherever he went in the house.

Pointy had consumed ten eggs by the time Vipin noticed. He'd been preoccupied with emptying the ashtrays and lining up the bottles in the veranda. He barged into the room and shouted at Pointy. "Man, don't you know how to break an egg? You crack it *over* the frying pan. Use a spoon or a spatula. Don't use the sides of the burner for Christ's sake."

Pointy said, "Sorry, dude," and stumbled back out, his belly full of eggs. He poured himself a whiskey and managed to spill some on Vipin's antique desk. Wringing his hands, Vipin said, "What's going on?! My table! My table! What do you think you're doing, Pointy?"

Pointy apologized and said, "So sorry, man. I know what to do. Do you have any vinegar?" Vipin, being a trusting sort, went to the kitchen and came back with half a bottle of vinegar. Pointy pulled out a face tissue from his pocket and set to wiping the table's surface. Once he'd wiped off the spilt liquor, a white stain, the size and shape of a wristwatch appeared on the table's varnished top.

"My table is ruined," screamed Vipin. "Hold on," said Pointy. "I know how to fix it." He pulled out another tissue, daubed it with the vinegar and vigorously began to rub the stain. The stain, for some reason, became even bigger. It was now the size of a wall clock. Vipin decided that damage control was the better option. If Pointy kept rubbing more vinegar into the stain it might just become the size of the clock on the clock tower in the heart of Dehradun. He modulated his voice so as to speak gently. "Chhoro yaar, forget it." Pointy said, "Well, I tried. I swear I was at my sister's place in New York and the same shit happened and I did the same shit as I did now. It worked that time I swear. Something's wrong with this Indian wood, man."

By now, the guests were fleeing the party like refugees. Some kind of tipping point had been reached. The two rooms emptied as quickly as they had filled up. It was only half-eight in the evening. One fellow called Sodhi stayed back. He'd been in the first batch of students that Vipin taught when he'd just joined. He was also the most loyal Pointy fan of them all.

Pointy said, "So let me play you guys some new tracks that I've been working on." "Yes, yes," said Sodhi, clapping his hands. Pointy walked over to the laptop, glass of whiskey in hand and plugged his hard drive into the USB port. He spilled some whiskey on the laptop keyboard just as the first track was starting up. "Damn," shrieked Vipin. "Hell no, my god." "Dammit," said a genuinely puzzled Pointy. "Fucking sorry, dude. I don't know what's happening today."

It was time for Sodhi to take charge. Two of his most favorite men in the world were in the same room together and they were making a meal of it. Sodhi suggested a change of scene: "Let's step out for dinner, guys." Vipin said, eggy rag in hand. "That's a very good idea. This rag smells of egg. My laptop smells of egg. My clothes smell of egg. The whole fucking house smells of egg."

༄

Vipin backed his battered Maruti 800 on to the road. Sodhi, ever the loyal fan, escorted an unsteady Pointy down the steps and into the back seat of the small Suzuki hatchback. Vipin sat leaning his chin on the steering wheel. "Where to, Sodhi? The usual?" The usual meant butter chicken at Hotel President. Pointy emitted a retching sound. Sodhi said, "But what if Pointy throws up on the table?" Vipin said, "Good point. Let's go to Ashnan's. We can sit outside there. Plenty of bushes to barf in." And so they went to Ashnan's.

They were about to walk into the restaurant when Pointy said, "I want to pee yo." He walked over to a shuttered shopfront, right next to Ashnan's, unzipped, jetted out an unending stream of urine in a rainbow arc, zipped up, stumbled back to the car, opened the back door, crawled back into his beloved backseat and promptly fell into slumber. A loud snore confirmed the fact that Pointy was indeed lost to the world.

Meanwhile, Mr. Ashnan came running out and started shouting at Vipin and Sodhi. "Why you are doing like this. This behavior not allowed. My restaurant very famous. Last week only Rocky and Mayur from NDTV eating here." He beckoned to them to step inside. "See, I have photo also," he said, pressing a grubby finger on a digital print pinned to the wall behind the cash counter. "From where your friend coming? Which country?"

"Queens, New York," said Vipin, modulating his voice to sound like a meek dormouse. "You can do all this in Amreeka," concluded Mr. Ashnan. "But not in Indeeya." He thought for a moment and added a corollary. "My brother in New Jersey. Nobody behaving like this in New Jersey."

Formalities over, Vipin and Sodhi stepped inside Ashnan's, leaving Pointy stretched out in the car. Unbeknownst to Vipin, Pointy had cleaned out a strip of Valium in between the whiskey and the Punjabi pop. He was going to be sleeping a while.

Vipin and Sodhi ordered a mutton kheema paratha each. Vipin said, "My laptop is ruined." Sodhi said, "Leave it upside down in the sun tomorrow. It'll dry up."

They got a paratha packed for Pointy. It was Sodhi's idea. "He'll wake up whenever and then he'll be hungry. You don't want him frying eggs in the middle of the night." "No," said Vipin. "Not after all the cleaning I've done today. I'm out of rags." Vipin started the car. "Shit," said Sodhi. "My phone's battery has died. My mum must be trying to call. It's eleven." They drove home with the packed paratha and still-snoring Pointy in the back, his sneaker-shod feet sticking out the Maruti's window.

Sodhi's mum was waiting for him at Vipin's gate. "What happened to your phone, gangster?" "Sorry Ma, the battery . . ." mumbled Sodhi, flushing red, embarrassed his mother had turned up like this. But he was used to it. She did this often.

The mother turned to Vipin. "How are you, Sir? When is school reopening?"

Mom Sodhi had never liked Vipin much. "What kind of teacher spends time drinking beer with his wards?" she'd complain to her husband. Her husband would say, "But Gita, our son has passed out of college. He's a grown man now. He's not Vipin's student anymore." "Still," persisted Gita. "But still. He's not married. God knows what he eats living by himself. He can't be a good influence on our Sachin. I don't want Sachin to end up like him." "Arré, Gita," said Papa Sodhi. "I told you, na. Sachin's not his student anymore. Why bother your head over a bachelor master?"

"Who's that?" said an alarmed Gita Sodhi, when she saw Pointy's sneakers peeping out of the Maruti, like two spoilt Pomeranians taking a joyride.

"That's Pointy the rapper," said Vipin, before young Sodhi could say anything. "Pointy has had one too many." Vipin didn't care much for Mrs. Sodhi either. He could sense her eyes settling in judgement on him. "Chalo, beta," she said. "Let's go home. Papa is waiting. Okay Mr. Dogra. Lovely meeting you. All the best. See you. Bye." As Sodhi walked past Vipin, Vipin whispered an SOS in his ear. "WhatdoIdowithPointy?" "Lethimbeinthecar," Sodhi hissed back.

Vipin Dogra was exhausted. It had been one of the longest days of his life. He wanted to lie down, shut his eyes and never wake up. Exactly what Pointy was doing.

At 3:00 a.m. Vipin was jolted out of his slumber by the incessant ringing of the doorbell. It was Pointy. "Dude, what happened?" Vipin was not at all happy at being woken up. He kept it short. "You slept. We went to Ashnan's." "You went where?" asked a bewildered Pointy. "Where was I?" "Ashnan's," replied Vipin. "Anyway, forget it, man. I got a paratha for you. It's in the fridge. You can heat it if you want. You know where the plates are. I'm sick of cleaning up after you, feeding you, picking up your clothes from the floor. Which reminds me, I've moved your knapsack to the veranda. It was cluttering up the room. See you tomorrow."

There. Vipin, the schoolmaster, had done it. He'd shot Pointy point-blank. That should teach him a lesson. A heavy load was off his chest. He went back to sleeping the sleep of the just. Pointy suddenly felt homesick. He wanted to speak to his mother. He called her up. It was three in the afternoon in Queen's. "Hello, Ma. Tussi ki kar rahe ho."

Vipin was so tired and hungover that he ended up sleeping for the better part of the next day. Pointy woke around noon. He hadn't had dinner. He was horse hungry. He wished human beings didn't have to feel hungry every few hours. He thought of making some eggs. He checked the fridge: no eggs. There was a tin of mackerel but Pointy was wary of touching it. Vipin had sounded so angry last night.

There was half a loaf of bread, no butter. He cut himself a thick slice and washed it down with a tumbler of water. He thought to check his email but Vipin had removed the laptop and taken it with him. Pointy's own laptop was at the bottom of the Ganges. He had an iPad but couldn't connect to the internet because he didn't know Vipin's password. There wasn't much to do.

He had music on the iPad. He lay on the bed and listened to Yo Yo Honey Singh songs. It was the spring of 2014 and Honey was all the rage. Pointy liked Honey's quaint sing-song style of rapping. He spent an hour listening to the hits of Honey: "Blue Eyes,"

"Bring Me Back," "Brown Rang," "Party with the Bhoothnath," "Char Botal Vodka" . . . He fell asleep listening to the songs.

Vipin woke at around five. He had been waking up intermittently since noon but had stayed in bed. The thought crossed his mind that he had a guest in the house, that as a host it was his duty to look after his guest. But then there was the matter of the broken chair, the wet laptop, the stain on the antique table and the eggs, how could he forget the eggs—he could still smell them on his fingers. He spoke to himself in capital letters: "STAY IN BED, DOGRA. POINTY CAN TAKE CARE OF HIMSELF. THERE IS A PIZZA HUT MENU LYING ON THE STAINED TABLE. THERE IS A MUTTON PARATHA IN THE FRIDGE."

After lounging in bed for a bit, Vipin got up and opened the door, only to walk into Pointy's hairy chest. Vipin said, "You okay, man. Eat something?" "Naah," said Pointy. "Survived on bread and water. And Honey Singh."

"Oh," said Vipin. "I'd left a Pizza Hut menu on the table. You could have called for a pizza. What about the mutton paratha?" "Forgot about that, man," said Pointy. "It's okay. Bread and water's just fine."

Now, Vipin felt guilty. He pulled out a button of hash from his jeans pocket and gave it to Pointy. "Roll one, bro. Then we'll go grab a bite somewhere."

꼭

They went to President where Pointy polished off a plate of butter chicken. Vipin sat around pecking half-heartedly at his starter. He had no appetite. This always happened to him when he ate at odd hours. Yesterday's paratha hadn't gone down too well; then he'd slept and missed breakfast and lunch. The skipped meals had somehow taken his hunger away. His stomach was in a post-hunger no-man's-land. All it could take was lung-fung soup.

Vipin decided to concentrate on the alcohol, starting with a couple of Buds, and moving on to Blenders Pride. "Liquid diet, eh," said Pointy, crunching chicken bone. Vipin grimaced while drinking the first pint. He knew this was a necessary phase on the road to feeling happy again. On a hangover, the first drink is the most painful. The second one slightly less so. And then you're fine. It's like you have been transported back to the previous night. It's like the drinking never stopped.

Since he wasn't eating, not even the complimentary bowl of salted peanuts, Vipin proceeded to get drunk very quickly. He fist-bumped Pointy and told him he was the best rapper on the planet. Vipin said, "Bro, sorry about last night. You can break every item in my house and I couldn't care less. You're the only truly famous brown rapper, man. You're the shit. I wish school was open. Would have loved to have you come to class, talk to the kids."

Pointy said, "It's all good, man. Here, have some butter chicken. It's really very good." Vipin's phone rang. It was Sodhi. It turned out his parents had left for Delhi by the morning Shatabdi. Sodhi was home alone. There was Scotch in Papa Sodhi's liquor cabinet. "Let's go," said Vipin to Pointy. "Let's go," agreed Pointy. "But, man, Vipin, are you sure you can drive?" "Yeah, Points," replied Vipin, asking for the bill. "Don't you worry. Dehradun's a toy town with baby streets. Yeah I can drive, fucker."

⁂

At Sodhi's, they finished a bottle of Glenlivet between them. It was 2:00 a.m. and Vipin and Pointy were about to leave when Sodhi said, "Hold on guys. I think I got some mushies." Pointy said, "Wow, yes! I haven't eaten mushrooms in ages'" Sodhi said, "Your last night in Doon. Go for it, bro."

They sat around chewing on muddy mushrooms and drinking water. The night was still and muggy. Not a leaf moved. They walked out to the garden and lay down on their backs. They gazed at the stars and chased their thoughts. Vipin felt like his head had severed itself from his body. Now the breakaway brain was up in the sky, circling the moon like a moth. The moon was his head was the moon.

Vipin said, "Let's go. Any later and I won't be able to drive." Sodhi didn't want them to leave. "Arré crash here, no. Folks are not back till Monday night." Vipin said, "Haan, but I like to wake up in my own bed." He turned to Pointy, modulated his voice to sound like a schoolmaster's, and said, "Let's bounce."

They'd managed to reach the Maruti when Vipin tripped on a protruding root and fell in a heap, arms and legs flailing. Pointy said, "Man, I'm not getting into that car. I got gigs coming up in Europe next month." Vipin, still on the ground, said, "Dude, I'm not drunk or anything. For fuck's sake I just tripped. Give me a hand somebody." Neither offered. Sodhi said, "Can you feel the mushies, man. It's coming in waves."

⁂

On the way back, Vipin took a wrong turn and they got lost in the valley town's bylanes. They could feel the mushrooms rising. Vipin felt he was driving in a maze. This couldn't be Dehradun. These were the narrow gullies of Benares. Pointy was atypically hysterical. "It's *your* fucking town, man. Just get me home. I don't care how." Vipin said, "You're fucking my trip, dude. Yeah, it's my town all right but I don't know every fucking street." They were driving blind. The cute toy town had transformed into a ghost town. Vipin collected his thoughts and took a U-turn. His gut told him this was familiar territory. He turned to Pointy and said, "I think I know where we are." Pointy grunted and shook his head. "God. Really." Vipin whooped with joy when he saw the clock tower rising at the end of the road, like a friendly lighthouse. "See, I told you. We'll be home in ten minutes."

⁂

Vipin and Pointy were friends again by the time they reached Vipin's house. All was forgiven between the two. They sat on the double bed in the guest room, sipping iced water. Pointy said, "Hell, yeah. What a ride. The high has worn off though. Where were we? Fear and loathing in Dehra fucking Doon."

He suddenly seemed to remember something. He went and fetched his knapsack from where Vipin had kept it in the veranda. He poked around in the pockets and pulled out a quarter of Blenders Pride. "Thought so," he mumbled triumphantly. "I was quite sure I'd bought two yesterday."

"Awesome," said Vipin. "Just what the doctor ordered." Pointy poured two stiff ones. Vipin downed his in one go. Pointy played some Honey on his iPad: "Aur seaside pe paani ka shor / Aaja meri baahon mein / Girl what you waiting for / Tujhko main leke chalun phir pyari si yacht pe / Ho jaayenge hum talli Malibu ke shot pe." While queuing tracks on the iPad, he said, "Bro, what's your password? I need to check my mail at some point." No answer.

Pointy turned around to find Vipin sprawled on one side of the double bed, the empty glass rising like a small chimney from the roof of his belly. "Damn," he muttered under his breath. "I really needed to check my mail."

He finished the Blenders Pride. He wondered what to do next. He thought to himself: "Should I go to his room and sleep? What if he wakes up in the middle of the night and wants his bed back? He told me expressly last night: 'Don't bother me.' That's why I had bread and water. That's the reason why I didn't touch his mackerel in tomato sauce. Jesus! He was so angry about the eggs and the frigging stain on the table."

Pointy thought to himself in capital letters: "I WILL STAY WHERE I AM. ON THIS DOUBLE BED. IF HE WAKES HE CAN GO BACK TO HIS OWN BED."

And so, Pointy lay down on the bed. Not since his hall-of-residence days had he shared a bed with another man. It made him uncomfortable. He wanted to be at the furthest edge of the bed, as far from Vipin as possible. Except that the human body is not exactly stationary when in sleep mode. It rolls, it moves, it changes positions constantly. At times your hand is on your forehead, at times on your chest, at times it's flat on the pillow. The back of Vipin's palm kept falling on Pointy's face.

At about four in the morning, Pointy woke. He sensed something was amiss. What could it be? He fumbled around for the bed-switch. And what was that smell, that familiar childhood smell. The smell of dampness. "Why am I wet?" thought Pointy, switching on the light.

He could now see the source of the mysterious wetness. They were both soaked in urine. Vipin had peed in his sleep. He must have taken a long one. Let it all out. The long piss goodnight. The wet patch extended to both sides of the double bed. By now, Vipin was making waking sounds. He sat up, rubbed his eyes. "What happened, bro?" He saw the damp puddle patch, felt the urine-soaked clothes on his skin. "Shit. Shit! Oh god."

Pointy was as calm as a hangman. He said in a matter-of-fact tone, "It's cool. Just pee. Nothing."

"No, no," said Vipin. "I'm so sorry. Not cool at all." He pulled the wet sheet off the bed and threw it out in the veranda. He picked up the mattresses and turned them over, dry side up. He went and got a fresh bed sheet from the linen cupboard.

"All right," ordered the schoolmaster. "You sleep now. I'll go sleep in my room."

"Sure," said the rapper. "Don't you want to change your clothes? They're soaking wet you know."

"Of course," said Vipin. "I will. Cheers. Silly me."

JEET THAYIL

from *The Book of Chocolate Saints*

This is the way the future arrives, flying low and fast, on silver wings that set the sign of the cross flickering over the business district. On a day like any other, a day like no other. You are one of the hundreds, one of the thousands hurrying to your place of employment. Above you the tower warms its skin in the falling sun, its steel core braced, the tower and its parallel twin built a segment at a time to withstand history. So when the plane appears the mind perceives it first as art. There is no other way to understand the images that follow: the clear blue sky, the clean line of flight, the way the plane tilts in the final seconds, the inevitability of impact. Later he will mark it as a premonition, the starting bell of the twenty-first century. And he will talk about eye-witnessing two kinds of terror, Islamic and white American. What he won't talk about is the woman, because it makes him ashamed that he could not save her.

From a walkway by the river Amrik sees smoke high on the north tower and then he hears the crash and a cloud of fuel boils into the sky. People stop moving, unable to supply a thread of logic to the scene: a plane-shaped hole in the side of the building. The first news van and television crew have arrived, a local station, and a police cordon is up, but where are the fire trucks? When the second plane appears the cameras are ready. He watches the aircraft's path into the new world, the scorched unstoppable gleam of it. Around him people are trying to get away or they are frozen in place, their heads tilted at identical angles, and he reverses direction to skirt the block. He's pushing his way through when the first tower comes down and people start to run.

The crowd is roiling off the buildings, the helter-skelter office workers in suits and dress shoes, the restaurant workers and tourists. He sees two men in running clothes standing frozen in place. He sees discarded backpacks and a pair of high heels and a single sneaker. A man takes off his scarf as he runs and the length of white wool joins the other detritus on the sidewalk. A delivery bike lies on its side, its rear wheel spinning.

The woman is the only one who isn't running, that is the first thing he notices. Hold this, she says, one second, and she hands him a small camera on a strap. Her eyes are lined with black and there is a leather tote on her shoulder and she's reaching for something inside when he hears a roar of bass that builds and holds and builds again. Advancing up the street is a solid cloud of smoke twelve stories high, the color of dirty snow. A heavy underground thump shatters glass all around them and the woman loses her footing and in an instant he loses sight of her.

Someone screams in short evenly spaced intervals, a woman's voice screaming, Mara, and there are shouts and sirens and his lungs are on fire. It isn't easy to absorb the moment: people concentrated on one task, the pumping of legs and the taking in of air and the deflection of thousands of arrows of information flying in from every direction.

This is how the future arrives, out of the bright blue sky. He knows this is the future but he cannot hope to understand it, not now, because something is about to yank him out of the moment and reduce him to a question of headgear. Across the street someone's yelling at him. Where did the guy come from? He is not a hardhat. He is not working in construction or any conceivable Wall Street job. He is a hooded sweatshirt and painter's jeans and he's saying something unbelievable.

"You, motherfuck terrorist, take the rag off."

Amrik's reflexes take a moment to kick in. The guy is still far enough away and the street is full of people moving in a jerky headlong rush, not a stampede or a migratory wave but a race kicking against oblivion, a collective hyperjump made up of many smaller ones. These are New Yorkers running for their lives and what he wants is to run with them, but he goes the other way, south, away from the two men, there are two now, who are following him.

"Yo, dune coon! Ali Baba, wait up!"

The sky is overcast but the sun is there too, or a simulacrum of the sun inside the thunderclouds that have landed on the street. A hawk of some sort flies across the avenue in a rough diagonal only a few inches above the crowd. The bird too is headed north. Somebody's mail whips by, and more paper, stapled pages and newspapers blowing down the street. The air is full of grit and Amrik puts his handkerchief to his mouth and turns west on the zebra at the end of the block. He heads south then west again and when the two men start to run he does too.

When they were picked on at school his brother's response was to say God-bless, if you say God-bless they will leave you alone. But his brother is a cut Sikh whose kesh is gelled to who knew how many points, a kid who gave up on the five Ks in college because his dream was bhangra. Amrik's dream is all-American. He is Brooklyn-born and Brooklyn-bred, a New Yorker with a doomed love of the Red Sox, and none of it means a thing because today he is nothing more than an animated logo. He is a running turban.

Above him the great buildings of the business district appear stricken, block after block of dead air, the city under attack. Within that attack another is taking place and Amrik is the sole intended victim. He unwinds his new turban as he runs, a length of crisp black cotton as stylish as anything in a midtown store. He will take off his turban and stuff it in his satchel and he will tuck his long hair into his collar and run.

This is an American, a New Yorker, on the day the new century arrives. See him ducking into a subway station. The ticket booths are empty. On the platform, people carry breakfast bagels and unread financial papers and dead cell phones. Some have just exited trains from Uptown, from Bronxville, White Plains and Riverside. He sees a tall blond man whose khaki shorts are wet with piss and the man makes no effort to hide the stain. A chain wrapped in blue plastic hangs from his fist.

The crack of the train comes scraping off the tiles.

When his pursuers jump the turnstiles their boots make a single whump on the sticky platform and such is the strangeness of the morning that no notice is taken of them or of the way they are walking through the crowd and scanning heads.

Amrik sinks into himself, becomes smaller, becomes absolutely still. He's taken off his turban and his jacket and tie but there is nothing he can do about his beard and skin color. He is the only person in the crowd who is not black or white but an unrepresented brown, provenance unknown, from some place off the census grid.

The air smells funny, thick with exhaust and rust and a metallic residue he can taste on his tongue. The doors ding open and he enters a car and goes to the far end where he leans against the connecting door. A woman in a blue jumpsuit and hardhat is watching him. She is big and dreadlocked, the color of black coffee with a drop of condensed milk, and he's the only one in the car, on the train, on the entire subway, whose color is off the grid. The woman takes off her hardhat and hands it to him.

"Put it on," she says.

He can see the two men on the platform and he can taste the metallic residue in the air. He notices the camera in his hand, the brand name inscribed in silver, the name rhyming with leaker or liker. He puts on the hardhat and waits for the doors to close.

"Philomena Debris," the woman says. "What I do all day? I ride the rails. I ride and watch. That's my name and job description. Philomena Debris, rider-watcher."

The name on her overalls is De Brie.

"My advice? Keep your head down. Don't look up, not now."

He keeps his head down; he doesn't look up.

Saturday morning. He and Sukh were on the six, *on the sex*, his brother called it, up in the first car because that had been their ritual when they were kids, up in front in sight of the motorman. There were seats vacant but they were standing, his brother hunched like he was already downtown at the Basement Bhangra spinning Punjabi remixes in his white K-Swiss. Amrik asked him once, how d'you keep them so white? He said, every night, before I sleep? I pray my *kicks* to keep.

"I were you I'd cut my hair," Sukh said. "Lose the turban, stop being stared at by the average white man."

"Turban's our pride," said Amrik. "I take it off, they win."

"Win? Shit," and Sukh laughed, "you can't win against a lynch mob."

"I thought about it, get a haircut and a shave. But racists see race, they don't see anything else."

"At this point and the historical process, race is everything."

"Why join them?"

"There's a war in America and like it or not you part of it. You being too idyllistic."

"You remember any Punjabi at all?" said Amrik.

"Bro, the pic, you want to or not? Gimme a peek? So I know what you're saying to me?"

"What I should be asking, you remember any English?"

"The pic, the snap, the grainy, you know, image."

Amrik dug the *Post* out of his briefcase, already folded to the page. Sukh stayed with the picture for a while, two white guys pointing at a word in red capitals on the front of a garbage truck, the guys wearing reflective sunglasses with straps, like they were on a skiing holiday. On Sixth Ave.

The caption said: *MAKE THAT DOUBLE FOR US. After more than three decades on the job, NYC sanitation men Phil Manzanera and Rick 'Raucus' Honeycutt (right) retire this week. After the catastrophic terror strikes of 9/11 they spray-painted their city vehicle with the motto above*: REVENGE!

"You sure these are the guys?"

"No question, wearing the same clothes."

"Same clothes when they're chasing you all over the subway system?"

"Yeah."

"Hoodies and Tims. White guys dressed like brothers. You in your Brooks Brothers and the towers collapsing."

"Sums it up."

"Amrik, their names are in the paper. You know we can find these guys and show them what the pagri stands for."

"I thought about it, got to admit."

"Bro, puttar."

"Turn the page."

Sukh turned to a double spread datelined Mesa, Arizona. He read the headline: *Trial Dates Set in Alleged Bias Killing of Sikh Immigrant*, and then the article quickly through to the end.

"Sukh, you get it?" said Amrik. "The bias killer shot him because he thought he was Muslim. It's happening all over the country."

"See what I'm saying? Lose the turban."

"No."

"What is it you're trying to sell me here?"

"Come to Arizona. The guy who did it, the bias killer? He's pleading not guilty due to insanity. I want to meet the family, show some solidarity at the trial."

"You see my new Ks?"

"I see them."

"You know what they are?"

"I know you'll tell me."

"Custom made. My K-Swiss with a upgrade on the classic style. All leather. See the one-piece rubber outsoles? Reinforced toe, five-stripe band, D-Ring lacing system?"

"What did it cost you?"

"Always with the most *un*important question."

"Okay, but what?"

"Senty dollars for the basic shoe. The customizing? Off the grid. Check the laces and the gold eyelets. Not available online, not available anywhere. And the straight Lydiard-type bar lacing, see that?"

"Yeah."

"Ok, but do you see the main thing?"

"Which one, there are so many."

"Don't belittle, bro, don't be little. Check the sleeves on the laces."

"The sleeves."

"The metal tube at the end of the lace, holds it together."

"Okay."

"Yeah, gold plated."

"I'm finding this hard to believe."

"And the color on the uppers, see how it's a different white from the shield on the tongue there? See how the toe and heel are a different white from the stripes?"

"Yes."

"Now look at that monogram there by the heel."

"What's it say? Sorry if I don't examine your sneakers up close on the subway."

"DJ Suki."

"Right."

"What I'm talking about. Customized. I'm not taking no three hundred dollar Ks to Mesa, Arizona, get my ass shot at by some alleged *bias* motherfucker."

"That's what I thought you'd say."

"And Rik? You ask me you shouldn't be going either. Who do we know in AZ?"

"Sukh, take a look at the picture of Balbir Singh, the gas station owner who got killed."

"See that double beard and jumbo turban anybody be scared."

"Funny."

"I'm on in thirty minutes, regular gig two nights a week. I'm getting it to work. I'm being responsible, unlike my older brother."

"I heard you."

"For real."

At City Hall the train's antique brakes shuddered and the crowd thinned out and Sukh picked up his CD cases.

"I'm supposed to be the rebel in the family but look at you. Quit steady high-paying job, check, try for job with reclusive artist, check, and now? You're taking off for Arizona just because you can."

"Balbir had just been to the local church. He made a Nine Eleven donation and he was planting flowers at his gas station when the guy shot him. Five shots from a car."

"Not now when my career's in take-off position."

"An hour earlier killer's sitting at Applebee's and laughing with the waitress. He tells her, I'm gonna go out and shoot me some towel-heads."

"Mesa, Arizona. What d'you expect? Tolerance and understanding?"

"Family man, Balbir. Who does he look like?"

"Who?"

"He could be anybody, could be Papa, or Jarnail Chacha in Amritsar. You see what I'm saying?"

"I see what you're—"

"Listen, put an ad in the *Voice* for me. Here's the copy."

Sukh read from the notepaper his brother handed him, " 'Seeking pinstriped woman I met on September 11. I'm the turbanned guy. You gave me your Leica to hold.' Yeah, okay, I can take care of it."

He jumped off the train at Spring Street with the cases clutched to his chest and Amrik noted his brother's unique running style. Sukh's upper body and thighs did little work; like a cartoon character the movement was all in the feet, it was all in the K-Swiss. No one on the platform gave him a second glance, just another city kid going about his business. Amrik would have been stared at because he had stayed loyal to the five Ks. Not that it was a flaw in the faith. How could Sikhism's founders have anticipated the ways in which their innovation would be viewed in the new world?

He found a seat and the compartment filled up again. The connecting door opened with a heavy crank and a man stepped in carrying a clutch of flags and baseball pennants.

He said, "Push in, push in, we're all American here."

Which wasn't necessarily true. There were several nationalities and races and combinations thereof. This was New York. The guy barreled down the aisle and stopped in front of an old couple with a Chinese newspaper spread on their laps. They were reading together, reading the same article and possibly the same sentence.

He said, "Be American, buy American."

The woman looked up and inspected the man and his flags and went back to the newspaper.

A bearded guy in a camouflage jacket nodded at the flag-seller.

The flag guy said, "Fight the Taliban. Buy American, be American."

The bearded guy said, "Buy the blood of Jesus Christ."

"Say what?"

"The blood of the Savior redeems me."

A ripple of movement, people looking for possible routes of escape, and the flag guy planted himself in the aisle two seats from the bearded man and three from Amrik. He looked at Amrik in his black suit and black shirt and black shoes with side buckles and his eyes lingered on the black turban and he offered a tiny pin, stars and stripes waving in an invisible wind.

He said, "Be American."

And the words shook Amrik out of his subway persona, the *don't make eye contact, don't talk, don't smile* shield he wore like armor.

He said, "I am American."

The bearded guy said to Amrik, "If thou has run with the footmen and they have wearied thee, how canst thou contend with the horses?"

The flag guy said, "Horse what?"

The guy with the beard said, "Old Testament."

Amrik said, "He's saying there's no point engaging with fools."

The guy with the beard said, "You think it didn't have fools in the time of our Savior?"

The guy with the flags said, "Fucking city, everybody's got a mouth."

But he went to the connecting doors and left the compartment.

Amrik thought, New York, where racism is an equal opportunity enterprise. It wasn't the first time he'd been sniped at by a black man, but it was certainly the first time he'd been defended by someone white.

You blurt it to a nut on the subway, but you don't articulate it otherwise. You are an American with a job on Wall Street and an apartment in Park Slope. People give you their money and you knead it like dough: you supersize it. You run in the park in a warm-up jacket with headphones strapped to your arm. You don't take sugar in your coffee. You don't eat white bread or potatoes. You don't drink beer. You have a body mass index calculator on your computer and it tells you your weight, real and ideal, in relation to your height. You take your coffee black. In your office there is a leather couch and two leather armchairs and a framed lithograph of the Brooklyn Dodgers signed and numbered by the artist. You are an American: a New Yorker: a Brooklynite. Then the towers come down and you find yourself on a plane headed west. It is 2003, wartime in America. You have to be wearing a turban and sitting on a plane to Arizona via Texas to understand the meaning of this.

They made him take off his shoes and socks. He placed his black leather Cordovans in a tray and stepped through a metal detector. They made him do it three times. He retied the laces the first time and then he left them untied, slipped on the shoes, slipped them off. Random checks, but he was the only passenger who had to remove his footwear more than once, who had to unwind his headgear. It was embarrassing. Also, downright fucking humiliating.

On the second leg, a small jet from Houston to Mesa, he was the only passenger who was not white, who was brown, hairy, gym-fit, and it made him wonder, what happened to the melting pot, the salad bowl, the mosaic? Fly out of JFK and the United States was a foreign country. You found ancient race anxieties. You found extreme weather and isolation and brutal long-distance terrain. All the way on the short flight he was aware of the other passengers' awareness. He was sitting in the front row and this too seemed to him a misfortune: he could feel them staring. He was happy his brother had not come with him. If one Sikh could be the cause of so much dismay, the two brothers would have caused a stampede. Out of his briefcase he pulled a copy of Newton's first book of poems, the cover a painted cross, chipped and blood-spattered. The title, *Songs for the Tin-Eared*, appeared above a banner that said POEMS, and he hoped it would occur to his fellow passengers that a man reading a book of poems in English would most likely not be planning to blow them out of the sky. He held the book high and buried his face in it, but the man beside him did not seem reassured. He seemed as nervous as when he'd first set eyes on his turbanned bearded seatmate. Soon Amrik put the book away and pulled out a copy of the *Wall Street Journal*.

He took a taxi from the airport to the hotel and kept it waiting while he had a shower and washed his hair and changed his clothes. He hung his suit in the closet and put on a short-sleeved white shirt and sandals and when he got back to the taxi the driver had a cigarette in his mouth and the radio tuned to death metal, a bottomed-out voice shouting GowBowBowBowBangBangGang into stop-start guitars. He killed his cigarette and flipped channels to a soft rock station. He was wearing plastic sunglasses turned the wrong way around and there were empty food containers on the dashboard and bits of debris on the front seat. From the upholstery a smell of antique smoke and dirty clothes. But the guy was helpful enough, he knew where the courthouse was and he didn't mind waiting.

"Thanks."

"Hey, you're welcome. Where you coming from, you don't mind me asking?"

"New York."

"The big bad city."

"Not so bad anymore."

"How's that?"

"The mayor did some housekeeping."

"Rudy Giuliani. Did a good thing, right?"

He drove with one hand on the wheel, his eyes squinted against the glare and his shades perched on the back of his head, twitchy and dry, with a reedy country-western voice.

"Depends who you're talking to. I'm not complaining."

"You're here for the trial, I'm guessing."

"That's right."

"It's all over the news, radio *and* TV. They're pleading insanity."

"Guilty except insane."

"Crazy like a fox. Guy knew what he was doing."

"Yeah, probably did."

"Are you a lawyer?"

"No, I'm here for the solidarity. See what happens."

"Right."

"Because I'm a Sikh, like the guy who was killed."

"Balbir Sodhi."

"Okay, you know his name."

"Hey, I've been to his gas station a few times. Ask me they should hang the shooter no questions asked."

~: 269

"Maybe they will."

"They're calling him the American murderer. What he's doing, he's giving Americans a bad name."

"And Arizonans."

"Guy isn't even from here, moved to Mesa from fucking Alabama."

"Can't hang a man for moving here. Sodhi came from the Punjab."

"Shoot a guy in the back? Dude *deserves* to hang."

The driver introduced himself as Charlie Moon, Mesa born and bred, driving now for three years. He handed out a card with the name and number of the taxi company. Amrik sat back and watched the city go by. Even the sun fell at an angle that felt strange to a man just arrived from a fortified borough on the coast. The streets were calm and orderly, raked gravel and wide sidewalks and no trash blowing against the storefronts. The desert was everywhere. On the traffic islands and street corners were stands of saguaro, stoic stumps reaching upward. Everything was beige or pink, the houses, the saguaro, the gravel, even the animal figures in people's yards: a hundred shades of pink and five hundred shades of beige.

When you are displaced in the world, displacement is its own reward.

He began to enjoy riding around the foreign city and looking at the sights and talking to Charlie Moon. Then they turned a corner and he saw a group of Sikhs in blue and red turbans. The headgear was vivid against their white clothes. A dozen men and women dressed in the Hindu color of mourning. Amrik stepped out of the car and a guy with a chest-length beard extended his hand and introduced himself as Lakhwinder, brother of Balbir. He said, welcome, from where are you coming? The Punjabi-accented English sounded strange in the American desert and then it didn't sound strange at all. Others came up to introduce themselves and shake his hand. There was a television crew and a woman who asked if she could speak to him later to get a comment about the trial, but he didn't get a chance to reply because now he was entering the courthouse at the head of a crowd of people he had never before met and he fitted right in with his saffron turban and white shirt.

[. . .]

Amrik's father wore a netted beard and elaborate turban, a soft-spoken man whose ambition had been to get out of the Punjab. He would have gone anywhere, Iceland, Argentina, Papua New Guinea; but he had relatives in Queens who found him work in a grocery store in Jackson Heights. He married a girl chosen by his uncle and named their son after his adopted country. Amrik's mother wanted a traditional name, something Punjabi, but his father got his way with their first-born. With Sukhwinder his mother got hers. His father became a Republican, because the elephant reminded him of India, and he stayed one all his life. How hard his parents worked, how happy they were with how little, and because they had been poor they did not take money for granted. They lived small lives with few comforts and thought themselves fortunate. Back home they were success stories. Even after all these years his father thought of the Punjab as home. He wore his Sikhism lightly: he said faith was a private thing and there was no point parading it on the streets for the world to see. He would as likely have talked about his wife's lovemaking habits as he would the nuts and bolts of his faith. What would he say to these men?

He'd say, *Eye for an eye makes the whole world blind.*

The Court TV crew has also been invited to dinner. People leave their shoes at the door and sit cross-legged on the floor to eat—black daal, rotis cut into wedges, tandoori chicken and fish kababs that are a bright unnatural shade of red. The Sodhis provide a quick house tour and Amrik understands that they are being savvy, working the media. Over dessert, the reporter asks Amrik what brought him all the way from New York to Mesa.

He answers truthfully that he has no idea.

"I guess I'm out of my mind," he says.

"Well, that's something. I think you should talk to me, tell your story to the world."

She gives him a card, *Cassandra Bird, Assistant Producer.* Call me Cassie, she says, her voice with a drop at the end. But Amrik does not want to talk.

He says, "And what brought you from NYC to Mesa?"

"I did a bunch of stories after Nine Eleven about people suffering from post-traumatic stress without knowing it. I interviewed rescue personnel at Ground Zero who suffered from insomnia, respiratory problems, anxiety attacks, and they wouldn't take sick leave. I spoke to a woman who'd lost her husband and her father. She was camped out there. She wouldn't go home. I kept meeting survivors who didn't come across like they'd survived, who."

"Right."

"I met a woman who was riding the subways all day long. She was a senior custodian in Tower One and lost her job, obviously. Rode the subways in a blue jumpsuit—"

"Wait a minute! What was her name? Black woman?"

"Don't remember the name. Big woman, black, gave great sound bites."

"That's her, Philomena Debris! I met her just after the towers went down. She gave me advice that maybe saved my life. Hey, this is fantastic!"

But Cassandra Bird isn't impressed.

She says, "That's what she does, she rides the subway and talks to people. That's her disorder."

She takes a sip of sweet milk tea and coughs.

"How does all that bring you to Arizona?"

"Tell the truth, I needed to get out of the city. I was tripping on other people's disorders. I'd done so many stories on trauma I was traumatized myself."

On the way back to the hotel his cell phone beeps with a text message from Sukh. *No need 2B a hero ok*?

Amrik asks Charlie Moon to pick him up early the next day. He won't go back to the courtroom. He can already see the outcome as a ticker on a screen. Sentenced to death. Balbir's family telling reporters that only partial retribution has been achieved and the debt will be paid in full when Frank is hanged, electrocuted, lethally injected, clubbed to death, executed by firing squad, lynched in a public square.

On the American flight out of Mesa he stands with his hands on his hips and examines himself in the toilet mirror. He looks at his careful clothes and groomed facial hair and tries to see himself as a stranger might. He understands that he is permanently displaced in the new America and the new New York.

The return trip is worse. The other passengers' stares are more pointed and the stopover in Texas is much too long.

He orders draft lager at a sports bar and grill and flips through a bar copy of the *Texas Times*. His eye, newly sensitized to *turban* and *Sikh* and *terrorist*, finds an article about the Sodhi trial. *Victims of Mistaken Identity, Sikhs Pay a Price for Turbans*. It opens with Frank Roque's contention as he's being arrested, "I'm a patriot. I'm a damn American all the way." The phrase plays and replays in Amrik's head and coalesces into a chanted anthemic *damngoddamnAmerican, allthewayAmerican*. The article is a piece of subtle alarmism. Sikhs are being singled out because they wear "distinctive turbans that resemble the head wrap of terror chief Osama bin Laden." Sikh temples and homes vandalized nationwide. A gasoline bomb tossed into a window and a three-year-old hit on the head. A woman arrested for trying to pull the turban off the head of a man at a highway rest stop. The attendant wrestles her down and his explanation coins a phrase. "Turban rage." The article ends with the following paragraph:

> An intense debate has begun among Sikhs. Should they shave off their beards and cut their hair? Should they differentiate themselves from Muslims? Or is this an act of cowardice?

Amrik reads slowly and sips his beer and orders another. The aquarium light of an airport bar in the middle of the day in America. No conversation. TV bolted to the wall above the counter.

There's no way to justify it, warriors making a virtue of fear to explain themselves to white Americans.

Don't shoot me. Shoot him. Shoot the Muslim.

He likes the way the lager is working on him. He takes a roast beef sandwich and another beer. Then he gathers his bag and newspaper and sunglasses and heads for security check. He takes his shoes off with a smile, and what's this, the security woman, is she giving him attitude?

"Sir, please don't take off your shoes until you are requested to."

"You're kidding me, right?"

"Sir, do not address me."

And there are three of them now, two men and the woman, suddenly there, all heavy in the same way, bulk without muscle or tone. And it could go any way. One word, a moment of unthinking loudness or annoyance or anger and the whole banal exchange will implode. He can see it in their faces, how pumped they are. This is what they've been training for, the chance to take down some belligerent Middle Eastern dude, take him down and put his lights out. He'll end up on the floor in a chokehold with his hands cuffed behind him. He'll end up in a room waiting to be processed, waiting indefinitely, nobody the wiser.

This is the new America. Except it isn't America at all. This is Post America, After America, the dream of equality curdled into race paranoia. Rights if you're white otherwise you take your chances.

He weighs his course of action. He thinks of Philomena Debris and the way she moves through the world, self-contained, graced, a black sailing ship, black dignity intact in the face of whiteness, accommodation without servility. And he's thinking of a story Sukh told him about a young software engineer waiting for a flight to Boston, detained at the airport because he was speaking Tamil to his wife on his cell phone. The story ended with the software engineer in tears, saying he wouldn't do it again, would not speak to his wife in any language other than English.

Amrik apologizes and puts his shoes back on.

RAVI MANGLA

Feats of Strength

A strongman is lifting my car, his hands bolted tight to the front bumper. His trunky thighs and buttocks are facing streetward, and several women in the neighborhood have set up lawn chairs and are watching the spectacle from their front yards. His grunts are loud, like falling timber, and the birds perched on the roof have fled in search of friendlier shingles.

We have remodeled our lives with family in mind. Out goes the air hockey table and bean bag chair, the ninja throwing stars and KISS commemorative guitar. The car, a cramped but capable two-door, is the last loose end, the sole remaining relic from our previous lives.

Yes, I want take it, the strongman says, extending and contracting the fingers on his left hand. (If I could, I would call him by his first name, but it's unpronounceable to those unaccustomed to the sounds of his language, a series of consonants arbitrarily arranged.) He rummages through his gym bag for his checkbook and upon finding it writes out a check for the requested amount. No haggling. We agree to sort out the title transfer and other details during the week.

Natalie stands in the window with our son. She smiles at me, since we now have the money to buy the minivan we've been eyeing. My son, in her arms, is trying to fit the head of a stuffed giraffe in his mouth. He couldn't be more pleased with himself.

Every couple of months Natalie has dinner with the supervisor from her work, a woman who lost her family in an accident. It happened the winter before last. Her husband was driving their daughter to a piano lesson when his car skidded over a patch of black ice and plummeted into freezing cold water. He was able to force open his door but drowned trying to unbuckle his daughter's seatbelt, which was stuck. This is the story the police pieced together from the remains. My wife brings our son along and each dinner the woman buys him a new toy, something bright and extravagant.

Natalie and my son have vanished from the window, departed for another room in the house, and I can't help but wonder what tragedies will confront us, what feats of strength I'll be asked to perform for my family. It's not a matter of *if*, but of *when*, and I only wish I knew how it will all pan out.

The first crib we bought for my son—his name is Dev, by the way—the first crib we bought for Dev was recalled by the manufacturer. A faulty latch. The drop-side, installed wrong or burdened with too much weight, was prone to loosening from the adjoining railing, or detaching completely. When Natalie found out about this, she cried. *How could we let this happen?* I didn't know what to say.

The strongman asks if he can walk the car home. I nod, absently, my head elsewhere. He untangles a complicated web of straps and ropes from his gym bag. With a tow hook, he attaches a thick rope to the underside of the front bumper. The other end of the rope is threaded through a climbing harness, which he belts around his waist and shoulders. He leans forward and takes several long, agonizing steps. The rope tightens. The wheels start moving. Slowly at first, and then a little more easily. His face is red and the veins around his temples push through the skin. His legs are pumping like pistons, churning forward, determined.

 Natalie comes outside and stands beside me. I pick up Dev and hold him against my chest. The strongman reaches a bend in the road, disappears behind a cluster of trees. The women fold up their chairs, but we stay outside and wave goodbye to the car, trailing behind with no one at the wheel, as if moving under its own power. We keep waving, the three of us, to all the things we've loved that have let us go.

ARUNI KASHYAP

from *The House With a Thousand Stories*

Some visitors from nearby villages had come around late afternoon with fruits, grams, coconuts and spotted senisompa bananas for us. Most of the people in the house were sitting on the veranda, listening to them. Mukut-khura, dressed in his dhoti, sat there on a chair too, recounting his first reactions, how he feared—after his brother had passed away—for the death of his old mother as well.

"Don't ask me what she did when she learnt that her eldest son had died! I thought—even Mai would leave us along with Bolenkai. He was the one who looked after her almost all the time. Checked if she had taken her medicines, heated water for her, took her out for walks. She was very attached to him. I thought she wouldn't be able to take this stab of destiny." He sighed.

He was so fat, but also so tall that his body didn't seem disproportionate. Still it didn't stop me from thinking the chair he sat on would break suddenly under his weight. He was so loud too. Aaita must have been in one of the nearby rooms. I wondered if she could hear him.

"I know, I know—" one middle-aged man agreed.

"I think her health deteriorated because of the trauma, not just because of the thick fog this year."

"For two whole days after his death we sat with her. It was as if she was leaving us. She coughed and coughed and was absolutely senseless for those two days. We were almost sure she'd succumb to the grief. When the sun rose on the third day, we brought her out and informed the relatives that she was leaving us, and they gathered soon. Some women had already started crying, and someone had poured out Ganga water into a bowl to feed her a drop before she went. But lying there under the sun, she stirred and said, 'Could I have some tea, please?'"

"*Nai, nai*, this old woman is not going to die easily. Maybe she'll live on to tell stories to Mridul's children too!"

The men started laughing.

Mridul came out of his room and asked me if I was ready. Mukut-khura looked at us when he heard him and Oholya-jethai shot us a stern look. She looked at Mukut-khura's face and, when she sensed no possibility of an intervention, she asked where we were going. Mridul said he wanted to show me around the village—the people, the stream, the temple and the marketplace. Oholya-jethai asked him to stay back; she said there was no need to roam around like that, especially when people were visiting. They would ask for the dead man's son. But Mridul's mother intervened. She asked Oholya-jethai to let him go in her meek voice, wondering aloud how long a young man like him could lock himself up at home. When we opened the bamboo gate of the compound, we heard Oholya-jethai's loud voice telling someone how young men might stray from the right way if they stayed out of the house for long hours. She said she wouldn't be responsible if the army interrogated Mridul or picked him up. Mukut-khura said something in reply, but by then we had walked farther away from the house, so we didn't hear what he was saying. But I was sure if Oholya-jethai had continued speaking, her words would have pricked us with the sharpness of shards of glass.

Suddenly I was filled with a sense of triumph. It was only a little later, when we reached the marketplace, I realized I had felt victorious because I had finally figured out that it was possible to do something against Oholya-jethai's wishes in that house.

The market was teeming with people. Among the well-dressed crowd, Mridul looked odd in his dhoti and shawl. He wasn't wearing a shirt. He was barefoot. Among the people buying vegetables, oil and meat from the shops, he looked out of place. With his tonsured head, he looked like a statue, a symbol of sacrifice, a Buddhist monk who had relinquished the pleasures of earthly life.

We had reached a large laburnum tree that stood beside the village road and just on the edge of the road there was an electric pole. I noticed that when he got near the electric pole, Mridul stepped away like a meandering stream of water to avoid treading on the portion just below and around it. I was behind him and he asked me not to step on the portion of the road that was just under the electric pole. I followed his instructions, wondering why.

"I don't think you should know the reason. You won't be able to digest it."

I was irritated. "Is this some kind of a joke? I have digested Oholya-jethai's words; I would be able to digest anything now. Tell me," I said.

Mridul looked at me, as if he was preparing to tell me something serious and didn't approve of my flippant manner. Without saying anything, he started to walk away; I followed him, asking more questions. He went to a shop where some of his friends were hanging out, chewing betel nuts. He introduced me to them. One of them was called Brikodar, whom he was particularly close to.

"Pabloo wants to know the story of the electric pole," Mridul told him, with a touch of mockery in his voice.

Brikodar laughed. He was taller than Mridul and plump. He looked like someone who wouldn't weave mysteries the way Mridul loved to. By telling me half stories, by asking me not to walk on a certain portion of the road without explaining why. Mridul laughed, too, at my confused state. I didn't like it. I didn't like it when his friends told me that I would have nightmares if I heard the story and laughed. I didn't like it when they asked me if I would be able to digest it. I felt annoyed because I couldn't tell them I would jolly well be able to, if I could digest whatever Oholya-jethai had been saying all day. I was humiliated because their laughter reminded me that I was younger than them and they had access to worlds I didn't. Worlds that Mridul wouldn't usually think twice before introducing me to.

But now those worlds were suddenly hidden away from me. I was suddenly reminded that I was four years younger than Mridul. I told Mridul politely that I wanted to go home. He was surprised, but didn't protest. He walked with me, said this and that, but I didn't respond. When we reached the electric pole, I saw him avoiding the portion under the pole. I wanted to defy him and walk on it but I felt, whatever the reason was, it wasn't funny; it was serious and he was scared of something, which is why he had walked like a meandering stream that had found an obstacle on its way and changed course. I realized that obstacle was invisible—the obstacle that made him avoid the portion of the ground just under the electric pole that stood just near the road, next to the laburnum tree that hadn't yet bloomed into flakes of gold.

The sun had set by the time we reached home and I thought about how long it took for the sun to set. On our way, I wanted to ask him again what the fuss over the electric pole was all about, but I was too proud. I was offended that he had reminded me of the difference in our ages by telling me I would be scared if I knew the real reason behind his peculiar behavior.

I could smell ghee. I could smell chopped coriander and chopped green chillies. I could smell boiled potatoes and grilled brinjals. Smell of slivers of lime that must be stacked on banana leaves beside a mound of stork-white salt. I knew that smell all too well. The smell of a mourning-house dinner, like when grandma had passed away, in 1993. When I had met Mridul for the first time. When I wasn't old enough to roam around the village alone, wasn't old enough to go to Mayong alone, but Mridul—who, at that point, had disrupted my ideas about the animal kingdom—was old enough to represent his family at a funeral. Dressed in a blue shirt and black trousers, he had looked so handsome that I had felt jealous, just the way I was jealous of his dimples.

"Mridul!"

Oholya-jethai's booming voice invaded the room.

I was sitting quietly on the bed, too proud to tell Mridul that I was offended. He must have been wondering what was wrong with me. So he didn't know what to say or whether he should leave the room. He had started arranging his books on his study table.

Mridul turned towards her.

"I need to tell you something. You will not mind, I hope. You will not pull a long face, I hope." He turned his back to her and started rearranging the already arranged books.

He didn't look at her.

"I don't like this habit of yours."

No one spoke. I looked at Mridul.

Oholya-jethai folded her hands and stood there, staring at Mridul. I don't know if he knew that she was staring at him. But her look was piercing and he must have felt it on his back, on his spine, on his neck, on his scalp, and so he replied after a few uncomfortable moments of silence, "Which habit?"

"You don't need to roam around like this in the market. There is no need to hang out with those losers like Brikodar, and I have always maintained you should stay away from their family. They might feed you some potion and you may end up falling in love with Brikodar's sister. They have been eyeing the men of our family for years now. And what is this carrom fascination? Have you forgotten? Last year, you failed your exams because you spent hours with them, playing carrom and strumming the guitar. It's just four days since your father passed away and you are already doing things that would have made him unhappy. You don't deserve to mourn him. Take off your mourning attire and change into jeans and T-shirt!"

She left in a huff.

Mridul leaned on the table. He didn't look at me. How cruel her words were. Just to prove her point, she could say anything. Just to strip her opponent of dignity, she said anything she could to hurt them. I was suddenly embarrassed for him because she had revealed secrets about him that I wasn't supposed to know. He hadn't told me he had flunked the previous year. Obviously he didn't want me to know. Perhaps he wanted to hide it from me so that I continued to like him, respect him, and didn't look down on him. And when he started crying not long after she left the room, I didn't quite notice it. I was still sitting on the bed and he had his back towards me. But his back was trembling and his head was bowed.

I went up to him, turned him around and looked at his face. He looked away, wiped his tears with the ends of his fingers. He didn't want me to see that he was crying, that he had lost control. I wondered if he was crying because she had scolded him or whether he suddenly missed his father who wouldn't have scolded him at all, who would have let him hang out with anyone he wanted to.

He wiped his tears and looked at my face. "You think I can't answer back? You think I can't say anything to her? I just want peace in this house. If you go out, it is the army's fear. If you stay in, it is Oholya-jethai's terror. For a while, the rebels have stopped coming to our house to demand food and shelter. And that was another kind of trauma. Where do I go? Where should I try to find some peace? If I play music, I have to consider what people will think because someone has just died in this house. If I play carrom, I am wasting time and not studying. How can I study? I still miss my father. It isn't going to go away, Pabloo. It will never go away, just like the fear that makes me walk in a curve around the electric pole on that straight road, avoiding the portion of ground just under the electric pole. And not just me, many of my friends do that too because we had seen it first."

He waited. His Adam's apple moved up, down, up. He wiped the tears with the tips of his fingers. It was a nice day, he said. Clear, blue skies. They could even hear the distant bleats of goats. They could see the kites flown by the young boys in the East Bengali village. It was a Sunday. So they had all woken up late but the younger ones had woken up first since they had planned to go fishing, get some crabs, get some pork from the Karbi village, prop up a hut in the middle of the empty fields and have dinner together that night. Eat forbidden food. The fields were bright yellow. The skies looked peaceful. Mridul had first gone to Brikodar's house to tell him about the plan. From there, they had walked down to Binod's house, and then to the market. No one was around. The dogs were barking so loudly.

And since the dogs were barking in the village, dogs from the neighboring villages had also gathered. But they were scared. They didn't come into the marketplace, into the terrain of the Hatimura dogs. They were barking from a distance. And there were the crows. In a chorus, they had shattered the beautiful silence of that morning.

Mridul said that he had wondered, when he reached Brikodar's house, why the crows and the dogs were making such a racket. Brikodar's mother had said probably *something* was dead. A dog. A crow. A big, fat fox. Something. You know, if you kill a crow, the rest of the crows caw like that. For days, you wouldn't be able to go anywhere near the dead bird because other crows would attack you with their sharp beaks and talons. When Mridul had gone to Binod's house, Binod's grandmother had said the same—why were the crows cawing like mad? Why were the dogs barking so much in the market? Probably something was dead. Something. A dog, a crow, a fox. A buffalo.

"We didn't care," Mridul continued. "It was far away—the shops, I mean, are far away from the houses. But we saw him first. I don't remember who informed the police. But we saw the body first. Only in his red underwear. He didn't have legs. They had been chopped off. He didn't have fingers. They had been cut off too. His face was twisted—as if he was repulsed by a bad smell. It was such a horrific sight! Hanging from the electric pole like a dead, electrocuted bat. He was from a nearby village—the brother of an ULFA member. Why did they have to torture him like that? Moina-pehi, who had also seen the body, couldn't eat for three days. She retched and retched. I couldn't sleep for many days as well. Moina-pehi was among the women who cried the most, wondering aloud if the man had loved someone, wanted to marry someone, if he had a sister. His only crime was that he was the elder brother of an ULFA member and the ULFA member, his brother, had refused to surrender to the government and take the money that the government was dishing out so that he could return to society by setting up a business.

"When someone climbed up the pole with a bamboo ladder and cut off the rope that had tied the corpse to the pole by its fingerless wrists, the body had fallen exactly on the portion of the road we avoid stepping on now. It's been almost three months since this happened. More killings are taking place every day.

"But this was the most horrific spectacle. The East Bengali villagers who use the Pokoria River most of the time say that they have started finding body parts of unknown human beings at regular intervals, almost every fortnight or so. They are so scared that they haven't even informed the police. But on that ground where that corpse fell—we still can't walk. Because we saw him first. I will never be able to walk on it. I feel his ghost will enter my soul. It is also a way of respecting the man, you know? His mother had cried so much. We hoped that she would faint and fade away and not have to go through the trauma, but she didn't. His wife did, though. The night before, four masked men had taken him away from his house. He was sleeping after a meal. There were guests. His wife howled, saying how much he loved the turtle curry. When the corpse fell, the blood had splattered around the pole, Pabloo. So much blood."

ANEES SALIM

from *The Blind Lady's Descendants*

In the summer after Sandip's brief liaison with Barbara, he was accepted back into the family. One morning, his father, wearing a cap that had a red anchor embroidered on its black visor, turned up at Mermaid Inn and surveyed the hut with a mixture of approval and disgust. The sea had been closer to turquoise than ever, and tourists had been pouring out of every train that stopped at our station and flocking through the town like it was the colonial times revisiting, an army of white people invading the warm curve of the golden beach, then wading into the lapis lazuli sea, watched over by coastguards. Mermaid Inn had never been livelier. All the three huts had been taken by a group of elderly Norwegians, who checked the harshness of the sun with a hand stuck out of the window before venturing out to the beach. Sandip spent his days on the hammock, his straw hat shielding his eyes. It was the summer when I made some money—guiding tourists around, running errands and pushing a bit of drugs—and kept Mother's grumbling at bay.

Sandip's father took a long walk through the plantation, sizing up his coconut trees. When he came around the huts again, Sandip was still on the hammock, blinded by the straw hat. He pulled up a chair and waited for Sandip to wake up; little did he know that Sandip was wide awake and probably seeing the brilliant fireworks cocaine had ignited under the mat-work of his hat.

"Good morning, Daddy," I said loudly, to warn Sandip.

It was a while before he recognized me. "Hello, Amar," he said coldly. "You have grown up. You too married?" Long years of sailinghad reddened his face and taken away much of his hair, but his air of sarcasm had been left untouched, if not sharpened, by the sea wind.

"I am not married," I said aloud again. But Sandip showed no sign of being warned.

"Why not?" he asked in a complaining voice. "How old are you? Much younger than your friend here?"

"I am twenty-four."

"Too late, Amar," he said, in a voice so rich with concern that I almost started to take him seriously. "Follow your friend's example. Get married. On my next vacation, I want to see you carrying a baby around."

A Norwegian crone came out of a hut in a burgundy brassiere and a white towel around her skinny thighs. She paused on the veranda and looked briefly at us before screwing up her eyes at the horizon.

"Is she my daughter-in-law?" he asked, putting his cap back and swaying lightly on the chair, as if he would get up and go to the hut if she were Barbara.

"No, she left." I lowered my voice.

"Oh, that is sad," he said, eyeing Sandip. "When did that tragedy happen?"

"A year ago," I was practically mumbling now.

"Good morning, handsome," the Norwegian in the burgundy brassiere greeted me as she sauntered past us to the cliff path, shading her eyes with a pale-skinned hand.

"Good morning, Mrs. Peder," I greeted her in a near murmur.

"Son," Sandip's father said in a conspiratorial tone. "She could well be Mrs. Amar if you try hard enough. She called you handsome."

We watched Mrs. Peder go to the cliff's edge and gingerly start the descent to the beach, clawing the side of the narrow stairway.

"When does your friend normally wake up?" he asked, strumming a string of the hammock with a finger. "I just want to have a word with him before I go back to the ship."

"You can talk to me," Sandip's lips moved under the rim of the straw hat. "I am listening."

Sandip's father cast a quick glance at me, surprised. Then he smiled at me, demanding a private audience with his son, but I, failing to see anything more than hurt in his smile, stayed put near the hammock.

"Amar," he said. "I think you should chase your Mrs. Peder. She must be waiting for you under the cliff."

I drifted to the cliff's edge and stood under the headless coconut tree while the two men chatted by the huts. On the sands below, sallow bodies lay on colorful towels, their backs turned to the fierce April sun; two policemen sat on the white rocks, shooing away peeping natives. Behind me, the father and son chatted on, patching up, fighting and patching up again. Then, after about half an hour of quiet arguments, Sandip's father left, waving at me as he started to walk through a grove.

As the summer turned hotter and the sea turned a paler blue, Sandip started to mount his sports bike and ride away to his home on alternate nights. Sometimes he stayed home on weekends, leaving the custody of the huts to me. I wandered down the beach, the top three buttons on my shirt undone and sleeves rolled up to reveal the cuts of my biceps. One afternoon, while strolling past the white rocks, I spotted an elderly couple sitting a good distance away from the sunbathers. They somehow had the look, even from a distance, of people who would readily adopt, having lived all their life without children. They were building a sandcastle, the one they probably had imagined their children would do before they came to know about their inability to reproduce.

My instincts told me they were my passport to another life, another land of sunshine and happiness. I walked to them, looking innocent and orphaned, squinting at my shadow, which appeared to be more eager than me to be with them. A thought struck me as I dragged myself across the hot sand: if they took pity on me and opted for an adoption, my shadow would be the only thing I would be taking to my new life. I could already see it thrown on unfamiliar landscapes, hovering around me in my new environs, sitting pensively by me as I happily wrote Mother a letter of fake nostalgia.

The man looked up from the half-finished castle, and I could not believe my luck.

"Professor Tim from London?" I asked him, joining my palms in the native welcoming gesture which the tourists normally returned in bad, and almost comical, imitation.

"Yes," he said, mildly surprised, a questioning frown forming on his bony face. The lady continued to work on the castle, slapping wet sand on the conical roof with infantile concentration.

"May I sit down near you, Professor Tim?" Many years ago I had picked up a shabby book on etiquette and had been diligently studying passages on good manners, just for a moment like this.

Professor Tim looked at the vast expanse of sand, doubtlessly wondering why I wanted to seek permission to sit down by him when liberal stretches of the beach were available for me. But he gave me consent all the same, with a nearly imperceptible nod of his head.

"There is no reason why you should remember me," I spoke out the words I had been rehearsing from the moment he had looked up from the sand castle.

His eyes were blue, almost the same shade the sea donned that season; I saw fine coral patterns shining in the depths of his eyes as he studied my face. "Obviously there is no reason," he said, rubbing wet sand off his palms.

I forced a short laugh. "More than fifteen years ago, you talked to a group of schoolchildren when they were on their way to school. But I don't expect you to remember it."

"How kind of you," Professor Tim said. Here was a professor very different from the one we had at home; old, overtly short-tempered and in no mood to feign magnanimity. I considered getting up and walking away, probably showing him the middle finger when the lady was not looking. But I had heard of people queuing up in front of embassies for hours, sometimes even a whole day, and failing at the end of it all to get the clearance to cross over to the land of their dreams. This old man's resistance was nothing in comparison; a minor hurdle I was confident of hopping across.

"You asked me why I was crying," I told him, laughing. "I was only a boy of seven."

"So?" he asked threateningly. My face fell.

"Give him a rupee and get rid of him," the lady told him in what was supposed to be a murmur, but I heard her loud and clear, and she knew I had heard her.

"And you told my sister that she looked like Sophia Loren."

The lady looked up sharply from the castle, not at me but at Professor Tim, who still seemed to be untouched by the information. "T," she said with an expression of wonder in her eyes. "She was the one you mentioned in your travelogue. A family of children going to school down a narrow road and a young girl who surprised you with her adorable Mediterranean features."

"No," he said, twirling the tip of his thin, gray moustache. "That was in Syria. In Damascus."

"No, T, that was indeed in India," she said, taking her hands off the castle. "In Damascus it was a group of children bunking school and playing marbles under a date palm. The Sophia Loren look-alike was in India."

"Really?" he held her gaze for a moment, then he turned his head to me with his cheeks lumping up in a smile. "Thank you for recognizing me after all these years."

At the far end of the beach, a catamaran was being pushed into the sea, and men were hopping in as it started to float. The couple watched the waves rock the catamaran and the men crouch when the surf towered over them. We sat watching the catamaran until it turned into a speck. The lady picked up bits of crab shell and poked them into the sand structure, riveting the doors of her lop-sided castle. Her architecture complete, she sat back, propping herself on hands that reminded me of Barbara's. Lost in admiration of their creation, the couple sat in silence, waiting for a wave to raze it. I rose to my feet, somehow comforted by the fact that the children of the Bungalow were immortalized in print; I wondered how those who read his travelogue pictured the four of us, dressed in green-and-white uniforms, carrying sand-colored satchels, heading hurriedly to the school that filled our ears with the sound of the sea. Maybe they just raced through the passage, not bothering to visualize us; maybe Professor Tim had buried us in the vivid description of the mud road lined with coconut trees, maybe in their imaginations we were faceless, a group of children springing up in the beginning of a sentence and fading out at the end of it. Lives lived between two tiny full stops. Nevertheless, I felt deeply gratified, and regarded it as a more meaningful discovery than the one that brought Javi to my life. I had forgotten to abide by the book of etiquette and was walking away without saying goodbye when I heard Professor Tim's voice behind me.

"You come to the beach often?"

I froze in my stride, pleased to know that the encounter was not yet over. "Yes, Professor Tim. I work as a tour guide. And that is where my office is." I pointed to the headless coconut tree slanting out of the cliff. "It is called Mermaid Inn. And I am called Amar."

"Nice meeting you," Professor Tim waved at me. "Thanks again for remembering me."

The next morning—Sandip was away as it was a Sunday and he now used Sundays to get deeper into his family fabric—I was watching the slivers of light glinting on the hut ceiling when the sound of footsteps drew me to the door. Professor Tim stood in the garden, the lady a few feet away from him, her hands crossed at the base of her spine. She was leaning over to sniff a blood-colored hibiscus, the long stamen of which was threatening to invade her wide open nostrils. There was a rolled-up sheet of paper in Professor Tim's hands, and a crinkled smile on his face.

"You are a guide?" he asked. "We would like you to take us around."

My heart sank a little, though I quickly put on the acquiescing smile of a tour guide as he climbed the steps to the veranda and unrolled the sheet of paper on the wooden table. A typical tourist's map, the places that caught his fancy were circled in red ink, a hill station here, a lake there, many ruined forts across its corrugated terrain. A big question mark had been drawn over our town, which appeared to be nothing more than a beach fenced around by coconut trees.

"We want to start with a trip around the town." He tapped on the question mark with the end of a sketch pen. "Tell me what there is to see."

Except for the beach, there was hardly anything worth seeing in our town, no charming ruins, no flowering gardens, not even a decent pond topped with water lilies. To the red question mark on the map, which seemed to ask *What is there to see?* the honest answer was *Nothing*. Unless you thought a few furlongs of darkness could attract these two aging Brits.

"There is a tunnel the British built nearly a century ago. And a few temples. You and I can see those from the outside, but are not allowed inside. And a fisherman's village around the rocks."

"An Englishman's tunnel seems to be interesting. My wife's father was an engineer who built bridges and tunnels in imperial India. What do you say, Nancy?" The lady was by his side now, the tip of her nose coated with yellow pollen from the hibiscus.

"You have my approval, T," she said. "But don't expect to see Dad's name on this tunnel. He has never been down south."

"So tunnel it is," Professor Tim confirmed. "When can we start?"

"Not today," Nancy said. "I have my yoga classes to attend."

"Well, tomorrow then," he said, rolling up the map and holding it behind his back. Halfway down the short flight of stairs, he paused and looked over his shoulder, as if I had called him from behind. "How is your sister, the Sophia Loren one?"

"She died long back,'" I found myself saying with a painful smile.

"I am sorry," said Nancy, looking genuinely so.

"What happened?" There was shock in Professor Tim's voice. His fingers fidgeted with one end of the rolled-up map.

"Drowned," I said without any qualms, remembering how she had stormed out of the Bungalow the day the timber merchant was at our doorstep.

"We are both really sorry," Nancy said. "We will start tomorrow after my morning yoga session. Nine o'clock sharp."

But the next morning, we had to wait almost half an hour outside the yoga center, a rectangular shed sitting on the edge of a coconut grove, before she emerged in a lilac frock, a handbag of the same shade dangling from the crook of her arm. Professor Tim had a camera slung around his neck; as we waited for Nancy to finish her yoga classes, he had stood back and taken pictures of the shed from various angles.

We drove along the laterite road, the same one Barbara had traversed after the wedding, with the blue of the sea shimmering in the distance. I heard the camera click several times in the backseat and knew he was photographing my profile with the windshield as the backdrop.

We entered the tunnel from the mosque's side and walked slowly into the thickening darkness. Me in front, holding a torch, Professor Tim and Nancy close behind me, holding hands, led by the weak circle of light I shone intermittently on the track. When they paused to glance up, I tilted the beam up and formed a circle of light on the ceiling.

"Awesome," Nancy exclaimed, as if she had seen paintings on the ceiling. Once we were halfway from the two circular points of sunlight, I shone the torch on a side wall near the shoulder of concrete and held the beam so steady for a minute that they screwed up their eyes to see what was there, other than stunted clumps of thistles.

"This was where my uncle's body was found many years ago," I said calmly, like describing a little-known tourist spot.

Even in the darkness, I could see them exchange glances.

"He killed himself."

"Oh," said Nancy.

"Why?" asked Professor Tim.

"I don't know," I said with dramatic indifference. "I was born on the same night he killed himself."

"Which is the shortest way out of this place?" Nancy asked after a short spell of silence. "I want to go out."

"Why, Nancy? It is quite interesting out here."

"Not for me, T." She had already started down the track, the lilac handbag rocking in the crook of her arm as she walked towards the red glimmer of the railway signal.

The sea-blue paint that had been put on the walls just before Jasira's wedding had turned a light brown, streaked with blotches of dirt years of rain had left on them. Many bars in the gate had started to rust; some spindly plants had taken root in the front garden and hid several ground-floor windows. The sorry state of the Bungalow inspired a new thought in me: this childless couple—by now I was sure that they did not have children—might take pity on me if they saw the ruins that surrounded me.

"This is my house." I pointed to the Bungalow as we walked past the signal post.

"Very nice," Nancy said. "Very tropical in design."

"Amar," Professor Tim said, addressing me for the first time by my name. "Isn't that your name? I was wondering if we could just sneak into your house."

I was completely unprepared for this. But I knew the coast was clear. Father was away at Uncle Syed's, Jasira had not called us since the last fight and Akmal must have left for the radio mechanic's shop. Bringing these tourists home was sort of showing Mother my work credentials. And the state of things inside the Bungalow could just work as a bonus.

"My pleasure, Professor Tim."

Mother, when she opened the door and stepped out into the portico, looked ready to faint. She just could not stop shifting her gaze from me to Nancy and back. Many young tourist guides who worked on the beach often brought home foreign wives, and when the news of Sandip's wedding reached the Bungalow, Mother had made me put a hand on her head and promise her not to turn a tourist into her daughter-in-law. Now at the mere sight of Nancy, who looked any day older than Mother herself, she stared as if I had gone back on my word and was trying to sneak Nancy into the Bungalow. She placed her hands firmly on the door frame, blocking the way, her eyes on the brink of brimming over. Then she saw Professor Tim standing near the portico pillar, taking pictures of the clump of sugar canes and the washing stone.

"They are tourists, Mother," I muttered. "Let them in."

A hesitant smile broke over her confused expression and she took her hands off the ledge and stepped aside. Nancy joined her palms and bowed slightly, and Mother held a hand to her lips and giggled through her fingers. Remembering the story in which the Sophia Loren of the house had drowned, Professor Tim dropped his chin to his chest.

"Our condolences," he said to Mother. She broke into a new fit of giggling.

"Welcome to our small home, Americans." Akmal stormed into the front room, rearranging the Kufi cap on his stupid head. It was a wonder how easily Professor Tim understood Akmal's jumble of an accent and replied promptly. He held up a victory sign to Akmal and said, "Two minor corrections. First, this is not a small house. I would like to call it a little mansion." He folded one finger. "Second, we are not Americans. We are English." When he tucked in the second finger, it looked as though he wanted to punch Akmal with the clenched fist.

"Same thing," Akmal mumbled. "What you do for your bread?"

"You mean how do I like my bread? Plain or toasted?"

"No, no," Akmal waved his hand across his lap. "I mean your job."

"Okay, how do I earn a living? I am a professor."

"What an accident!" Akmal exclaimed. "My brother-in-law is also a professor."

"Yes, a pleasant coincidence," Professor Tim stroked his camera. "Tell me what you do for *your* bread."

"I am a radio mechanic," Akmal announced proudly. "My mechanic shop is closed today." There was a new quality of calmness in his voice, a new discipline to his smile, which he kept lit on his lips as he sat chatting to Professor Tim, and brightened up by a few watts when, just before they were to leave the Bungalow, we lined up around Grandma and stood still in front of Professor Tim's camera. It was Nancy's idea.

"T," I overheard Nancy as Professor Tim was about to click. "I have a caption for this picture, if you are going to put this in your book."

"I haven't decided yet," Professor Tim said pensively, his finger hovering over the button.

"Would you care to listen to the caption?"

"Go on," he mumbled, his eye glued to the viewfinder.

"Blind lady's descendants," she said it like a short prayer and the flash washed over us like a muted thunderbolt. We broke up shyly and escorted them out of the house.

It was then, at that instant of the camera clicking, the flash blinding us for a moment and Nancy pronouncing a title for the photograph; it was then that the seed of this memoir was sown in me. I instantly decided to write it in English, not because I was good at it, but because I thought of it as an appendage to the picture Professor Tim had taken and would probably put in his new travelogue. The title, thanks to Nancy, was ready. In the days that followed, I thought of starting to write it, but not until a couple of months ago did I find the right beginning and commence writing it, a running commentary of our commonplace lives. And not a single day has passed since without a new page being written, for I feel if there is nothing more to add, I am as good as dead.

K. R. MEERA

Ave Maria

Translated from Malayalam by J. Devika

The day PG forswore EM, rage welled up again inside Immanuel. Storm clouds piled heavy as he got off the bus at Moscow Junction. Thunder rumbled beneath his footsteps as he strode towards Chorakkod, the house. Jumping over the fence, a flash of lightning, he climbed on to the veranda's mud floor. "Thieving whore!" he roared. Sixty-five-year-old Anna ran to the neighbor's. Sixty-four-year-old Mary hid beneath the cot, muttering terrified prayers. On her coir cot, poor paralytic fifty-nine-year-old Lourdes wet herself again. Immanuel's varicose legs furiously kicked open the door, already reduced to mere planks by kicks and more kicks of the past. Inside, as his weak, long-sighted eyes searched in the dark, Immanuel bellowed, "DIRTY WHORE! Come out, Mariakutty, comrade Mariakutty, soviet Mariakutty, socialist Mariakutty, republic Mariakutty, Chinese Mariakutty, YOU WON'T SEE ANOTHER SUNRISE! I'LL CUT OFF YOUR HEAD! PULP YOUR WOMB! GULP YOUR BLOOD! WASH THIS HOUSE WITH IT! MAKE A COMMIE RED GARLAND OUT OF YOUR BLOODY GUTS! THEN SURRENDER TO THE POLICE. THE POLICE ARE PEANUTS, YOU BITCH!"

Immanuel can't see in the dark. Mariakutty lay quiet, pressing herself to the ground. Immanuel's cracked feet would search the floor. Bursting with anger, they would hit against each wall. They would kick at every corner. Sometimes at Anna's torn mat, folded up. Sometimes at Marykutty's bundle. Or at a dried-up coconut found somewhere, fallen off a tree. Or a piece of yam, begged off the neighbors. In between these Mariakutty would lie curled up like an iron sickle. Immanuel would not see clearly. He would kick everywhere. Crush and bruise anything that resisted. Keep on spewing curses. And then, sometimes, she would be found. Hauled up on a single arm. Just about ten kilos. Nine kilos of bones. The meat, just a kilo. Skin. Eighty-nine years. They are all like that. Age goes up, weight goes down. When bones age, the flesh hangs. Immanuel would toss them around, playing the cat's game with the mouse. Crush them. Grind them to the ground. Kicking, hitting, throwing, Immanuel would tire. His dhoti would loosen halfway down. His shirt would be soaked, sweaty. Sweat drops would roll on his bald head, like on a lotus leaf. Eyes would redden and half close. About to collapse, he would stop. Get out. Go the way he came, head bowed. Anna would come back from her running away. Mary would chant aloud, Praise the Lord, Praise the Lord. Lourdes, relieved, would wet herself again.

At night, Immanuel would return, like a lame dog. Anna and Mary and Lourdes would have slept. He would sit on the soiled armchair on the veranda. In his tired voice, he would call, "Mother . . ." Pull out the rum bottle from his dhoti. Pour out the liquor into a clean or not-so-clean glass kept underneath the armchair. Sit there without sipping, staring into the darkness. Mariakutty would then slowly raise herself up, along the wall. Come out carefully, measuring the floor with her weak eyes. A bit of lime pickle in her broken-edged tin plate. Or a washed green chilli. Sliding the plate close to Immanuel's feet, Mariakutty would sit on the floor, leaning against the wall, silent. Immanuel would take in his drink slowly. Suck at the pickle, in between. Stare at the dark, thinking of the concrete houses sprouting up in the fields, or of the battery factory where the communist paccha weeds thrived. Drink a bit. Think a bit. Drinking, thinking, drinking, thinking, he would fall asleep. Legs would be raised up on the chair. They would curl up when the sleep thickened. He would curl into a C, like a tiny baby in its cradle. Suck his thumb in slumber deep. Sob in his dreams. Shake with laughter. Then Mariakutty would stretch her bones and get up. Cover him with her cloth. Wipe the spittle oozing on his grayed beard. Close the open liquor bottles, straighten up the fallen-down ones, push them behind the chair. Creep back inside with the curry plate. Get herself down on the floor with effort. It is then that heavy tears condense. "IngilaSindaba . . ." she would chant in a shattered voice.

That's an old habit. Something that Cholakkot Varkey taught her. Varkey, the son of a Varkey, who was the son of an earlier Varkey, of Cholakkot. Known those days as Cholakkodan. Until Putuppally and Toppilaan got to him. Chorakkodan, afterwards. Born rebel. He saw Mariakutty, whose parents had died, now bullied by sisters-in-law. Got her a new blouse stitched out of thick white mulmul. Took her to church to marry. Taught her to cook chilli-and-tapioca. To fry beef with pepper. To reap. To winnow. To be tickled, and to laugh. To play at tiffs and to fret. To give birth to chubby little ones every year. Anna, Mary, Magdalene, Maria . . . when Lourdes was in her womb, Putuppally, Toppilaan and Potty Sir started appearing. Bidi lights glowed among the tapioca. The kerosene lamp Maria lit began to hear controlled whispers. Anna's slate began to know the shape of the sickle. Baby Maggie began to lisp, IngilaSindaba. He brimmed over when asked about the meaning of it. Mariakutty, golden one, hot-sweet love, my own wine glass, my daily bread, holy mother. That is a novena. A novena to recite, to call upon. Call upon? Who? Call upon good times. A good time. A time when no one will be sad. Be warned, the police's blows will come—yes, some will come; be warned, the jail—yes, that'll happen; and what about the kids and me? That's what I'm sad about. Why sad? I can also take a few blows. Hey Mariye, you silly, these are police blows. Oh, big deal, I've had five or six kids! But, Mariye, still . . . Oh, if no one will go hungry, what's the big deal in suffering a few blows?

So you bred like swine, didn't you? Immanuel spat out as he delivered another kick. You put together wizened old crones, not worth five rupees, didn't you? Why? Couldn't you kill them? Cut them into pieces and fry them in pepper? No, I'll do it myself, I'll kill these swine myself. He ran after his sisters. The kidney patient, Anna. Her swollen body. She would run, and she would fall. The tattered nightgown, the neighbor's gift, would tear. She would scream aloud. The mental patient, Mary. She would tug hard at her gray hair. He cometh to deliver the sinners, she would yell. Lourdes would wet herself in fear. The son's roaring. The daughters' screaming. Mariakutty shut her eyes tight. Eyes grown rheumy from seeing, seeing. Eyes rusted from crying, crying. They are all like that. Rust to iron. Termite to wood. They would crumble, speck by speck. Break off, inch by inch. The night the policemen bit the dust at Sooranad. The beginning of the flight. Five tiny kids. Three small bundles. A babe in the left arm, still at the breast. A toddler in the right. Children, left and right. Don't cry. Don't play. Don't laugh. Don't make a sound. Don't say Mama's and Papa's name. Walk. Walk fast. I'm hungry, Mother. A little water, Mama. Anna wants to lie down. Mary wants to be picked up. Maria wants beddie-bed. The January sun beat down. The children wilt. Fall. First, Adoor. From there, Kottarakkara. Be careful. There's a reward on Chorakkodan's head. A thousand rupees. A cool thousand. The never-fully-counted one thousand of those days. The heart beats hard, seeing someone on the way. If he looked again, the knees knock. Walk, walk, and finally a house at Valakam. Cooked gruel under the coconut tree. Laid out the mat on the step of the cowshed. The children slept like logs. The eyes then shut, with ears open, and hear muffled sobs. Mariakutty, my jar of wine, sweet grapes . . . let's go—the kids are sleeping, let them. Take only the infant. What are you saying?—No other way. They are my mark. Five children.—Oh, my womb burns.—Mariye, call out, IngilaSindaba.—My heart will smoulder.—IngilaSindaba.—Our Annakutty. Marykutty, little Maggie, Maria-baby . . .—Mariye, IngilaSindaba . . .—the tiny girl, Maria . . .—IngilaSindaba . . . our Maria . . . Ingila . . .

IngilaSindaba. Immanuel was finished, shattered. He panted from the labor. Pulled up his dhoti and got out. Mariakutty lay on the cold ground and chanted.—IngilaSindaba. She didn't know he had left. Her mind was at the hilltop. Life in hiding. Tears, like rain, so copious, one drop would fill a pot. Little ones, four little ones. Scattered. Three were lost. Little Maria fell. Little Maria, who held out the light for Putuppally and Toppilaan. Little Maria, who had lisped and giggled, Ingila. Hungry, worn, crying, crying, crying, mama, mama, mama, delirious little Maria. The police waited, she was the bait. At night Papa stole in. Swooped her up. Gave the slip to the police. A whole day and night inside the brushwood. He came, with dried blood stains all over. On Papa's shoulder lay Maria, like a wilted vine. Opened her eyes at Mama's touch. An upward glance, like the dying flame's leap. She was buried on the hilltop. The arrest came that night. The police growled all around the bottom of the hill.—Mariakutty don't give in. They'll catch me. Beat me up. Kick me. Even kill me, perhaps. But if I'm alive, I'll come back. You must hang on.—I will, don't flinch. No, we'll all go. But the good time will come, it will.

Back at the village. Where it was home. No walls, door, just the foundation. The wife of Chorakkodan, murderer of six policemen. No warmth in anyone to offer a drink of water. No spunk to offer work. Only the police came. Six or seven, can't remember right. The blouse got torn off. The dhoti flew off. The wailing baby flew, too. It broke its back on the hard ground outside. That infant never crawled on fours. Didn't sit. Walk. That's Lourdes. The kid who peed in laughter, in tears, in terror. Nothing to eat. To wear. Nothing to feed the half-paralyzed baby sucking hard at shrunken breasts. The police came in turns. Handcuffed her, and then raped. She shut her eyes tight and prayed—IngilaSindaba. They dipped the broken-down infant in water to produce different kinds of screams. People gaped. Communist wench. Hardy stuff. The ploughed-up soil sprouted. People laughed. Did you hear? The wife of the jailed comrade is pregnant. That's socialist pregnancy. Communist pregnancy. Just wait, the kid's going be born with a hammer and sickle. She gave birth, all alone, inside a thatched parting. Cut the umbilical cord by herself. A boy. The Virgin hath given birth. He was named Immanuel.

No one would give her work. But visitors arrived at night before the broken-down door of the house. Chorakkodan's wife Mariakutty thus became socialist Mariakutty. She wandered in search of her lost children. Found them, in the end. Anna, at Alleppy. A servant in a house. Mary, at Ambalappuzha. Begging. Anna came running, shouting aloud, Mama, Mama . . . Mary stared for a while. Then collapsed in a faint. Maggie wasn't found. Lost, somewhere. Where? Taken by the beggars? Thrust into some churchyard to beg, with legs broken, eyes gouged? The womb burned. Nipples smouldered. Maggie, Maria, babies borne in the womb all ten months. Babies brought forth in pain. Babies fed at the breast to the heart's content. Little fingers that caressed Mama's face, and tiny mouths pressed around nipples. Tiny mouths that pulled off the breast without warning and shaped into roguish smiles. The marks of Papa's love. The tokens of Mama's devotion. My Maggie, my Maria, my Immanuel. Two years, thus. He came back. The man who went inside unbowed. He came out bowed, crooked. They looked at each other, intently, for a long time. His lips moved. She didn't hear. Maybe it was to call her, Mariye, my own. My Mariakutty, my jar of wine, my wine glass, maybe all this. Didn't hear. Mariakutty handed him the child. Chorakkodan took him. Pressed him to his chest. The husband broke down and wept. The wife murmured—IngilaSindaba.

Immanuel walked to Moscow Junction, exhausted. The long gray hair swung, touching his shoulder. He scratched the bald patch, in between. Immanuel. He whispered. Bastard. The seed of six policemen. Six men. Immanuel spat out in hate. Revolution, his mother's cunt! Chorakkodan, son of a thief. Didn't let me call him father. Called him Comrade, only that. Never called me son. Only Comrade. Grew up hearing a new story every birthday. People pointed to him each of the six. Put bets on whose resemblance was clearest. As Immanuel grew, Chorakkodan waned. More of silence, less of talk. The night the Party split, he got mightily drunk. Came home with a big bottle. Called to her one more time, Mariakutty, my own wine-jar. Cook me some tapioca. Told jokes from the lock-up. Described the different blows in jail. Relished Mariakutty's chilli-and-tapioca doused with oil. Got the kids together around him one last time. Caressed them all one last time. Kissed Mariakutty one last time. Lay dead the next day, blood seeping from the corner of his mouth.

Acchu's petty shop. Immanuel bought a bottle. The illicit stuff. Walked back, stuffing it in his dhoti. His first drink was from what was left in the bottle Chorakkodan brought before his death. The first sip was sour. He felt, then, that it would be the last. Got a job in the factory. Fell in love with the girl who worked with him. Was shattered when she said, "I don't want a bastard." He went to a whore that night, in rage. When she shut the door and slipped off her clothes, he saw his mother. Six policemen. Mother, all alone. Mother, naked. Blood-soaked. The Ingila rang in his ears. He heard the infant's scream from the front yard. He ran out, frenzied. He tried again and again. Many experiments. Many whores. Women of many kinds. But when each woman shed her clothes, he collapsed. Was shattered in the dark, in the light, at night, in the day. Each time he went back to beat up Maria. Drank in the veranda till daybreak. Called Mama for company. Mariakutty came out, silent. In the white tin plate, there would be meat, sometimes, sometimes fish. Or mangos. Or just green chillies. Immanuel would stretch in the armchair. Sip his drink, slowly. Forget that he beat up his mother. Mother would forget the beating, too. Staring into the dark where the crickets raised slogans, Maria would wait. Then, gradually, he got off women. In between there was a strike in the factory. A lockout. He lost his job. Immanuel tried many things. Was never able to stick to anything. Never got a decent wage. Never managed a full stomach. Never calmed his mind. Wants lay stagnant. Whenever he saw a jatha, heard slogans or a speech, he went berserk. Maria would be pounded on those days.

The house was near. Immanuel became enraged, again. Thunder rang in his swollen feet, again. A storm gathered on his face. He jumped over the fence, into the veranda. Reached out for the Furedan, bought from Vijayan's manure shop. Shook half of it into the glass. Sat back in the armchair and called Mother. Maria, ten kilos heavy, eighty-nine years old, wobbled out. Pushed the white tin plate with the last green chilli to his feet. Immanuel took in his drink, drained out. Maria waited, silent. Everyone will forswear someone one day, before the cock crows. Everyone will crucify someone between two thieves, one day. Will make someone drink sour wine. Stab someone in the breast. Throw someone into a tomb carved in the boulders. At the door of the vault, some Maria alone will wait, weeping for the man she loved.

Notes:

The day PG forswore EM: PG and EM refer to two communist stalwarts in Kerala: the highly-respected communist party intellectual, P Govinda Pillai aligned with the Communist Party of India - Marxist (CPM), and the leading figure of the communist movement and Kerala's first Communist Chief Minister, E. M. S. Namboothiripad. Pillai's critical remarks about Namboothiripad in an interview he gave to a literary magazine in 2003—claiming that the latter lacked originality and vision—roused a storm in the CPM and was perceived as almost patricide.

IngilaSindaba: from the Urdu/Hindustani phrase "Inquilab Zindabad" which translates as "Long live the revolution."

babies borne in the womb all ten months: in Kerala, the period of pregnancy is referred to as "paathu maasam" or ten months.

jatha: demonstration.

SEJAL SHAH

Climate, Man, Vegetation
for LeeAnne

It was our country at night. We were walking toward the water and I could hear the runners beginning to run. We were walking toward the row of cars and soon you would find your car and I would have to find mine. It smelled like summer in the suburbs: rhubarb and forget-me-nots. Day turning to night, and me looking for my car keys, holding you up. You had the look of someone who would later buy apples and forget the loaf of bread. After class, the jangle of car keys, the bloom of sweat between your breasts, across your back like silent wings: this is what I remember.

Do you know that smell? You said it smelled like dill. I said no, rosemary and pavement. You said it smells like water rising. I said thyme, black pepper. You said it smelled like grass. Boiled carrots, I said. Cut grass and carrots.

This was the summer I couldn't get up most days. I saw you maybe three or four times. You were getting ready to move.

They said it was sciatica, but I knew it started in the brain. My brain was stuck. It said to itself over and over, it smells like the suburbs at night! This made sense to me.

At night, before bed, I read an old world geography book. It is predisposed toward mountains. "Mountains," it says, "always stand boldly, form the relief in the landscape." I read about the vertical distribution of mountain vegetation and the importance of trade. I read that south of the polar tundra is the taiga. Different things grow there. There is no relief.

It was a book from a school district that no longer exists. It was a book that came from a library sale. Of course, the countries had different names.

I see the girl who thinks she looks like you. I used to hate her. I used to try and say hello. Now, she laughs when I pass and I can't think of anything to say. She picks at her hair and laughs and laughs. Her mouth is a blot of lipstick. She is proud of her boyfriend. She shows us a ring of keys, heavy with her keys, heavier with his. Her mouth is bougainvillea: common, red.

It's no one's fault. They said take this pill. This one or that one, two before sleep. Take four: in the morning or at night. It's best to avoid alcohol. May cause drowsiness, nausea, lack of appetite, lack of useful secretions, the presence of useful inhibitions. These things, they said, happen sometimes. There is no relief.

Your husband has finished his degree and you are getting ready to move. I will have to return your black shelves and the lamp that needs re-wiring. I used the lamp to hang my hats on. Four hats and three of them are dark colors. Each time we talk on the telephone, words fly faster and faster. I imagine them to be bubbles in water. Each word a country, inhabited and blue. These words: they are nearly beautiful that way.

GAIUTRA BAHADUR

The Stained Veil

Ramchand's death, in Connecticut, in his late sixties, was unexpected. He was a diabetic, but one who watched what he ate, strictly monitoring his calories, and who walked every day at the same hour, clocking his time precisely. He retired even earlier than usual that evening, complaining of indigestion. When his wife Rani followed an hour later, she found him gasping for air on her bed. They slept in the same room, but they had not slept together for many years. Later, the emergency room nurses found thousands of dollars in immaculate $100 notes, stuffed into his trouser pockets. Ramchand distrusted banks. His account had been seized by the government when they fled their country, so he kept a substantial amount of cash hidden in their bedroom in Bridgeport. Even Rani didn't know where. Although Ramchand had gone into cardiac arrest with no history of heart trouble to warn him, somehow he understood that his time had come. He understood enough to lie on that bed, hers not his, with money enough on his body to bury him.

At the funeral home, she betrayed little emotion as she received the procession of relatives who had come to pay their respects. They had come from up and down the East Coast and a few from as far away as Florida and Toronto to say goodbye. As they filed past, they registered her otherworldly quiet, an eerie halo encircling her as she sat in the front row. A niece knelt beside her to whisper a consoling memory of Ramchand, the year he was mayor, riding around on a bicycle with a basket in front to meet his constituents in the little market town near their village. Remembering how seriously he had taken to his role, Rani smiled to herself. He had been a figurehead, really, a token Indian in the ruling African party.

"Uncle Ram gone," she said, squeezing the girl's hand.

There was only the slightest quiver in Rani's voice. Her children did not know what to make of her composure. Over the years, they had seen her entire body shake with emotion, during almost epileptic breakdowns. Perhaps the anti-depressants had numbed her. Even at the crematorium, as the mechanical maw closed around the coffin and their son flipped the incinerator's switch, turning on the wails of the women in the room along with the flames, Rani shed her tears silently.

In the car, on the way back to the house, she told her son-in-law how pleased she was with the memorial service. So many people had come from so far away—and once she reprimanded their eldest grandchild, who didn't want to deliver a eulogy, the young woman had complied, finding between grief and shyness a few words of strangled tribute. Her granddaughter had done her duty as the firstborn, and this had satisfied Rani's sense of *dharma*. If the girl had not found her voice, Ramchand would not have liked it.

After this terse expression of approval, Rani retreated into herself, humming. She looked out of the window, beyond the narrow streets and the row of houses leaning together for support, beyond the squat city of ruined factories and empty warehouses where they had spent the last twenty years, their American years. The song she was humming took her back to a place where she could be alone with the task of remembering Ramchand.

The turning point in their marriage had happened before they emigrated. While at first he could not ration his glasses of rum, in later days he was frugal to a fault, counting closely the coins he earned as a shopkeeper as well as the affection he gave as a husband. Ramchand had gone from excess to austerity, and each had been cruel in its own way.

As a young man, he had been fond of race horses and drink. Sometimes, he lost himself so deeply, he threatened violence. On too many afternoons, dread coiled in their house on Cloud Nine Avenue, like a cobra that had somehow stolen in.

To keep him from the rum-shop, their eldest daughter would lock herself in their bedroom with his clothes. When he was forty-one, he quit drinking, yet the attention he paid Rani was no less measured out. He transferred his fervor from the bottle to Hinduism; clasped his faith with the same desperate logic and need for solace as his daughter used to clasp his clothes behind a barred bedroom door. From the moment that Ramchand found the gods, for the rest of his life he would be their devotee, just as Rani was, and would continue to be, his.

She had spent almost all her life by his side. All her years, except the first sixteen, had belonged to Ramchand, to his shop, to his children—the three who survived and the four who didn't. Grief would collect beneath her bones in layers, a still but gestating thing, gathering and sedimenting with each infant's loss. This kind of mourning, this slow and silent unbecoming wasn't one she could ever have imagined in her first sixteen years.

Those years had unfolded in the shelter of a father enlightened enough to let Rani stay in school, just long enough to learn to read and write and count—skills that later served her well as a shopkeeper's wife. She had been the cosseted darling, the youngest and the prettiest of the Mohabir daughters, the one who most gracefully wore the dainty shoes, respectable handbags and store-bought dresses that were the relics of her family's faded prosperity.

In those sixteen years of rooted innocence, she had known place and its boundaries intimately. There was her family's rice mill, where cattle moved in circles in the yard, crushing paddy underfoot around a threshing pole. On Saturdays, she would go to Miss Evie's bungalow—Miss Evie who taught her to sew and knit, whose son, Esau, would one day become a composer of classical music in another country. Once, she'd peeked through a back window of the Kali temple down the road, only to run home sick to the stomach at the sight of the blood of a sacrificed goat. That was the extent of her transgression and thrill.

The village sat unassumingly on the edge of endless rows of flowering cane, but hidden in its tall quiet, it contained too much drama for the good of its inhabitants. Too much story, coiled like snakes in the cane. Her father used to say in rounded and swaying dialect, while observing his girls in some fracas, some private disagreement that had embroiled them: *Ayu get too much o' story wid ayu self.*

That's what it was like in Lovely Lass.

Rani crossed the boundaries of this world for the first time when she married Ramchand. Whim, his village, was a half-day's journey from hers, near the next big sugar estate down the coast. Her father had chosen for her a young man from a devout family, high-caste but humble before god. What Rani had noticed was how handsome he was, his features symmetrical and angular, his face cut with precision, like a dark jewel. He was as dark as she was fair.

When decades later, she and Ramchand left for America in late middle age, she would remember this first migration from her father's home to her in-laws'. There was nothing that could match it for daring. It was the most routine, inevitable thing a girl could do. And the most terrifying. After that, what move could possibly be as bold?

Rani didn't understand it at the time, but ever since she was a child, the older women at work in the rice fields and the kitchens were singing her fate just as they sang their own. So many of the folk songs they taught her had been about a bride going to her in-laws' house, and a stained veil had often featured in them. It would be her destiny as it had been theirs.

Their in-law songs, those *sasurals*, held a heroine's fear and wonder on crossing an unspeakable threshold. The songs had featured in the Bollywood movies screening at The Astor, the cinema house in New Amsterdam, the town nearby. Of course, Rani was not there to see Meena Kumari as the courtesan in *Dil Hi To Hai*, crooning "Laaga Chunari Mein Daag" with eyes that mourned, yet feet that stamped and hips that pivoted. The boys in the village would skip school to catch the pivoting hips, but that was their privilege. As a girl, how did she dare? She wasn't at the matinees, as the boys were, over and over again, to hear the sensual tragedienne sing: "How will I go to my in-laws with a stained veil?"

A good girl from a good family, she would never settle into a scarlet cushioned seat next to boys who might wonder how precisely the veil had become stained: Was it from sex or violence? Did they know yet that the two could exist together, in the same moment's loss?

The image had come from Kabir, a saint-poet from the land that her ancestors had left generations ago. As Rani sewed in the yard, or helped her mother grind *dal* in the kitchen, she would chant:

> *You must leave your home forever*
> *Putting on a veil you will go to meet your beloved*

> *You must leave your home forever*
> *This veil of yours is stained*
> *The neighbor women jeer*

These words written some four centuries earlier would fly away from her as she formed them, their meaning difficult and strange. When she was big enough, the old women tried to tell her how to make sense of the poems. Imagine the father's house as the world we know, the earth, they said—and trust that the husband's house is a higher reality, the mystical. Trust was their instruction and refrain. When you go to your marriage bed, they explained, the stain will be the spot that proves you are pure; but know also what Kabir knew, that the besmirched veil is the physical world, the impure body that we must all cast off in death. Rani was perplexed. Kabir didn't seem to know the difference between a dirge and a bride's ballad. Did death and marriage call for the same song? Rani might have been forgiven for wondering, as she intoned:

> *You will never escape this body's betrayal,*
> *Wrinkling and bunching with time.*
> *You must leave your home forever.*
>
> *Kabir says: when you seek to understand*
> *You will always fail.*
>
> *Kabir says: any song your body sings*
> *Is a death song*
> *What bride wears her veil*
> *In the presence of her beloved?*
>
> *Cast it off.*
> *You must leave for your real home.*

When Rani arrived at the little white house standing on stilts, so like the bandy-legged egrets that alighted in the rice fields, her in-laws were kind. They were not the cruel ones foretold in so many *sasurals*, the ones where mothers-in-law slapped their daughters-in-law for failing to make perfectly round *rotis* or fathers-in-law loomed, with the rancid smell of stale bush rum on their breath. Ma and Pa doted on her. Ramchand was both loving, and not. It was easy to admire him. He looked like a matinee idol, with thick, oiled curls and a cocksure grin that betrayed his knowledge of just how convincing his jawline was; on his face light and motion played, in eternal boyishness. What dealt the final blow, making him irresistible, was the vulnerable undertow in otherwise scampish eyes.

Ramchand's father had sweated in the cane fields, and so had his mother. They wanted better for him—and Rani was definitely that. Her family had some position. Their business, though struggling then, had once been robust. As early as the thirties, Mohabir Enterprises was exporting rice overseas, all the way to the islands; they had an office in New Amsterdam, and it even had a telephone.

At eighteen, what did Ramchand have, besides his ambition and eyes that seduced? When she arrived, with a spangled *chunari* too proud to be stained, he had Rani. To have her, as his wife, was one path to the prosperous world that his confidence had marked as his own. Success was rightly his. And when he removed her veil that first night, it was with a tender kind of possessiveness. Whose woman was she? She and all that she represented was his, to do with as he pleased.

It's hard to know how he learned what he pleased to do that night. He could not have learned it from the Bollywood movies at The Astor, with their strategic cutaways, leaving kisses suspended in the imagination, somewhere between intention and execution. There were no scripts for it there, nor in the songs that Rani was taught. Or perhaps she just hadn't known how to decode them. She knew only that she liked Ramchand and wished to please him. She knew, too, that blood rushed to her shoulders when he took her by the hand and led her into their bedroom. The sensation was bewildering, a strange kind of levitation, as if she were both anchored in her body and floating outside it.

"Come," he had said.

The command was gentle. And he spoke softly to her, admiring her beauty, expressing wonder at the depth of innocence in her eyes, telling her how proud it made him to nuzzle a nose as sculpted as hers. Her fair shoulders, again, blushed. He undid her blouse to reveal them, a few shades less scarlet than her sari, and instead of turning those innocent eyes away, she looked directly into his own. They had a liquid quality that made her dissolve, but in that instant they crystallized with purpose, as if before him lay an impossible target that he had to apply every muscle and all his wits toward hitting. It was that single-minded look, fixed with determination on his sudden goal that she would most remember about their wedding night.

This stalactite quality in the eyes would appear again during the course of their marriage. It was there when, on the edge of orgasm, lying on top of her, he yanked at her hair, giving her an unexpected thrill. And it would be there the time he had her on her hands and knees, and she looked back over her shoulder, to hear him express an intention that she could never have imagined him expressing, much less with such blunt, profane brutality. Then his eyes became something darker, fired by entitlement, stunned by disbelief, as she said "no" and turned over. How dare she deny him? In a fit, faster than either of them could register it, he completed an act that he would, much later recognize, required forgiveness.

It wasn't Rani that he ultimately asked for forgiveness. In prayer, seeking quiet in his conscience, he acknowledged to himself: "She said no, but I turned her back over, and took it anyway."

It provided some comfort to him to remember that, afterward, he had held her, stroking her hair as if she were a bruised child. He had been, at once, her violator and her protector. And she, like him, would for a long time afterward tether and untether feeling to fact: her pride in who she was to what she had allowed him to do, her adoration of him to what he had been capable of doing. How could she have fought him? Wouldn't resisting have made his actions even more wrong, his character even more compromised? And how untethered would she have been then?

Under his spell, she had gone to a place where ego had not mattered. She had climbed down into the unconfessable cave of what it meant to be in love: to be willing to submit, even to choose it. Was she mirroring what the world told her she was, as a woman? Was she choosing a psychological prison like the many legal and physical ones that society had constructed for her? What he did that night wasn't a crime. They were married, after all. And he never did it again. Once he had asserted his right, he never again exercised it. The world was what it was: paddy did not grow without flood. Sita did not let Ram go into exile alone—no, a good Hindu woman never abandoned her husband. Nor did she refuse him. Love was its own dictatorship. Of this, she had no doubt.

When they came to America, Rani and Ramchand were running from a political dictatorship which they had resisted in modest ways. When the police came to his shop, and tried to seize his goods as contraband, Ramchand jumped on top of the counter to stop them. He had performed many such acts of bravery, shopkeeper's bravery, during the days that flour, potatoes and imported brands were banned. In the end, their greatest act of resistance was to leave. Like everyone else, they had queued outside the American Embassy. Sponsored by their daughter in Connecticut, they waited long, drowsy years for their green cards.

Driving home from the crematorium in Bridgeport, Rani traveled back to the day that finally convinced them it was time to go, the day of Ramchand's first brush with death. Flashbacks often found her there, remembering how a bullet found its home beneath his left shoulder blade.

When the robbers arrived at Cloud Nine Avenue, Ramchand was pulling shut the shop's wide, barn-like doors to reveal the faded "Pepsicola" ad painted across them. The bandits came with guns in the middle of a crime wave, a spree of what the papers called "choke-and-rob." The opposition parties, in the underground pamphlets they pressed secretly into receptive palms, declared petty Indian shopkeepers the targets, and the dictator, the prime mover behind the scenes.

The family responded as if they had expected their turn at any moment. Rani was in the back of the house, in the kitchen, attacking dough with a rolling pin, and the children were upstairs at their evening routines, the girl ironing her school uniform and the boy cradling his shortwave radio, his ear cocked for the cricket scores. When she heard the gunshots, and the screaming, the girl undid her golden earrings shaped like bells, placed them gingerly on her tongue and hid behind the clothes hanging in her mother's wardrobe, as terrified of swallowing the *jhumkas* as of being discovered. The boy slid under the bed, pressing his rail-thin body into a corner, trying to make himself even smaller than he was. Rani had run out into the front yard with her rolling pin still in hand, raised as if to defend her family. She was in time to watch Ramchand reach beside the shop door for the cutlass that always waited there, its long, curved blade too rusty to be any real threat to the six armed young men she saw encircling him.

"Coolie man, nah even try da," one warned, drily.

Even though they wore red kerchiefs with white polka dots across their mouths, Rani recognized the robbers as village boys, barely out of their teens. The one who cautioned Ramchand with such composure was the son of the bowlegged policeman at Whim station. And the one who shot Ramchand was the old lady Winifred's nephew, the light-eyed one everybody called Hazel. The first Sunday of every month, at four o'clock, Rani went to Winifred's house to receive phone calls from her daughter in the States. Had Hazel overheard Rani talking about the black market flour and Enfamil formula hidden behind the parlor cases displaying pine tarts and Chinese cakes? Had he been there when Rani described the baby bangle, a slender, fretted rope specially ordered from the goldsmith for her first grandchild, born in America?

It was Hazel who fired when Ramchand grabbed the machete. The slur had made her husband act the hero. She was sure of it. The insult must have wounded him as deeply as the bullet. His attackers didn't address him as Mr. Maraj or Uncle Ram or Mayor, or even Bicycle Uncle, as the village boys sometimes mockingly called him. Instead, as he reeled from the bullet's impact, Ramchand heard: "Coolie man! Nah man! Keep de cutlass fo' you wife."

His entire life, Ramchand had been belittled by that epithet. He had inherited the hurt from his parents, who had been branded the same by plantation overseers. Ramchand couldn't seem to save—or marry or Brahmin—his way out of the shame of it. Not even joining the ruling party had helped. And it didn't seem to matter that he sold the banned wheat flour to Winifred too, to Indian and African alike. He was from cane country, a son of indenture, lacking high school or Christ, town ways or creolized polish, and no one was ever going to let him forget it, certainly not his neighbors who had come to rob him. As he lay there bleeding and humiliated, just another coolie with a cutlass in his hand and a bullet in his back, the bandits shot his sister to death. She had bolted out of her house next door, yelling bloody murder from her veranda when the first shots rang out.

Rani was too stunned to scream. In her trance, the men took easy charge of her, disarming her of the *belna* before taking her by the elbow and leading her into the house. "Where de gold, auntie?" Hazel asked.

All Rani could see as she took him to the room where her jewelry and the last of her children were secreted was Ramchand collapsing. His eyes were open when he hit the ground. Where, she wondered, was the stalactite in them then? That afternoon, the robbers almost added another layer to Rani's grief. Among the things they carried away that night were her wedding *jhumkas* and *mangal sutra*, the necklace of sovereigns that her mother had thrice pawned when the family rice mill had failed, the bangle for the baby in Connecticut, jute bags filled with flour and sugar and all the petty cash in the register; but they did not succeed in taking Ramchand's life.

In the years to come in America, whenever the illness that never stopped growing inside seized her, she would ransack every room searching for lost jewelry. The police had ultimately rounded up the thieves and recovered the precious necklace strung with pound sterling coins, a rarity from plantation days, and the rest of the stolen goods—everything but the money. Rani remembered going to the station to identify the young men and her things, but it had done no good. The police released the robbers and kept the jewelry.

Afterwards, whenever depression took hold, she would hunt madly for bangles that were exactly where she had left them. She would phone her children, accusing each in turn of taking the jewelry without asking. Rani repeatedly acted out the loss of what she still possessed, as intensely as if she were mourning the proud man cut with precision who once made her shoulders blush, as if the robbers had in fact stolen her dark jewel that day, as if he had departed long before he lay down on her bed to die.

When his soul was actually about to depart, his ashes in an urn on her lap, she found herself returning to those two other thresholds in their lives. As she remembered leaving for marriage half a century before and for a new country more recently, she sang of stained veils. It seemed appropriate. Had there not been blood, both times? Weren't both migrations tarnished with violence? So Rani sang the verses that the old women had taught her. *The bride cries, she must go to her lover's. She cries because she must go.* She was an old woman now. *My love will beat me with a bamboo rod. My love will hold me by the neck and beat me.* Finally, she understood what the words meant.

She hummed to herself until she saw before her eyes Ramchand, wearing *jhumkas* and a red *chunari* with golden beadwork. He looked young again, his curls blue-black and glistening under the veil, his eyes rimmed with *kohl*, a bride before the gods, ready to go to his last home. His lips moved, forming the words "laaga chunari mein daag," and he danced with bells on his ankles, the spark coming from his hips, the grace from the nimble flight of his hands. Their coquette's tracery framed his eyes, those eyes that had always contained want and wrong and the fire of this world. The vision tossed its head. *How will I go to my in-laws / With a stained veil.*

Ramchand threw off the veil, slowly crossing over to another realm.

And Rani, forgiving the body's betrayal, let him go.

Note:
The verses from Kabir that appear in this story are translations by the poet, Rajiv Mohabir, from his chapbook, "A Veil You'll Cast Aside" (Anew Print, 2015).

KUZHALI MANICKAVEL

The Statue Game

Anjali always pointed to her teeth when she tried to sell her appendix.

"Canadian teeth," she would say, giving them a tap. "Romba strong. If the teeth are this good then imagine what my appendix must be like."

Unfortunately, nobody wanted to buy her appendix and she couldn't understand this because people in India were buying and selling body parts all the time.

"I don't think there's a market for appendixes," I said. "Try selling your kidneys. Or your liver."

"Why should I? Appendix is just as good as kidneys," she said. "I think I'm being blacklisted because I'm Canadian. If I didn't have this accent I would have sold my appendix a long time ago."

"It's not your accent, it's because you're kind of pink and muscly," I said. "Most Indian women aren't pink and muscly. It makes people suspicious."

I wanted Anjali to go home. I couldn't think of a better place for a Canadian than Canada, but she was very comfortable here. She stayed in a small room down the road from my grandmother's house and spent her time sending postcards to the folks back home. She wrote about how this was a real-deal Indian town that didn't have many cows but there were lots of black pigs and goats that never stopped farting. Water only came out of the taps twice a day and you couldn't drink it because it was filled with malevolent strains of cholera, malaria and small pox. She wrote about how she saw dead rats in the daytime, how people peed at the side of the road, how the electricity came and went as it pleased. Once a month her sister wired her fifty dollars, but Anjali wanted to expand her horizons and you couldn't do that on fifty dollars. This is why she wanted to sell her appendix. One afternoon she came to my grandmother's house and started tugging at the front door.

"What do you want?" I said from the window. I didn't want to let her in because it would take a very long time to put her outside again.

"My sister's coming," she said. "Is the door locked? Why's the door locked?"

"Will she take you back to Canada?"

"I think she's just wants to make sure I'm alright and everything. You know."

"Where are you going to keep her?"

"I was thinking since you've got extra rooms here—"

"No."

"Okay. Well I guess she could stay with me then. I could rent an air conditioner or something. Are you going to open the door?"

"How long is she staying?"

"I don't know. Hey, maybe you could meet her."
"Maybe she'll take you back to Canada," I said.

∽

My grandmother died in her sleep in a white Ambassador car, somewhere between Tirunelveli and Nagercoil. When we finished burning her, I was asked to go to her house and settle the "little things," though I wasn't very clear about what these "little things" were. Her house was sparse and mysterious, littered with chairs and straw mats. There was also a broken gramophone player, a cupboard of old silk saris, cooking pots, and a crumbly statue of Krishna that was the size of a small child. He was chipped all over, as if he had been pecked at by millions of tiny birds. Both his hands were missing and there was a large hole where his right knee should have been. His flute had been reduced to a rusted mess of wire that stuck to his cracked lips.

"Give it to me," said Anjali.
"Why?"
"Because I'm totally into Krishna. And it would look really cool in my room."
"Five thousand rupees."
"I'll give you a hundred. Once I sell my appendix."

A builder wasp darted in and out of the hole in Krishna's knee. I wondered what had happened to his hands. It looked like they had been broken off.

"So can I have it?" asked Anjali.
"You can have him for five thousand rupees."

∽

The shopkeeper across the street was the custodian of my grandmother's house and the official keeper of the house key. As far as I could tell, he didn't like me for three reasons:

1. I didn't know how to add up my change.
2. I still got "left" and "right" mixed up.
3. I only knew how to count to ten in Tamil.

"I have a question," I said to him one morning. "What can I do with an old statue?"
"Throw it out," said the shopkeeper.
"Isn't it wrong to throw out statues of God?"
"Shouldn't you have mentioned that? How am I to know it's a statue of God?"
"It's a statue of God."
"You need to put it in a river."
"Will you put it in a river for me?"
"No."

∽: 305

"My grandmother would have wanted you to."
"Why are you lying like this?"
"I'm not lying."
"Yes you are."

I went home and sat on the back porch with the statue on my lap. It was the weariest statue of Krishna I had ever seen. The tiny gouges in his eyes made him look vampiric and blind at the same time. His smile seemed to be waiting for the right time to fall off and join the broken hands, wherever they were.

"You remind me of that guy," I said, peering inside the hole in his knee. "The one who couldn't die and they turned him into a grasshopper. Which I never really understood. Why would you turn something into a grasshopper?"

I spent my days walking around the house, looking for the little things, carrying the statue on my hip like a broken child. I found wooden boxes shoved under the beds, all of them locked. I wondered what was inside them but was too lazy to try and open them.

"I don't think there are any little things in there," I said. "People don't lock up little things."

I noticed that some rooms had windows that opened into other parts of the house. They were fitted with green and orange glass and the window panes had been painted white then green then brown. I imagined the disappointment of a house guest opening one of these windows, hoping to see the sun or the sky. Instead they would have seen another room, possibly with an old person breathing noisily in a corner. I put Krishna's head next to a window pane.

"There's something very dirty and suspicious about inside windows," I whispered. "Don't you think?"

His head began to rhythmically knock against the pane. It looked like he was trying to split his head open.

"I have a cousin who used to do that all the time when he was small," I said. "I think he still does."

It soon became clear that Anjali's sister was not coming on a social visit. She was coming either to take Anjali home or to cut her off because whatever well of affection had spurred her to send fifty dollars a month had completely dried up.

"If I could just sell my appendix I wouldn't give a fuck if she came or not," said Anjali. "She's such an asshole. She's the biggest fucking asshole you ever saw."

I ran my finger along the chips in Krishna's face and hair. Some seemed to have flaked off but there were a number of tiny pits dotting his face like angry, black freckles.

"It's like he was attacked by a bunch of tiny spoons," I said, tapping the gouges in his cheek.

"Let me hold it," said Anjali.

"No."

"For Christ's sake, my sister is going to come here and ruin my fucking life and no one will buy my appendix and I just want to hold the fucking thing, let me hold it."

She held the statue on her lap, then on her hip. She traced his eyebrows and the garland that was melded onto his chest.

"Give it to me," she said. "I mean you don't want it, I'll take it, what's your problem?"

"I have to put it in a river or something. It's very complicated."

"What's so complicated?"

"It's an Indian thing. You wouldn't get it."

"Well fuck that, you think I can't just take it?"

"You know what you should do? Buy yourself a nice Krishna statue. With hands and kneecaps and stuff."

"I think I should just take this one."

"I think you should get your own statue. And then you should go back to Canada."

∞

I didn't see Anjali the next day. I asked the shopkeeper if he had seen her and he said he had better things to do than keep track of all the people who came and went in the local vicinity.

"I didn't mean it like that," I said. "I don't think anyone keeps track of things like that. Except maybe the police."

"Was there anything else you wanted?" asked the shopkeeper.

"Do you want to know what else I found in the house?"

"I'm very busy."

"There are all these windows that open into other rooms. I can't understand why anyone would do that. Unless they wanted to spy on each other in a very obvious way."

"If there's nothing else you wanted," he said, pulling out an account ledger. I went home and sat by the window, watching Anjali's house. Then I decided to hide the statue in the old car shed.

"They should ban foreigners from coming here, India makes them crazy," I said, placing him behind the shed door. "They get sunburned and sick and they just go crazy."

I looked up and saw the bats hanging like tiny folded umbrellas from the rafters. I had seen them here before, when I was seven. A boy had rattled a huge bamboo shaft against the rafters, making the bats swish back and forth in the dusty sunlight. I had remained near the doorway, ready to run if they decided to charge us. And here I was, grown up and brave enough to walk in all the way.

"You know, I'm just going to keep you in the house," I said, picking up the statue by the head. I spent the rest of the day sitting at the window. People walked past carrying wire baskets, looking at their watches, talking about how many things had disappointed them recently.

"Why do they do it?" I said. "When they can have barbecues and boyfriends and jobs, why do they come here and make themselves miserable? Although I have heard India is very big with junkies and pedophiles. And spiritualists."

The statue stared blankly out the window, his cold, molded head leaning against my cheek. He did not seem apprehensive of any of these things, not even of Anjali and the prospect of her pink, muscly arms whisking him away. He wasn't even looking at her house.

॰ुः

Anjali reappeared the next evening, reeking of artificial cherries, her eyes angry and slightly unfocused.

"You smell like candy," I said.

"Benadryl. Z-Coff. Somethingsomething," she said. She sat cross-legged on the floor and leaned against the wall. I sat across from her on a plastic chair, holding the statue on my lap.

"I'm going home," she said.

"Good."

"My sister's coming. And we're putting everything in the car. And then we're going home. Do you know what I'll do when I get home?"

"Eat bagels for breakfast. Take your dog to the vet," I said.

"No."

"You'll watch hockey games in bars and drink beer."

"That's so fucking stupid. Is that what you think we do all day?"

"Yes."

"That's so fucking stupid," she said, shaking her head. She stood up, steadying herself against the wall. Then she walked over and placed a finger on the side of Krishna's head.

"What a scummy statue," she said, gently rocking it back and forth.

"Chippy. Not scummy," I said.

"It's fucking scummy. Believe me."

"Well why do you want it if it's so fucking scummy?"

She shrugged and pushed at his head like she was pressing a button. The statue swayed, then slid down and hit the floor with a dull, weary crack. We looked at the pile of broken arms, legs and face.

"Sorry," said Anjali. "I didn't mean to."

She began sweeping up the stray pieces with her foot, pushing a piece of his shoulder with her toe.

"No big deal," she said. "I can buy myself a new one."

⌘

Anjali left with Krishna's rusted flute sticking out of her back pocket. I collected the remaining pieces, put them in a pista-green plastic bag and walked around the house with the bag hooked over my shoulder. I prodded the locked boxes with my foot and tried to open some of the inside windows, but they were nailed shut. All the nails had been hammered in sloppily and their rusted heads were curled against the window panes like they were sleeping.

"You know what this means, right?" I said. "Someone took a stand against the inside windows. Someone said enough is enough."

I could feel the pieces rolling and shifting against my back. There had been a length of rusted wire in there somewhere and I wondered if it would scratch me and give me tetanus.

The next morning I locked the house and went to the shop across the street.

"Here," I said, sliding the house key across to the shopkeeper.

"You're leaving?" he said. "You've settled everything?"

"Yes," I lied, placing the plastic bag on the counter. "This is the statue I was telling you about," I said.

"I don't want it."

"I'm not giving it to you."

"You can't keep it here."

"I'm not going to. I just want you to know that crazy foreigner girl broke it yesterday. She came in my house and just broke it with her finger. For no reason."

"And what do you want me to do about that?"

"Well I'm just warning you. She might come into your store and break everything. She might just come in and start knocking things down with her finger and then what will you do? Because that's what she did to me," I said.

Half an hour later I was on a bus, sitting beside a woman who repeatedly asked me what time it was, even though I repeatedly told her I had no watch.

"Don't you have a cell phone?" she asked.

"No."

"Why not? My daughter has a cell phone." When her stop came, she brushed past me, leaving behind a heavy space filled with the scent of dead jasmines and vethalai. I placed the bag on the seat where she had been sitting, even though I knew it must be hot and damp and disgusting. Two people came and asked me to move the bag so they could sit down. I said I couldn't and they moved away, muttering bad things about me and my upbringing.

When I was in the auto on the way home, I realized I had left the bag on the bus. For some reason I looked behind me as if I expected to find it there.

"Forgot something?" said the auto driver.

"My bag."

"Your purse? Was there money in it? Cell phone?"

"I don't have a cell phone," I said.

I knew someone would find the bag and open it, possibly with two fingers while they crinkled their nose. Then they would see the clay pieces and say *chee, mannu* and be relieved and disappointed. Or they would see the broken arms and face and say *ada*? Later, when they got to wherever they were going, they would remember this and tell whoever was next to them, *ada, you know what happened on the bus? You know what I found*? They would start a rumor that anti-Hindu factions were leaving broken statues of gods on state buses.

But before all that happened, they would toss the bag out the window, with enough push so that it fell at the side of the road. They would look back to make sure it was really out there and hadn't redoubled inside through the back window or stuck somewhere between their fingers and the atmosphere.

And then they would see it, receding in the dust like it had been there all along with the malnourished water buffalos and clumps of hair.

SUBIMAL MISRA

Wild Animals Prohibited
Translated from Bengali by V. Ramaswamy

Any person bringing, keeping or raising in urban areas categories of animal or animals notified as dangerous vide government gazette notification, in contravention of regulations promulgated by the government, or in violation of the rules and conditions of the licence, shall be fined an amount not exceeding rupees two thousand.
—Clause 71 (a) of the Bengal Law no. 4 of 1966

When Jodu arrived with his wife in the evening, we got started. Ram and Shyam had come by late afternoon and were sitting around, making conversation every now and then. Every once in a while they said: "We're gonna have a helluva time today!" At three-thirty, when it was time for the daily water supply, my wife entered the bathroom with a loosely draped sari around her and a towel and soap-case in hand. When she emerged an hour later, her body exuded the fragrance of sandalwood soap. I often feel like biting her exposed shoulder but don't, thinking it would be improper. But as soon as Amala emerged and my old maidservant went into the bathroom with a pile of unwashed plates and utensils, I took advantage of the privacy to fondle my wife a little. But Amala was largely preoccupied with getting dressed or doing up her face, she didn't give me much time. Yet I took the opportunity to lick and lap up as much as I could. Ram and Shyam called out from the next room a couple of times, "There are some squeaky sounds coming from your room, what are you up to, Madhu?" Making no bones about it, I replied, "I'm kissing." They got excited and said, "We wanna kiss too." In response, I tried to explain the situation to them. I counselled them to wait: "Gently into the night."

And thus the evening advanced. Ram and Shyam looked at their watches, they were getting impatient and restless. They knew things couldn't begin before Jodu and his wife arrived. In the other room, Amala daubed color thickly on her cheeks and face. The old maidservant shuffled back after washing the dishes. I shouted at her: "What's with you, you whore, you take so long to wash the dishes—come on now, hurry up and pour the liquor into the glasses." The old woman was afraid of me. She quickly busied herself with fetching the liquor from the cupboard. In whispers, I indicated to the others the authority I wielded in my house.

The evening grew darker and the lights were turned on. Sipping our drinks, we waited in silence for Jodu and his wife. They arrived after a while, sat down, had a drink. I closely observed Jodu's wife, Kamli—how she sat, how she spoke, the way she laughed animatedly at every turn, almost to the point of keeling over. My wife Amala joined us after a while. She brimmed over with laughter at every word, her entire torso from waist to shoulder swaying lustily, the anchal of her sari slipping off time and again to expose her breasts. We carried on talking while we drank.

Ram asked: "Is the revolution advancing?"

Shyam replied: "I don't know."

Jodu asked: "How many salary increments did you get?"

I replied: "Three."

"What are those people doing?"

"They keep playing cards, sitting beneath the mezzanine veranda upon newspapers spread out under the tube light."

"What do they do?"

"Sometimes when we are rapt in pleasure, they climb the stairs and knock on the door, they look here and there suspiciously and with angry expressions they ask, 'What's happening here?'"

In the midst of such talk the flower seller's cry could be heard: "Bel, buy bel-flowers!" Hearing the word "bel," the women got excited. I called the flower seller upstairs and bargained with him. Then I bought two strings and we fixed it on the women's hair, me on Jodu's wife's, Jodu on my wife's. They were beside themselves with joy and let us kiss them right there in front of the flower seller.

After sending off the flower seller, while some of us were kissing—were getting ready to, rather—standing at the door was the young beggar girl from the bottom of the stairs, dressed in dirty rags, holding in her arms a rickety baby just a few months old. She wailed: "Ma, a roti for me, ma!" And I don't know why but I thought of the people sitting beneath the mezzanine veranda on spread-out newspapers, silently playing cards under the tube light. Sometimes my wife gave her a roti or half a roti and sent her off before her incessant wailing began to get on our nerves. But most days she got nothing and she stood at the door for a long time, pestering us. Sometimes we teased her: "Hey girl, wanna come and drink some booze?" She stared at us with wide eyes as we fondled each other. Sometimes one of us got up in exasperation and twisted her arm. She would turn blue in pain and her eyes saw only darkness as she tried to protect her now withered young breasts as well as her baby. Sometimes we chucked whatever we could find at her—pieces of stone, for instance. We even spat at her. Some days my wife took the situation into her own hands. When the water in the kettle boiled she splashed it on the girl's body, and when the girl and the baby screamed at the sudden attack, we enjoyed it.

The disturbance of the flower seller and beggar having passed, the night advanced. We kept waiting, kept getting ready. There were bits of stray conversation. We talked about how the number of our female members could be increased with the addition of at least two more persons, and our wives protested loudly at the suggestion. They said, "Getting more girls is not permitted. How are we inadequate in any way?" We laughed, and through our laughter we enjoyed their talk. "Compared to other countries, we simply haven't become civilized"—we talked about all that too, about social norms and taboos on sexuality being a sign of backwardness, and we talked about the many countries in the world that had left these behind long ago. Our women expressed their views on how outrageous the ban on the import of foreign lipsticks into the country was. Sometimes it was "contraceptives need to be more reliable." They talked about things like that. Ram and Shyam wanted to talk about those four people, the ones beneath the mezzanine veranda, who kept playing cards silently under the neon light, sitting on spread-out newspapers. We knew very little about them, and consequently our discussion lacked substance. Jodu said, "Those people are extremely unsocial, they don't say anything even when we walk past them." My wife said, "They're men, after all, the day you bring them under control they'll talk your head off."

The night progressed. We couldn't stand any more useless chatter. I said, "Let the real thing begin now. What's the use of sitting around anymore?" Hearing me, everyone sat up. Everyone wondered what today's item would be. After some discussion, the day's program was decided upon. Given that there were four men and only two women, there was some argument and bargaining and laying down of conditions. But eventually everyone was reassured that they would get their share in the next session, and the matter was more or less resolved for the day. But on some days, there was a toss, and those who won the toss got the chance to get the women. Then the bright lights were turned off and a dim blue low-voltage lamp was lit, because if anyone outside found out or suspected anything, it could be dangerous. I had locked the old maidservant up in the tiny store room. I had told her, "Sit quietly, you old woman, don't you dare shout and scream!" Each time I locked her up like this, I inevitably felt a surge of emotion, and in that agitated state, I felt like landing two blows on her face. Damn her, how long would she oppress us like this?

And so, taking care of everything in this way, we got ready. We took the time we needed because if one was not well-prepared, if the chase was not undertaken, the whole thing got diluted. It became unappetizing. For instance, we always kept in mind the fact that there were four guys here and only two women, so when it came to taking off the women's clothes and all that, we never had them do it themselves. After all, even a tiny bit of excitement is achieved with a lot of trial and effort, so how could it be wasted just like that! Take those who didn't win the toss, or those who wouldn't get a chance that day. We gave them the chance to do a little bit in the beginning of the session, so they too got some crumbs of pleasure. And thus did we advance and become advanced in our quest for pleasure. The door to the house remained closed, we were shut out from the world outside, engrossed only in ourselves.

Sometimes there were hindrances in our work: those four people, the ones beneath the mezzanine veranda, who keep playing cards, sitting silently on spread-out newspapers under the neon light. They come upstairs with an air of enquiry. When I open the door, they come near and, wearing a grave face, want to know, "What are you people doing?" We are busy, and I say so, and not getting any cue from us they make their grave faces graver still and descend the stairs. Sometimes there's the sound of many feet arriving together and halting in front of the locked door, and in our languid embrace we wait in the dark with thumping hearts. But there is no knock and the moment passes. We suspect someone found out about the whole affair, that they spread the story in the entire neighborhood. But there was no reaction, no one came to apprehend us. We had been frightened in vain. No one in the neighborhood suspected anything about us. Those four grave-faced people who kept playing cards under the neon light did not suspect anything yet.

But sometimes, late in the night, after we have finished our business, when, on tired legs, I go down to see off our guests, I see the beggar girl in rags, lying in the dingy darkness on the last step of the staircase, holding the baby in her arms to her breast. Seeing her, my words suddenly choke in my throat. I feel a peculiar uneasiness rising within me, I can't make any parting talk. As quietly as possible, without waking them up, I run upstairs, my chest heaving in fear. As I climb the stairs, I feel the clutch of the desolate midnight in my heart. Observing my fear, my freshly fornicated wife says testily, "Just forget about it. I'll pour a pot of hot water on them tomorrow and the whole lot will be set right at once." It is this statement of my wife's that I am unable to rely on. I get scared, and on such nights I continue to feel scared. I go to the bathroom and splash water on my face and eyes to drive out the fear; I try to forget the whole scene. But try as I might, I can't. Fear roams through the recesses of my heart. Hearing the sudden screech of brakes of a speeding car in the desolate midnight, I sense that same fear awakening once more in my heart.

GEETA KOTHARI

I Brake For Moose

Friendly's 1:30 a.m.

We're sitting at a booth, brown vinyl with scratches and holes burned into it from too many careless cigarettes over the years, shooting M&Ms back and forth across the table. My cigarette burns close to the filter, still I take a drag, too tired to care that I'm into my second pack of the day. I will quit when we get back to New York. I will quit the next time I hear the band's single on the radio. I will quit the day Gus and Jeremy show up anywhere on time. All remote possibilities, too distant to measure anything by.

"I read this article about these Indian guys who dump their American girlfriends to marry wives their parents pick for them," Joanne says. She looks like a ferret, dark eyes ringed hollow with thick eyeliner that never smears, no matter how hard she dances, how late we stay up. Her face is small and pointy, her brown hair cut in layers, short and crooked, close to her scalp. Her skin is sallow, washed out like salted cod soaked for too many days.

It is 1986. I've been reading about the depletion of cod in the Grand Banks, the migrations of the fishing industry up and down the coast. I've been reading about the Acadian Forest, where descendants of Frenchmen fleeing the British in Canada still speak French. I've been reading about Baxter State Park, where moose and other wildlife roam freely. Joanne's reading her horoscope in a magazine, which is where she comes across the article.

"Some of them get married and then pick up with their girlfriends as if nothing's changed."

Scientists say that in order to conserve cod, fishermen would have to reduce the allowable catch by half, but Joanne doesn't want to hear this any more than I want to hear about Indian men.

"I've only met Gus's parents twice," she says. "You know, in the whole time we've been together, I've only met them. Never eaten with them, had a drink, nothing. Isn't that weird?"

I know girls who live with their boyfriends and have two separate phone lines. I know girls who outright lie; they tell their parents he's the roommate's brother, a nice guy from a good family. But we're talking about Joanne, Joanne and Gus, the Romeo and Juliet of the road. I don't have to answer her, just look sympathetic and eat her leftover fries.

"More coffee?"

It's Alma, our waitress, blond hair cut short like a cap. She's too young for such an old name, and I feel sorry for her, so I nod even though my stomach is burning; the inside probably looks like the bench we're sitting on right now.

Waiting is what we do best, all for the privilege of being able to say, "I'm with the band," and to walk past the red velvet ropes and other girls as if we've done something special. This has happened only twice in the six months I've been around, once in Boston and once in New York, when we opened for a better known band. "We" is what Joanne, official girlfriend of the lead singer, says. We are with the band, she says, and the way she says it, rhythmically, with resonance, it's like a mantra she must tell herself when I'm not listening.

How I Got Here

My parents want to know what kind of an Indian name is Gus.

"I don't know."

A boy from a good family, last name known to my parents, caste equal to ours, theirs not mine since I don't understand any of that stuff—that is Gus, and I should feign more interest in him as he is the reason I am "allowed" to go on the road with the band. I tell my parents I'm the treasurer since I have a head for numbers.

"One last fling," I promise, as I did four years ago when I dropped out of grad school in Pittsburgh and fled to New York.

"But they can't say anything," Joanne says. "You've been supporting yourself since you graduated."

"It doesn't work like that."

She says, "Oh?"

And then I have to explain, explain that immigrant children are expected to succeed and capture all the remaining bits of the American dream that eluded their parents. They are not expected to drop out of business school, work a series of clerical jobs, send home a new address and phone number every six months, promising that this time the apartment will work out. It's not like Joanne can't understand. Her father tells her he didn't slave in a mill for thirty years, just outside of Worcester, so she could go to Smith and become a friggin' secretary, working the night shift at a production company that does special effects for TV commercials.

We were bored, Manhattan was hot, and the band had a single that was getting some airplay. It was time, Gus said. Time to hit the college circuit and build up a following. We were heading north and would be back before Christmas.

This is what I tell my parents, promise to call them collect: I tell them about the articles I'm reading. I tell them about the Grand Banks, the impending cod apocalypse. I tell them Gus is a nice guy, the brother I never had. I tell them the band is on the verge of success, almost famous. I tell them the boys all went to college, Ivy League schools up and down the East Coast.

What I Don't Tell My Parents

Kenny, the drummer, is twenty-nine, six credits short of a degree in something he can no longer remember. He's damaged, but good drummers are hard to find.

On and off stage, Gus moves like someone who thinks he's a star. He has a mop of black curly hair, high cheekbones and brown eyes like pools. That's how Joanne describes them, pools of dark light she'd like to drown in. I think she got that from one of her magazines. On the road, people assume Gus and I are brother and sister even though we look nothing alike: my skin is lighter, my nose flatter, and my face rounder. My hair is straight and long, and the closest we get to being brother and sister is that we both sound the same, products of private schools and New England colleges.

When we first met, we quickly realized that our parents move in the same circles and this knowledge becomes a sheer curtain between us. We got into a fight about the money some towns back and didn't talk for a few days, but Gus knows I'm right—band expenses are not the same as personal bar tabs. We've sized each other up several times now and keep a wary distance like dogs on alert.

The rules are simple: the band comes first and personal conflicts must be contained at any cost.

I should tell my parents about Mike, the guitarist, who's from Minnesota. He's short and stands a bit like a duck, all swayback and butt, but it's not something you'd notice when he's on stage. He wears plaid and thermal and hiking boots. His girlfriend, Christine, works on Wall Street and thinks Joanne and I are losers.

Did I mention that we all went to Smith? Women's college, serious degrees: Economics, History, Math? Did I mention that Christine has a job on Wall Street?

Finally, I don't tell my parents the real reason I am here, sitting in a Friendly's with winter breathing down my back. I don't tell them about Jeremy, the long summer nights we spent drinking Bohemia and watching the sun set over the Hudson from the sixth-floor walk-up Joanne and I shared, and the short autumn nights now, when we turn our backs to each other and fall into troubled, restless sleep. I don't tell them about those days when I used to stand in front of the stage and watch the top of his blond head, bent over that bass like he was studying for an exam, and how I stood and waited for the small flicker of recognition, the smile, the wink, the nod that would come when he finally looked up and saw me. Perpetually tan, long and thin, he was sunshine in those dank basement bars, a rock steady beat in the chaotic boredom of my carefree life.

And now I felt the chill of unrelieved togetherness like a layer of snow over the first spring daffodils. Everything that had been good and fun between us droops, heavy with cold and frost.

Friendly's 2:00 a.m.

We're still waiting, coffee grown cold at the bottom of white cups stained with lipstick and bits of tobacco. Mike dropped us off at one, then went back to finish packing up. With girls milling around, breaking down the equipment always took longer than it should. We got paid, and I stowed the cash in a cloth purse around my neck, in between my T-shirt and my wool sweater. I divide it five ways: Mike, Kenny, Gus, Jeremy, and the band. A percentage always goes to band costs, which includes my nominal under-the-table salary.

Alma smokes a cigarette at her station. Another waitress says something to her. Alma looks over at the door and shakes her head. She stopped asking if we wanted more coffee some time ago.

"We should pay," I say. "Let her go home." There's something familiar about her, but I can't place her face.

Joanne shrugs. She has an amazing capacity for long hours of doing nothing. She doesn't overeat, drink, or chip her nail polish. She was a history major, someone who memorized scores of dates and facts and stories about things everyone else has forgotten, and now she sits here without a thought in her head.

"Do you think Gus will leave me for an Indian girl? Some nice virgin his parents find?"

So this is where we are.

What Else I Don't Tell My Parents

When I called my parents yesterday, I told them everything was fine, the foliage was beautiful, and the sun was shining on the water, a perfect blue sky day. I told them the band was playing well, that we would soon be in Canada, New Brunswick to be precise, then Nova Scotia where Gus had friends, and after that we'd head back home. We'd played harvest parties, half-empty bars and wedding receptions. On the way back, a couple of Christmas parties and then we'd be home. I said it like that, we'd be home, as if I too were part of the band.

I don't tell them I have to drive because Kenny has no sense of direction, and the last time we let him drive the van, he passed three exits before he realized he should have gotten off the highway thirty miles ago. I don't tell them about the marijuana seeds on the floor of the van. I don't tell them I'm tired, that my back hurts and my stomach feels hollow most days.

And I won't tell them about the day before, about how we got three rooms at the HoJo's when we arrived at dawn, and how Jeremy stayed in Gus and Joanne's room while I crawled into bed in the same smoky T-shirt I'd been wearing for the last twenty-four hours and popped two Benadryls and still couldn't sleep.

A couple of hours later, as light begins to seep in through the sides of the curtain that doesn't quite cover the window, Jeremy sags into bed, his clothes still on. We say nothing, which is mostly what we do these days when we're alone, exhausted, wrung out, this has not been as much fun as I thought it would be, and Jeremy feels the weight of that. It's not his fault, but in that musty, overheated room with its worn blue carpet and ashtray full of someone else's butts, there is no space to say what I feel.

After a while, he says,

"What are you thinking?"

I'm thinking about August in the city, the claw-foot tub in the kitchen and the old black-and-white TV on the dining table. He'd come in, after practice or a double shift at the diner, and I'd run the bath. Joanne was working late or at Gus's, and in the glow of the TV, I'd lean into Jeremy and watch our shadowy limbs in the cold water. My fingers studied every hair and sinew and vein on his arms, the arms that cradled that bass, and I felt no jealousy, only envy at the sureness with which Jeremy played.

The hotel bed is soft and wide, with enough space for both of us to sleep comfortably. We try, curl up against each other, then shift and return to the edges, as far away from the dip in the middle, the one I hadn't noticed when I lay down alone. After a few hours, Jeremy gets up to take a shower and when he comes out, he finds me staring at the ceiling.

"What are you thinking?" he asks again. His green eyes are miserable, but I can't look at him for I don't want him to see mine. Not dark pools of light but murky bog land from which nothing emerges.

We cannot break up on the road, disturb the tender ecosystem we have struggled to maintain for the last two months. But we can find a space apart. So, in the afternoon, when Joanne says she wants to hang out at the hotel until the party starts, Jeremy agrees and I take off with Kenny and Gus. Mike will stay behind, make sure everything's good to go. We plan to meet at seven, then head over to the student union to set up.

The sun sets behind the trees that loom sky-high on either side of the tiny road, and it's dark by the time we stumble on a bar in a clearing. Young men in ill-fitting pastel-colored tuxedos and women, girls really, in matching dresses shaped and cut like elaborate lampshades mill about the wood-paneled room.

Before I can decide if I want to stay, Gus hands me a beer, and Kenny disappears. Dazed, mildly drunk people brush past me. I feel conspicuous, Gus and me dark blips on white landscape.

"The bartender said we could hang," Gus says, wielding a roll of quarters. "It's his cousin's wedding."

Into the jukebox, five dollars' worth of quarters, all oldies, the songs the band used to cover, years before my time. Gus and I exclaim over our favorites, forget the arguments, the money, the mutual suspicions that have dogged us since the day we met. The Stones, Janis Joplin, Marvin Gaye, Aretha. Led Zeppelin and T-Rex, for the sake of high school.

"Only girls listen to T-Rex," Gus sneers, as I hit the button.

Gus dances with me, passes me off to Kenny, dances with the bride, the groom, and his best man, and a blonde girl, more than once. She is lithe and small, petite like Joanne. I watch them from the bar, turn around for another beer, and when I look into the center of the room, they're gone. It's only six, and I'm not worried, just glad to be away, away from Joanne and her endless inquiry into a future I cannot see, away from the broken wings of my relationship with Jeremy. Then T-Rex is on and Gus pulls me out onto the dance floor. When the song turns into a slow one, I feel his warm palm on my back, my cold hand in his.

He folds my fingers into his. He's only a couple of inches taller than me, and I focus on the patch of skin between his neck and his chest. And then the song is over, and in the distance a bottle crashes against the wall. The wedding party is drunk. Night has fallen, and if we stay another minute, I won't be able to get us back to where we came from. So I take Gus's hand and pull him through the mass of people packed around us. Near the door, he drains his beer, and Alma—whose name I didn't know, who I wouldn't recognize hours later at Friendly's—gossamer-winged angel in pink netting and taffeta, steps out of a group at the bar and hands Gus a folded piece of paper.

"Later?" she says.

He puts the paper in his shirt pocket and pats it reassuringly, reaches over to touch her cheek.

Outside, Gus says, "She thinks you're my sister." We're still holding hands. The air is a cold shock, but the sky, the perfect star-studded sky edged with the ragged tops of pine, spruce and fir, this sky stops us in our tracks. Gus squeezes my hand.

"Jeremy," I say.

"I know," Gus says, and squeezes my hand again. I start crying. I see Jeremy, frozen in a photograph wearing the shirt I bought him before we hit the road, and I wonder if sadness will always look like a light-blue shirt with small paisleys in red and green. Finally, Gus kisses me, gently but not in a brotherly way, not in a way I could later justify to my parents, Jeremy, myself or Joanne.

"That was a stupid thing to do," I say and blow my nose.

Perhaps Joanne is right, the only way to get to the border is to turn your eyes back to your magazine, look away from the intensity of these boys who know exactly what they want.

"You think too much," Gus says.

"Or maybe not enough," Kenny says, from the back seat. He hands me a roach.

I stub it out in the ashtray.

"Tell me you didn't smoke that whole thing by yourself," Gus says, worried now about the gig. The girl at the bar, the kiss at the door, we've been filed and forgotten.

I pull out of the parking lot, the taste of beer and smoke on my lips, along with something foreign I cannot name. "When we get home," Jeremy keeps saying, as if somehow that will erase the nights of sleeping in our clothes, on beds that sag in the middle but still do not bring us closer together. When we get home, I'll still be smoking. When we get home, I'll still be looking. When we get home, Jeremy says, everything will be better, you'll see this will all be worth it.

The van hurtles down the winding road, brights cutting a path through the darkness. I want to blame someone for my insides hollowed-out, but when I look around, there's no one, just myself.

Friendly's 2:30 a.m.

We're waiting, and by now I've realized that Alma is the girl from the bar and she's waiting too. I want to leave, but Joanne won't have it. Her job is to wait: she waits for the set to start, then she's the first one on the floor, close to the stage where she can smile at Gus when he looks at her. Then, after the show, she waits—she doesn't help load out, she just waits, watches the action through the smoke generated by endless packs of cigarettes.

"Do you think Gus wants a traditional Indian wedding?" she asks. "What are they like?"

"Lots of standing around and waiting for something to happen."

"It could be fun." She looks at her watch, then the door. A heavy man in a fur cap sweeps in.

Our job is to wait. Waiting is what we do best.

How We Get There

After the bar, Kenny and I dropped Gus off at the hotel for a quick shower and picked up Mike.

"See you in ten," Gus said.

Mike looked at his watch and muttered, "Ten years or ten hours?"

The harvest moon hangs low, as if the world is coming to an end, then it disappears behind the trees and shrubs on the side of the road. It emerges a few miles later, glowing like a pearly orange. We park behind the student union. Mike taps the back of the seat with his fingertips, going over music only he can hear. Part of his ritual prep for each gig involves listening to no other music for the hours preceding it, which means when I drive him and Kenny, I'm pretty much listening to the voices in my head.

We wait for fifteen, twenty minutes, wait for Gus and Jeremy to pull up in the station wagon Gus's dad gave him.

Kenny fires up the roach in the ashtray.

"Jeez, Ken," I say.

Mike plucks the roach from Kenny's hand, and stamps it out on the van floor.

The purse hanging from my neck settles against my chest, as if contains gold coins rather than a handful of twenties, all that's left until we get paid tonight. I blow my bangs out of my face, curse Gus and Jeremy for being late, and pull open the doors to the van. A guitar stand crashes to my feet.

"Watch out," Kenny says. He elbows past me, mad about the dope, even though it's Mike who took it away.

The steel door screeches, and a kid, pimples and long stringy hair, waves us in. He wears worn topsiders without socks and a thick blue sweater.

"Need some help?" he asks. Puffs of smoke fill the air between us. and I hand him Jeremy's bass.

I'm the girlfriend, I tell myself. I'm with the band, not in the band. I should be sitting in some VIP lounge sipping cocktails, smoking imported cigarettes. I should be wearing a black-and-blue tie-dyed miniskirt with thick black tights and blue jellies, not jeans and scuffed Doc Martens, sticky with beer and spiked fruit punch.

I run into a stand of evergreens to the right of the parking lot. Through the dark branches, there is sky, spotted with stars, white flecks of paint against an illuminated blackboard. The crisp air smells of burnt wood, apples and pumpkin pie. I want to disappear into the trees, merge with them like moose so that no one would ever find me.

And then I hear tires on gravel, a door opening, and voices that crack the silence like brick through glass. The world is not coming to an end, I am not a moose, and the boys have arrived.

The Best Years of Our Lives

The boys play "Twist and Shout." Gus engages in unnecessary stage banter. They play their hit single, then the B-side. Three people dance, including Joanne. I stand at the back of the auditorium, crush my cigarettes in a red plastic ashtray that Will, the guy who let us in, found for me.

He says, "It's still early. More people will be here soon."

He says, "These are guys are wicked good. Glad we could get them."

He says, "You and the lead singer—you guys related or something?"

"Or something," I say, and drink the tepid beer in my hand.

In the dark room, kids lurk in the shadows, with plastic cups of beer and red wine. Track lights illuminate the platform where the band plays under a big painted harvest moon, complete with craters and pockmarks. Orange and brown streamers hang from the molding.

Jeremy tunes his bass with the mic on. Kenny blows big pink bubblegum bubbles in between songs. He winks at someone I can't see. Gus and Jeremy talk; the play list, peppered with more originals than covers, has once again been abandoned. They play two more songs, Rolling Stones and The Who. Mike says something about moose, Minnesota and Maine, but now there are thirty people on the dance floor, twenty-nine for whom each cover sounds new and fresh. Some of the girls wear wraparound skirts over long johns, heavy boots that make the floor vibrate when they do the pony. The boys jerk stiffly or flail their arms wildly. They are pale from days and nights in a place where winter comes early, and summer comes late. They are in the middle of the best years of their lives, only none of them will know this until that time has passed, and one morning you wake up in a room the size of your college dorm closet, kill another cockroach in your bathtub, and open an empty refrigerator, not because payday is two weeks away, but because the depression that sits on you like an oppressive New York summer day hasn't lifted, and it's now the middle of winter, and you're still saying, it will be okay when summer comes. And summer comes and goes, and your fridge is briefly filled by love and a new boyfriend, but even this is not enough, so you take a trip, thinking if you can leave it all behind somehow you'll find what you're looking for.

And what you realize is this: loneliness feels the same no matter where you are, and the ecosystem you're now part of is so delicate a sneeze could blow it apart. Kisses under a star-strewn sky mean nothing, friendships are for the moment, and each stop—marked not by lobster pots, or moose or the birch and spruce and pine that tower over the road, but by the red-and-yellow striped cheeriness of Friendly's—blends into the next and soon all the songs on the playlist sound the same.

Friendly's 3:00 a.m.

Two plates of fries and a gallon of coffee later, the guys show up. Jeremy slides in next to me, Gus next to Joanne, then he says, "Hey, let me sit next to my sister." They switch, and Joanne laughs, a deep, husky laugh. Alma is now in Jeremy's line of vision, hidden from Gus by my head and the partition between the booths. I wonder what he'll do when she comes to our table.

What he does is what he always does: he and Jeremy order grilled cheese and bacon sandwiches, fries, and two Cokes. He smiles at Alma, puts his arm over the back of the booth, rests his fingers lightly on my shoulder.

She bites her lower lip, holds her pen tight between her fingers and thumb, pressing down on the pad. What did Gus say to her on the dance floor as he held close and stroked her cheek? What promises did he whisper in her ear that made her hand him that piece of paper? And who is she that she can imagine a future in his words?

All night I've been looking for the words to tell Joanne that if Gus leaves her, it won't be for a mysterious fresh-off-the-boat virgin. She knows as well as I do that the day she stops showing up at the front of the stage, the day she starts standing at the back of the room, smoking and drinking as if she's heard these songs before, the day she emerges from her world of magazines and remembers she graduated from college with honors, that's the day he'll leave her, and it won't be for some girl like me or a better version, handpicked by his parents. It will be for Alma, the young girl who imagines that all things are possible if you attach yourself to the fender of a car that's going somewhere. She doesn't see the way night closes in on us early these days, a blink and the sun is gone, or how the trees press down on us on a dark single-lane highway that cuts through a forest of secrets we already know.

When Gus leaves, he will leave for Alma who still imagines a future open with promise and opportunity like a brand new calendar on New Year's Eve.

How I Leave

I get on a bus. At six in the morning, the depot is closed, the air is cold, but there are people waiting for the first bus to Portland, so I know I've come to the right place. In the reflection of a window, I see dark circles under my eyes, dry chapped lips, and the hollow look of a girl with nothing left to give.

When I shut the door of our room, I imagined Jeremy reaching for my side of the bed in his sleep. But as I lean against the brick wall of the depot and sip vending-machine coffee, it's the boy with the wild black hair I'm thinking of, the wide hand on the small of my back, the black hair in the V of his shirt, its whiteness crisp like snow against the darkness of his skin. I feel his hand in mine, as I pull him through a pack of people, and when I turn back to look, he's gone, and my hand is empty.

Daylight creeps in. We speed by thickets on either side of the highway, and in a clearing, a young moose, small and vulnerable, stands and watches us go by. It happens so quickly, I'm sure I imagined it, but the woman in front of me shrieks "moose!" and taps the window.

I think about what I'll tell my parents, and what I'll tell them is this: I saw some moose, some stars, and some trees. I'll tell them I got tired of waiting. I'll tell them that for one brief moment I could say "I'm with the band" and that perhaps that's all I needed: a moment so brief that years from now, when they tell me Gus is getting married, I'll nod as if I still remember him and go back to whatever it is I'm doing.

SAIKAT MAJUMDAR

from *The Scent of God*

Sushant Kane was going to destroy everything. In class he recited poems he'd written, love poems like these:

> The bleating ram of my soul
> Is tied to the lamp-post of your heart

Such poems caused the boys pain. They did not know whether to laugh or cry. Was it poetry or a joke?

Sushant Kane looked so hip that it was absurd. He was a skinny man with hollow cheeks covered with acne-marks and a trimmed beard. He was the Class 7 English teacher and the debate coach. He wore tight shirts and trousers that flapped loosely around the ankles. It was easy to imagine him in dark sunglasses even though no one had ever seen him wearing any.

He spoke about everything outside the ashram—city buses and plays, exhibitions and advertisements, movies and books they didn't know could exist. He made it all sound real, even though they knew they were stories. Like this play he saw last Saturday in the city, where a lone woman played all the roles. It was the story of the *Mahabharata*, told by Draupadi, the wife of the five princes, how she was given away as property lost in a wager over a game of dice, fought over, insulted and attacked. There was no one else on stage the whole two hours. She even played an army and battle stallions.

Sushant Kane was a mathematician of grammar. Everything about him was pointed, his cheekbones, the end of his beard, the rhythm of his poems and the chalk with which he split complex and compound sentences on the board. Complex sentences into a principal and a subordinate clause, compound sentences into two principal clauses with a finite verb each. Nothing else existed.

He was one of the ashram stories. There were three Marathi brothers—Sushant, Prashant and Ashant—who were adopted by the monks. They were probably orphaned or something like that, nobody really knew how the story began or trailed off. Prashant was a brute with a balding head who ran the early-morning PT and late-afternoon naval cadet training drill as if he was following Hitler's orders. Ashant was popular with the sporty boys; he was a lighthearted loafer who coached the football team and zipped around the ashram on his snazzy yellow Yamaha motorbike. Most of his fans had been won by the bike. Ashant wore sunglasses while riding the bike and usually forgot to take them off while at lunch in the hostel dining hall.

Sushant Kane was different. He was pale like his brothers but different in every other way. He wasn't well-built like them. He was too thin; his limbs were long twigs. Prashant and Ashant were ashram boys; they breathed its air. They sang Sanskrit hymns and tortured the students till they got the marching drill exactly right for the Independence Day and Republic Day parades. They were big brawny men who became little boys before the Great Monk—the secretary of the ashram. Sushant Kane did not change. His acne-marked cheeks wrinkled the same way before the monks as before the boys in his seventh standard English class. Neither the boys nor the monks knew for sure if the trimmed beard hid a kind or a cruel smile. That's probably why he got the nickname Senior Kane, even though he was the middle brother.

Senior Kane, SrK.

SrK belonged to the ashram, like his brothers. And yet, unlike them, he did not belong here. He made the world outside real and fantastic at the same time. For his brothers, there was no world outside.

He talked a lot. He spoke slowly. Sometimes you felt he was asking you to get out and run.

༄

The boys' rooms did not have fans. They spent most of the year in these rooms that had large windows but no electric fans. They went home for summer vacations during the hottest weeks of the year. At home, they could lie on their beds and stare at the electric fans whirring overhead. There were heavy, old-time fans that swallowed the entire ceiling and became a blur; and new, tiny white ones that were like cute, deadly animals swooshing out swirls of air that felt absurd coming out of their little bodies. Even table fans like grim night nurses.

Sometimes, when the boys came back to their hostels after summer vacation, they stayed up late into the night and chatted dreamily about the different kinds of fans they had seen that vacation. At homes, in doctor's waiting rooms, even in railway waiting rooms. The night air in their rooms was deadly still. It was still summer. Sometimes they could smell monsoon in the air that crept up from the Bay of Bengal down south, rainy wind on its way to Calcutta further north. Sometimes they dreamt so hard that the cool air entered their rooms and danced softly over their beds.

Daytime was different. The boys barely spent any time in their rooms. They flew from one hall to another: prayer hall to study hall to dining hall. And school and the football field. Football was sacred, as the young saffron prophet had said that you'll be a lot closer to God if you played football than if you read the *Gita*. Always in motion, the boys felt wind on their skin. But there was to be no fan in the boys' rooms. It was the time to build character and the breeze from electric fans was an indulgence. The monks liked the boys sweaty and breathless. That was the true path of Yoga.

Something strange happened to Anirvan every time he walked past Sushant

Kane's room at the end of their block in Bliss Hall. Whenever Sushant Kane was inside, the door was bolted shut. They saw him quietly walk across the block, a white prayer chador flung across his slim-fitting shirt, walk into his room and bolt the door. He went to the prayer hall. Every teacher had to go.

Anirvan walked up and down the block balcony during Sunday morning "room study." He was reading *Our Living Planet*, their Geography textbook. Ontario, Erie, Michigan... Ontario, Superior... Ontario. The paragraph on agricultural produce. He had to memorize that whole chapter. The trick was to read it once, and then try to repeat it without looking at the book, and then read it again. And repeat the whole thing, and keep repeating the sentences till you could say the whole paragraph without looking at the book. Whoever could remember would go far in life, the monks always said.

Anirvan hadn't realized that he had stopped walking. He was remembering furiously. There was corn, and there was... what else was there? Suddenly his feet wouldn't budge. A blast of cool air hit his face. He looked up and stared at Sushant Kane's window. It was open. Inside, it was dark, and quiet but for a steady whirring sound. The electric fan spread cool air inside, and every time he came close to the window it blasted his face.

It was July but they had only a few days of rain. The leaves on the trees had stopped moving and the sun glared everywhere. The boys had to keep the windows of their rooms open or otherwise they would die but the open windows made the rooms hotter and many of the boys just lay with thin wet towels on their faces which dried up in a few minutes. On these weekends, they missed the coolness of the school and study halls. The prayer hall, with its heavy fans and dark curtains, was heaven.

The window revealed a dreamhole. Dark and cool and full of the steady music of the electric fan. Anirvan could stand there forever. He wanted to thrust his face against the bars and let them leave dents on his cheeks. He stood close and breathed deeply. Cigarettes. He couldn't see Sushant Kane through the window but could hear the rustle of paper.

Kamal Swami did not have an electric fan in his room. The monks never did. They smiled through the pain. For them, it was no pain. Though everybody knew that the house of Atal Swami—the secretary of the Mission—was fully air-conditioned and also had a swimming pool because there were many foreign visitors who came and stayed in his house. The boys had never seen that house but they knew, especially about the white women who swam in the huge blue swimming pool. But the teachers all had fans in their rooms. They were not monks. They were human beings. The boys had never been inside the room of any of the teachers. Standing before Sushant Kane's window, Anirvan knew why.

Room 25, Block 5. The room was there but not really there. It smelled different. Of cool air and cigarette smoke and darkness at noon. Standing in front of the room, Anirvan knew things were scattered and unkempt inside. He peered inside the room.

The smoke smell hit him with a coarse sweetness. He felt dazed and knew that he had left the hostel already. He was home.

Home was the whir of the fan but also the rough sweetness of the cigarette smoke. Sushant Kane was nothing like Anirvan's father but they smoked the same cigarette. Charminar. His father was not bony like Sushant Kane but smooth and pale and delicate. Everything about him was round and soft and slow, versus Sushant Kane's clicking pointiness. But they smoked the same cigarette. As Anirvan flattened his nose against the window bars, he caught the silhouette of Sushant Kane's outstretched legs. He was lying on the bed in his pajamas smoking a cigarette. Anirvan's father did that too. The smoke twirled around in the dark and quickly got lost in the breeze of the fan.

He walked along the corridor, remembering the paragraph about grain production in the Great Lakes Region. He hummed the lines as he walked. His feet picked up the rhythm of the song and his flip-flops dragged to the beat on the floor.

But he slowed down every time he came close to Sushant Kane's room. He thirsted for the blast of cool air and the bitterness of cigarette smoke. He paused again.

There was a click at the door.

"What's up?" Sushant Kane's voice floated out. "Come in."

Anirvan stepped inside. His eyes were riveted on the red spark that glowed in the darkness. As Anirvan walked inside, Sushant Kane stubbed it out on the ashtray. A wisp of blue smoke wafted away.

Anirvan stared at the ceiling fan. Sushant Kane followed his eyes and looked above, staring for a moment. Quickly, Anirvan's eyes closed.

"Come, sit," Sushant Kane pointed Anirvan to a chair under the fan.

Then he stepped out of the room.

The dark room was now faintly lit up by the light from the half-open door. It looked like an old library.

Books were everywhere. On the shelves and heaped on the table and the bed. And newspapers. Piles and piles of newspapers. Where did he get them? No newspaper ever came to the ashram.

Sushant Kane came back. His face was wet. Water dripped from his hair.

"It's burning outside," he said.

He stared blankly in Anirvan's direction, at his hair being ruffled by the wind of the fan. His voice softened.

"Ah, the exam warrior!" He looked at Anirvan as if he could finally see him.

Anirvan smiled a little.

"You were sharp in class this week," Sushant Kane said with a mild frown. "People rarely see what odd fun language can be."

Anirvan nodded. He felt overpowered by the breeze of the fan. He felt if he tried to speak the words would fly away.

"But grammar's just a game," Sushant Kane said. "That's not how you master a language."

"But you know that." He added, staring at Anirvan. "You speak beautifully. That's the most important gift."

He did? But he did, indeed he did! Anirvan's body throbbed.

"I . . . I," he stammered. "I really like your class."

Sushant Kane nodded. In that half-darkness, he looked like a ghost.

◆

Sushant Kane's class was in the afternoon the next day. Afternoons felt sated and sleepy, the right time for his classes. It was not the right time for the important subjects, like mathematics or physics or biology. But Anirvan liked SrK's English grammar class on Monday afternoons. They were precise and angular, like SrK's cheekbones. But they were not real math; Anirvan couldn't have solved them if they were. They were just a game. Being good at English grammar was a useless skill. It had nothing to do with real merit, which was about being good at physics, algebra or biology, real subjects that created success in life.

But that afternoon Anirvan felt a whir of laughter behind the cracking of clauses. Sushant Kane did not look his usual sharp and angular self. There was something cool about him, like there were ways of beating the afternoon heat that his body knew but he couldn't tell them. Anirvan felt a smile dance through SrK's beard. Was it a smile or something else? It was strange, as he was not someone who smiled much. But he said things that made the boys smile.

Anirvan spoke a lot in class that day. Suddenly, his heart beat faster. He tossed the clauses back and forth with SrK as the rest of the class stared at them, looking amused and bored at the same time. But SrK rarely looked at Anirvan. He never looked at anyone, even while talking to them. But Anirvan hoped that he would look at him.

Rajeev Lochan Sen stared at them for a long time, looking back and forth between Sushant Kane and Anirvan. He was a thin boy with sharp wit and a girlish voice from a hilly town in north Bengal. He had clever things to say in every class, things which had little to do with the subjects being taught. He sang beautifully and had a voice carved with affection.

"Does clause analysis make you clever?" He sounded lost as he asked the question.

"Not the way chess does," said Asim Chatterjee, the big boy who had failed a few classes and dropped down to theirs. Nobody had ever seen him play chess, and he hated clause-analysis. "Chess makes you the smartest."

Anirvan laughed. Kajol turned and stared at him. He sat across the aisle. Kajol had large eyes that looked moist when he stared at someone, and he looked at Anirvan every now and then, their eyes meeting. Anirvan wanted to look away and look back at the same time.

"Chess." Bora, a dark and dangerous boy from Guwahati, whistled. "Chess." He studied Hindi instead of Bangla and hence had that posh-dumb accent when he spoke Bangla. "Not true! Algebra is for the sharpest people."

"Cracking clauses makes you better at cracking clauses." Sushant Kane stared at them. "Playing chess makes you a better chess player. If you're sharp at algebra, that's what you are sharp at."

The boys waited. This could begin another poem about rams and lamp-posts.

"There is no cosmic intelligence," he smiled through his sharp beard and Anirvan imagined beautiful smoke rings curling out of his nose. "Every skill is just that. The skill at doing just that thing."

"No such thing," he said, savouring his joke the way he savoured his love poetry. He glanced at Anirvan for the fraction of a second, but quickly, his eyes were lost. "Nothing cosmic at all."

It was a strange thing to say. Strange, and scary.

SAMPURNA CHATTARJI

Insectboy

Outside the coffee shop in Colaba where the light-haired tourists with their skin boiled raw took refuge from the October sun, Insectboy sat arranging his useless legs. Arranging and rearranging them on the little rack with wheels that he used to get around. Until his stick-thin shanks were displayed at just the right angle, no one would take a look.

"Ready for battle?" Fluteman asked, as he wafted past, his back bristling with bamboo flutes. "All set?"

Insectboy nodded. No words were necessary between Fluteman and him. Fluteman rarely spoke, he let the flute in his hands do that for him. Insectboy approved of wordless communication. He himself was a man of few words.

Insectboy was anywhere between nine to fifteen years old. His father sat outside the J.B. Petit girls' school with a weighing scale in front of him. His father had no legs at all. Between the two of them, it was Insectboy who earned more. Insectboy knew very well it wasn't the keychains that earned him the money. Which didn't mean he neglected them. Oh no, display was everything, that much he had learned in all the nine to fifteen years of his life. Now that his legs were done, he set to work with busy fingers, hanging the bunch on a wire that he twisted into a hook on the outside of the MTNL telephone box. The keychains shook in the very slight breeze. They were made of thin, cheap plastic, but when they shook and shone, they were irresistible, he knew it. They looked like gold and silver, like metals that hadn't yet been invented, slippery pink and green and blue metals to match the women who walked past, their dresses, their bags, their mobile phones.

He loved this place. This triangle that was his world. The fruit stall outside Mondegar, the newspapers and magazines on the ground next to it, the long chains of junk jewelry that hung like curtains on either side of the dark door like a mouth to a cave of people, sitting in a wash of noise and music, drinking, eating, laughing, the taxis that waited behind him, always the same three, Amjad, Ali and Abu, Indiamap with his rolled-up maps walking up and down up and down, Pantshirt taking a small rest on the ledge outside the coffee shop, waiting for fresh young tourist girls to hire as extras, his back to the big glass window that Insectboy sometimes watched TV through, Billi who was small and crippled like him and who spat and fled if anyone tried to feed or pet her, Amma who sat with her daughter and grandson, beating the boy with her coconut-shell hands every time he cried, Didi who brought plastic bags of dal, rice and roti for them all, and sometimes tinfoil packets of food from the Chinese restaurant.

His people, his home. If he suddenly lost both eyes, like Kalu when the pataka burst in his face, he would still be able to see it, imprinted exactly as it was.

Sometimes, especially when he was trying to settle down for the day, Insectboy felt he had more than two legs. It was the way they folded and unfolded, like an unsteady camp bed. The way they scampered, sideways, without warning. Sometimes he felt he was sprouting knees like knobs on the doors of dreams. Sometimes, when rearranging his legs, a knee hit him on the chin with the aim of a champion boxer. They were useless only when it came to walking.

Balloonist went by, looking like he might fly off any second, tethered to his enormous helium heart. Dholki accosted two white men in soiled clothes with fake rudraksha beads around their necks and wrists, and played a witty taal. The dirtier of the two men stamped his feet and flung his arms about as if in response. Then they laughed, shook their heads and crossed the road.

A white woman came out of the coffee shop, lit a cigarette and sat down, not where Pantshirt had been sitting two minutes ago, but on the very narrow ledge in front of the MTNL telephone box, right next to Insectboy.

He steadied his legs and widened his eyes. Careful now, he said to himself. This could go wrong.

"Hello," he said. "Like to buy?'"

She looked up from her cigarette like he had burnt her with it. Her eyes were a muddy brown, with things swimming in them, like little golden worms.

"Hello," she said, a little sadly, Insectboy thought. She hid behind the smoke that she let out from her nostrils and her mouth, almost simultaneously.

"Like to buy?" Insectboy persisted.

She shook her head. She hadn't even looked at what he was selling.

Insectboy took down the bunch of keychains from the hook he had so painstakingly hung it on.

"See?" he said. "Nice? Like to buy?"

"Nice," she echoed, absently.

"See?" Insectboy said again, as if explaining things to a very dumb child, taking out one of the keychains and shaking it in front of her. "Pretty? Buy?"

He had decided she didn't understand proper English. Keep it simple, he decided. Show, not tell. One word at a time. She must be from those other countries where they spoke languages that sounded like rocks breaking. He had heard them talking as they walked by, those aliens.

She shook her head. Insectboy couldn't tell if she was shaking it because she didn't want to buy, because she didn't find it pretty, or simply because she was disagreeing with some voice in her head.

"Got cigarette?" he said, changing tack, waving two fingers in front of his mouth in a puffing motion, in case she didn't understand.

Wordlessly, she took out a pack of Classic Milds and offered it to him. The whole pack! He took it delicately, tapped out one cigarette and gave the pack back. Let her notice his manners.

Before he could make another mime of match striking box, she was flicking her lighter on under his nose. He hastily tucked the cigarette into his mouth and breathed deep.

They smoked, she on her second cigarette by now. The minute she finished she would get up and his first possible customer would be gone.

"In another life, I'd like to be a peacock," she suddenly said. Or that's what Insectboy thought she said. Her accent was funny.

"You?"

She turned those wormy golden eyes on him.

Was she mad? Had she said *peacock*? As if to tease him, at that very moment Mayur went by with his fan of peacock feathers. He swirled past, shaking his hips, but he didn't try to impress the woman or distract her with his wares. No one did that. You didn't steal from your own kind.

She was still looking at him, waiting for his answer.

Insectboy thought for a second.

"Businessman," he said.

It was a serious, practical answer, so he was irritated when the white woman began laughing. A high pained laugh, as if someone was tickling her all over with a needle.

It must have showed on his face, because she stopped as abruptly as she had started.

"I'd like to be a peacock and dance," she said, looking away, inside herself. "In the rain. Have you seen a peacock dancing in the rain?"

Insectboy shook his head. Who had time for peacocks dancing? Where were the peacocks anyway? The closest he had come to a peacock was in Mayur's cane basket.

Besides, this was not the point of his conversation with her.

"Peacock!" he said brightly, picking out another one from the bunch. "See?"

It was the blue keychain. Surely, now that he knew her secret dream, she would buy?

"No thanks," she said, looking sadly at the bauble as it shivered between his fingers. "It's pretty, but I don't need one. Threw all my keys away."

Isn't it odd, Insectboy thought, that no matter how strangely she speaks her words, I understand them?

"Why?" he asked.

"I'm not going back," she said. "I will never go back."

"Why?"

"Because . . ." she said, and she shivered like a bauble in her tinsel top. A picture of Shiva was stretched across her breasts. Shiva's cheeks and blue brow glittered with gold make-up. She must have bought it at one of the stalls outside Mondegar or Leopold. Her sandals, with pink toes sticking out of them—she had clean feet unlike a lot of the foreigners who passed by—her sandals were also from Causeway. Her left arm was noisy with silver bangles. Her right ankle had a wire around it. Her nose had a pin through it.

How old was she? He could never tell. Sometimes the young ones, young in their tight calves and thighs, had such wrinkled leathery faces when you looked up at them. Skin aged differently in different parts, in different parts of the world.

"Because?" he repeated.

She was silent. Her third, or was it fourth, cigarette was lit between her slack lips.

"Once," Insectboy said, abandoning the enticement of English and speaking in his own tongue. "Once, there was a boy with the longest legs of steel. He was so tall he could see over the tops of buildings. At night when the city was asleep he walked around, stepping over the buildings as if they were road dividers. GPO, VT, Laxmi Building, BSNL, InterContinental, President, Museum, Gallery, Taj, Maker Tower, Oberoi, Ambassador, Gateway of India, Afghan Church, Mantralaya, High Court, what part of his world had he not seen from the sky? He saw such strange things on the tops of buildings—motorcycles and rooms filled with pigeons and garden chairs growing around pots and pots of flowers. He saw very young women and very old men dreaming on the rooftops, and he never disturbed them. He saw a fire eating a very tall building once, and from the roof, he lifted a whole family that the firemen had forgotten to save, or been unable to reach even with their longest ladders. He put them down, all the way down near the sea, where they could forget the smell and the sound of burning.

"It was only at night that the boy could stand up to his full height because there was no room in the crowded city for him to unfold and unfold and unfold his mighty steel legs in the day. Put them away, his mother shouted. Shut up and sit down or I'll break your legs, his father yelled. Mummy, his sister screamed, he's kicking me again in his sleep. They lived under a plastic sheet in the rain, under the sky in the summer, only his father had a cot, his mother, his sister and he slept on the piece of pavement that they considered theirs. Down the road from their home was the Sterling picture hall where he had never seen a picture. He sat on the clean white steps whenever he could, he watched the lines of people going in, he watched the big boys selling tickets in black, he imagined what the seats were like and how far they would tilt back and how close the screen would be. He hid away his secret all day. At night, he went home, made himself small, and when they all finally slept, he woke, and stretched and stretched and stretched."

She was silent, but her lips were no longer slack. They were listening, like the rest of her tense, pinned, wired little white body.

"One night, the boy decided to go farther than he had ever gone before. The piece of sea he loved the most was the one garlanded by the Queen's Necklace. But there were other parts of the sea he had never been to. Haji Ali, Worli, Bandra, the names were like a necklace too. He had only heard of them, the sea in which the holy mosque floated like a miracle at high tide, the sea along which people walked on rock, the sea beside which whole families played on sand and in which only the daredevils swam. The city was separated by so many seas! So many cities separated him from that one sea

". . . He would cross from one to the other, he would make this important journey. He knew his legs were long enough to dig right down to the bottom of the water, no matter how deep. He would not take the land at all. From water to water, he would move like a giant god. He liked the idea of the waves splashing against his mighty steel legs.

"So he started stepping over the heads of the buildings, the Maidan, the Station, the Stadium, splash, he was in the middle of Backbay. Looking back at the lights, he felt dizzy with the beauty of it. But he had to go forward, not back. Extending his mighty legs, he walked, in three steps he was rounding Raj Bhavan, where was the magical mosque? He saw before him the way the sea curved and curved, beckoning him.

"He walked, not forgetting to look at the land, where there were parks, there were buildings that might have hidden so many beautiful things, he had heard of the tank where the water never dried, where Ram's arrow had fallen, where lamps were floated every year, he wished he could step ashore for a second and see it. But he had promised he would take the sea, not the road! Banganga would have to wait for another night. He walked with giant strides and then right before him was the Dargah. It was like a fairy tale, an island of light in the middle of the dark water. It was so small, a small sparkling white stone of worship, but it looked like nothing could damage it, not even the greatest storm. He bowed his head, like his mother had taught him, then stepping reverently around it he walked into what seemed like the longest stretch of all.

"The road ran all along the sea. No one was walking on it. He was alone in the night, the lights were not as dazzling here, he missed his part of the world, he wondered if he should turn back, was this Worli, hadn't he journeyed far enough? He wondered if he could already smell Mahim, or if he was only wishing he could smell it because that would tell him how far he had come, when suddenly, the water changed.

"The waves became warmer, heavier. They felt alive, like hands and tongues. He felt the hands slapping his legs but not pushing him away. They liked him! He felt like giggling as they tickled him, he felt aroused, as if any minute now he might burst open. He felt the tongues pushing into him, tasting the strength of his legs all along their length to his knees. He felt like kissing the surface of the water that pleased him so much. He bent down. He bent down down down from his enormous height until he felt the crack in his waist that warned him not to bend any more. His face was skimming the surface of the sea. His legs were dug deep in, steady as pillars. Hands touched his face, drew away from it invisible threads of silk, he was the finest strongest silk, and they were unweaving him, they were drawing him across the surface of the sea in a net that would span the earth, they were playing him like a giant harp through which the wind would blow and make a music sent from heaven, he was being broken apart by soft and skilful hands, no longer flesh and blood and bone, but silk and steel and stone, he was being shaped and reshaped into an arch of light, he was breaking slowly into an endless, inhuman joy that would destroy who he was, who he had been, and hold him in this strange new pose, his arms so intensely far away from his legs, his heart no longer only at the center of him but all over his new body, his body laid down like a bridge across the water, this warm dark living water that he now stretched across as if he were a supple wire along which humans could safely glide. He would never go back to the southern tip where he had lived all his short, secret life, he would stay here forever, rooted in the sea, this strange new enormous beautiful thing he had always wanted to become, no need ever again to be small and folded, no need to hide, here he would stay for all the world to see, linking two parts of land to two parts of sea for ever."

Insectboy stopped speaking, and looked at her. The white woman was weeping silently, her tears seemed golden as they streamed down her cheeks, and fell on her T-shirt. She made no attempt to hide them, to wipe them.

Insectboy looked openly at her weeping face. She had understood. Or maybe not. Maybe his voice speaking a language she did not understand had sounded like the kind of sad music women in her country listened to when they needed an excuse to cry.

He hung the bunch of keychains back on the hook of the MTNL telephone box. She would cry. When she had finished crying, she would get up and leave, and go back into the coffee shop where smoking was not allowed, back to her hotel, back to wherever she came from, even if she did use that word "never" with such certainty. But not before laying on his knees the cool glance of her pity for his stick-thin shanks, not before laying unobtrusively, on the ledge next to him, as if for some unseen god at the shrine of the telephone box, a little bit of money, which would be more than a little for him.

Before she had a chance to do any of that, before things returned to the way they were, Insectboy slipped the blue keychain into the cloth bag that lay open at her feet.

Dance, he thought, in the rain.

Contributors' Notes

ANDAL is a ninth-century Alvar saint of South India who is credited with composing the Tamil works *Thirupavai* and *Nachiar Tirumozhi* that are still recited to this day. Eschewing earthly marriage, Andal "married" the god Vishnu, both spiritually and physically, and is considered an incarnation of the divine in many parts of South India, especially in Tamil Nadu in general and Srivilliputhur, her birthplace, in particular where there is a large temple dedicated to her.

USHA AKELLA has authored nine books. Her most recent collection of poetry, *The Waiting*, was published by Sahitya Akademi. She earned a Master's in Creative Writing from the University of Cambridge. She is the founder of Matwaala (www.matwaaala.com), the first South Asian Diaspora Poetry Festival and an interview site, www.the-pov.com.

MEENA ALEXANDER (1951–2018) was an award-winning author and scholar. She was Distinguished Professor of English at Hunter College and the Graduate Center of the City University of New York. Her published works include *Atmospheric Embroidery*, *Birthplace with Buried Stones*, *Quickly Changing River*, *Raw Silk*, and *Illiterate Heart* (winner of the PEN Open Book Award), all published by TriQuarterly Books/Northwestern University Press.

ETHIRAJ AKILAN translates from English to Tamil. His translations of Ahmet Hamdi Tanpinar's *The Time Regulation Institute*, Halldór Laxness's *The Fish Can Sing*, and Orhan Pamuk's *The Black Book* have been published by Kalachuvadu Publications. His translation of Ma Jian's *Stick Out Your Tongue* has been published by Adaiyaalam India. He is currently translating Michal Ajvaz's *The Other City* and Matthew Alper's *The "God" Part of the Brain*.

KAZIM ALI was born in the United Kingdom and has lived transnationally in the United States, Canada, India, France, and the Middle East. His books encompass multiple genres, including several volumes of poetry, novels, and translations. He is currently a Professor of Literature at the University of California, San Diego. His newest books are a volume of three long poems entitled *The Voice of Sheila Chandra* and a memoir of his Canadian childhood, *Northern Light*.

ANAMIKA is a Delhi-based Hindi poet, novelist, translator and professor of English.

Her national award-winning poetry collections are *Khurduri Hatheliyan*, *Doob-Dhan*, and *Tokri Mein Digant*, and her novels are *Dus Dwaare Ka Pinjara*, *Tinka Tinke Paas*, and *Ainesaaz*. Her translations of Rainer Maria Rilke, Pablo Neruda, Doris Lessing, Octavio Paz, among others, have been published by Sahitya Akademi, HarperCollins, Katha, and Penguin. She is a trained Kathak dancer.

GAIUTRA BAHADUR is a Guyanese American writer and assistant professor of journalism at Rutgers University–Newark. Her book *Coolie Woman* was shortlisted for the Orwell Prize. She is the recipient of literary residencies at The Bellagio Center in Italy and the MacDowell Colony, where she began "The Stained Veil." She is twice winner of the New Jersey State Council on the Arts Award for Prose and a winner of the Barbara Deming Memorial Award for feminist writers.

SUBHRO BANDOPADHYAY is the author of four books of poetry in Bengali, one of which fetched him the Sahitya Akademi Yuva Puraskar in 2013, while three were translated into Spanish. He received the Antonio Machado International Poetry Residency Fellowship from the Government of Spain (2008) and *Poetas de otros mundos distinction* from Fondo poético internacional, Spain. He has been invited to distinguished literary festivals around the world. He teaches Spanish at the Instituto Cervantes, New Delhi.

SOHINI BASAK's first poetry collection, *We Live in the Newness of Small Differences*, was awarded the inaugural International Beverly Prize. She studied literature and creative writing at the universities of Delhi, Warwick, and East Anglia, where she was awarded the Malcolm Bradbury Continuation Grant for Poetry. She won a Toto Funds the Arts award for her poetry in 2017.

SUJATA BHATT's latest books from Carcanet Press are *Collected Poems* and *Poppies in Translation*. She has received numerous awards including the Commonwealth Poetry Prize (Asia) and a Cholmondeley Award. In 2014 she was the first recipient of the Mexican International Poetry Prize, *Premio Internacional de Poesía Nuevo Siglo de Oro 1914–2014*. Her work has been widely anthologized, broadcast on radio and television, and has been translated into more than twenty languages.

SHELLY BHOIL is an Indian poet and independent scholar living in Brazil. Her publications include two poetry collections, *An Ember from Her Pyre* (2016) and "Preposição de entendimento" (forthcoming). She has also edited two reference books on Tibet, *Tibetan Subjectivities on the Global Stage* (Lexington Books 2018) and *New Narratives of Exile Tibet* (Lexington Books 2020).

JASWINDER BOLINA is author of the essay collection *Of Color*; three full-length poetry collections, *The 44th of July*, *Phantom Camera*, and *Carrier Wave*; and a digital chapbook, *The Tallest Building in America*.

MICHELLE CAHILL writes poetry and fiction. She is the 2020 Red Room Australian Poetry Fellow. Her prizes include the Kingston Writing School Hilary Mantel International Short Story Competition, the Val Vallis Poetry Award, and the NSW Premier's Literary Award for New Writing. Her poetry collection, *Vishvarupa*, was shortlisted in the Victorian Premier's Literary Award. *The Herring Lass* is her most recent book. Her novel "Woolf" is forthcoming with Hachette in 2021.

PRIYA SARUKKAI CHABRIA is an award-winning poet, translator and writer of nine books of poetry, speculative fiction, literary non-fiction, translation and, as editor, two poetry anthologies. Her books include *Andal: The Autobiography of a Goddess* (translation), *Sing of Life: Revisioning Tagore's Gitanjali* (poetry), *Clone* (speculative fiction) and *Bombay/Mumbai: Immersions* (non-fiction). She has studied Sanskrit rasa theory of aesthetic and Tamil Sangam poetics, and collaborates with photographers, filmmakers and dancers. She is the founding editor of Poetry at Sangam. See more at www.priyasarukkaichabria.com

NIRENDRANATH CHAKRABORTY (1924–2018) was a poet and litterateur who published widely and wrote extensively across genres. He won many awards for his poetry, including the Sahitya Akademi Award (1974) for *Ulongo Raja*, the Tarashankar Literary Award, the Ananda Puroshkar, the Sunil Gangopadhyay Memorial Award for Excellence in Bengali literature in 2012, and the Banga Bibhushan Award in 2017.

AMARJIT CHANDAN is a Punjabi writer, editor, translator and activist. He has published eight collections of poetry and five collections of essays. His work has been translated into many languages including English, Arabic, Brazilian Portuguese, Greek, Italian, Slovenian, and Turkish. He has translated the works of Bertolt Brecht, Pablo Neruda, Yiannis Ritsos, Nazim Hikmet, John Berger, Martin Carter, and others into Punjabi. He was poet in residence at the University of California, Santa Barbara, in 2014.

CHANDAK CHATTARJI is a poet, translator, and retired educationist. A product of Shantiniketan and Calcutta University, his recent publications include a bilingual poetry collection, *Summer Knows / Les savoirs de l'été* (Poetrywala 2021), translated by Roselyne Sibille; a skill-builder for all ages, *You Can Do It! Be a Grammar Champ* (HarperCollins 2021); as well as translations of Jibanananda Das's short fiction, *Three Stories* (Paperwall 2016), and *Six Bangla Poets* (Poetrywala 2017).

SUMAN CHHABRA is a multigenre writer and the author of *Demons Off* (Meekling

Press 2015). She is a Kundiman Fellow and her work has been supported by The Poetry Foundation, Vermont Studio Center, Ragdale, the anthologies *Asian American Literature: Rethinking the Canon* (The Massachusetts Review and the Smithsonian) and *New Poetry from the Midwest* (New American Press) among others. She attended the University of Michigan and received an MFA from the School of the Art Institute of Chicago. Chhabra teaches courses on Asian American literature at SAIC.

ROHAN CHHETRI is the author of *Slow Startle* and the chapbook *Jurassic Desire*. His second book of poems, *Lost, Hurt, or in Transit Beautiful*, is forthcoming from Tupelo Press and HarperCollins India in 2021. His poems have appeared, or are forthcoming, in *Paris Review, New England Review*, Literary Hub, Poetry Society of America, and have been translated into French for *Revue Europe* and *Terre à ciel*.

MANGALESH DABRAL (1948-2020) published six books of poems, three collections of literary essays and sociocultural commentary, a book of conversations, and two travelogues. A selection of his poems in English translation appeared in the volume *This Number Does Not Exist*. He was a fellow of the International Writing Program at the University of Iowa in 1991 and received numerous awards, including Shamsher Sammaan (1995), Pahal Sammaan (1998), and the Sahitya Akademi Award (2000).

MUSTANSIR DALVI is an Anglophone poet, translator and editor, with three books of poems in English, *Brouhahas of Cocks, Cosmopolitician* and *Walk*. His poems have been translated into French, Croatian, and Marathi. Dalvi's English translation of Muhammad Iqbal's *Shikwa* and *Jawaab-e-Shikwa* from the Urdu as *Taking Issue* and *Allah's Answer* has been described as "insolent and heretical." He is the editor of *Man Without a Navel*, a collection of translations of Hemant Divate's poems from the Marathi.

KEKI N. DARUWALLA has published twelve poetry volumes, the latest being *Naishapur and Babylon: Poems 2005–2017*. He is the author of three novels, most recently *Swerving to Solitude: Letters to Mama*. He won the Commonwealth Poetry Award (Asia 1987) and Padma Shri 2014. He returned his Sahitya Akademi Award in protest against intolerance. Daruwalla was a member of the National Commission for Minorities (2011–2014) and writes the political column "Musings and Maledictions" for *Tribune*.

NABINA DAS is the author of the poetry books—*Sanskarnama, Into the Migrant City*, and *Blue Vessel*; a short fiction volume titled *The House of Twining Roses*, and *Footprints in the Bajra*, a novel. Das is a Charles Wallace, Sangam House, and Sahapedia-UNESCO fellowship alumna, and an MFA from Rutgers-Camden. She is editor of

Witness: The Red River Book of Poetry of Dissent (2021). Her poetry volume *Ani[l]ma and the Narrative Limits* is forthcoming from Yoda Press in 2022.

LAL DED was a fourteenth-century Kashmiri mystic and poet fondly known as "Lalla." A spiritual questor who composed a memorable corpus of *vaakh*s or quatrains, Lal Ded was a bridge figure between Kashmir's millennial Hindu-Buddhist tradition and the Islamic practices that began to evolve in the Valley during her lifetime. Nourished by the heritage of Yogachara Buddhism and Kashmir Shaivism, Lal Ded inspired Kashmir's distinctive Rishi lineage of Sufi practitioners.

JAY DESHPANDE is the author of *Love the Stranger* and *The Rest of the Body* (both from YesYes Books) and *The Umbrian Sonnets* (PANK). His poems have appeared in *American Poetry Review*, *New England Review*, *AGNI*, *Denver Quarterly*, and elsewhere. He is the recipient of a Wallace Stegner Fellowship and teaches for Brooklyn Poets.

IMTIAZ DHARKER was awarded the Queen's Gold Medal for Poetry in 2014, has received the Cholmondeley Award and an Honorary Doctorate from SOAS, is a Fellow of the Royal Society of Literature, and is on the editorial board of Poems on the Underground. Her six poetry collections include *Over the Moon* and *Luck is the Hook*, both from Bloodaxe Books, UK.

TSERING WANGMO DHOMPA is the author of the poetry books *My Rice Tastes Like the Lake*, *In the Absent Everyday*, and *Rules of the House* (all from Apogee Press, Berkeley). Dhompa's first nonfiction book, *Coming Home to Tibet*, was published by Penguin India in 2014 and in the US by Shambhala Publications in 2016. She teaches in the English Department at Villanova University.

HEMANT DIVATE is an award-winning Marathi poet, editor, publisher and translator with six poetry titles. His most recent publications in English translation are *Struggles with Imagined Gods* and *Man Without a Navel*. His poems have been translated into French, Italian, Slovak, Japanese, Persian, Maltese, Serbian, Hungarian, Turkish, Slovenian, Greek, Galician, as well as many Indian languages. He is the founder-editor of Marathi little magazine, *Abhidha Nantar*, and the independent poetry imprint, Poetrywala.

ROSALYN D'MELLO is a writer, editor, and art critic. She is the author of *A Handbook for My Lover*. She writes a weekly feminist column for *Midday* and is a regular columnist for the web-based publication, *STIR*, and the weekly magazine *Open*, where she writes about her visits to artists' studios, the subject of her forthcoming book for Oxford University Press, India. She was nominated for the Forbes' Best Emerging Art Writer Award in 2014.

TISHANI DOSHI is an award-winning poet, novelist, and dancer. Her most recent books are *Girls Are Coming Out of the Woods*, shortlisted for the Ted Hughes Poetry Award, and a novel, *Small Days and Nights*, shortlisted for the RSL Ondaatje Prize and a New York Times Bestsellers Editor's Choice. She is a visiting professor of creative writing at New York University Abu Dhabi, and otherwise lives on a beach in Tamil Nadu, India. See more at www.tishanidoshi.com.

MONICA FERRELL's most recent collection, *You Darling Thing*, was a finalist for the Kingsley Tufts Award and *Believer* Book Award in Poetry. Her novel, *The Answer Is Always Yes*, was named one of *Booklist*'s Top Ten Debut Novels of the Year. She has been recognized with residencies at the Civitella Ranieri Foundation and the MacDowell Colony, a Wallace Stegner Fellowship, and a Discovery/*The Nation* Prize. She teaches Creative Writing at Purchase College (SUNY).

SHAMALA GALLAGHER is the author of *Late Morning When the World Burns* (The Cultural Society 2019), a poetry collection set in the end times of the lush, still-segregated American South. Her poems and essays appear in *Poetry, Black Warrior Review, The Rumpus, West Branch, The Offing*, and elsewhere. She lives in Athens, GA.

JOY GOSWAMI has published over fifty titles. His poetry in English translation is available from HarperCollins—*Selected Poems* (2014, 2018) and *After Death Comes Water* (2021). His many awards include the Ananda Puroshkar, the Bangla Academy Puroshkar, the Lifetime Achievement Award from the Bharatiya Bhasha Parishad in 2011, and the first Tata Literature Live! Poet Laureate Award in 2014. He was a fellow of the International Writing Program at the University of Iowa in 2001.

RANJIT HOSKOTE is a poet, cultural theorist, translator, and curator. His books include *Vanishing Acts: New & Selected Poems 1985–2005, Central Time, Jonahwhale, The Atlas of Lost Beliefs, Hunchprose*, and the translation of a Kashmiri saint–poet, *I, Lalla: The Poems of Lal Ded*. Hoskote was a fellow of the International Writing Program, University of Iowa, and writer in residence at Villa Waldberta, Munich. He was curator of India's first-ever national pavilion at the Venice Biennale (2011).

MUHAMMAD IQBAL (1877–1938) was a preeminent poet of India in the early twentieth century. His collections of poetry include *Bang-e-dara* (1924), *Javed-nama* (1932) and *Baal-e-Jibreel* (1935). In his later years he was an advocate for Muslims in India, whose causes he represented through his writings, particularly *The Reconstruction of Religious Thought in Islam* (1930), his poetry and public speeches. Iqbal is best remembered in India for "*Saare jahaan se achchha*," recited to this day as an alternate national anthem.

J. DEVIKA is a social researcher, historian, translator, and teacher, presently working at the Centre for Development Studies, Kerala, India. She has written on the intertwined histories of gender, politics, culture, and development in Kerala and has translated literature from Malayalam to English, and social science from English to Malayalam. She offers social commentary on Kerala at kafila.online.

K. SATCHIDANANDAN writes poetry in Malayalam and prose in both Malayalam and English. He is also a critic, playwright, translator, and essayist. Representative translations from his poetry have appeared in the collections *While I Write*, *Misplaced Objects and Other Poems*, *The Missing Rib*, and *The Whispering Tree*. He has won several literary awards including the Sahitya Akademi Award and the World Poetry Peace Prize from the United Arab Emirates.

K. SRILATA is a professor of English at IIT Madras and has been writer in residence at the University of Stirling, Scotland; Yeonhui Art Space, Seoul; and Sangam House, Bangalore. She has five collections of poetry, the latest of which, *The Unmistakable Presence of Absent Humans*, was published by Poetrywala in 2019. Srilata has a novel titled *Table for Four* (Penguin, India) and is co-editor of the anthology *Rapids of a Great River: The Penguin Book of Tamil Poetry*.

K. R. MEERA is the author of more than a dozen books in Malayalam including novels, novellas, short story collections, essays and children's literature. Her novel *Aaraachaar* has won several awards in Kerala. It was translated into English by J. Devika as *Hangwoman* and shortlisted for the DSC Literary Prize. *The Poison of Love* was longlisted for the DSC Literary Prize and *The Unseeing Idol of Light* (both translated by Ministhy S.) shortlisted for the Crossword Translation Award.

KALIDASA (fourth century CE) is widely regarded as the greatest poet and dramatist in the Sanskrit language. Over the centuries, his work has been cited, celebrated and served as a benchmark for poetics and aesthetics in literature. His best-known works are *Abhijnana Shakuntalam*, *Ritusamharam*, and *Meghadutam*.

SUBHASHINI KALIGOTLA is a poet and art historian of premodern South Asia. Author of the poetry collection *Bird of the Indian Subcontinent* (2018), she teaches at Yale and lives in New York City.

MEENA KANDASAMY has published two collections of poetry, *Touch* (2006) and *Ms Militancy* (2010). Her critically acclaimed debut novel, *The Gypsy Goddess* (2014), narrated the 1968 Kilvenmani massacre. Her second novel, a work of auto-fiction,

When I Hit You: Or, The Portrait of the Writer as a Young Wife (2017), was shortlisted for the Women's Prize for Fiction 2018. Her latest novel is *Exquisite Cadavers* (2019).

KIRUN KAPUR's latest book, *Women in the Waiting Room* (Black Lawrence Press, 2020), was a finalist for the National Poetry Series. She is the winner of the Arts & Letters Rumi Prize and the Antivenom Poetry Award for her first book, *Visiting Indira Gandhi's Palmist* (Elixir Press, 2015). She serves as editor at the Beloit Poetry Journal and teaches at Amherst College, where she is director of the Creative Writing Program.

ARUNI KASHYAP writes fiction in English and Assamese. He is the author of the short story collection *His Father's Disease* and the novel *The House With a Thousand Stories*. He currently works as an Assistant Professor at the University of Georgia, Athens.

RAFIQ KATHWARI, the first Kashmiri American recipient of the Patrick Kavanagh Poetry Award, obtained an MFA from Columbia University. His new collection of poems is *My Mother's Scribe* (Yoda Press 2020). He divides his time between New York, Dublin, Cairo, and Kashmir where he was born and raised.

AKHIL KATYAL is a writer based in New Delhi. His second book of poems, *How Many Countries Does the Indus Cross*, won the Editor's Choice Award from The (Great) Indian Poetry Collective and his third book of poems, *Like Blood on the Bitten Tongue: Delhi Poems* (Westland-Context), came out in 2020.

TABISH KHAIR's latest novel, *Night of Happiness*, appeared in 2019. In June 2020 he published an e-book, *Quarantined Sonnets*, containing rewritings of Shakespeare's sonnets in the context of the virus crisis, with the profits donated to a charity. Winner of the All India Poetry Prize, his fiction has been shortlisted for the Man Asian Prize, the DSC Prize, the Hindu Fiction Prize, Sahitya Akademi Award, Encore Award, among others.

GEETA KOTHARI is the nonfiction editor of the *Kenyon Review*. Her writing has appeared in various anthologies and journals, including *New England Review, Massachusetts Review, Kenyon Review*, and *Best American Essays*. She is the author of *I Brake for Moose and Other Stories*, and teaches at the University of Pittsburgh and in the MFA program at Carlow University.

MONIKA KUMAR teaches British Poetry and Indian Writing in English at the Regional Institute of English, Chandigarh. She writes in Hindi, Punjabi, and English. Her poems have been translated into English, Maltese, Croatian, Slovenian, and Galician.

She has translated the poetry of Zbigniew Herbert, Tomas Tranströmer, Antonio Porchia, and Roberto Juarroz into Hindi.

AMIT MAJMUDAR is a poet, novelist, essayist, and translator. His recent books include *Godsong: A Verse Translation of the Bhagavad-Gita, with Commentary* (2018) and the poetry collection *What He Did in Solitary* (2020). Novels forthcoming in India include *The Map and the Scissors* (HarperCollins India, 2022) and *Heroes the Colour of Dust* (Puffin India, 2022). The former first Poet Laureate of Ohio, he is also a diagnostic nuclear radiologist in Westerville, Ohio, where he lives with his wife and three children.

SAIKAT MAJUMDAR is the author of four novels—*The Middle Finger* (2020), *The Scent of God* (2019), *The Firebird* (2015), published in the US as *Play House* (2017), and *Silverfish* (2007). He has also published a book of literary criticism, *Prose of the World* (2013), a general nonfiction book on higher education, *College: Pathways of Possibility* (2018), and a co-edited a collection of essays, *The Critic as Amateur* (2019). He is Professor of English & Creative Writing at Ashoka University.

RAVI MANGLA is the author of the novel *Understudies* (Outpost19). His stories and essays have appeared in *Kenyon Review, Cincinnati Review, Quarterly West, Mid-American Review*, and *Los Angeles Review of Books*. He lives in Rochester, NY.

INDERJEET MANI is a retired professor and scientist based in Thailand, the setting of his novel *Toxic Spirits* (Calumet Editions 2019). He has published six scholarly books, including *The Imagined Moment: Time, Narrative and Computation* (Nebraska 2010). His short stories and essays have appeared in *3:AM Magazine, Aeon, Apple Valley Review, Cargo, Drunken Boat, Eclectica, New World Writing, Nimrod, PANK, Short Fiction Journal, Slow Trains, Storgy, Unsung Stories, Word Riot*, and many other venues.

KUZHALI MANICKAVEL's short fiction collections *Things We Found During the Autopsy, Insects Are Just like You and Me Except Some of Them Have Wings* and chapbooks *The Lucy Temerlin Institute for Broken Shapeshifters Guide to Starving Boys, How to Love Mathematical Objects*, and *Eating Sugar, Telling Lies* all appeared from Blaft Publications, Chennai. Her work has also appeared in *Granta, Strange Horizons, Agni, Subtropics, Michigan Quarterly Review*, and *DIAGRAM*. See more at www.kuzhalimanickavel.com

SHARANYA MANIVANNAN is the author of several books of fiction, poetry and children's literature, including *The High Priestess Never Marries, Mermaids In The Moonlight* and *The Queen of Jasmine Country*.

SHIKHA MALAVIYA is co-founder of The (Great) Indian Poetry Collective, a mentorship model press publishing voices from India and the Indian diaspora. She has been a featured TEDx speaker, AWP mentor, and was selected as San Ramon, California's Poet Laureate. Her book of poems is *Geography of Tongues*.

ARVIND KRISHNA MEHROTRA is a poet, translator, and scholar. He has recently published *Translating the Indian Past and Other Literary Histories* (Permanent Black 2019), *Selected Poems and Translations* (NYRB 2020), and (with Sara Rai) a translation of Vinod Kumar Shukla's stories, *Blue Is Like Blue* (HarperCollins 2019). He lives in Dehradun.

PALASH KRISHNA MEHROTRA's debut story collection, *Eunuch Park* (Penguin India), was a finalist for the Shakti Bhatt First Book Prize and the Hindu Prize for Fiction. His first work of nonfiction, *The Butterfly Generation* (Rupa-Raintree), was a finalist for the Crossword Book Award. He is also the editor of two anthologies, *Recess: The Penguin Book of Schooldays* and *House Spirit: Drinking in India*. He is a columnist with *The Economic Times*.

LEEYA MEHTA is a prize-winning poet, fiction writer and essayist. She is the author of *The Towers of Silence* and *A Story of the World Before the Fence*. Leeya writes a column on the literary life, *The Company We Keep*. She lives in Washington DC where she works in international development. She has finished a novel, *Extinction*. See more at https://leeyamehta.com.

SIDDHARTHA MENON has published three collections of poems, *Woodpecker* (2010), *Writing Again* (2012), and *The Owl and the Laughing Buddha* (2016). His poems have appeared in journals and anthologies published in India. Since 1991, he has been working at Rishi Valley School and other schools run by the Krishnamurti Foundation India. He balances poetry, as best he can, with teaching, school administration, and long distance running.

VIKAS K. MENON is a poet, playwright, and songwriter. His poems have been featured in *Chicago Quarterly Review*, *Indivisible: An Anthology of South Asian American Poetry*, and *The HarperCollins Book of English Poetry*. He co-wrote *Priya's Shakti* (www.priyashakti.com), the first of a series of award-winning augmented reality comic books that address gender-based violence. He was one of the co-writers of the shadow-play, *Feathers of Fire: A Persian Epic*.

SUBIMAL MISRA is considered the father of the experimental novel in Bengali and has written exclusively for little magazines since the 1960s, with several volumes of stories, novels, plays and prose to his credit. Translations of Misra's work in English by

V. Ramaswamy, his chosen translator, include *The Golden Gandhi Statue from America: Early Stories* (2010), *Wild Animals Prohibited: Stories, Anti-Stories* (2015), and *Actually This Could Have Become Ramayan Chamar's Tale: Two Anti-Novels* (2019).

MONICA MODY is a transdisciplinary poet whose recent work is rooted in earth-based worldviews. She is the author of *Kala Pani* (1913 Press), *Bright Parallel* (Copper Coin), and three chapbooks including *Ordinary Annals* (above/ground). She has been a recipient of the Sparks Prize Fellowship (Notre Dame), the Zora Neale Hurston Award (Naropa), and a Toto Award for Creative Writing.

RAJIV MOHABIR is the author of *ANTIMAN* (winner of the 2019 Restless Books' New Immigrant Writing Prize), *Cutlish*, *The Cowherd's Son* (winner of the 2015 Kundiman Prize) and *The Taxidermist's Cut* (winner of the Four Way Books Intro to Poetry Prize), and translator of *I Even Regret Night: Holi Songs of Demerara* (Kaya Press 2019). Currently he is an assistant professor of poetry in the MFA program at Emerson College and translations editor at *Waxwing Journal*.

SHARMISTHA MOHANTY is the author of three works of prose—*Book One*, *New Life*, and *Five Movements in Praise*, and most recently of a book of poems, *The Gods Came Afterwards*. She has also translated a selection of Tagore's fiction, *Broken Nest and Other Stories*. Mohanty is the founding editor of the online literature journal *Almost Island*, begun in 2007. Mohanty taught at the Creative Writing MFA, City University of Hong Kong, from 2009 to 2016.

ARYANIL MUKHERJEE is a bilingual poet, translator and editor who has authored fifteen books of poetry and essays in English and Bengali. His poetry has been included in several anthologies in the USA, India, and Spain, discussed in the Best American Poetry Blog and has been translated into Hindi, Spanish, and Danish.

VIJAY NAMBISAN (1963–2017) was a poet, writer of nonfiction, critic, journalist, and translator. His debut collection, *Gemini*, a shared edition with Jeet Thayil, was published in 1992. His second collection, *First Infinities*, appeared in 2015. He published two acclaimed nonfiction books, *Bihar Is in the Eye of the Beholder* (2000) and *Language as an Ethic* (2003), as well as *Two Measures of Bhakti* (2009), comprising translations of the devotional poetry of Poonthanam and Melpathur Narayana Bhattathiri.

KUNWAR NARAIN (1927–2017)—a poet, writer and thinker—published in Hindi. His diverse oeuvre of seven decades includes poetry, epics, stories, criticism, essays, diaries, translations of poets like Constantine P. Cavafy, Stéphane Mallarmé, Jorge Luis Borges, Zbigniew Herbert, and Tadeusz Różewicz, and writings on world cinema and the arts. His honors include the Sahitya Akademi award and Senior Fellowship, the

Padma Bhushan; Warsaw University's medal; Italy's Premio Feronia for distinguished world author; and India's highest literary prize, the Jnanpith.

APURVA NARAIN is Kunwar Narain's son and translator. His translations include the poetry collection, *No Other World*, the co-translated story collection, *The Play of Dolls*, and the poetry collection, *Witnesses of Remembrance*. Several literary journals have carried his work. He has professional interests in ecology, public health, and ethics; and writes in English.

VIVEK NARAYANAN's books of poems include *Universal Beach*, *Life and Times of Mr S*, and *After*. His honors include fellowships from the Radcliffe Institute for Advanced Studies and the Cullman Center for Writers and Scholars at the New York Public Library. He teaches at George Mason University in Fairfax, Virginia.

RALPH NAZARETH is the author of *Ferrying Secrets*, *Cristal: Poemas Selectos*, *Between Us the Long Road*, and *Dropping Death*. He has taught in schools, colleges, universities and prisons. The Managing Editor of Yuganta Press, he also heads GraceWorks, Inc., an international nonprofit foundation. He lives in Stamford, CT.

ROBIN S. NGANGOM writes and translates in English and Manipuri. He is the author of three poetry books—*Words and the Silence*, *Time's Crossroads*, and *The Desire of Roots*. His poems have appeared in *The New Statesman*, *Planet: The Welsh Internationalist*, *Verse*, and *Literary Review*. He teaches literature at the North-Eastern Hill University, India.

NIRALA was the pen-name of Suryakant Tripathi (1899–1961). His family was from the Kannauj region of Uttar Pradesh but had migrated to the small princely state of Mahishadal in Bengal, where his father was a court official. In a literary career spanning four decades, Nirala published novels, short stories, and books of essays, in addition to a dozen volumes of poetry. He is widely seen as the greatest Hindi poet after the sixteenth-century Tulsi Das.

SASHA PARMASAD has an MFA from Columbia University and is the author of the poetry collection, *No Poem*. Her novel, *Ink and Sugar*, was placed third in the national First Words Literary Contest for South Asian Writers, and she stood first in the annual Poetry International competition. Her poetry has been published in the US, India, and the Caribbean, and she has designed and taught academic and creative writing courses, and Transcendental Meditation courses, in programs at Columbia University.

SURJIT PATAR is one of Punjab's most celebrated poets. The range of his poetic forms includes very strict meters as well as blank and free dramatic verse. He has published seven collections of poetry, translated three tragedies of Federico Lorca as well as poems by Bertolt Brecht and Pablo Neruda into Punjabi. In 1995 he was given the Sahitya Akademi (Indian Academy of Letters) Award and the Saraswati Award by the K. K. Birla Foundation in 2010.

GIEVE PATEL is a writer and painter. He has published three collections of verse; a volume of his *Collected Poems* appeared in 2017. His paintings are in various collections including The National Gallery of Modern Art, New Delhi, and the Peabody Essex Museum, Salem, Massachusetts. *Mister Behram and Other Plays*, a collection of his performed plays, was published in 2007. He has worked as a medical practitioner in rural and urban India.

SALEEM PEERADINA is the author of six books of poetry including *Final Cut* (Valley Press 2016) and *Heart's Beast: New and Selected Poems* (Copper Coin 2017), and a prose memoir, *The Ocean in my Yard* (Penguin 2005). He is Emeritus professor of English at Siena Heights University in Michigan, USA.

ARJUN RAJENDRAN is the author of *One Man: Two Executions* (Westland, 2020), *Snake Wine* (Les Editions du Zaporogue 2014), *The Cosmonaut in Hergé's Rocket* (Poetrywala 2017), and the chapbook *Your Baby Is Starving* (Aainanagar/VAYAVYA 2017).

LALNUNSANGA RALTE works as an assistant professor of English at Martin Luther Christian University, Shillong. He is a member of the North East Writer's Forum and has participated in various literary events. His poems have been published in various online magazines and anthologies. He was part of the Poets Translating Poets project organized by the Goethe-Insitut, Mumbai, and was invited to read his poems in a poetry festival in Germany.

VINITA RAMANI explores myth, ritual, and sexuality through words and sound. A former music and film journalist, she previously headed her own NGO that represented victims of mass crimes before the UN-backed Khmer Rouge Tribunal in Cambodia.

MANI RAO has ten poetry books including *Sing to Me* (Recent Work Press, Australia), *New & Selected Poems* (Poetrywala, India), *Echolocation* (Math Paper Press, Singapore), and *Ghostmasters* (Chameleon Press, Hong Kong). She has two books in translation from Sanskrit—*Bhagavad Gita* (Autumn Hill Books, USA and Fingerprint, India) and *Kalidasa for the 21st Century Reader* (Aleph Books, India). Her latest book is *Living Mantra—Mantra, Deity and Visionary Experience Today* (Palgrave Macmillan 2019).

SRIKANTH REDDY's latest book of poetry is *Underworld Lit*. He is the author of

Voyager, named one of the best books of poetry in 2011 by, among others, *New Yorker*. His first collection, *Facts for Visitors*, won the 2005 Asian American Literary Award for Poetry. He has received fellowships from the Guggenheim Foundation and the National Endowment for the Arts, and is Professor of English and Creative Writing at the University of Chicago.

KUTTI REVATHI is the author of fifteen collections of poetry in Tamil, including the controversial *Mulaigal*, five short fiction collections, and a novel. She is also a filmmaker, film lyricist, anthologist, editor of a Tamil literary magazine for women's writing (Panikkudam) and a doctor trained in the traditional Tamil Siddha system of medicine. Her directorial debut was the Tamil feature film, *Siragu* (2019).

ARUN SAGAR has published two books of poems, *Anamnesia* (Poetrywala 2013) and *A Long Walk in Sunlight* (Copper Coin 2020). His work has appeared in numerous literary journals from India and abroad. He currently lives in Sonipat where he teaches law.

ANEES SALIM's published works include the novels *Vanity Bagh* (winner of The Hindu Literary Prize for Best Fiction 2013), *The Blind Lady's Descendants* (winner of the Raymond Crossword Book Award for Best Fiction 2014 and the Kendra Sahitya Akademi Award 2018), and *The Small-town Sea* (winner of the Atta Galatta-Banaglore Literature Festival Book Prize for Best Fiction 2017). His works have been translated into several languages.

JASON SANDHAR teaches courses in critical race theory and postcolonial literature at Huron University College in London, Ontario, Canada. In 2019, he completed his PhD in English Literature at Western University. His work has appeared in numerous literary journals and anthologies.

IRWIN ALLAN SEALY is the author, most recently, of *Zelaldinus*, a verse novel. His novel *The Trotter-Nama* is regarded as a modern Indian classic. Other works include the novels *Hero*, *The Everest Hotel*, *The Brainfever Bird*, and *Red*; *The Small Wild Goose Pagoda*, a memoir; and the travelogues—*From Yukon to Yucatan* and *The China Sketchbook*. He has won the Padma Shri, the Sahitya Akademi Award, and the Commonwealth Writers' Prize.

SEJAL SHAH is the author of the award-winning essay collection, *This Is One Way to Dance* (University of Georgia Press), named an NPR Best Book of 2020. Her writing, spanning multiple genres, has appeared widely online and in print including several anthologies. She is the recipient of a New York Foundation for the Arts Fellowship in fiction and fellowships from the Kenyon Review Writers' Workshop, Kundiman, the Millay Colony, and The Virginia Center for the Creative Arts.

RAVI SHANKAR has published, edited or has forthcoming over fifteen books, including the Muse India award-winning translations of ninth-century Tamil saint-poet Andal, *The Autobiography of a Goddess*, *The Golden Shovel: New Poems Honoring Gwendolyn Brooks*, *The Many Uses of Mint: New and Selected Poems*, and W. W. Norton's *Language for a New Century*. He currently holds an international research fellowship from the University of Sydney and his memoir *Correctional* appeared this year.

MANOHAR SHETTY's *Full Disclosure: New and Collected Poems* (1981–2017) was published by Speaking Tiger in 2017. He has edited *Ferry Crossing: Short Stories from Goa* (Penguin India) and *Goa Travels: Being the Accounts of Travellers from the 16th to the 21st Century* (Rupa). He has been a Raza Foundation, Homi Bhabha, and Sahitya Akademi Fellow. He lives in Goa.

VINOD KUMAR SHUKLA's first collection of poems was a twenty-page chapbook, *Lagbhag Jaihind* (Hail India, Almost, 1971), the ironic title marking him out as a new voice in Hindi poetry. He novels include *Deevar mein ek khidki rehti thi* (A Window Lived in a Wall 1997), which won the Sahitya Akademi Award, and a volume of stories, *Blue Is Like Blue* (2019), translated by Arvind Krishna Mehrotra and Sara Rai.

MEDHA SINGH is a poet, translator and editor. She edits Berfrois (London) and sits on the editorial board at Freigeist Verlag (Berlin). Her books are *Ecdysis* (Paperwall, 2017) and *I Will Bring My Time: Love Letters by S.H. Raza* (Vadehra Art, 2020). She was nominated for the TFA awards in 2019 and 2020. Her work has appeared widely between India, the UK and the US. Her second collection of poems, *Afterbody*, is forthcoming. She is currently at University of Edinburgh.

RAHUL SONI is a writer, editor and translator. He has edited an anthology of Hindi poetry in English translation, *Home from a Distance* (2011), and translated Shrikant Verma's collection of poetry, *Magadh* (2013), Geetanjali Shree's novel *The Roof Beneath Their Feet* (2013), a selection of Ashok Vajpeyi's poetry *A Name for Every Leaf* (2016), and Pankaj Kapur's novella *Dopehri* (2019).

EUNICE DE SOUZA (1940–2017) was a poet, fiction writer, and academic as well as an anthologist of several collections of poetry, the latest being *These My Words: The Penguin Book of Indian Poetry* (2012), with Melanie Silgardo. Her debut *Fix* (1979) was followed by *Women in Dutch Painting* (1988), *Ways of Belonging* (1990), *A Necklace of Skulls* (2009), and *Learn from the Almond Leaf* (2016). She has also written two novels and several books for children.

ARUNDHATHI SUBRAMANIAM is the award-winning author of twelve books of poetry and prose. Her most recent collection, *Love Without a Story*, published in India in 2019, is forthcoming from Bloodaxe Books, UK. Her previous collection, *When God is a Traveller*, won the inaugural Khushwant Singh Prize and was shortlisted for the T. S. Eliot Prize.

ANAND THAKORE's poetry collections include *Waking in December* (2001), *Elephant Bathing* (2012), *Mughal Sequence* (2012), *Selected Poems* (2017), and *Seven Deaths and Four Scrolls* (2017). Also a Hindustani classical vocalist by training, he studies, performs, composes, and teaches Hindustani vocal music. He is the founder of Harbour Line, a publishing collective, and of Kshitij, an interactive forum for musicians. He lives in Mumbai and divides his time between writing, performances, and teaching music.

ANITHA THAMPI is a poet from Kerala who has been translated into several languages. Her collections of poetry are *Muttamatikkumpol* (While Sweeping the Frontyard 2004), *Azhakillaathavayellam* (All That Are Bereft of Beauty 2010), *Alappuzha Vellam* (Alappuzha Water 2016), and a trilingual co-authored collection, *A Different Water* (2018). She has translated Juan Ramón Jiménez, Les Murray, Mourid Barghouti and others into Malayalam.

JEET THAYIL's first novel, *Narcopolis*, was awarded the DSC Prize for South Asian Literature and was shortlisted for the Man Booker prize. His five poetry collections include *These Errors Are Correct*, which won the Sahitya Akademi Award (India's National Academy of Letters). As a musician, his collaborations include the noise quintet Still Dirty, the experimental trio HMT, and the opera *Babur in London*. His most recent novel is *Names of the Women*.

ROBERT WOOD is interested in enlightenment, suburbs, and diaspora. The author of four books, Wood is Creative Director of the Centre for Stories on Noongar country in Western Australia. His latest collection of poems is *Redgate*, translated into Hindi by Abhimanyu Kumar and available from Red River in New Delhi. Find out more at www.robertdwood.net.

V. RAMASWAMY has been engaged in a a multi-volume project to translate the short fiction of Subimal Misra. *The Golden Gandhi Statue from America: Early Stories* was published in 2010, *Wild Animals Prohibited: Stories, Anti-Stories* in 2015, and *Actually This Could Have Become Ramayan Chamar's Tale: Two Anti-Novels* in 2019. He was a recipient of the Literature Across Frontiers–Charles Wallace India Trust Fellowship in 2016. He lives in Kolkata.

PRAMILA VENKATESWARAN is co-director of Matwaala: South Asian Diaspora

Poetry Festival and author of *Thirtha* (Yuganta Press 2002), *Behind Dark Waters* (Plain View Press 2008), *Draw Me Inmost* (Stockport Flats 2009), *Trace* (Finishing Line Press 2011), *Thirteen Days to Let Go* (Aldrich Press 2015), *Slow Ripening* (Local Gems 2016), and *The Singer of Alleppey* (Shanti Arts 2018). She teaches English and Women's Studies at Nassau Community College, New York.

SHRIKANT VERMA (1931–86) was a central figure in the Nai Kavita movement in the late 1950s and early 1960s. He published two collections of short fiction, a novel, a travelogue, literary interviews, essays, and five collections of poetry including *Jalsaghar* (1973) and *Magadh* (1984). Verma won the Tulsi Puraskar (1976), the Kumaran Asan Award, and the Sahitya Akademi Award (posthumously, for *Magadh*, in 1987).

MONA ZOTE's poetry has appeared in *Cordite Poetry Review, Carapace, Poetry International Web, Indian Literature,* and *The Indian Quarterly*, as well as in *Dancing Earth: An Anthology of Poetry from North-East India*. She lives in Aizawl.

Credits

"The Song to Kamadeva, God of Love" and "Take Me to His Sacred Places" by Andal reprinted with permission from trans. Ravi Shankar and Priya Sarukkai Chabria, *Autobiography of a Goddess* (New Delhi: Zubaan 2016).

"Nov 1/16" and "Nov 2/16" reprinted with permission from Usha Akella, *The Waiting* (New Delhi: Sahitya Akademi 2019).

"Little Burnt Holes" and "Fragments of an Inexistent Whole" first appeared in *Atmospheric Embroidery*. Copyright © 2018 by Meena Alexander. Published 2018 by TriQuarterly Books/Northwestern University Press. All rights reserved.

"Divination" reprinted with permission from Kazim Ali, *Sky Ward* (Middletown: Weslayan University Press 2013).

"Hands Up" printed with permission from Anamika.

"The Stained Veil" reprinted with permission from Gaiutra Bahadur, *Adda* (September 15, 2016).

"Glass Pronouns," "Dog Days," and "About Presences" printed with permission from Subhransu Banerjee and trans. Ranjit Hoskote, *Kacher Sarbonam* (Kolkata: Kaurab 2014).

"Future Library: Some Anxieties," "Future Library: A Footnote," and "Future Library: Alternative Ending" reprinted with permission from Sohini Basak, *We Live in the Newness of Small Differences* (London: Eyewear Publishing 2018).

"A Neutral Country" and "Notes from the Hospital" printed with permission from Sujata Bhatt.

"the way we write" reprinted with permission from Shelly Bhoil, *40 Under 40: An Anthology of Post-Globalisation Poetry* (Mumbai: Paperwall Media & Publishing 2016).

"Country, Western" reprinted with permission from Jaswinder Bolina, *Fanzine* (February 4, 2013).

"Red Scarf" printed with permission from Michelle Cahill.

"Great Mosque, Xian" and "Prayer as Three Camera Movements" reprinted with permission from Priya Sarukkai Chabria, *Calling Over Water* (Mumbai: Paperwall Media & Publishing 2019).

"Being Means," "Hello Dum Dum," "Amalkanti," and "Flag" by Nirendranath Chakraborty reprinted with permission from trans. Chandak Chattarji, *Six Bangla Poets* (Mumbai: Paperwall Media & Publishing 2017).

"Insect Boy" reprinted with permission from Sampurna Chattarji, *Dirty Love* (New Delhi: Penguin Books India 2013).

"Home Body" and "this life is mock containment" printed with permission from Suman Chhabra.

"The Blueprint among the Ashes" and "Visitation" reprinted with permission from Rohan Chhetri, *Vinyl* (October 14, 2016) and *Prelude* no. 3 (2017).

"Description of the Mad" printed with permission from Mangalesh Dabral and trans. Arvind Krishna Mehrotra.

"Effigy Maker" and "Teo'ma" reprinted with permission from Mustansir Dalvi, *brouhahas of cocks* (Mumbai: Paperwall Media & Publishing 2013).

"Winston to Cyril" and "Some Poems for Akhmatova" reprinted with permission from Keki N. Daruwalla, *Naishapur and Babylon* (New Delhi: Speaking Tiger 2018).

"Anima Walks Borderless" printed with permission from Nabina Das.

Lal Ded's verses 13, 14, 64, 111, 140 and 142 reprinted with permission from trans. Ranjit Hoskote, *I Lalla: The Poems of Lal Ded* (New Delhi: Penguin Books India 2011).

"Page Ripped from Rockbottom's Own Invented Book of Prayer" and "That's the American Dream, Is to Have a Green Lawn" reprinted with permission from Jay Deshpande, *Blunderbuss Magazine* and *Denver Quarterly*, 51, no. 3 (2017). "Pennsylvania, Pittsburgh" printed with permission from Jay Deshpande.

"The Knot" and "Out of Line" reprinted with permission from Imtiaz Dharker, *Luck is the Hook* (Newcastle: Bloodaxe Books 2018).

"After Sunset" and "Before Sunrise" reprinted with permission from Tsering Wangmo Dhompa, *Indian Quarterly* 6, no. 2 (January–March 2018).

"Praha, I'll be Back" and "What Happened to Language?" reprinted with permission from Hemant Divate and trans. Mustansir Dalvi, *Struggles with Imagined Gods* (Mumbai: Paperwall Media & Publishing 2013).

"Something New, Something Borrowed" printed with permission from Rosalyn D'Mello.

"O Great Beauties!" and "The Women of The Shin Yang Park Sauna, Gwanju" reprinted with permission from Tishani Doshi, *Girls are Coming out of the Woods* (Port Townsend: Copper Canyon Press 2018).

"In the Fetus Museum," "A Funfair In Hell," and "Savage Bride" from *You Darling Thing* © 2018 by Monica Ferrell. Appears with permission of Four Way Books. All rights reserved.

"Mooncalf" reprinted with permission from Shamala Gallagher, *Black Warrior Review* 42, no. 1 (Fall/Winter 2015).

"50" reprinted with permission from Joy Goswami and trans. Sampurna Chattarji, *Selected Poems* (Noida: HarperCollins India 2014).

"Sand," "Market," "Shoe," and "Hunchprose" reprinted with permission from Ranjit Hoskote, *Hunchprose* (New Delhi: Penguin/ Hamish Hamilton, 2021).

"Ghazal" by Muhammed Iqbal printed with permission from trans. Mustansir Dalvi.

"The Unknown Tongues" and "An Old Poet's Suicide Note" printed with permission from K. Satchidanandan.

"Breasts/*Mulaigal*," "Because I Never Learned the Names of Trees in Tamil" and "A Brief History of Writing" printed with permission from K. Srilata.

"Ave Maria" by K. R. Meera, translated by J. Devika, *Yellow is the Colour of Longing*, 2016. Reproduced with permission of the publisher Penguin Random House India.

"From *Meghadutam*" by Kalidasa reprinted with permission from trans. Mani Rao, *Kalidasa for the 21st Century Reader* (New Delhi: Aleph Book Company 2014).

"Interior with Particulars" and "Grammar Lesson" printed with permission from Subhashini Kaligotla.

"Celestial Celebrities," "Eating Dirt," and "Things to remember while looting the burial ground" reprinted with permission from Meena Kandasamy, *Ms Militancy* (New Delhi: Navayana Publishing 2010).

"Girls, Girls, Girls" reprinted with permission from Kirun Kapur, *Agni* online (July 1, 2014).

"From *The House with a Thousand Stories*" reprinted with permission from Aruni Kashyap, *The House with a Thousand Stories* (New Delhi: Penguin Books India 2013).

"The Day I Was My Sister's Chaperone" and "For My Nephew Omar on his Engagement to Nadia" printed with permission from Rafiq Kathwari.

"Dehradun, 1990" reprinted with permission from Akhil Katyal, *Guftugu: Culture Matters* no. 4 (July 2016).

"Who in a Million Diamonds Sums Us Up?" reprinted with permission from Tabish Khair, *Man of Glass* (Noida: HarperCollins Publishers 2010).

"I Brake for Moose" reprinted with permission from Geeta Kothari, *I Brake for Moose and Other Stories* (Braddock: Braddock Avenue Books 2017).

"On Seeing a Watermelon" and "Window Seat" reprinted with permission from Monika Kumar and trans. Sampurna Chattarji, *Songs of the Shattered Throat: Modern Poetry in Translation*, 1 (2017).

"The Gita Variations: Gloss 10" and "Godhra Sequence" reprinted with permission from Amit Majmudar, *Poetry International* 25/26 (2019); *The Hopkins Review* 10, no. 4 (Fall 2017).

"A Dreamhole" reprinted with permission from Saikat Majumdar, *The Scent of God* (New Delhi: Simon and Schuster 2019).

"Feats of Strength" reprinted with permission from Ravi Mangla, *Tin House* online (May 10, 2013).

"Ali G does Kabir" reprinted with permission from Inderjeet Mani, *Lakeview International Journal of Literature and Arts*, 4, no. 2 (August 2016).

"The Statue Game" by Kuzhali Manickavel, first published in *AGNI Online* (July 2010). Reprinted with permission from Blaft Publications, *Things We Found During the Autopsy* (Chennai: Blaft Publications 2014).

"Botany 101 (For India's Daughters)" reprinted with permission from Shikha Malaviya, *Chicago Quarterly Review*, 24 (2017).

"The Chicken Trusser" reprinted with permission from Sharanya Manivannan, *Dark Sky Magazine* (April 2011).

"Three Questions for Prabhu S. Guptara . . ." and "Ballad of the Black Feringhee" reprinted with permission from Arvind Krishna Mehrotra, *Collected Poems* (New South Wales: Giramondo, 2016). Translations from *The Absent Traveller: Prakrit Love*

Poetry from the Gathasaptasati of Satavahana Hala reprinted with permission from Arvind Krishna Mehrotra (New Delhi: Ravi Dayal 1991).

"Double Bed" printed with permission from Palash Krishna Mehrotra.

"Black Dog on the Anacostia River" reprinted with permission from Leeya Mehta, *District Lit* (Fall 2015).

"Eclipse," "Evening," and "Retired Swami" reprinted with permission from Siddhartha Menon, *Woodpecker* (New Delhi: Sahitya Akademi 2010).

"Devayani" printed with permission from Vikas K. Menon.

"Wild Animals Prohibited" reproduced in arrangement with HarperCollins Publishers India Private Limited from the book *Wild Animals Prohibited* written by Subimal Misra and translated by V. Ramaswamy, first published by them in 2015. All rights reserved. Unauthorized copying is strictly prohibited.

"Vapsi: Return," "A Mnemonic for Survival," and "Underwater Acoustics" reprinted with permission from Rajiv Mohabir, *Asian American Literary Review* 8, no.1 (Spring/Summer 2017); *The Collagist*, Issue 68.

"What Holds Together" reprinted with permission from Sharmishta Mohanty, *Five Movements in Praise* (Mumbai: Almost Island Books 2013).

"Stayed Home with Language" reprinted with permission from Monica Mody, *Burning House Press* (October 25, 2019).

"From *code memory: dead fish buoy above the living*" printed with permission from Aryanil Mukherjee.

"On First Looking into Whitman's Humour," "Lint," and "Bhima in the Forest" reprinted with permission from Kavery Nambisan, *These Were my Homes: Collected Poems* by Vijay Nambisan (New Delhi: Speaking Tiger 2018).

"Reaching Home" and "They are not crowds, they are us" by Kunwar Narain reprinted with permission from trans. Apurva Narain, *No Other World: Selected Poems* (New Delhi: Rupa Publications 2008).

"Poems After Valmiki" reprinted with permission from Vivek Narayanan, *Oxford Poets 2013* (Manchester: Carcanet Press 2013); *Indian Literature* 61, no.1 (197, January–February 2017); Indian Cultural Forum (November 23, 2016).

"Song of the Plumber" reprinted with permission from Ralph Nazareth, *Between Us the Long Road* (Owlfeather Collective 2017).

"Marriages and Funerals," "St. Edmund's College" and "Understanding" printed with permission from Robin S. Ngangom.

"The Village" printed with permission from Sasha Parmasad.

"The Magician of Words" reprinted with permission from Surjit Patar and trans. Amarjit Chandan, *Modern Poetry in Translation* 3, no. 14.

"Postmortem," "The Multitude Comes to a Man," and "Of Sea and Mountain" reprinted with permission from Gieve Patel, *Poems* (published by Nissim Ezekiel, 1996); *How do You Withstand Body* (Bombay: Clearing House 1976); *Mirrored, Mirroring* (New Delhi: Oxford University Press 1991).

"Heart's Beast" reprinted with permission from Saleem Peeradina, *Heart's Beast: New and Selected Poems* (Ghaziabad: Copper Coin 2017).

"Mail from San Juan," "Sea World," and "Refilling" reprinted with permission from Arjun Rajendran, *The Cosmonaut in Hergé's Rocket* (Mumbai: Paperwall Media & Publishing 2017).

"Wildling" printed with permission from Vinita Ramani.

"We are women with three breasts!" and "Spectral Horse" reprinted with permission from Kutti Revathi and translators Ethiraj Akilan and Vivek Narayanan (with Padma Narayanan), *Indian Quarterly* 5, no. 3 (April–June 2017); *Asymptote* (January 2017).

"Black Leather Shoes," "Naming," and "The Fourth Day" reprinted with permission from Arun Sagar, *Anamnesia* (Mumbai: Paperwall Media & Publishing 2013).

Extract from *The Blind Lady's Descendants* (2014) by Anees Salim reproduced with permission of the publisher Penguin Random House India.

"oak creek: 5 aug 1919" printed with permission from Jason Sandhar.

"crossing the line" reprinted with permission from Irwin Allan Sealy, *Zelaldinus* (New Delhi: Aleph Book Company 2017).

"Climate, Man, Vegetation" reprinted with permission from Sejal Shah, *Drunken Boat* 13 (2011).

"Taverna" and "Carried Forward" reprinted with permission from Manohar Shetty, *Baffler*, no.22 (April 2014); *The Common*, Issue 3 (April 1, 2012).

"The man put on a new woolen coat . . ." by Vinod Kumar Shukla, reprinted with permission from trans. Arvind Krishna Mehrotra, *Collected Poems* (New South Wales: Giramondo 2016).

"Chair" and "An Answer" reprinted with permission from Medha Singh, *Nether* 2 (2011).

"Disillusionment of a Courtesan from the Time of the Buddha," "Trauma" and "Return" by Shrikant Verma, reprinted with permission from trans. Rahul Soni, *Magadh* (Mumbai: Almost Island Books 2013).

"Learn from the Almond Leaf," "Compound Life" and "Western Ghats" by Eunice de Souza, reprinted with permission from Melanie Silgardo, *A Necklace of Skulls: Collected Poems*, (New Delhi: Penguin India 2009).

"When God is a Traveler," "How to Read Indian Myth," and "Leapfrog" reprinted with permission from Arundhathi Subramaniam, *Love Without a Story* (New Delhi: Westland-Context 2019); *When God is a Traveller* (Newcastle: Bloodaxe Books 2014); *Where I Live: New and Selected Poems* (Newcastle: Bloodaxe 2014).

"Fak You," "Dear Baruk," and "Afzal" reprinted with permission from Lalnunsanga Ralte, Poets Translating Poets, Goethe Institut, Mumbai (2016); *Indian Quarterly* 8, no. 2, (January–March 2020).

"From *Echolocation*" reprinted with permission from Mani Rao, *Echolocation* (Singapore: Math Paper Press 2014).

"*Scarecrow Eclogue*" and "from *Voyager: Book One*" reprinted with permission from Srikanth Reddy, *Facts for Visitors* (Oakland: University of California Press 2004); *Voyager* (Oakland: University of California Press 2004).

"Elephant Bathing" reprinted with permission from Anand Thakore, *Poetry Wales*, 38.1 (Summer 2002).

"Alappuzha *Vellam*" reprinted with permission from Anitha Thampi and trans. J. Devika, *Indian Quarterly* 5, no. 4 (July–September 2017) and *Songs of the Shattered Throat: Modern Poetry in Translation*, 1 (2017).

"From *The Book of Chocolate Saints*" reprinted with permission from Jeet Thayil, *The Book of Chocolate Saints* (London: Faber and Faber 2018).

"We Seed," "Week of Rose," and "To be Rice" printed with permission from Robert Wood.

"From T*he Singer of Alleppey*" reprinted with permission from Pramila Venkateswaran, *The Singer of Alleppey* (Brunswick: Shanti Arts 2018).

"Rez" reprinted with permission from Mona Zote, *Borderlands of Asia: Culture, Place, Poetry* (Amherst: Cambria Press 2017).

About the Editors

ANJUM HASAN is the author of the novels *The Cosmopolitans*, *Neti, Neti: Not This, Not This*, and *Lunatic in my Head*, the book of poems *Street on the Hill*, the short story collections *Difficult Pleasures* and, most recently, *A Day in the Life*, which won the Valley of Words Fiction Award, 2019. Her books have also been shortlisted for the Sahitya Akademi, Hindu Best Fiction and Crossword Fiction awards. She is currently a New India Foundation Fellow and lives in Bangalore.

SAMPURNA CHATTARJI's twenty books include a short story collection about Bombay/Mumbai, *Dirty Love* (Penguin); two novels, *Rupture* and *Land of the Well* (HarperCollins); translations of Joy Goswami's poetry—*Selected Poems* and *After Death Comes Water* (Harper Perennial); and ten poetry titles, the most recent being *Over & Under Ground in Mumbai & Paris* (Westland-Context) and *Space Gulliver: Chronicles of an Alien* (HarperCollins). Her translation of Sukumar Ray is a Puffin Classic. She was Poetry Editor for *The Indian Quarterly* (2017–2021); and currently teaches writing to design students at IIT, Bombay.